"*House of Windows* is a beautifully observed narrative of two marriages and the darkness underlying the relationship between fathers and sons. John Langan continues his impressive assault on the genre's heights with his story of a Dickens scholar's timeless predicament."

—Lucius Shepard, author of *Softspoken* and *Viator*

"The academic novel meets the ghost story (with a pinch of Dickens thrown in) in this tale of the mutual torment that can occur between fathers and sons and the aftershocks such torments can cause even after death. A smart, entrancing book, *House of Windows*, is a strong first novel."

—Brian Evenson, author of *Last Days* and *The Open Curtain*

"John Langan has established himself as a master of weird fiction and horror literature."

—*New York Journal of Books*

"Think Henry James and Joyce Carol Oates with just a few paragraphs of Joe Lansdale...the novel, as a whole, is thought provoking, satisfying and, at times, frightening...If you appreciate the more traditional ghost stories of James, Dickens, and even Peter Straub—and, yes, you need to like the academic style of writers like Oates—here is a novel to enjoy as you sit by a fire in the dark of night."

—Tor.com

"The best parts of this novel, however, are the visits of the ghost... it's mere presence is a sledgehammer to the mind and to sanity...For a lover of ghost stories such as myself I found this novel particularly satisfying but I th̶ ̶ ̶ ̶ ̶ ̶ ̶ ̶ ̶ ̶ ̶ ̶ood story will love it as well."

—*SFF World*

"[Langan] presen̶ ̶ ̶ ̶ ̶ ̶ ̶ ̶ ̶ ̶ ̶ ̶narrative infused with the belief in the power of art, namely literature, to transform and shape a life... *House of Windows* is a haunted house story of the highest order, and it offers plenty of mysteries and scares. But it is also a celebration of literature, of the power of words themselves. "

—*Strange Horizons*

HOUSE OF WINDOWS

JOHN LANGAN

INTRODUCTION BY ADAM NEVILL

DIVERSIONBOOKS

Diversion Books
A Division of Diversion Publishing Corp.
443 Park Avenue South, Suite 1008
New York, New York 10016
www.DiversionBooks.com

This is a work of fiction. Names, characters, places and incidents either are the
product of the author's imagination or are used fictitiously. Any resemblance to
actual persons, living or dead, events or locales is entirely coincidental.

For more information, email info@diversionbooks.com

First Diversion Books edition July 2017.
Print ISBN: 978-1-68230-812-7
eBook ISBN: 978-1-68230-811-0

For Fiona

INTRODUCTION

In a much-denigrated field that was overrun by works with an intense focus on gruesome action, dialogue-heavy narratives, simplified language, and the discourse of straight-to-video ideas, with added implausibility and poor writing, I walked away from horror for a good ten years, a self-imposed exile that began in the early nineties. The kind of horror I really liked was still written and published here and there, or was called by other names, and I've mostly read year after publication, but the more sophisticated horror fiction was hard to locate before the internet really spread its wings.

But in the Anglosphere something very interesting began to occur off-radar in the long night of horror's literary exclusion that began in the early '90s. Once horror had become *persona non grata* in traditional publishing (and for about fifteen years), and once the readership for literary horror aimed at adults switched, seemingly overnight, to serial killer thrillers, crime, and dark literary fiction, a new generation of horror devotees with literary aspirations began thinking about horror differently and brought new influences to their writing. To my eye, John Langan is one of the significant voices in what I term "The New Wave of North American Horror" that really seems to have placed its clawed feet upon the ground post-millennium.

House of Windows was the first book by this author that I read, and I recall getting very excited when I began reading. I discovered the book online while browsing others in the same cosmic horror field that I had enjoyed and come to quite late. Excited in a way that I reserved for writers of a certain cast, with a particular set of aesthetic goals and literary skill.

Primarily, my interest was stimulated because of the quality of the actual writing; the novel attains an equivalency with America's contemporary literary fiction authors. I sensed this was an author with a great deal of reading behind him, both in and out of the horror genre. This was also an author with a fine mind, one that stretches itself courageously into new ways of depicting horror, both in subject matter and in style, structure, and voice. There is an academic's understanding of craft and the tradition of literature across multiple fields. The author writes with intelligence, insight, moral complexity and depth, and the way that his narratives are composed seems as important and vital as the stories.

He is one of those writers who whittles rods to sting his own back, because he is ambitious and even radical in the way that he approaches horror fiction and extends its borders. And despite their regular claims to the contrary, John Langan is probably the exact opposite of what most big commercial publishers seek for their lists. A tragedy for horror, but we can be encouraged by the fact that it doesn't stop writers of his calibre producing fascinating and inspiring bodies of work, nor many readers from craving fine writing.

So why write a complex novel that attempts so much within its carefully considered and, I suspect, exhaustively revised pages? Would it have been be so much easier for a writer to not examine grief, America's seismic wars in the Middle East, family relationships, parenthood, literary criticism, and all at the same time, within a haunted house story that strives to create that memorable fusing of terror with awe and wonder?

But a real writer, in any field, writes what they are compelled to write, as well as fashioning a view of their own time and their own interpretation of the best that has gone before them in their chosen literary tradition. This purpose and integrity struck me about John Langan as soon as I began reading his work.

With *House of Windows*; his collection, *The Wide Carnivorous Sky*; and with his next novel, *The Fisherman*; I think readers who appreciate quality horror, appreciate having their imaginations and horizons stretched while witnessing just what can be done with horror fiction, will find a favourite writer in John Langan. He should be read and collected and given the greatest gift that any writer can receive: *word-of-mouth*.

I recall a review on Amazon for one of my own books that said, "No Zombies chasing cheer-leaders here". It made me laugh, but I thought it revealing. Sometimes the dead need to do more in fiction than wear plaid shirts, stagger around, and ask for brain matter; sometimes the cheerleaders need to stay home or on the field; and there are other ways of catching our attention without cranking the chainsaws. *House of Windows* is a good example.

Adam Nevill,
January 2017,
Devon, England.

ACKNOWLEDGMENTS

I wrote the first draft of this novel in the tiny laundry room of the house my wife and I were living in with our then-infant son. Like all new parents, we were stressed and sleepless. Yet every morning, for anywhere from an hour to an hour-and-a-half to two hours, sometimes, Fiona occupied David while I worked on adding one more page of legal paper to the pile on my wobbly desk. Then, when the manuscript was done, typed, and printed, she read it and commented on it, twice. At the time, I don't think I was as profoundly grateful for all of that as I should have been. But without my wife, this book wouldn't be here, so thanks, love.

Once the novel was done, it was read by a lot of people, including my younger brother Rob, John Joseph Adams, Keith Badowski, and Helen Pilinovsky, all of whom offered support and encouragement at times it was very much needed. The first section of the novel benefited from the careful critical attention of the Wallkill (Zombie) Writers Workshop, composed of Brett Cox, Heinz Insu Fenkl, Roseda Molina, Veronica Schanoes, and Robert Waugh (whose wife, Kappa, was very patient with the lot of us); because of their ruthless counsel, this book contains 50 percent less semicolons.

I began this novel as a break from another I was writing; when I realized that what I had thought was a novella was in fact going to become a novel, my agent, Ginger Clark, fearlessly went along with what was in fact a profound change in the game plan. Ginger has championed this book from the get-go, and she's a good part of the reason you're reading these words now.

This book had a hard time finding a home: the genre people weren't happy with all the literary stuff, the literary people weren't happy with all the genre stuff. Jeremy Lassen at Night Shade Books read the novel, understood and appreciated what I was trying to do in it, and acquired it. To say I'm grateful is an understatement, especially since Night Shade is also responsible for publishing work by such fine writers as Laird Barron, Graham Joyce, Joel Lane, and Lucius Shepard. It's nice company to find yourself in. I also owe Ross Lockhart a debt for putting up with my insane demands.

My family—my sons Nick and David, my Mom, my siblings, siblings-in-law, hordes of nieces and nephews—have supported me in a multitude of ways great and small. I've benefited from the friendship of Laird Barron, Mike Cisco, Sarah Langan, and Paul Tremblay. The last few years, I've been the beneficiary of kindnesses from a number of more established writers: Brian Evenson, Jeffrey Ford, Elizabeth Hand, and Lucius Shepard among them; I'm happy to acknowledge them here.

Finally, there's you, whoever you may be, who have allowed me your time and attention, both of which, I know, are never in great supply. You make a novel like this possible, and I'm grateful to you for it. Now, take my hand and I'll try to offer you something worthy of what you've offered me.

The figure of my sister in her chair by the kitchen fire, haunted me night and day. That the place could possibly be, without her, was something my mind seemed unable to compass; and whereas she had seldom or never been in my thoughts of late, I had now the strangest ideas that she was coming towards me in the street, or that she would presently knock at the door. In my own rooms, too, with which she had never been at all associated, there was at once the blankness of death and a perpetual suggestion of the sound of her voice or the turn of her face or figure, as if she were still alive and had been often there.

—Charles Dickens, *Great Expectations*

So, pursuing the one course of thought, he had the one relentless monster still before him. All things looked black, and cold, and deadly upon him, and he on them. He found a likeness to his misfortune everywhere. There was a remorseless triumph going on about him, and it galled and stung him in his pride and jealousy, whatever form it took: though most of all when it divided with him the love and memory of his lost boy.

—Charles Dickens, *Dombey and Son*

PRELUDE

A FACE JUST OUT OF VIEW

"Everyone asks me what I 'think' happened to Roger," said Veronica Croydon, "and if I don't supply them with an answer immediately, they're only too happy to offer their own. Could he have had a heart attack while he was out for one of his walks? As if the police hadn't thought of that already, and there hadn't been that enormous search for him in the woods off Founders. And as if, because he was six-ty-five, his heart was a ticking time-bomb. If not a heart attack, then it's a stroke or something similar, an aneurysm. As if Roger didn't run five miles every day; as if he didn't have the body of a forty-year-old. Trust me, I know." She raised her hands from the sink, and passed me a plate.

Taking it into the dishtowel, I said, "Surely you can understand—"

"That people assume I wore him out?"

"No," I said; although I supposed there was sufficient truth to her statement. Veronica Croydon had begun her relationship with her eventual husband as a graduate student; she had been more than three decades Roger's junior—closer to four—younger than the son of his first marriage. "No," I repeated, setting the plate in the cupboard, "I was thinking that heart attacks happen at every age."

"Maybe," Veronica said, "but I doubt it. If you could hear their voices, the way they drop an octave, as if they're broaching a delicate topic—the details of our sex life, which they are, indirectly. They sound so greedy.

"Not that those people are the worst," she continued, handing me another plate. "That would have to be the ones who look me straight in the eye and declare that Roger 'obviously' left me for someone else. About seventy percent are in favor of him returning to Joanne; the remaining thirty think it was someone even younger. As if Roger and Joanne hadn't been over for years before I ever met him; as if she didn't do her best to make us miserable once we were together, even though they were basically divorced and leading separate lives. Have you met her? Have you seen her? Of course you have. Why would Roger want to exchange me for that? And someone younger? Please—as if that's all our relationship was, Roger living out a dirty old man's secret fantasy."

All of these possibilities had occurred to me and Ann, my wife; I believe they must have occurred to everyone in the English department at SUNY Huguenot, to anyone who had known Roger Croydon. Hearing them from Veronica's lips, however, I felt myself accused. In the immediate aftermath of Roger's disappearance; in the subsequent year and a half; we hadn't communicated with Veronica, hadn't sat down at the computer to send an e-mail, much less written a card or letter or picked up the phone to call her. We hadn't talked to her, but we had talked about her, to each other and to our friends, discussing the various scenarios she had enumerated along with other, more fanciful explanations for her husband's disappearance. He'd joined a cult; he'd run afoul of drug dealers; he'd lost his mind and been secretly institutionalized. Such discussions had been a de facto party game for months, and whatever twinge of distaste I might have felt had not prohibited me from joining in. That Veronica was not, had never been, the easiest of people to get along with—that it was easier to talk about her than it was to talk to her—suddenly seemed the thinnest of excuses. Placing the plate on top of its fellows, I said, "It's just that Roger's behavior had been so…erratic. Since Ted was killed."

At the mention of her late stepson's name, Veronica paused, her arms submerged in soapy dishwater up to the elbows, her gaze focused on the window directly over the sink. Night and the kitchen lights had transformed the window into a mirror, and all she could be staring at was her reflection: longish red hair pulled back into a ponytail, angular cheeks carefully made up (though it had been only the six of us and the baby for dinner), brown eyes greened by colored contacts, ears hung with dangling earrings that terminated in small, circular mirrors. Her mouth, lipsticked muted red, pursed, and she said, "Ted."

"I didn't mean—"

Veronica waved me to silence, showering suds across the counter. "I know," she said. "It was real. It happened. And yes, it did send Roger around the bend." She laughed humorlessly. "You have no idea how far it sent him." She turned, and I was shocked to see tears spilling from her eyes. "Everyone asks me what I 'think' happened to Roger," she said, "and the thing is, I know what happened to him."

"What?" Stunned, I stood there, while Veronica wiped her eyes with the back of her hand, sniffed, and resumed dishwashing. That she knew what had befallen her husband, yet, as far as I knew, had said nothing of it to the police or anyone else was...was incredible. Only when she held out the last plate to me without looking and it slipped from her fingers, so that I had to leap forward to catch it from smashing on the tiled floor, did I find my voice. Holding the plate in both hands, I said, "You know?"

"I do."

"But," I gestured with the plate. "Why haven't you told anyone?"

Veronica went to pass me a handful of cutlery. Seeing that I had not finished with the plate, she returned the knives and forks to the sink, took a breath, and said, "Because it's impossible. What happened to Roger is impossible."

"I don't understand," I said, finally setting the plate down and closing the cupboard door. "If you know where Roger is—"

"Roger's dead. He died two years ago."

Either Veronica was playing an unpleasant joke on me, or her words were meant to express some oblique truth. Ted had been killed in Afghanistan two years ago; perhaps that was what she meant.

After a pause, she said, "Pretty nuts, huh?"

I decided to risk honesty. "I don't think I understand."

"No," Veronica said, handing me a bundle of silverware, "you wouldn't." While I dried the cutlery and set it in its drawer, she added, "Don't feel bad. No one would understand. Well, it's not so much no one would understand; it's more no one would believe. And I can imagine what they'd say. There's been enough talk about me already. The last thing I need is everyone looking at me and saying, 'Oh, there goes crazy Veronica. Did you hear what she said happened to her husband?'" She gave me the remainder of the silverware and released the water from the sink. Rinsing her hands, she asked, "Is there any wine left?"

"There's a little white in the fridge."

"Great." As she retrieved a glass from the cabinet and sought out the wine, I finished my duties as dish-dryer and hung up the dish-towel. "I guess I'll turn in," I said, turning to the stairs.

"Hey!" Veronica said. "Where are you going?"

"To bed," I said. "It was a long drive here, and Robbie's been a bit restless, lately—he's still teething—so I want to be there in case he wakes up."

"Come on," Veronica said. "Don't go up yet. Stay and have a glass of wine."

"Thanks," I said, "but I'm not much for wine. My stomach—"

"Have a glass of water, then. I can't believe everyone's gone to sleep. It's barely nine o'clock."

"Everyone's had a long day," I said. "There is cable—"

"I don't want to watch TV. I want someone to talk to."

I was on the verge of answering that there was a phone, too, but something in Veronica's tone, a plaintive undercurrent, made me hesitate. Noticing this, she said, "Tell you what: stay up with me for a little while and I'll tell you what I meant just now. I'll tell you what happened to Roger. You write those weird stories, don't you? Then you have to hear this. It's right up your alley."

"I'm sorry?" I wasn't sure what was more confusing: the offhand, breezy way in which Veronica had offered a story that not five minutes past she had insisted she would never disclose—a story that could only be unhappy—or the fact that she was offering it to me, here and now. We were not even friendly acquaintances; my offer to dry the dishes had been put forth before I knew she would be washing them. If I had talked to her while we performed our respective duties, it was out of generic civility. It was hard to believe that my infrequent responses to her nearly continuous monologue could have earned me the right to hear her story.

Apparently, however, that was the case. "I said I'd tell you what happened to Roger. It's been a year and a half, and I'm wondering if I need to tell someone about it, regardless of what they'll think. It's like—are you Catholic?"

"Episcopalian."

"Do you guys have Confession?"

"Yes."

"Okay. It's like, I need to Confess, you know? Not that I did anything wrong—I just have to say what took place out loud. I have to hear myself say it to someone else."

"Fair enough," I said, "but why me? Couldn't Addie—"

"Addie would think I had lost my mind," Veronica said. "You probably will, too, but she's one of the only friends I have left, and I couldn't stand that. If you think I'm nuts, it's no big deal. Basically, you're in the right place at the right time."

"Aren't you concerned I'll tell someone?" I asked.

"You could," Veronica said. "But I'm asking you not to."

"All right," I said, after reflecting that, sitting in the living room, we'd be directly beneath Ann's and my bedroom. If Robbie cried, I'd be able to hear him and run up the stairs before he'd worked himself up too much. "If you're sure—"

"Don't worry," Veronica said, "you won't believe what I'm going to tell you, anyway." Carrying the bottle of wine in one hand, her glass of it in the other, she led the way from the kitchen through the dining room and into the living room. While I seated myself in the rocking chair, she set the bottle and glass on the low coffee table in front of the overstuffed blue-and-white-striped couch. For a moment, Veronica gazed at the windows over the couch, then, turning to me, said, "Tell you what. Before I start this story, I'm going to take a quick shower. To unwind, you know? Don't go anywhere. I'll be right back." Without waiting, she headed for the downstairs bathroom, on the other side of the stairs. A moment later, I heard the bathroom door shut.

I was sufficiently annoyed to stand up and cross to the foot of the stairs before curiosity made me pause. Never refuse a story: How often had I offered that as a maxim to my creative writing students? Here I was, being offered a narrative that promised the seed of a story, at minimum, possibly a novel, and I couldn't wait ten minutes for it? I returned to the rocking chair.

This was not how I had anticipated spending tonight. Ann and I had made the five-hour journey from our home in Huguenot to our friends Harlow and Addie's vacation house on Cape Cod as a treat to ourselves—our variation on the spring break our students at SUNY were spending in Florida and Mexico—and because we'd wanted to introduce Robbie, our ten-month-old son, to the place that had come to mean so much to us, the house where the seeds of our marriage had been sown and to which we'd returned in the years since. We had known we'd be joined by our friend Leigh, escaping

Manhattan for a long weekend, but we hadn't realized Veronica would be staying with us until we'd driven up the house's sandy driveway and seen her red Jetta parked in front of it. Veronica's presence was testament to Addie's unfailing generosity of spirit. After Veronica had replaced Roger Croydon's first wife—an affair that was a good deal more fraught and messy than Veronica had pretended—Addie had been the only one of Roger's former friends not to abandon him, and her loyalty had been sufficiently expansive to include the former student over whom he and Joanne were divorcing. Following Roger's disappearance, Addie had visited and had Veronica over to visit her and Harlow. When I had remarked to her that doing so must count as some act of mercy—whether corporal or spiritual I wasn't sure— Addie had sighed and said, "Underneath it all, Veronica is really very sweet. She's just been through a lot. She refuses to talk about it right now, but it's clear that things between her and Roger had gotten very bad. From what I can gather, before he left, he was in the process of an extended breakdown, which she did her best to cope with, but which was too much for her. I think she blames herself for his leaving."

While it was true that Veronica had compressed what should have been the experiences of twenty years into barely a quarter of that time, I was less inclined to Addie's charity. My aversion to Veronica wasn't rooted in any slight or wrong she had done me; to be honest, I hadn't known her well at any point. It was more basic than that. We had met during her first semester in the Master's program, at an English department party. I had spoken with Veronica briefly, and been struck by the fact that she was, literally and figuratively, over-dressed for the occasion. Where the rest of the party-goers alternated among thirteen ways of appearing casual, Veronica had chosen a black cocktail dress, high heels, and a pearl necklace and earrings. Where the clusters of people around us complained about apathetic students and poor pay, Veronica's conversation with me had circled a line of Emily Dickinson's poetry she said she had been "contemplating": "There's a certain slant of light / Oppresses, like the heft of cathedral tunes." In the course of our brief discussion, Veronica had mentioned that she had graduated—magna cum laude—from Penrose College, where she had written her senior thesis on Dickinson and Hawthorne, and at first I had attributed her mannerisms to the lingering effects of four years spent on the other side of the Hudson, wandering ivied halls. When I considered the students and faculty from Penrose I'd encountered before Veronica, however, that notion dissipated. If anything, they were more proletarian than we at SUNY Huguenot, albeit in a more self-conscious and -satisfied way. It had occurred to me that Veronica—who at that point was still "this graduate student" to me—was carrying on her fantasy of what an English department faculty party should be, insisting that the rest of us conform to her vision. Later, when I had made a few acid remarks about her to Ann, my then-fiancée had given her a name: Veronica Dorian, and laughingly declared that I was just jealous to have discovered someone who was more of a snob than I was. Ann, who shared Addie's generous perspective and who had Veronica as a student in her Contemporary American Novel class, had agreed that Veronica was full of herself, but added that her remarks in class and written work showed genuine acuity of thought. "I am not a snob," I had replied, "I just have standards," and then changed the subject.

(Although, during tonight's dinner, whose conversation had almost inevitably been taken up with the merits or lack thereof of the war in Iraq—whose one-year anniversary was later this week—Veronica had been oddly quiet, refusing to engage the topic in any but the most cursory fashion.)

Veronica's intelligence had caught Roger Croydon's notice right away. Roger was the resident Victorian scholar; he also was one of our more accomplished members, having published upwards of fifty articles and half a dozen books, one of which, *Dickens and Patrimony*, was standard reading for students of Dickens. Why a man of his achievements hadn't been snatched up by one of the major universities was something of a mystery—until, that is, you met Joanne. She and Roger were like a pair of minor characters from one of Dickens's longer novels. Her face was long, its most prominent feature her large, liquid eyes; his face was more square, marked by a nose that had been broken some time in the past. Where she was tall, broad-shouldered, lean, he was short and slender. She sported designer outfits; he favored plain white shirts and chinos. Where she delivered her sentences in the broad accent of old Manhattan money, he spoke with the nasal twang of the South Carolina mountains. Theirs was a famously unhappy union—according to Roger, at least, who rarely missed the opportunity to drink too much at the parties they held at their large house and complain to whoever would listen. He never drank enough to name the specific cause of his general unhappiness, but the looks he cast at Joanne, standing across the room serenely ignoring him, left little doubt. The Croydons had one child, Ted, who I understood from older members of the department had been "wild" as a teenager, but who had calmed down considerably after enlisting in the Army on his eighteenth birthday.

Although Roger was by far the more flamboyant of the pair, given to expansive gestures and loud exclamations, Joanne was in charge of the marriage. She liked Huguenot. It was close enough to Manhattan— an hour and a half down the Thruway—for her to keep in easy contact with her family and the life of playgoing and gallery browsing with which she'd grown up; yet far enough away from the City for her to indulge the notion that she was living "in the country." (I've noticed that, as a rule, the inhabitants of New York City consider everything beyond Westchester "the country" and "upstate.") Anyone who saw the Croydons' house, however, an enormous, three-storey stone and wood edifice on Founders Street just shy of being a mansion—anyone who saw the house the Croydons called "The Belvedere House," after a minor painter who had summered in the place a half-century prior; much less walked its wide, polished hallways, stood in its high-ceil-inged rooms, looked out its tall windows to the mountains behind the town—that person might have thought, *If this is country living, then sign me up*. It didn't require much imagination to understand why Joanne would be reluctant to leave such a house, and when you learned that the place had not always been in such condition, that she and Roger, newly married and arrived in town, had found the house for sale and in a state of almost total disrepair, borrowed the money from her father to purchase it, and then spent literally years restoring the place to its former glory, you understood how deep her attachment to the place ran. Belvedere House was where the Croydons had raised their son; it was where Roger had written most of his articles and all of his books; it was where Joanne had entertained the half-dozen charity and social groups to which she belonged.

The house was a striking, even peculiar structure. Its first storey was built of the same gray fieldstone as the other houses on Founders; its second, third, and attic storeys constructed of wood painted dark brown with forest green trim. Its upper storeys were full of windows, most of them long rectangles, with a few circles and half-circles in amongst them. The first time I had seen the place, I had thought of it as the house of windows—the phrase had come unbidden to me—and that name had lodged in my memory. I understood that its architectural style was more properly referred to as Queen Anne, but I'm not sure what of its features—gables, portico, eaves—that description encompassed. From that initial encounter, the house had had the strangest effect on me. There are many houses whose fronts suggest faces—windows for eyes, door for a mouth—but Belvedere House was the only residence I've seen whose front suggested a face hiding amongst its windows and angles, just out of view.

I glanced with impatience toward the downstairs bathroom, from whence I could hear, faintly, the continuing hiss of the shower. So much for being right back. For a second time, I considered climbing the stairs and leaving Veronica and her story. Had it not been for the fact that she was only going to be here for a day or two—over dessert, she'd told us of her plans to visit Provincetown tomorrow, and possibly Boston the day after—and had this not been perhaps my only chance of hearing this story, I might have done exactly that, and felt self-satisfied at having taught her that she couldn't take advantage of me. As it was, however, my curiosity still outweighed my annoyance, so I stood and wandered out of the living room, back through the dining room, into the kitchen. Retrieving a glass from the cupboard, I filled it with seltzer, adding a slice of lemon from the plastic bag on the refrigerator's top shelf.

Glass in hand, I turned to the kitchen's wide open space, which morning would fill with sunlight through the windows over the counters. With its open floor plan, its expansive rooms, its plenitude of windows, the entire house was friendly to the sun, and if that same abundance of windows meant that now night pressed in on us from all corners, the house was decorated with sufficient cheer and charm to balance it. It was hard not to compare it to Belvedere House, whose excess of windows never seemed to admit sufficient light to dispel the shadows cluttering its high ceilings. That said, Ann and I would have traded our undersized house, whose eight hundred square feet had been too small for one person, let alone two adults and a baby, for Belvedere House's expanses, however shadowy, in a heartbeat. If I could have had my dream house, though, it would have been the Cape House. "It's next to a cemetery," I had said to Ann on more than one occasion. "What could be more fitting for a guy writing horror stories?"

Belvedere House had witnessed many of the Croydons' most

significant moments, including the beginning of Roger and Veronica's affair, and the subsequent end of Roger and Joanne's marriage. Roger was well-known in the English department for his "crushes": younger, usually attractive women whom Roger took it on himself to mentor. You would see them in one of the local bookstores, Roger expounding on this or that novel his mentee should have read; or in the Main Street Bistro, Roger proclaiming this or that opinion on literature, music, or art while the mentee sat silently sipping a cup of tea; or in Roger's office, Roger recounting his jousts with this or that critical rival as he passed his mentee copies of articles to read. So far as anyone knew, these relationships had been strictly Platonic, at worst *affaires de coeur*. Certainly Joanne always treated them with good-humored irony. When Roger started popping his head in my door, asking me how I was doing and then launching into rapturous descriptions of this new student before I had supplied an answer, I was almost comforted by the return of a familiar ritual. Roger's last crush had graduated the previous spring; he was due to find someone new. My reaction was, by and large, typical.

This latest crush of Roger's, however, was not. I'm not sure when it became apparent to the rest of the department that things between Roger and this latest mentee were different, but for me the revelation came shortly after my first meeting with Veronica. While browsing the Poetry section at Campbell's, the used bookstore on Main Street, I overheard a pair of whispered voices engaged in a furious debate. After a moment, I recognized one of the contestants as Roger, and after another, Veronica. Leaning around a tall bookcase, I saw the two of them standing in the midst of General Fiction, Roger's arms flailing like a man scything wheat, in constant danger of sending books tumbling from their shelves, Veronica's hands propped on her hips, an openly skeptical expression on her face. Roger was vigorously extolling the virtues of Melville, the sole American contemporary of Dickens who could hold a candle to him, if only in *Moby Dick*. Veronica overrode him to insist that Melville was verbose and overrated: there was more value in *The Scarlet Letter* than in all of Melville. To which Roger replied that Hawthorne had been so constipated by the Puritan guilt that was his principle diet that he'd been incapable of squeezing out any but the most trite and conventional of sentiments.

And so on. I withdrew and resumed my browsing, unable to avoid eavesdropping on their argument as its volume steadily increased, then did my best to leave the bookstore unobserved—not difficult, really, as the two of them were still in the thick of their debate. That night, over dinner, I recounted the scene to Ann, who raised her eyebrows and said, "Well. It looks like Roger has finally met his match."

It appeared he had. The sound of him and Veronica disagreeing, so close to outright argument as to be indistinguishable from it, became familiar, and to Veronica's credit, she held her own. I had known Roger long and reasonably well-enough to be acquainted with most of his opinions and ideas, and I don't think I heard one of them with which Veronica agreed. What was more, her disagreements were usually cogent. You might have thought Roger would grow tired of such constant contradiction—as the rest of us did of having to listen to it—but he thrived on Veronica's challenges. His eyes alight, his step light, he looked less like a man at the far end of a distinguished career and more like one whose star has just started its rise. A new mentee always brought about some measure of regeneration in Roger, but this was the most dramatic example of it I had witnessed. Roger's enthusiasm carried over into his classes, where his students were more impressed and inspired than they had been in some time; and into his writing, where he was halfway through a new essay on the role of young women in Dickens's life and works.

As for Veronica: if what all of us overheard was any guide, then she was eminently up to the challenge of Roger. Indeed, after one afternoon of her and Roger's voices echoing up and down the English department's corridors, I recalled my first conversation with her and my thought that she had been living out her ideal of what English students and professors discussed: with Roger, she had found that ideal made real.

Given the intensity of their relationship, it shouldn't have come as that much of a surprise when the heat of their intellectual engagement sparked other fires. If every profession is accompanied in the popular imagination by two or three stereotypical images, then that of the (male) professor's affair with the younger (female) student must be among ours; the advent of feminism and sexual harassment legislation has blunted the stereotype only slightly. That said, Joanne's suddenly leaving Roger the following spring caught everyone off-guard. Ann called me from the office to share the news. Supposedly, the cause of Joanne's departure was her having discovered Roger and Veronica *in flagrante delicto*, but that I could not credit.

When Roger left Belvedere House to move in with Veronica less than a week later, however, the rumors were confirmed. While I've heard of quick, even friendly divorces, I've never actually seen any, and Roger and Joanne's split was among the most bitter. The scholar of the great melodramatist had enrolled himself in a modern variety of the form, the soap opera, and not an especially original one at that.

Throughout the two years it took them and their lawyers to work through their divorce, Belvedere House stood first empty and then rented. It was perhaps the only point on which Roger and Joanne were able to agree: their reluctance to part with the house. Eventually, they rented it to a young heart surgeon and her family.

Veronica continued taking classes, working toward her Master's. I was more than a little surprised at this. Given the storm of gossip that continued to swirl around her, I would have expected her to withdraw from the program and seek another, preferably in Manhattan or Albany. But she decided to brazen it out, completing her coursework during the first year of Roger and Joanne's divorce, then writing a thesis during the second year. What was more, she attended the department's social events with Roger, walking into whatever house it was at his side with a nonchalance that suggested she'd been doing this for years. Many of the senior faculty were as scandalized as Roger and Joanne's old friends had been; though in several instances, it was a case of the kettle calling the pot black. Unlike those friends, however, they had no choice but to continue to see and deal with Roger, so, in the end, an effort was made, if not exactly to welcome Veronica, then at least to acknowledge her. By the time Roger was officially divorced, Veronica had earned her degree and had been hired to adjunct back across the Hudson at Penrose.

I finished my seltzer, and shot another look over at the bathroom door. At least I could no longer hear the shower; though Veronica seemed no closer to reappearing. The second I started up the stairs, I knew, she would emerge. *In for a penny*, I thought.

This current visit was not Veronica's first to the Cape House. She had come here with Roger a year and a half ago, in the week or two immediately preceding his disappearance. Roger had been, to put it mildly, in a bad way: Ted had been killed while serving in Afghanistan earlier that year, and his death had undone his father. In an instant, the excess of vitality with which his affair with and marriage to Veronica had endowed him disappeared, drained out of him by the wound of his son's death; indeed, if anything, Roger appeared even older than he was, the poet's tattered coat upon a stick. He sagged inward, the way an old house whose frame and foundation are failing does, and though Veronica did her best for him, it was the equivalent of splashing a fresh coat of paint in some garish color across the façade of a dilapidated old house: hiding nothing, it instead calls attention to the structure's decay. The fires that had burnt in Roger had been blown out by the gust of his son's death, leaving only ashes and gray smoke. He and Veronica held a memorial service at the Dutch Reformed Church on Founders Street, but it was sparsely attended, most of his former friends having chosen to be present at the service Joanne arranged in Manhattan. Ann and I went, as did Addie and Harlow, and it was painful to witness. The worst moment was Roger's attempt to deliver the eulogy, a speech that began with his memories of a much younger Ted breaking his arm in an attempt to scale the wall of Belvedere House, drifted into his attempt to read Dickens to Ted when Ted was more interested in Spider-Man, and dissolved in his effort at reciting Houseman's "To an Athlete, Dying Young."

After that, reports of Roger's continuing downward slide reached us in stages, like bulletins from the site of some distant and ongoing disaster. He was missing classes and, when he was present, either obviously unprepared for the subject at hand or silent for extended periods of time. Finally, the President of the college had him up to her office. Grief-addled though he was, Roger recognized the lifeline that was being thrown to him and took it, turning over his classes to a couple of adjuncts and locking the door to his office behind him.

Until we saw Roger's face on the evening news, that was about the last word any of us had of him, except for one, final piece of information: he and Veronica had moved into Belvedere House. Apparently, Joanne hadn't contested the idea; and Dr. Sullivan and her family had been given one month to locate suitable replacement lodgings. At the end of that time, Roger and Veronica had left her small apartment behind for the spacious house. For a week or two after they moved in, a rumor circulated that Veronica was planning a house-warming party, but it proved unfounded. I don't believe anyone saw Roger for any length of time before the broadcaster was saying, "Police are investigating the disappearance of SUNY Huguenot professor Roger Croydon…"

I'm not sure what the consensus was on Roger's fate. From the start, I had a bad feeling about it: it seemed to me the last act in what was emerging as Roger's tragedy of dissolution. Ann was of the opinion that Roger had taken off for a time to parts unknown in order to rest and regroup himself. After the initial searches for Roger—for his body, really—by the police failed to turn up anything, the possibility of his death—and, lurking behind it, of his suicide—receded; though I don't suppose it ever disappeared entirely. The scenarios Veronica reported being forced on her were valid enough, but they were also indexes of the lingering resentment towards her harbored by Roger's old friends, who traced the origin of all his troubles to his move from being one half of Roger-and-Joanne to one half of Roger-and-Veronica.

The bathroom door clicked open, and at long last Veronica emerged. She had replaced the short brown dress she'd worn to dinner with a long plush robe the same cream color as the towel turbanning her hair; she'd also replaced her contacts with a small, rectangular pair of glasses; her earrings, I noticed, still caught the light. "Okay," she said as she took up her seat on the couch, folding her legs as she reached forward for her glass of wine. She took a long drink from it. "Like I said, this is a pretty weird story. I won't say even I don't believe it, because I was there and I saw it. It's more that I don't want to believe it, if that makes any sense. It will. I read that story of yours—the one about the mummy, or whatever you'd call it—so I'm thinking that you'll at least have an open mind about what I'm going to tell you. What's so funny?"

"I'm sorry," I said, "it's just that, when people learn I write horror stories, they tend to one of two reactions. Either they tell me they don't read them—don't like them, usually—or they feel compelled to tell me one of their own. I wonder if the same thing happens to mystery writers, or romance writers?"

"Right," Veronica said. "Even before Roger—even before his disappearance, I was trying to arrange what was happening to us into some kind of coherence, into a narrative that would make sense. After he was gone, it became a kind of obsession with me. No matter where I was or what I was doing—driving the car, watching TV, doing laundry, teaching a class—I would be going over what had happened, drawing connections among what seemed to be unrelated events, inferring motives and reactions, sometimes inventing scenes that I knew had to have taken place. For about a month—it was the first

Christmas after Roger was gone—I wrote everything down. I spent day after day filling marble notebooks. I think I topped out at about four hundred pages of very tiny script, and I still hadn't come to terms with everything we'd been through. I still didn't understand it all. Every now and again, I go back to those notebooks; I revise them: crossing some words and sentences out, adding others in the margins, and in-between lines. By now, I'm not sure they're legible to anyone but me; their pages look more like some kind of abstract art than they do writing.

"Just now, in the shower, I was thinking about where to begin, wondering if I could take a short cut to the end. I was remembering the last full night Roger and I were together. About three in the morning, Roger left the bed and went outside. He was sleepwalking, which wasn't such a big deal—he'd been up at three to wander the house for weeks. This was the first time he'd walked out the front door, however, so I followed him. He walked around the house a few times, then stopped at the back lawn. Although it was the middle of summer, the air was freezing cold, winter-cold. Fifteen feet from where we stood, our breaths making white plumes, there was darkness. Not the normal dark of three a.m., but solid black, truncating the yard from right to left in front of us. It was the source of the tremendous cold, as if someone had erected an enormous wall of black ice behind the house.

"By this point, I was not as shocked at the sight of a huge black curtain hanging in my backyard as I otherwise would be. A lot of weird, which is to say, completely terrifying, stuff had been happening. Still, I moved closer to Roger, who was staring into the blackness as if he could distinguish something in it. 'There it is,' he said.

"I said, 'What is it?'

"'It's mine.'

"I didn't think I'd heard him. 'What?'

"'Me.' He continued gazing into the blackness.

"'You're yours?' I asked.

"'It's mine,' he said, and I understood him. 'Oh,' I said, 'you mean this.'

"'Me.'

"'It's yours and it's you.'

"'Where's my boy?'

"'Ted?'

"'We're supposed to work on his slider,' Roger said, hesitated. 'He never comes to see me.'

"'Ted.'

"Now Roger turned to me, although his eyes were blank. 'Do you know my boy?'

"'Not really.'

"'He used to be so good. We used to have such a time together. Not anymore.'

"'What happened to him?'

"'He died.'

"For reasons that had become important by then, I asked, 'How did he die?'

"'I locked him away,' Roger said. 'Threw away the key. Then he died.'

"'And he's still locked away?'

"From the corner of my eye, I saw movement. The wall of blackness had shifted, rippled as if it really was a gigantic curtain. If every square inch of my skin hadn't already been rigid with the cold, the sight of that shifting would have brought it out in instant goosebumps. Through the blackness, I thought I could see something—was that a person standing there? It was, a tall figure that seemed to be both behind and inside the curtain. I looked away. Now I was afraid, fear surging up the middle of my back, sending my heart galloping. I looked at Roger, who hadn't responded to my last question.

"He shrugged. He said, 'I have to assume. He won't tell me anything. He won't speak to me at all.'

"I didn't want to, but I glanced at the black wall. The shape there was drawing closer, growing more definite. My mouth was dry. 'Roger,' I said, 'Ted—'

"Roger's face twisted, and he was shouting. '*Where is he? What have you done with him? Where's my little boy? Where is my little boy? Where is my little boy?*'"

PART 1

MUTUAL WEIRDNESS

Instead of enormous black curtains hanging behind my house (Veronica said), begin with someone banging on my apartment door so loud it woke me out of a deep sleep. Beside me, Roger was already sitting up. I said, "Roger, what?" and checked the digital clock on the nightstand. Three a.m. Roger slid out of bed, stood up. I asked, "What is it?"

"I don't know," he said, and went to answer it.

"Wait," I said, because when is someone hammering on your door at three in the morning ever a good thing? Roger ignored me, crossing the tiny living room to the door, which was jumping under the blows of whoever was on the other side. Now I was out of bed and going for the phone, wondering if I'd be able to dial 911 before myself and my new husband were horribly murdered.

"Yes, yes," Roger said, unlocking the door. He swung it open, and there was Ted.

It was the first time I'd seen him in person. His face—he favored Joanne, those same long, horsey features—his face was contorted, red—scarlet—all the way from the bottom of his neck right up to his crewcut. I'd never seen anyone look so angry. In his right hand, he held the wedding announcement I'd sent him. He was in his fatigues, the green ones with the brown and black spots. Roger was not expecting to find his son on the landing in the middle of the night; you heard it in the way he said, "Ted!"

"I got your message," Ted said—snarled, really.

Roger didn't know what he was talking about. Did I mention

17

that I hadn't told him about sending Ted our announcement? He said, "What? What message?"

"This!" Ted shouted, holding up the card as if he was the district attorney and this exhibit A in a capital trial.

Roger wasn't wearing his reading glasses. He had to hunch over a little and squint to see what Ted was showing him. "Why, how did you get this?" he asked.

You could see that Ted thought Roger was mocking him. "From you!" he said, jerking the card back.

"I never," Roger started, and stopped. He'd guessed how the card came to Ted. Instead, he said, "Ted. What is this about?"

That was the invitation Ted had been waiting for. He said, "This is about you leaving my mother for some teenaged slut. This is about you breaking up a thirty-eight-year marriage so you could get your dick wet. This is about you spitting in the face of the woman who gave her life to you."

"Now wait just a minute," Roger said, but Ted shouted him down.

"This is about you bringing dishonor to our family. This is about you making yourself a laughing stock."

"That is enough!" Now Roger was shouting. He drew himself up to his full height—which still left him a head shorter than Ted. "I am your father, mister, and you will speak to me with respect. My business is my own, and you will respect that as well. I do not expect you or anyone else to judge me."

"Respect!" Ted answered. "Like the respect you and your whore showed my mother?"

"You are speaking about my wife," Roger said, "you had best change your tone."

"Or what? You'll leave me for another son?"

"This is ridiculous," Roger said. "You are ridiculous. Your mother and I have been separated for over two years, son, and this is the first you come to see me about this? At three a.m., screaming and yelling? Oh, very good. Exactly the way to impress me with whatever point it is you think you're making."

"Me?" Ted said. "I was happy to let you ruin your life. Mother's better off without you. But you couldn't leave well enough alone, could you? You had to rub my face in it." He brandished the announcement.

Roger bowed his head and said, "That was a mistake."

"You're damned right it was!"

I watched their argument unfold from the bedroom doorway. When Roger opened the door and I saw Ted standing there, I was going to go up to him and introduce myself—for about a nanosecond, until I saw his face and realized this wasn't a surprise visit. Well, it was, but more in the way an ambush is a surprise. I stopped where I was. Probably, I should have gone back to bed, but how could I sleep with the two of them yelling at each other? Things had heated up too fast. Ted's face looked like it wanted to tear itself apart—his whole body was vibrating like a wire—while Roger's hands kept clenching and unclenching. I couldn't believe that two grown men were about to start fighting because of a stupid card—I mean, it was supposed to be a nice gesture.

With every word they said, though, they edged closer to the moment I was going to have to call the cops. I'd already picked up the cordless and was holding it at the ready. Ted was yelling that this was just like Roger, he'd always thought of himself first, last, and in-between. Roger was yelling back that Ted was forgetting himself, and he'd had just about enough of this adolescent grandstanding. Finally, Roger shouted, "This conversation is over!" and went to slam the front door.

As he did, Ted stepped forward. The door bounced off his shoulder, back into Roger's hand. "This conversation is over when I say it's over," he said, taking another step. "You are not going to tell me when to leave. I am going to decide when I want to leave."

Roger pushed him. He tried. It was like pushing a tree. Ted swayed backwards, then forwards, pushing Roger on the return. Roger went over on his butt.

For Ted, this must have been a fantasy come true. Here he was, able to hold his own with his father. When Roger sat down—hard—Ted's face completely relaxed. It was still beet-red, but he looked more like a guy who'd just been exercising than someone out for retribution. He seemed surprised at how easily Roger had fallen—I think he forgot what he was about to say.

Before he could remember, Roger threw himself up off the floor and drove his head into Ted's gut. All the breath left Ted—he was like a cartoon character, his eyes big, his mouth a little "o." It was his turn to go down. On the way, he caught Roger's t-shirt and took him with him.

That was that. They went at each other full-out, rolling around the floor together, punching and kicking. I didn't bother trying to stop them. The cops took about five minutes to arrive; by which time, Roger and Ted had totaled that part of the apartment. They knocked bookcases over; they smashed the TV; they broke a lamp. It was pretty horrifying; although, I'll tell you, all the time they were pounding one another black and blue, I was thinking that, if this had happened when Ted was seventeen, it probably would've been a good thing. The cops grabbed hold of them and tried to pull them apart, but that didn't work so well. One guy got a black eye for his trouble. He pepper-sprayed the two of them. Have you ever smelled that stuff? God. I can't believe the cops are allowed to use it indoors. Roger and Ted shot away from each other, howling and rubbing their eyes furiously. They were cuffed and hauled down the stairs to the police car. I didn't feel especially bad about that. I knew I'd have to drive over to town hall to bail them out in the morning, but for the moment, it was a relief to have them out of there and in a place where they couldn't hurt themselves. I walked around the apartment opening windows to air the place out, threw an extra couple of blankets on the bed, and tried to go to sleep.

The operative word being "try." As you can imagine, sleep kept its distance. We hadn't been married a month, yet, and I had just called the cops on my husband because he was fighting with his son, for God's sake. It's pretty hard to drop off after something like that. I would've sat up watching TV, but oh yeah, I no longer had a TV, because my stepson put one of his boots through it while he was grappling with his father. I turned on the bedside light, piled Roger's pillows on top of mine, and did my best to read—Dickinson's poems, if anyone's asking—but I was no more successful at that than I was at unconsciousness. What should have been my favorite poetry was cryptic phrases and too many dashes:

"One need not be a Chamber—to be Haunted—
"One need not be a House—
"The Brain has Corridors—surpassing
"Material Place—"

I put the book down, leaned back on the pillows, and closed my eyes. I was thinking about going to bail out Roger and Ted in a few hours.

I was thinking about everything that had led up to this point.

• • •

Roger told me about Ted the second night he stayed over at my apartment. We were up till dawn talking, telling each other about our lives, our families. For all the time we'd already spent in conversation, it was amazing how little we actually knew about one another's lives. I could've told you Roger's choices for Dickens's top five novels, and his reasons for every ranking, but I still wasn't sure if he had one child or two. I'm sure he felt the same about me. We were sitting at the kitchen table, splitting a bottle of red wine. I had no kids, I said, what about him?

"One son," Roger said. "Edward Joseph—we call him Ted."

"How old?"

"Twenty-eight."

"What does he do?"

"He is a sergeant in the United States Army, Special Forces."

"Wow."

Roger grunted.

"So tell me about him."

For the next couple of hours, Roger did. He began with Ted's fifteenth birthday. There's an age, isn't there? Some point in your teens where you reach critical mass, where everything that's been simmering inside you boils over, and you metamorphose into the stereotypical teenager. Literally the day I turned thirteen, I realized my parents and most of my immediate and extended family were the biggest idiots who'd ever walked the face of the earth. I adjusted my behavior accordingly. It made for a fun few years—fun the way slow death by torture is fun. If you're lucky, you pass out of this stage in a couple of years, but as long as you're in it, you're useless to anyone else except maybe your closest friends.

Roger had seen this kind of behavior before. We all have, I guess. There are more than enough college students who haven't reached the end of it. On some level, he recognized it for what it was: this typical, almost impersonal response to everything. At the same time, he was deeply hurt by Ted's rejection, and he couldn't separate himself from that hurt, no matter what he knew about its cause. His son had been replaced by a sullen stranger who wore his hair long and over his face, answered every question in mumbles, and wore the same sweatshirt and jeans for days at a time.

In response, Roger became the disciplinarian. He tried, anyway, because the more he insisted on his rules, the more Ted flouted them. He abandoned his tutors, slacking off at school to the point he was constantly in danger of flunking out. He started smoking a lot of pot, and hung out with the other kids who smoked a lot of pot. He tried to sneak a girl into his room, and when Joanne and Roger caught him, stormed out of the house. He was picked up for shoplifting a couple of times; although Joanne had enough pull to make sure the charges were dropped. Time went on, and his antics worsened. He skipped school for days at a time. He came to dinner drunk or stoned or both. He did his best to hotwire Joanne's car when she refused to let him take it out for the night—but he didn't know what he was doing, and left a mess of cut and stripped wires dangling from under the dash of her Mercedes. Roger wanted to send him to military school— Roger! Can you believe it?—Joanne wanted to send him to a cousin in the south of France. They couldn't agree, so Ted stayed there with them and continued to test the limits. It was Ted's complete lack of interest in anything except getting high and hanging with his friends that really got to Roger. Out and out rebellion, angry, argumentative resistance, a coordinated rejection of his and Joanne's values, *that* he could've dealt with. You know how he loved to argue. Apathy, however, was beyond him. He did not know how to deal with someone who didn't care. I think Ted must have realized this and seen it as his most effective weapon.

Much too quickly and easily, Ted went from being the apple of his father's eye to the worm in the apple. There was no big confrontation—not then. His heart hardened, and he did nothing to stop it. Sometimes, they watched baseball; one of their oldest activities together. The week of the World Series was a time for détente, if not out-and-out peace, and there were moments when Roger, hearing Ted rave about a double play, his disaffection momentarily shaken by some amazing feat, would feel his heart start to soften, feel the stone cracking and something green and alive struggling to reach the surface. But then Ted would catch himself actually talking to his father like a human being, duck his head and say, "Or whatever," and slouch back in front of the TV. Maybe Roger could've said something—who knows what? maybe he could've praised Ted, told him that was a good point—maybe he could've made an effort to build on the foundation Ted had laid—but he didn't. It was too much; Roger let it be too much. His heart crusted over again, the green was smothered, and that was that.

Roger always was a bit of a fatalist. His parents died while he was young: his father of lung cancer when Roger was sixteen, his mother four years later of breast cancer, during his third year at Vanderbilt. They were both heavy smokers. His younger brother became an alcoholic young and didn't dry out for the next twenty-five years. His sister made an early, bad marriage that only ended when her husband drove into a tree and put himself into a coma that lasted a year. There was more stuff, too, more to do with his parents—his dad, especially—but I'll get to that later. Suffice it to say, his father was not the most supportive of men. Roger denied his family having any effect on him whatsoever, but obviously, watching everyone he loved relentlessly ground down affected him at the very deepest level. It was why he responded so strongly to Dickens, all those children in danger, all those families in jeopardy. You know it lay behind his drive to succeed, this overpowering desire to be different from the rest of his family. It also left him with a lasting certainty that the worst not only could happen, it would, and, more often than not, it would come out of your own actions. Why else did he stay with Joanne for so long? I'm sure that, from the second Roger first held Ted, he was bracing himself for the moment everything he was feeling—all the love, joy, pride—would sour. When it did—or, when he panicked and thought it did—Roger jumped the gun, decided to write the end to what he'd already decided was the latest chapter in the history of his life's defeats.

Ted never knew any of this at the time. I doubt Roger himself was fully aware of it—not that it was unconscious, just that he was always good at not thinking about things he didn't want to think about, especially if they made him look bad to himself. In all fairness to him, I'm not sure it would have made much of any difference to Ted if Roger had told him how he was feeling. Most likely, he would have snickered and walked away.

Probably the last major event in their relationship—before I came along—was Ted's joining the Army. Both Roger and Joanne were surprised—shocked. Ted hadn't given the slightest indication he was thinking about the military to either of them. He wasn't exactly what sprang to mind when you thought of soldier material, you know? Joanne took his decision hard, worse than Roger. She had thought that she and Ted had a special relationship, that she was the parent he talked to. Right. She was just the parent he came to when he needed money. Roger wasn't happy—he always said the military was for those who couldn't stand the burden of thinking for themselves—but he was satisfied, in a grudging way, to see Ted doing something, making a choice, however misguided. He didn't argue with Ted. Joanne was more than happy to spend hours doing that. He did, however, think that his son was even more different than he'd known. Within the week, Ted shipped out for basic training, and that was that.

By the time Roger was telling me about him, Ted had been in the Army for ten years. He'd been part of the Gulf War; although his unit had missed the major combat. He'd advanced rapidly through the ranks. I think he made sergeant within about three years. His superiors wanted him to train to be an officer, but he turned them down, said he was happy being a sergeant. What he did was move from Infantry to Special Forces. Roger and Joanne visited a couple of the bases where he was stationed. Those trips never went well. Joanne couldn't get used to the drabness of it all, while Roger couldn't stop himself from arguing with anyone who spoke two words to him. Someone would say, "Nice day," and he'd say, "Not really." You don't have to be Sigmund Freud to know he was displacing a whole heap of unresolved anger onto whoever was unfortunate enough to talk to him. After their second trip, during which Roger's continuing and unrestrained displacement almost earned him a beating from a pair of MPs, the three of them agreed that, in the future, it would be better if Ted came to see *them*.

From what Roger said, it sounds like the Army was the right place for Ted. I've never been a big fan of the military, either, but it works for some people, and Ted was one of them. Roger couldn't handle that. He said he wanted his son to live his own life, but what he meant was that, if Ted had wanted to get his Ph.D. in Melville instead of Dickens, he could have lived with it. His expectations for his son circled a fixed point, which was academia, and the military was light years away from that. If Ted had decided to move up to being an officer, it wouldn't have mattered. Roger would have taken that as further proof that Ted was wasting his abilities.

• • •

I rolled over and consulted the clock. Four-thirty, and while my body felt the hour, as far as my mind was concerned, it might as well be noon. Maybe some warm milk would help. I threw back the covers, hauled myself out of bed, found my robe, and padded out to the kitchen. On the way, I shut the living room windows, which had helped dissipate the pepper spray; although faint traces of it stung my nose. I took down a large mug from the kitchen cabinets and opened the fridge for the milk, thinking that Roger's bad memories helped explain why he and Ted would end up beating each other senseless on my living room floor, but that they weren't all. I had said so, that second night, said I couldn't believe things had always been so bad. The very fact that they had deteriorated so dramatically was proof that, once upon a time, they must have been very good, because isn't that the way these things work? You don't go from apathy to anger; if you want to find hate, the surest route's love. "What about before Ted became the teenager from hell?" I had said. "What about when he was a baby?"

Ah, Roger had said, that was different. His eyes had lost their focus—

• • •

—and in an instant, he was back in the delivery room at Penrose. Joanne screamed, the doctor said, "Here he is!" and Roger beheld his son, naked, wet, and crying. He and Joanne had been trying to have a baby for a long time—they were married almost ten years when she found out she was finally pregnant—and for that child to be a boy—well, you know what an old patriarch Roger was. Here was his son and heir, and all that. Not to say that Joanne didn't love him too—in her own, distant, icy way—but from the instant Roger first held Ted and looked down into his eyes, newly opened to the world, he fell in love, you know? You must have felt the same thing with your son.

For the first years of Ted's life, he and Roger were inseparable. They went everywhere together, did everything. From the time Ted was old enough to watch TV and understand what was going on, he loved baseball. Roger couldn't explain it, since he'd always preferred basketball, and as for Joanne—you can't imagine her family's got the genes for anything besides polo. Roger would turn on the TV, and Ted would crack himself up watching this game. Once Ted could stand and throw, Roger bought him his own glove and ball, a bat, the whole works—and he bought himself a glove, too. You've seen the lawn around Belvedere House. It's practically big enough for a baseball diamond. For about ten years, as soon as the weather was warm enough, the two of them went out there and threw the ball to one another. When they were tired of that, Roger pitched and Ted batted; then Ted pitched and Roger batted. And when they'd had enough of that, they went back to throwing the ball back and forth. They were a neighborhood fixture, the short guy wearing the dress shirt and slacks he taught in, the long, lanky kid in his t-shirt and jeans. Roger had never been what you'd call an athlete, and he was amazed at how much enjoyment he got from something as simple as sending the ball through the air to Ted. Ted played little league, and Roger was there for every game. By then, he had enough clout to insure a teaching schedule that wouldn't interfere with his watching Ted play. He even tried out as assistant coach for a season, but that was a disaster. Enthusiasm, he told me, is a nice supplement to ability, but it's no substitute for it. I gather he tried to inspire a team of nine-year-olds with quotations from Tennyson: "Into the valley of death rode the six hundred," and all that. He went back to cheering on the bleachers, which made everyone happier.

There was more to their relationship than baseball—a lot more. Roger read to Ted. Every night he spent at least an hour sitting at Ted's bedside, taking him through *Treasure Island, The Hobbit, Ivanhoe*: boys' books. Joanne was the one who was supposed to help Ted with his homework, since that's what she'd majored in in college, primary education, but can you imagine her with a class of first-graders? There's a horror story for you. She wasn't much good at explaining things—surprise, surprise—she could show Ted how to do a math problem, but he was the kind of kid who wants to know why, and that was too much for Joanne. So although Joanne insists she was responsible for Ted's education, that's not true. Roger was the one who had to leave the papers he was grading in his office on the third floor to come down to the kitchen to explain why Jefferson made the Louisiana Purchase. He sat with Ted watching his favorite cartoons; he took Ted to see the latest movies. He hadn't been prepared, he told me—he'd been completely taken by surprise by how completely besotted he was with this little boy.

There were the usual ups and downs. Ted broke his arm when

he tried to play Spider-Man and climb the walls of the house. He had the typical assortment of childhood diseases, including, Roger said, the single worst case of chicken pox he had ever witnessed. He spent most of fourth grade in an on-again, off-again fight with the class bully. There were more serious problems, too. Ted wasn't a great reader. He'd sit and listen to Roger read to him for as long as Roger wanted to, but he showed little interest in opening a book on his own. Roger bought him all kinds of books on all kinds of subjects. If Ted wouldn't look at a history of the Yankees, though, there wasn't much chance of him rushing through *Oliver Twist*. His report cards reflected his lack of interest in reading: good grades in math and science, poor and sometimes failing grades in English and social studies. Ted tried. He spent hours at that kitchen table, laboring over his reading and writing assignments well into the night, sometimes. Roger sat up with him, doing his best to explain what to Ted seemed an increasingly complex and confusing system. He continued reading to Ted, though he prefaced each night's selection by asking Ted if he wouldn't rather read it himself. Ted always refused, and Roger made less and less pretense of hiding his disappointment, thinking he could guilt Ted into reading. He instituted a daily reading period for Ted, an hour that Ted had to spend wrestling with something Roger had selected for him. Before Ted could go outside, go to his friends' houses, even do his actual homework, he had to sit in the living room where Roger would watch him struggle through *David Copperfield*—which, over the course of two years, Roger made him read cover to cover. Once Ted was done, Roger would quiz him, ask him about trivial details to be sure Ted hadn't been daydreaming. It was the kind of tactic Roger employed with his students. If Ted couldn't answer the question to Roger's satisfaction, he'd be sent back to the couch for another hour. Joanne intervened when Roger's regime interfered with little league, but all that did was make him switch the time to after dinner.

It was years before one of Ted's teachers suggested that Roger and Joanne might want to have Ted tested for dyslexia, which I can't believe. I think he was in the seventh grade at that point, twelve years old. Doesn't say much for the teachers in grades one through six, does it? Doesn't say much for Joanne, either. I'm sure she must have had some training in recognizing learning disabilities. If she spent as much time with Ted on his homework as she says she did, how could she not have picked up on his? Once the diagnosis was made,

Roger and Joanne spent all kinds of money on tutors for Ted, and his reading skills rapidly improved. But no matter how much his ability improved, his interest didn't. Ted was not a reader, and you can imagine how Roger—who liked to describe himself as a reader first, last, and in-between—took this. They played baseball together, watched TV and movies together, and Roger hoped there would be a time they'd sit in the library reading quietly together. He hoped too much, if you know what I mean, spent too much time brooding over this small but to him crucial difference between them. And then Ted hit fifteen, and any and all reading schedules flew out the window.

• • •

My hot milk was gone, and I was as awake as ever. I rose from the same kitchen table at which Roger had narrated his history with his son to me, deposited my mug in the sink, and returned to the bedroom. It was just past five; the sky was paling. In a little while, the sun would be up, and this weird night would be over. I sat on the bed. Roger and Ted's fractious relationship was one half of what brought Ted to my front door. As for the other—I don't know how much you know about Roger and me. Your wife's a faculty member; so are you, I guess. You know the scandal. You know how Roger and I got together; although, like I said, it wasn't as sordid as everyone pretended.

• • •

His and Joanne's marriage was over, had been for years, ever since she'd slept with a professor in the Anthropology department. I bet you didn't know that, did you? No one did, because she swore to Roger it was a mistake and he forgave her, brushed the whole thing under the carpet. None of you knew how much he put up with. You all saw him almost-drunk at one of their parties while Joanne stood there looking as cool and composed as a mannequin and you thought, "Oh, poor Joanne; look what she has to deal with." Please. Tell me the last time you saw a smile cross her face. With all the face-lifts she'd had, I'm not sure she could smile: that much pressure and the whole façade would've come tumbling down.

When everything between Roger and me began—the first time he stayed at my place—I know how lame it sounds to say it was an accident. I mean, we were together all the time, hanging out in Roger's office, drinking coffee at the diner, going to the movies—but I honestly didn't think it was anything more than—I don't know—a friendship. I'd met his wife, for God's sake, and seen the condescending smirk she gave me. She obviously didn't view me as a threat.

I had heard about Roger Croydon while I was at Penrose. Our Victorianist had a minor obsession with disproving everything Roger had written, and in the privacy of her office was quite happy to talk about Roger's "young honeys." "You just know he's sleeping with them," she'd say. "God! I thought this kind of behavior went out with the stone age." When Roger and I argued, I used some of her points against him. They didn't work; they weren't very good, really. Anyway, when I decided I was going to pursue the MA at Huguenot, I knew I was going to have to take a class with this guy. After all I'd heard, how could I not? I'd read a few of his articles, and what he had to say wasn't all bad.

What I wasn't prepared for was him, his presence. The class was his Studies in Dickens, and it was held in one of the basement classrooms in the Humanities Building—you know, no windows, low ceiling, a claustrophobe's nightmare. Not to mention the décor: molded plastic seats, folding tables, cheap walls—what I think of as civic bland. And then Roger strode in. He walked right to the front of the classroom, this short guy built more like a prize fighter than an English professor, threw his briefcase on the table, and went right into his lecture. In an instant, everything changed. The uncomfortable seats, the fluorescent lights buzzing overhead, the guy to my left coughing every two seconds, all of that vanished, or might as well have. There was only this man in tan chinos, a white dress shirt, and a fawn blazer, his hair gray but still thick and in need of a cut, his face creased and worn but animated, full of what he had to tell us about Charles Dickens.

For a while, I could recite large chunks of that first lecture; I still remember most of it. "Dickens melodramatic?" Roger asked, one eyebrow raised. "Yes, of course! What else are we to call the murder of Nancy Sykes, the death of Little Nell, the pursuit of Lady Dedlock? If melodrama abounds in Dickens's work, it is because he saw melodrama abounding in his life, in the world around him. From the beginning of his life, when he was yanked out of his routine and sent to work at a blacking factory, to its end, when he survived a train accident in France, Dickens was stalked by melodrama. So are we all, though much that passes for literature and literary criticism would like to close its eyes to it." Towards the end of the lecture, he quoted Graham Greene. "This is why, as Greene says, a novel like *Great Expectations* gives us the sense of eavesdropping on the narrator, listening to the conversation he is having with himself. Dickens's narrators create themselves through the stories they tell us; as, indeed, did their author."

Well. How could I not be impressed? Yes, I knew Roger was full of himself, but so what? He obviously knew what he was talking about. It didn't hurt that, from the start, I was his favorite. The first night, he stayed after class to talk to me; I showed up at his office hours the next day to continue the discussion. We met for coffee at the Plaza Diner the day after that. I went into what I suspected might be developing with my eyes open. While I attributed my Penrose professor's gossip to professional jealousy, that didn't mean there was nothing to it. Roger introduced me to Joanne the second week I knew him, however, which didn't seem like the kind of thing you'd do to someone you were planning to sleep with. The moment I met Joanne, I disliked her, and I'm sure the feeling was mutual. She was wearing this navy blue pantsuit with a blue and white striped scarf that was supposed to suggest she was ready to take the wheel of her yacht. All she needed was a captain's hat. She was so skinny, that semi-emaciated look some women embrace in middle-age as a way of convincing themselves they are, in fact, entering the prime of their lives. She was civil enough, but underneath her pleasantries, I could feel her sizing me up, turning me over the way she'd inspect a figurine she came across antiquing. It didn't take her long to decide I was a mass-produced knockoff, not worth worrying over. After that, I saw her a couple more times, and each one, she looked right through me.

All of which is to say, my suspicions of Roger receded pretty quickly. Nor did I have any designs on him. I found him incredibly attractive, more so than I would have expected I could a man his age. I didn't know exactly how old he was, but he had to be at least the same age as my mother, and I've never been one for crushes on my parents' friends. As a group, they've pretty much seemed...old. Not that they don't have their virtues, but the times I met my dad's work buddies, they all seemed distant, preoccupied, which no doubt they were, with their jobs, their families, paying the mortgage or the car. Roger was different. He was so—dynamic, and he had the ability to make you feel that all of that energy was focused on you. He had these green, green eyes. It was not hard to imagine those eyes looking into yours. That's why—when a woman becomes involved with an older—a much older man, the conventional wisdom is that she's looking for her father. Otherwise, how could she possibly be interested in this guy? I can't speak for everyone, but in my case, nothing could have been further from the truth. If I looked hard enough, I'm sure I could find similarities between Roger and my dad, but the point is, I'd have to make an effort to find them. Dad was low-key, funny in a goofy sort of way, a huge sports fan—when he died, one of my biggest regrets was that he never made it to the Super Bowl, or the World Series. He read, but it was mostly James Clavell and James Michener, big fat bug-crushers that he liked for what they told him about the Space Program, or Alaska, or Feudal Japan.

Whatever I might have felt, I was sure there was no way Roger would be interested, so I put any thoughts in that direction away. And for the longest time, nothing happened. When I invited Roger over to watch *Nicholas Nickleby* on Turner Classic Movies, there was no ulterior motive. It's funny. I still remember the date: March 1. From the moment I opened the door, he seemed awfully nervous, and I couldn't figure out why until, on his way out the door, he leaned over and kissed me. What a kiss that was. It was like, my eyes opened and I thought, "Oh." All the pieces fell into place or something. His breath tasted of the wine we'd been drinking. I kissed him back, and he put his arms around me. We—he didn't make it home that night, or the next one, either, which was no big deal, because Joanne was staying at her sister's in Manhattan for the week. Who knows what would've happened if she'd been at home? No, that's not true. Roger and I were inevitable. If it hadn't happened then and there, it would've someplace else.

That first night, afterwards, when we were lying in my bed together, holding each other the way you do after your first time with someone, I asked Roger if he'd planned this.

No, he said, although he'd hoped.

Had he done this before?

Never.

Then why now? Why me?

"I had to take the chance," he said.

• • •

By now, the sun had put in its daily appearance, the apartment filled with brightness. On their way out the door, the cop without the black eye had told me I could come for Roger and Ted at nine a.m. I supposed there was still enough time for a couple hours' nap if I felt like it, but I didn't, so I headed for the bathroom and the shower.

• • •

From the start, Roger's and my affair burned pretty hot. We couldn't get enough of each other, and discretion was not our strong suit. It only took three weeks for what was going on between us to come out, and, in retrospect, I'm surprised we managed to keep it quiet that long. There were a few close calls. You know that Roger and I were discovered by Joanne—"caught," was what she said when she opened the door to his study. She gasped and said, "I caught you!" Like a line from a bad play. She'd probably been rehearsing it. She had to have suspected something. Roger was gone from the house for more and more of each day; he returned later and later each night; he seemed happier than he had in years. How could Joanne not think he was seeing someone new? This part of our relationship—I don't know. When it was taking place, our affair seemed like the most important thing in the world. It had a consecration of its own. It was new and fresh and sure this kind of thing had happened before—how many of the college's faculty are on their second or third marriage?—but not like this, not in this way. I would think that it was like *Jane Eyre*. Here I was, the bright young independent woman, and here was Roger, Rochester, older, kind of cantankerous, living in this big house with an awful wife. Yes, I know the comparison's a stretch, but that was okay. If I couldn't find an exact parallel for our situation, that only emphasized its originality, you know?

Then Joanne walks in on us on the fold-out couch in Roger's office and it's, "I caught you!" and suddenly I didn't know what to think. Maybe my—our story wasn't that new. Maybe it was more a farce than a romance—some kind of second-rate *Peyton Place*. It turns out there is a precedent for what you've been doing. You just didn't see it because you were looking for it under literature, and it's filed under trash. Didn't Tolstoy say that God is a lousy novelist? Seems like it, sometimes, doesn't it?

Joanne was wearing a vanilla blouse and brown slacks. She stared at us trying to wrap this tiny blanket around ourselves; she hit her mark and delivered her line; she walked out. Roger was buttoning up his shirt when we heard her Mercedes start. He ran for the door, but Joanne put the pedal to the floor and peeled out of there. We stayed where we were, Roger, his shirt half-buttoned, untucked, no socks or shoes, his hand outstretched for the doorknob, me, still holding that blanket up in front of me, my hair in my eyes. For the last twenty-one days, we'd been living in our own private world full of secrets, secret signals, secret jokes, secret meetings. The rest of the world—what I thought of as the real world, which is strange, now that I think of it, because what we were doing was as real as it gets—the real world felt incredibly far away. We were living—if I call it a fairy tale, I'm not trying to be sappy or romantic—I mean, Roger was a little old to be playing Prince Charming, and my credentials for the part of Snow White were seriously lacking. It's just there was that same sense you have living in a fairy tale that here is a world that operates according to different rules than the ones we're used to. Mirrors can answer questions; animals can speak; there are dwarfs and witches and glass slippers. When we could tear ourselves apart for a minute—usually at the diner—we'd talk about where this thing was leading. We knew there would be consequences to what we were doing—we knew it, though we didn't really believe it. Consequences was just a word.

When Joanne stood there looking at us, however—when she tore out of that driveway like a bat out of hell—it was like our private fantasy world came smashing into this one. All the things we'd talked about, the possibilities we'd discussed, up to and including Roger leaving Joanne and moving out to my place, went from so many words to real possibilities. Yes, we had what we wanted. Isn't there a curse that goes, "May you get what you want"? Here we were, where we wanted to be, and it froze us.

But we thawed. I fully expected Roger to panic, say, "This has been nice, but I have a marriage to think about." I'm no fatalist, myself. It's just, they'd been together for thirty-five years. When Roger and I started sleeping together, I'd promised myself I wouldn't be stupid. I knew how I felt about him, and I thought I knew how he felt about me, but love doesn't always win the day, does it? I'd take this for what it was worth, get what I could out of it, but I had no doubt it was temporary. Even during our most—intimate moments together, this little voice in the back of my head kept reminding me, "This won't go on forever."

How shocked was I when Roger turned to me and said, "Get dressed: we have to go to the bank immediately"? All their accounts were joint, and he was afraid Joanne was on her way to empty them. "In case she's been there already, how are you for cash?" he asked as I pulled on my jeans, and it was with that question that I realized I'd been wrong. This wasn't over; this was on its way to something else entirely. I finished dressing in a hurry. We went to the bank. Joanne hadn't cleaned out their savings, so Roger took half of what was there and opened his own account. We returned to the house, and sat in the kitchen eating left-over fried chicken. Later, we watched TV in the living room. Everything was so real. It was as if we'd been living in a Monet, all fuzzy edges and warm glows, and suddenly been dumped into one of Lucian Freud's hyper-real canvases. I had this feeling—I was aware of shifting from one state to another, in a way I've been only a couple of times in my life.

A week later, Roger moved in with me. He and Joanne commenced their long and messy divorce. I became the Whore of Babylon. I'd rather not rehearse those couple of years. It would take me the rest of the night to catalogue what a complete and total bitch Joanne was. I mean, she broke into my apartment, for God's sake, and tossed it like some kind of amateur private eye. All the while, Roger and Joanne's old friends took her side, as if they had any idea what that marriage was really like. I guess the women were all afraid their husbands saw Roger as a secret hero, and the men were afraid they did, too. It was like high school, all over again. I always thought that, when you got older, you matured. How wrong was I? Here were these people two and three times my age, and we might as well have been passing notes in study-hall. Honestly, Roger and I were happy—you wouldn't believe how happy—but this childish stuff did get to us, sometimes.

The only people who weren't complete jerks to us were Addie and Harlow. I can remember how surprised—how pleasantly surprised I was the Saturday afternoon my phone rang and it was Addie, whom I didn't know, inviting us over for dinner. There was half a second when, as I was climbing the front stairs to their house, I panicked and was sure her invitation had been some kind of trap, and Joanne would be waiting for us, but I needn't have worried. Dinner could have been awkward—I mean, these guys went back to Roger and Joanne's arrival in Huguenot—but from the start, Addie made everything pleasant and comfortable. Thank God for her.

• • •

Even after an extra-long shower, there were more than three hours to go before I'd see Roger. I could have started to clean up the mess he and Ted had made, but I was more inclined to save that for him. I didn't want to be in the apartment anymore, however; so I decided that there were worse ways to kill some time than reading that day's *Times* over breakfast at the Plaza Diner. It took me a while to dress, since I wasn't sure whether casual or formal was more appropriate for picking your husband up from jail. In the end, I decided on formal, a robin's egg suit with a white blouse. I put my hair up and left my glasses on, both to make me look older and more serious. Then I left the wreckage of my living space for an early-morning drive to All the News that's Fit to Print and a plate of eggs Benedict.

• • •

The whole time his parents' divorce was being fought out, we never saw or heard from Ted. I was sure he'd at least call or write a letter— this was the end of his parents' marriage, after all, and you know the first thing Joanne did the day she left was phone Ted and give him her version of what had happened. I wanted Roger to call him and explain his side of things. Otherwise, I said, it made it look as if Roger was admitting he'd done something wrong. No, no, he said, it was already too late. Ted would be only too happy to believe his father was the villain. I didn't argue with him—he'd obviously made up his mind, and we had other things to worry about—though I thought about writing to Ted myself. Roger deserved to have someone offer his perspective. But when I sat down at the computer, I didn't know what to say. I couldn't figure out how to begin. "Hi, this is the woman your father left your mother for"? I couldn't see how to present Roger's version of events without seeming totally self-serving. I didn't want to do what Joanne had done, you know? There's still a file on my hard drive called "Ted Letter." Open it, and you see a blank screen.

No, all the while Joanne was breaking into my apartment, and sending me hate mail, and calling and screaming at me, we didn't hear from Ted. The times I brought him up to Roger, he said that Ted's silence spoke volumes, didn't it? All the bitterness and anger he'd felt about Ted as a teenager hadn't left him. He'd stored it, put it in boxes and tried to forget it, until he went looking for it again and found it was still bright and shiny as ever. This was when I understood how much Ted had hurt him—over a morning cup of coffee, I realized that he despised his son. It was frightening, to think that a parent would feel that way about their child. I mean, from everything Roger told me, Ted wasn't half as bad as I'd been when I was his age, and my parents never despised me. (I don't think they did, anyway.) If we hadn't been where we were—if those feelings hadn't come out of storage so recently—maybe it wouldn't have bothered me as much. But I felt like I was living with someone who had a loaded gun by the side of the bed.

(What is it Chekhov said? If you're going to introduce a gun in act one of your drama, it must be fired by act three? Something like that.)

And then came the wedding. Roger and I weren't planning it. He was barely out of his first marriage; I was content to wake up next to him each morning. We didn't need to get married. The next thing, I found out I was pregnant. We'd been rolling the dice—Roger wasn't much good with condoms, and I honestly didn't think anything would happen. Yes, stupid—and wrong. It was after the divorce was finalized. Roger had given Joanne everything—he said he wanted to make a clean break—everything except the house. That was what made the divorce take twice as long as it should have: Belvedere House. As if it hadn't seen enough misery, already. First Joanne wanted it and Roger thought it should be sold. Then he wanted it and she thought it should be sold. Then they both wanted it sold but couldn't agree how to split the proceeds. And so on. Finally, they negotiated this ridiculously complex deal, the upshot of which was that the house wasn't sold. It was rented, with the profits put into three accounts, one each for Roger and Joanne, and one for maintenance of the place. I'd suggested that exact solution to Roger a year before, but did he listen to me? No.

Anyway, I started to feel nauseated. After about three days of being unable to keep down anything more substantial than water and saltines, I started to suspect I might be pregnant. I was in denial for the next week, then I bought a home pregnancy test and confirmed it. That's the reason I married: my sixty-four-year-old boyfriend knocked me up. Neither of us was brave enough not to marry. For Roger, it had to do with the way he'd been brought up, which it did for me, too—but there was more to my decision. Once I'd decided I was going to have this baby, the prospect of everything ahead of me was overwhelming. I felt alone and terrified. Had Roger not proposed to me—which he did when I brought the home test out of the bathroom to show him: he looked up from the couch and said, "Does this mean you'll marry me?"—if he hadn't popped the question, I probably would've kicked him out.

As it was, he did, so the next day, we went to get our marriage license, and the day after that, at Town Hall, Judge Carol Tuttle officiating, I became the second Mrs. Roger Croydon. I wore a slate blue dress with a pale yellow jacket. Roger wore a shirt and tie and that blue blazer every English professor seems to have—they must get them with their doctorates. I was feeling pretty sick, and dizzy besides. I was afraid I was going to throw up on the judge. She was pretty annoying. Throughout the ceremony, she kept looking at us as if we were a sideshow attraction. "Come and see the woman who's marrying a man old enough to be her grandfather." Gasp. She was probably a friend of Joanne's.

For our wedding meal, Roger wanted to take me to the Canal House. It would have been a waste. The sight of anything more than crackers and a little clear broth was enough to send me running for the bathroom. Instead, Roger ordered a veal parm sub from Manzoni's, and we spent our wedding night curled up on the couch, watching an *Outer Limits* marathon on channel 11. At some point, Roger carried me through to bed, but it was just to tuck me in.

We kept the news of our marriage quiet, at first. It was nice to share a secret, again. We didn't tell anyone I was pregnant, either. We figured they'd know in due time. After a couple of weeks, when more people were noticing the plain gold bands on our fingers, we sent out notices to our families and friends. They were just plain white cards that said, "Roger and Veronica Croydon will be residing at 308 Springgrown Road, Huguenot, N.Y., 12561." Roger insisted on adding the first line of the Elizabeth Barrett Browning sonnet: "How do I love thee? Let me count the ways," which I thought was too much, but he wanted to make a point. Almost everyone ignored us, except for Addie and Harlow, who sent a beautiful card, a massive floral arrangement, and a cappuccino machine. Oh, and my mother called from California.

I haven't said that much about her, have I? Suffice it to say, I've pretty much been on my own since I was sixteen. Until then, we'd had your more-or-less standard nuclear family, dad, mom, kid. Then the dad died, the mom went to pieces, and the kid was left to fend for herself. You know who got me into Penrose; who filled out the admission forms, the financial aid forms; who went to meeting after meeting with this financial aid person and that scholarship representative? It wasn't Mom. Until the middle of my freshman year at college, she didn't do much more than sit on the couch and watch old videos of her and Dad. Nobody's grief was as profound as hers. She loved to say, "My father died, too, so I understand what you're going through. But you've never lost a spouse." I swear, I could have screamed. Anyway, over Christmas break, my first year at Penrose, she decided she'd been in mourning long enough and what she needed was a change of scenery. Her younger sister, Aunt Shirley, had invited her to come out to Santa Barbara for a while, maybe think about relocating there. Mom expected me to come with her. I had no intentions of leaving school. There was a huge fight, the upshot of which was that she moved to California, I stayed where I was and got an apartment, and we didn't see or hear that much of one another. I must've talked to her during the time after Roger and I got together, but it wasn't more than half a dozen times, and never for very long. I'd mentioned I was involved with someone, and pretty seriously, but she hadn't shown any interest beyond a, "How nice for you," so I hadn't felt obliged to fill her in on the details.

I shouldn't have been surprised when I picked up the phone one Monday morning and heard her voice saying, "You're married?" But I was, so instead of saying, "Why Mother, how nice to hear from you," I said, "Mom?"

"What have you done?"

"What do you mean? I got married."

"Yes, so I see—from a card, Veronica. I found out about my only daughter's marriage—not even about her marriage—I found out she got married, who knows when, to a man I've never heard of, from a card in the mail."

"Things happened kind of fast," I said. "I told you about Roger."

"Not that he was your fiancé."

"I told you we were living together."

"You most certainly did not."

"Yes, I did. It was a couple of phone calls ago."

"You may think you did, but, believe me, if you had told me you were living with a man, I would have remembered."

"Whatever, Mom. I know what I said."

"And I know what you didn't. Well, I guess I'll just have to accept the fact that my daughter got married and I wasn't there. Who is this Robert? Have you known him long? I hope so, if you've been living with him."

"It's Roger," I said, "Roger Croydon. We've been together a couple of years."

"Croydon? What kind of a name is that?"

"I don't know. English, I think."

"You don't know?"

"Mom."

"What does he do?"

"He's a professor at the college."

"I see. Was he your professor?"

"I did take a class with him—"

"And this is how you earned your 'A.'"

"Mom!"

"I'm sorry, it's just—how old is this man?"

"Old enough," I said.

"Why don't you want to tell me?"

"Because it's none of your business."

"Oh, I see—like your getting married was none of my business, apparently."

"Fine. Roger's sixty-four."

"Sixty-four?"

"Uh-huh."

"Veronica, you do realize that's older than I am?"

"Yes, Mom. It doesn't matter."

"Oh, I'm sure. Let me see if I have the details right. Aunt Shirley will love this. You've married your sixty-four-year-old college professor. Is there anything else? Are you pregnant?"

For an instant, I was going to tell her. Why not? It wasn't as if I was going to change the way she had already decided to think of me.

Why not go all the way, give her the whole, sordid story? At the last second, though, my, "As a matter of fact, Mom, I am," became, "No, of course not." Not because I was ashamed, but because I wasn't going to use my unborn child as a weapon against its grandmother. I would tell her when my due-date was closer—or, Hell, I could mail her an announcement for that, too. She'd love that.

So maybe sending people—certain people—marriage announcements wasn't the smartest move. After the phone call, I didn't hear from my mother for another six months. If I needed any confirmation of that opinion, I received it when Ted showed up at our front door, furious.

• • •

My eggs Benedict were a yellow smear on the plate, my toast a sprinkling of crumbs, and I'd had three cups of decaf and two trips to the bathroom. I'd read all of the paper I cared to, and fiddled with the crossword. I checked my watch. By the time the check came and I paid it, it would be time to fetch Roger. I folded the paper and signaled my waitress.

• • •

After our marriage, Roger had no intention of communicating with Ted at all. He assumed Joanne would've passed the information along—not that Roger told her, either. She found out from a friend who knew the Town Clerk the same day we filed for our marriage license. Can you believe it? The joys of living in a small town. Joanne called my apartment that night and left a nasty message on my answering machine. The funny thing was, she accused Roger of getting me pregnant, which was just her trying to be mean, but which was absolutely right. We should've been angry—Roger was, a little—but it was too funny. I thought we should make an effort with Ted, try to reach out to him. I didn't feel like I could call him, not if Roger wouldn't, but sending him a card seemed within the bounds of propriety. I mean, he was as much Roger's son as he was Joanne's, and I didn't see why she should have the monopoly on him. If they could share the house, for God's sake, they could share their child. From everything Roger had told me, Ted sounded like a bright guy—I was sure he'd appreciate the effort.

When I'm wrong, I'm wrong.

• • •

Once I walked into town hall, I was directed to the courthouse, where I waited fifteen minutes, until Roger and Ted were led in, then another ten until the judge arrived. Father and son had spent the night in a couple of cells in the back of the police station. Neither looked the better for it. Roger was obviously exhausted—and still furious. So was Ted. I swear, if the cops hadn't been right there, they would have started all over again. At their arraignments, I stood up and spoke to the judge—not the woman who married us; this was a guy, Brace—and did my best to explain everything in a way that pointed most of the blame at myself. I said that Ted's father and I had gotten together under difficult circumstances, which Ted must have found extremely painful. When we were married, I had sent a wedding announcement to Ted as a goodwill gesture. Without any context for my action, though, he had taken it as an insult, which was understandable and which I should have anticipated. Of course he was angry. As for Roger: I hadn't told my husband I was sending the card to his son, so there was no way for him to be prepared when Ted appeared on our doorstep, furious. The situation had spiraled out of control. Roger reacted to his son's anger; the next anyone knew, the police were there. Yes, the two of them had behaved like kids, but it was all a misunderstanding. I put in a pretty good performance, enough so that the judge let them off with a "don't-ever-do-this-again." I always knew I'd make a good lawyer.

On our way to the car, Ted came over to us. I don't know what he was going to say. His face wasn't exactly friendly, but it had lost its previous fury. He caught Roger's arm and said, "Wait."

Roger stopped and said, "Take your hand off me," in a voice as cold as outer space. It was so—different, so dark that I stopped walking, too. I swear, I'd never heard him speak like that before. I'd never heard anyone speak like that. The air froze and crackled around his words. Ted jerked his hand back. Roger went on in that same, absolute zero voice: "Boy, the best part of you dribbled down your mother's leg. You have always been a disappointment to me, from your inability to read even a simple book when you were a child, to the self-indulgence of your adolescence, to the blind surrender to authority that you call a career. You are an embarrassment and a disgrace. Your life has been nothing; it is nothing; it will always be nothing. As of this moment, I am no longer your father; you are no longer my son. I disown you; I cast you from me. All bonds between us are sundered; let our blood no longer be true. And when you die, may you know fitting torment; may you not escape your failure. You are a stranger to me. Good day, sir." Eyes straight ahead, Roger limped toward the car, leaving Ted and me standing there. I went to say something to Ted, but before I could, he spat, "Fine," and stalked away.

It was ridiculous—the whole thing was like a bad joke. Who disowns anyone? If what Roger said wasn't so terrible, if I hadn't heard that arctic voice, I would have laughed the whole thing off. He disowned Ted? Who did he think he was, King Lear? Really. That voice, though. Standing there in the parking lot behind town hall, watching Roger reach the car and lean one arm against it, while Ted strode in the direction of the bus station, I was overcome with fear—not of Roger, but for him. That, and I was angry at him. However ridiculous it was, you don't say that kind of thing to your child. It was the first time I was honestly upset with him. We'd disagreed a lot—we still did, at times—but over piddling stuff. This was serious. I ran to catch up with him. He'd opened the car door, but was still leaning with one hand on the roof. When he turned his face to me, it was gray and he was panting. He said, "Honey, I believe I'm in the middle of a heart attack. Would you please drive me to the hospital?"

My dad had a heart attack; it was what killed him. I recognized the same symptoms in Roger. I wanted to call an ambulance; he refused. "Not in front of the boy." Can you believe that? Ted wasn't in sight anymore. No matter. He insisted no ambulance. Struggling not to panic, I drove Roger to Penrose at roughly a hundred and ten miles an hour. We blew past the state trooper barracks on 299, but it was at exactly the right moment. There was no one out front to see us. All the time, I'm trying to do fifteen things at once. I'm trying to keep the pedal to the floor—because speed is of the essence, right?—both hands on the wheel, both eyes on the road. I'm trying to pass whomever I can as quickly as I can. I'm trying to pay attention to Roger, who's leaning back in his seat with his eyes closed and his mouth open, so that I'm afraid he's dead and have to say, "Roger? Can you hear me?" I'm ready to take one hand off the wheel to poke him when he says, "I hear you." When we hit the Bridge, it's a wonder we don't slide right off.

As it turned out, Roger did have a heart attack—plus three broken ribs, and a bruised hip and kidney. Not to mention bruises and cuts over every square inch of his body. The heart attack wasn't that serious. The cardiologist told me it was, "worse than mild, but not up to medium." Roger didn't want anyone to know about it. While we were waiting in triage, he took my hand and said, "Don't tell anyone."

"About you and Ted?" I said. "Because it's kind of late for that."

"About this," he said, tapping his chest with one finger. I've never liked when people do that, knock on their sternums. It creeps me out—makes you sound as if you're hollow.

Although I didn't see what the big deal was, I respected Roger's wishes. The people I told about him being in the hospital assumed it was due to the fight—which, let's face it, was pretty much true. You think it's coincidence he rolls around on the floor with Ted, beating and getting beaten up by him, and the next thing his heart's saying, "Sorry, no can do"? I stayed with him that first night and the seven more he was there. To start with, he was pretty doped up, so I sat beside his bed, staring at his bruised face. The bruises were red and deep blue, and they streaked his face in a way that made me think of war paint. They made him look fierce, even asleep. I had the urge to hold his hand, to stay in contact with him, but now that the worst danger was past, I kept hearing what he'd said to Ted—which I was already thinking of as Roger's curse on him. "I disown you; I cast you from me." I wanted to laugh at it, but that was harder than you'd expect. I was sure he couldn't have made it up himself. I was certain he was quoting someone. He did that a lot, quoted Dickens or Browning or someone else without telling you he was quoting. It was like his way of saying, "Look how smart I am," and, if you didn't recognize the person he was quoting, "Look how stupid you are." I used to call him on it all the time. For a little while, I did my best to guess the source of his curse. There was enough Dickens I hadn't read for Roger to have plucked it from the pages of one loose, baggy monster or another—oh yeah, there's some pretty fierce stuff in old Charles. Have you read *Little Dorrit*? There's a line in there: this mother is trying to threaten her son into doing what she wants, and she tells him that if he disappoints her, then when she dies and he kneels in front of her corpse at the wake, it'll bleed. Very pleasant. The curse didn't feel like Dickens, though. It felt more like something you'd read in Faulkner, all that stuff about family and disappointment and doom. I couldn't remember what Faulkner Roger had read. He claimed he read nothing written after 1914, but that was mostly a pose.

The games English majors play, right? Everything's a text, or relates to one. It didn't take too long for me to tire of "whence the curse." Where he'd pulled it from didn't matter. What did was that he'd used it, on his son. Every time I remembered the look on Roger's face as he'd pronounced it—the sound of his voice—I put my hand over my belly. Yes, I believed this child's relationship with Roger was going to be different. Roger was not the same as he had been when Ted was a teenager. He was older, mellower, most importantly, happier. We had a better marriage than he and Joanne; already, that was obvious. We had fun—and you can be sure there's a blank spot under that word in Joanne's dictionary. Things would be better for us—for the three of us. All the same, those words: "I am no longer your father; you are no longer my son."

...

I never got the chance to find out what kind of father Roger would have been to our child. Late that first night in the hospital, I woke from where I'd fallen asleep sitting beside him with terrible cramps. I knew—even before I was completely awake, I knew. I tried to stand, to reach the call button clipped to Roger's blanket, but the pain took my legs out from underneath me. I fell and lay there on the floor. I couldn't catch my breath; the giant hand squeezing me wouldn't let me. All I could see was the space under Roger's bed. No, I thought, *no no no no no*. I closed my eyes, tried to fight what was happening. Yes, my body said, and the hand tightened, another round of cramps wracked me. I opened my eyes. They were streaming tears; my nose was running, too. The underside of Roger's bed wavered then blurred. I closed my eyes again as the giant hand contracted tighter. *Oh God*, I thought. *Oh please*. I could feel—I could feel things loosening inside me. Things starting to slip away. The sensation was obscene. I opened my eyes—

And instead of Roger's bed, I was looking at a flat surface—at a wall. It was maybe thirty, forty feet from me, much further than the walls of the hospital room. The floor had gone from pale tile to dark hardwood. Despite the pain, I turned my head.

Roger's bed—his room, were gone. I was in a huge, empty space like a church. No, not a church, the design was wrong. This was more like a house if everything inside, all the rooms, the halls, had been removed, and only the outside left. The crazy thing was, even with the agony digging into my belly, I recognized this place. It was the house, Belvedere House, Roger's house.

The scene lost focus as a fresh flood of tears poured into my eyes. It was harder than ever to breathe. I blinked, was still inside the house. Its walls—what I had taken for shadows crowding them I saw were openings, doorways—the interior was honeycombed with them. Inside each one, there was—

A face. Lurking at the verge of each and every doorway was a face so large it filled the space—dozens of enormous faces. Sweat had broken out all over me; now, I started to shake as the pain deepened. The faces were all the same, the nose long-broken, the heavy creases beside the mouth and over the brows, the thick hair that needed cut. Half a hundred copies of Roger's face gazed out at the vacant interior of Belvedere House. Their lips were moving, the space echoing with their vast whisper. In the general murmur, I could pick out individual phrases. "Your life has been nothing; it is nothing; it will always be nothing." "This is ridiculous. You are ridiculous." "What is it you want?" "And when you die, may you know fitting torment; may you not escape your failure." "Anything—take whatever you need."

I was losing my mind. I had to be; it was the only explanation available. This was too vivid to be a dream. The faces—there was something wrong with each of them. Where its eyes should have been, this one had empty sockets. This one's skin was peeling off in large patches, revealing what looked like scales underneath. This one spoke, and blood ran out of its mouth and down its chin. I shut my eyes and thought, *Oh God. Oh God.* The pain hit a high note, held it. I turned my head to the floor and kept it there, eyes still closed, as my body finished what it had begun.

By the time the night nurse found me and called for help, it was gone, the baby I'd barely started to think of as mine was gone. I felt someone shaking me, heard a voice saying, "Can you hear me?" and opened my eyes to a broad, middle-aged woman's face frowning with concern. I was back in the hospital room. There was a lot of blood.

The air was thick with the stink of it; the floor was covered in it; my suit sodden with it. The nurses helped me clean up and found me someone's old sweatsuit. They wanted me to see one of the hospital's doctors—they insisted—but I refused. Yes, I understood the risks they ticked off on their fingers. I told them I'd see my own doctor first thing in the morning. For now, I didn't want to leave my husband—which wasn't exactly true. Roger had slept through my entire ordeal. He was hooked up to machines that registered his condition. He had a floor full of nurses to look after him. It was—I couldn't stand the thought of going to a doctor and having him tell me I'd had a miscarriage. I knew that was what I'd been through. I knew I'd been pregnant before and wasn't now. To hear it from a doctor, though—to hear it officially—that was too much to deal with. Neither nurse was happy about my decision, and they made me promise, repeatedly, to see my own MD the next day.

For the second day in a row, I spent the deep hours of the night awake, my body shaking, it was so desperate for sleep, my brain unable to shut down in the face of what I'd lost. Not to mention, what I'd seen while I was losing it. That—I didn't know what to call it. Hallucination was probably the appropriate word, but it didn't feel right. I didn't know what did. I would close my eyes, and I would see the empty house, the doorways, the faces. I would hear Roger saying, "Boy, the best part of you dribbled down your mother's leg." I would relive my baby sliding out of me. Every half hour, one nurse or the other poked her head in the doorway, saw I was awake, and asked me how I was feeling. I didn't know how to answer. What I was mostly was empty. Aside from my tears while I was losing the baby, I hadn't cried as much as I would have expected. I hadn't gotten that used to being pregnant in the first place. It had seemed incredible that there was another living being growing inside me. I guess it's different once you can feel the baby move. I sat beside Roger and thought, *Today, he's lost both his children.*

I waited until he came home to break the news to him. For the first couple of days he was at Penrose, I was afraid for his heart. The doctor told me everything was under control and Roger was going to be fine, but I didn't want to tempt fate, you know? I kept my promise to the nurses and saw my ob-gyn that following morning. He was more sympathetic than I expected, so much so that I started bawling in front of him. He made a speech about this being difficult but for the best—nature's way of sparing a life that couldn't have survived on its own. I nodded, drying my eyes and blowing my nose on the tissues he'd had ready at hand. The most important thing, he said, was that I appeared to be all right physically, and that that continue to be the case. I had to take care of myself. Mentally, it was normal to be depressed, even angry. He gave me the card of a Dr. Hawkins, a psychiatrist he'd referred patients to in the past, and made me promise to call her if I was having trouble handling this. I swear, the air the last couple of days seemed to be full of promises. I promised to call the psychiatrist if things started to get too bad. When I got in my car to drive back to the hospital, I had the strangest thought. I sat there with both hands on the steering wheel, looking into the windshield, where I could see my reflection, this woman who'd been a mother-in-process and who now was not, and I thought, *This is the price of Roger's words*. For a second, that idea took hold of me—I was absolutely convinced it was true—I saw Roger's face framed by a doorway, eyeless, the skin peeling away, blood pouring from his mouth. As quickly, it was gone. I shook my head, started the car, and drove back to the hospital.

• • •

Roger recovered rapidly. I probably could have said I'd lost the baby right away. By the time I was more sure of his condition, the hospital seemed like the wrong place. Roger knew I was keeping something from him. He kept asking me what was wrong. Nothing, I said, it was only the strain of everything. "Don't let yourself get too stressed," he said once, his second-to-last day there, "you've got someone else to think about." Somehow, I managed to smile at him.

The afternoon we came home, I told him. He was on bedrest for another week, which frustrated him. "I've been in bed a week already," he complained to the cardiologist, who told him to do as he was instructed or they'd be seeing each other again a lot sooner than either of them wanted. Having a heart attack made Roger nervous, you know? Before, you said that it can happen to anyone, at any age, which is true—and which was what Roger was trying to convince himself of the time he was in Penrose. A thirty-year-old can have a heart attack, but how do you react if they do? You're surprised. You say, "Wow, that's young for a heart attack." Because you associate heart attacks with being old. How many times have you heard someone talk about turning forty or fifty as entering heart attack country? Throughout his week in the hospital, Roger said, "I can't believe I had a heart attack." The second or third time I heard him, I realized what he was actually saying was, "I can't believe I'm old." I reassured him, told him yes, it was crazy that a man in his shape could have this happen to him. Secretly, I thought about his love for cheese, and cream sauces, and ice cream.

We came home, with instructions for a new diet, and I put Roger to bed with the latest issue of *Dickens Quarterly*. The apartment was still a wreck from Roger and Ted's excursion into ultimate fighting. I'd returned for a couple of hours the day before to clean up the worst of it, but the place was a mess, books all over the place, glass in the carpet, bloodstains on the floor. I dug out my cleaning supplies from under the sink, got down on my hands and knees, and started to scrub the floor. It's therapeutic, cleaning—it is for me, at least. From the bedroom, Roger called, "Honey? What are you doing?"

"Cleaning," I said.

"Are you sure that's a good idea?" Roger asked. "In your condition?"

My condition. My condition which wasn't a condition; a condition of wasn't. I stood and went through to the bedroom, where Roger lay on the bed, pillows piled up behind him, his cheap half-glasses on. He was wearing an old conference t-shirt with Dickens's faded face on it. Without removing the rubber yellow gloves I'd pulled on—a wet sponge in one hand—I sat down on the end of the bed and said, "Roger, I lost the baby. I'm sorry."

"Oh, honey," he said, dropping the journal and leaning forward, his arms open. I moved into his embrace. "When?" he asked.

"While you were in the hospital."

I felt him nod. I was expecting him to ask me why I hadn't told him, which I didn't want to have to answer. He didn't, just kept his arms around me. I'd also assumed I would cry when the words came out, but my eyes stayed dry. What I felt was more relief, relief and calm. Roger sniffled, and suddenly was weeping freely. I wound up consoling him, saying, "It's all right," repeating my doctor's words to me about nature sparing a life that couldn't have survived on its own. If I didn't entirely believe that—if I couldn't stop from connecting the miscarriage to Roger's cursing Ted—I didn't let on to him. I tried hard not to think about it.

Overnight, everything changed. Not in a big, dramatic way. It was more like sadness had entered our lives—our life. Until that moment Ted banged on the door, we'd had tough times, some very tough times, but no matter what happened—if all Roger's old friends ignored us; or Joanne called us every hour on the hour every night for a week; or she showed up at the front door of the motel we'd thought we could escape to—oh yeah, she was insane, all right—but it didn't matter if she was, not really, because she was on the outside. She could do whatever she wanted, she could say whatever she wanted, but she couldn't get between the two of us. I'm sure she realized this, and it drove her nuts. That combination of events, though, Roger's disowning Ted, his heart attack, and especially losing the baby, did what Joanne couldn't. It found its way into what we shared and—it didn't ruin it, no—it kind of tarnished it. Things were no longer as joyful. It wasn't as if I took up drinking, or Roger stayed out all night, or the two of us fought all the time. You noticed it in more subtle ways. We didn't wait for each other to be awake to have breakfast, anymore. We didn't read the Sunday *Times* together. We watched TV while we ate dinner. None of it was anything anyone would have worried about— we weren't in any danger of going the same way as Roger and Joanne. Things were different, that was all.

Although I struggled not to, at odd moments, I would hear Roger's curse. I would be driving across the Bridge, on my way to teach at Penrose; or I'd be in the fruit aisle at Shop Rite, wondering whether the Fuji or the Golden Delicious looked fresher; or I'd be walking back from the mailbox, sifting through the day's tally of bills and junk—and that zero-degree voice would burn my ears. "You are an embarrassment and a disgrace." "All bonds between us are sundered; let our blood no longer be true." The space I'd seen the night I lost the baby—that other Belvedere House—would crowd my vision, those doorways, those murmuring faces. Then they were gone, the sounds, the sights, and I was at the wheel, behind the shopping cart, holding a half-dozen envelopes. Probably, I should have talked to Roger about it. Scratch that: definitely, I should have talked to him. It was just—we hadn't said anything to one another about his disowning Ted—Roger's heart attack, and its attending drama, had pre-empted any and all other discussions, and by the time he was home again, there was the miscarriage to talk about, and the further we went from that parking lot, the harder it was to bring up. I assumed Roger would chalk up his words to the heat of the moment, and as for what I'd seen—I really didn't want to contemplate what that might mean for things like my sanity.

. . .

Hard as it was to believe, the world continued around us. When I'd entered the MA program, the economy had been going strong. We were almost at the end of the internet boom. By the time Roger and Joanne signed their divorce papers, the economy was folding in on itself and the 2000 election was stuck in recount. Roger couldn't stand Bush. He never got so caught up in the divorce that he couldn't rail about what an idiot the guy was. He used to say, "If we must have a Republican for president, why on God's green earth couldn't it be McCain, and not that vacuous boob?" I voted for Nader. All of it— politics, the economy, world events—took place in the background, if you know what I mean. We paid attention to the bombing of the *Cole*, to the start of the recession, but none of it compared to what we were undergoing—good and bad—none of it was very real to us.

Do I have to say that changed on September 11? What I remember most about that day—aside from the images on TV—was frantically trying to reach Ted. We were under attack. Planes had crashed into buildings. No one knew how many more might be on their way to what targets. Anything was possible. It was completely reasonable whoever was doing this would want to aim for military bases as well. The thing was, we didn't have Ted's phone number anymore. Roger had torn it out of all our address books after his return from the hospital. I tried calling information, but couldn't get through. Roger was in class. I actually dialed Joanne's number—that's how desperate I was—but it was busy. She lived in Manhattan, remember. Midtown, but who knew how safe that was? No doubt everyone in her family was calling her. I was frantic, pacing the apartment, listening to the beeping of one busy signal after another. I decided I was going to ask Roger for the number when he came home. He had a great memory for that kind of thing, and however hard he would have tried to pry Ted's number from his mind, I knew he'd be able to retrieve it if I insisted.

About ten minutes before Roger ran in the front door saying, "Oh my God, honey, have you heard?" I tried information again and got through. In a remarkably calm voice, the operator asked me what number I wanted. I told her. She gave it to me and told me to have a nice day. Bizarre. I punched in Ted's number, and waited. I was sure the line would be busy, if it was working at all. It wasn't. After what felt like hours, it started to ring. It rang, and it kept on ringing. I wondered if I'd dialed the number correctly; I wondered if it would still ring for me if the phone on the other end had been destroyed. It kept on ringing, what had to be fifty, sixty, seventy times. I considered hanging up and trying again, but was afraid I wouldn't be able to get through. I was hoping that, if I let the phone ring long enough, someone would pick up and I could ask them if Ted was okay. All the while, in the background, the TV was full of the pictures of the Towers burning, the Pentagon burning, of huge plumes of black smoke pouring into the sky. You could hear various talking heads saying they didn't know who was behind this; they didn't know the extent of it.

Finally, the other end picked up and I heard Ted's voice say, "Hello?"

I was so relieved I didn't even take the time to feel relieved. I practically shouted, "Ted! It's Veronica—your father's—Roger's—are you all right?"

There was no reply.

"Ted?" I said, "Can you hear me?"

He hung up.

When I called back, Ted's number was busy. I wasn't surprised he'd hung up; though I hoped maybe that wasn't the case, maybe wires had crossed somewhere and severed our connection. No—I knew he'd done it. But at least I'd heard his voice. I replaced the phone in its cradle, and Roger rushed in full of disaster. I didn't tell him about the call I'd just made. I thought I should wait for him to bring up Ted. He didn't. We spent the rest of that day glued to the TV as it replayed the same awful sights over and over again. Everyone, all the reporters and anchors and pundits, kept saying that what had happened was unimaginable. No, I thought, it's only imaginable. This is the kind of thing you read about, that's supposed to remain safely confined to the pages of a Tom Clancy novel.

Roger never once mentioned Ted—or Joanne, for that matter. It's strange to say, but what I realized on 9/11 was how completely my husband had rid himself of his former life. I was disappointed that he didn't suggest calling Ted—to tell the truth, I was the tiniest bit upset he didn't try to call Joanne, either. I mean, sure, she'd been a monster to us, but on a day like this one, you could look past those kind of things, at least to make sure of something as basic as whether people were alive. I could've come out and said I'd attempted to contact both of them, but each hour that passed without Roger uttering their names made what I'd done seem increasingly weird.

Do you remember what it was like, those days immediately after the attacks? I had been working on an article on Hawthorne, so I had reread a bunch of his stories and was about to begin *The House of the Seven Gables* for what must have been the twentieth time. The morning of the eleventh, I'd read the first couple of pages of the book when the phone rang and my friend, Alicia, was asking me if I had the TV on, a plane had crashed into the World Trade Center. I put the novel down and didn't pick it up again for the rest of that day. Later—I think it was the following morning—I noticed it lying where I'd left it. I tried to go on from where I'd left off, old Maule's curse on Judge Pyncheon: "God will give him blood to drink." I couldn't do it. The words on the page refused to add up to anything. My eyes kept returning to that pronouncement. "God will give him blood to drink." Eventually, I gave up on Hawthorne and cleaned the apartment, instead. When I was done, I was tired and sweaty and didn't feel any better, but I'd found a way to pass a couple of hours. During the week that followed, I cleaned the apartment every day, sometimes twice the same day. I emptied out cabinets and scrubbed them and their contents. I rearranged the furniture in the living room. When I heard Roger say, "I disown you; I cast you from me," when I saw that whispering space, I ignored them and put my back into shifting the couch. I unscrewed the light fixtures and soaked them in the kitchen sink to remove the layers of accumulated grime. I rearranged the furniture in the bedroom. When I saw the words, "God will give him blood to drink," I ignored them, too, and tugged on the bed. I emptied out the closets, and put Roger's clothes in two piles, one to keep, and one for the Salvation Army. Roger saw what I was doing and didn't comment. His response to the disaster was to focus his complete attention on his classes. He sat at the kitchen table for hours with oversized photocopies of key passages from the books he was teaching, filling the copies with notes in half a dozen different-colored pens—one for each theme he was pursuing. By the time he put them aside, they looked like a strange combination of map and modern artwork.

One afternoon that first week—I'm pretty sure it was Friday—I drove into town for more cleaning supplies. On my way back, there was an accident on Main Street and the detour the cops had set up sent me down onto Founders, past Belvedere House. Do you know, it had been months since I'd seen it? In person, I mean. None of the routes I routinely traveled took me onto Founders, and I didn't exactly go out of my way to drive it. Now here to my left was this huge house squatting in the middle of its lawn like—like I couldn't say what. It wasn't empty; I knew that. I'd been inside it, had been with Roger in it. The house was practically a labyrinth, stuffed full of furniture and decorations. Few places were less empty. And yet, as the light shifted on its windows, I was absolutely certain that, were I to pull over, cross the lawn to the front door, and walk inside, I'd find the whole thing hollow, only walls and ceiling. I kept driving.

• • •

Pretty early on, I had a feeling that, when we went to war—because, right away, it was obvious to me that we were going; it was only a question of who and when—I had this feeling—a conviction—that Ted would be sent. I wasn't sure exactly what Ted did. I knew he was a sergeant in the Special Forces, but I wasn't clear what that meant. I'd asked Roger, once, what Ted's job description was. He'd said, "He and his friends do the secret things," as if I had any idea what those kinds of things might be. I'd pursued the question, asked him what "secret things" were, and he'd said, "Infiltration, reconnaissance, sabotage, assassination, that business." I didn't know how accurate Roger was— though I've since learned he was more or less on target—but I knew that Ted had been in the Army for a while, which I assumed meant he was experienced at his job, which I assumed put him at the top of the list of the people who'd be sent.

I was right. When the soldiers put their boots on the ground in Afghanistan, Ted's unit was among them. I'm not sure exactly what he did in the early days of the war, only that he was part of a lot of very intense stuff. That's how his best friend described it to me. Yes, I talked to Ted's best friend, a guy named Gene Ortiz; although he told me everyone calls him Woodpecker. I contacted him after Roger disappeared, when I was trying to fit what had happened to us into some kind of sense. I had questions about Ted, about his time in Afghanistan, so I did some research, found out who his CO had been, and called him. When he heard I was Ted's stepmother, he was very helpful. No doubt because he couldn't see me and think, "You're Ted Croydon's stepmother?" I'd been afraid he'd think my request to speak with someone who'd served with my stepson was morbid, but he said he completely understood. Specialist Ortiz and my stepson had been close to the point of inseparable, the CO said, he was sure the specialist would be happy to provide me any information I might need. "And Mrs. Croydon," the CO said, "may I just say how sorry myself and the rest of the men are about Ted? Your stepson was a model soldier—I don't think there was a man who knew him who didn't admire him. Working with him was a pleasure and a privilege." I thanked him. It was kind of nice to hear someone saying all this. The CO added that he'd tell Specialist Ortiz to expect my call and assist me in whatever way he could.

I was surprised at how nervous I was making that call. My hands shook so much that I had to punch the number in four times. I wasn't sure what Ted would have told his best friend, but it wouldn't have been too flattering. According to Gene, it wasn't; although he refused to say anything more than that Ted had been very, very angry with me. "Almost as angry as he was at his old man," he said. None of which—fortunately—made any difference to Gene. He appreciated me wanting to find out about Ted. We talked for a good couple of hours, about Ted, what he'd been like, some of the crazy pranks he'd pulled, how he and Gene had become friends. Gene didn't want to talk about Afghanistan very much. Their unit had gone in ahead of the main invasion force to, as he put it, "set up the party." "Mazar-i-Sharif, Kabul, Kandahar, Tora Bora: you name it, we were there first," he said. "We did what we did and I'm proud of it, but I'm happy I'm home and I'm sorry T.D. isn't." That's what they called him: T.D.

It took a lot of convincing, but I did get Gene to tell me about Ted's final patrol. "You don't want to hear about that," he kept saying; to which I kept answering, "Yes, I do." They had been out in Kabul, sent out to investigate rumors of Taliban holdouts. The air was abuzz with all kinds of crazy stories, but Bin Laden and Mullah Omar and more of the Taliban than should have been were still running around, so the Army took whatever information came their way seriously. It was late at night, the moon full and shining brightly. Their patrol had taken them to what all previous reports had indicated was a quiet neighborhood. Ahead, the street they were on opened into a square fed by a dozen other streets and alleys. After a quick inspection, they decided it looked safe and moved forward. When they were a little more than halfway across, they heard a loud wailing. Instantly, their guns were up and pointing at its source, an old man who came running out of one of the alleys, waving his hands. Ted swore and advanced to meet him.

That was when the ambush happened. Gene said he heard a whoosh, then the rocket-propelled grenade hit the spot where Ted and the old man were standing. "That was it for T.D.," Gene said. "The old guy, too. If it helps any, it was over before he knew it." The rest of the men spent the next fifteen minutes in a furious firefight with their attackers before killing them. "All of them?" I asked him.

"Yes, ma'am," he said.

"Good," I said, and meant it. The things you never think you'd say.

The first Roger and I learned of Ted's death came via a call from Joanne. For a change, I was the one out teaching—I had a pair of back-to-back sections of Intro to Lit at Penrose—and Roger was home. He didn't tell me about it for a full twenty-four hours. I knew he was acting differently. He was quiet, always the sign that something was wrong. I asked him if he was feeling okay. Fine, he said, fine. I didn't press him; everyone has times they feel like being quiet, right? Anyway, I had papers to grade.

At dinner the following night—we were having Chinese—I was eating cold sesame noodles. I glanced over at Roger—who if anything had been more silent today—and saw tears streaming down his face. He wasn't making any noise, just sitting there eating his chicken with snow peas while his eyes overflowed. I thought he must have been crying for some time, because there were a pair of dark patches on his shirt—he was wearing a denim shirt I'd bought him. I reached across the table and put my hand on his shoulder. He continued eating and crying. I said, "Roger, honey: What is it?"

"Ted," he said. In the sound of that one syllable, I knew; I heard Ted's death.

I said, "Oh. Oh, Roger."

"Joanne called to tell me," he went on. "She said he was on patrol and they were attacked. That's all she knows. That's all anyone is saying right now."

"Honey," I said, "I'm so, so sorry."

"That's the end," Roger said, beginning to sob. "That's the end of my little boy."

It was the end of Roger, too. Not right away, but if I want to point to the moment when he set out down the road to his own end, that would be it. Although maybe not completely. I can't discount the effect returning to Belvedere House had on him.

He arrived at that decision by himself. If we had discussed it, I would have told him that I was fine with leaving the apartment—it was too small, and shrinking every day—but for God's sake, let's find somewhere new. I don't know if it would have helped us to have packed our bags and gone someplace completely different—another state. I'm sure Roger could have gotten a position at a place like BC or UConn no problem. A move like that might've caused its own problems—but whatever those might've been, they couldn't have been any worse than what we found waiting for us in the corridors of that house.

Roger was all right—well, he was functional for a couple of days. Shock. I was in shock, too, but it was a completely different kind of shock. What I was experiencing was what you go through when some-one famous and distant dies. It was like the afternoon Kurt Cobain killed himself. I couldn't wrap my mind around it. Here was this guy whose music had meant so much to me—who seemed like he'd writ-ten the soundtrack to my life, you know? And he put a shotgun to his head. It's a loss, no doubt about it, but what you lose is what you've made of this person you've never met. From the way things had been left between Roger and Ted, you might have expected Roger to feel sad, upset, but not overwhelmingly so. He at least appeared to have distanced himself from Ted considerably. That was an act. Whatever the bad stuff between them, there was all this good history to balance it. Even after that last, awful confrontation, I'd walk into his office at school and catch him looking away from the picture of Ted in his baseball uniform he hadn't gotten around to taking down from his bookcase. Who knows? Roger could have been brooding over what a lousy son Ted was. The point is, he hadn't succeeded in severing himself from his son as completely as he wanted to think. It gave me hope that maybe he and Ted would be reconciled, eventually. It also meant that there was a lot more sentiment than anyone suspected waiting to rise up and carry Roger away.

That was how I thought of the change in Roger, that his grief over Ted's death was carrying him away from me. It was as if we were standing on an ice flow that was gradually breaking up; every day, he receded a little bit farther. He cried a lot at first—we both did. I'd never seen a man cry that hard or that much. He couldn't sleep. We sat up most of the night channel surfing; or Roger went out for these long walks that kept him away till dawn. I waited for him, trying not to be as anxious as I was, wishing I'd insisted on going along. I couldn't figure out where he was walking.

Now, I'm sure his destination must have been Belvedere House, the place where he and Ted had been happiest together. I can picture him standing there on the edge of the lawn, dressed in the gray sweatshirt and -pants that were his nighttime attire whether he slept in them or not. He's panting. His eyes are wide. He's remembering tossing the ball back and forth with Ted so vividly he can see them in front of him, the ball a white blur in the air. And there's the spot where he'd found Ted writhing on the ground, his arm broken after he fell off the roof. And there's the tree that still bears the black mark from where the teenage Ted, drunk on wine coolers, smacked into it with Joanne's Mercedes. Roger stares at the house's stone walls as if he could look through them to the interior he knew, to the kitchen doorway where he marked Ted's height, or the banister Ted delighted in sliding down, no matter how many times Joanne yelled at him for doing so, or Ted's room—rooms, really, because once he'd turned twelve, he convinced his parents to let him move to the third floor. Now Roger's climbing the narrow stairs that connect the second to the third floor. Now he's standing at the threshold of Ted's room, glancing at the posters of Yankees players in action that crowd the walls, at the Oxford Dickens Roger gifted him neatly arranged on the desk, at the bed unmade from when Ted last slept in it. Now he's crossing to the bed and lowering himself onto it. His nose wrinkles at the sharp bite of the Old Spice Ted has taken to wearing in imitation of one of his favorite players, beneath which are the softer odors of Ivory soap and Ted's skin. He rests there, outside and inside the house, calm if not happy, until a car passes by, startling him back into himself and his grief.

• • •

He would return an hour before dawn, full of words. I'd be staring out the kitchen window, wondering where he'd gone, and the lights in the yard would click on, announcing his return. Or I'd be asleep at the kitchen table, and the squeal of the front door opening would wake me. Roger would half-stumble to the couch, his face bright with sweat, his chest heaving. His heart attack was fresh enough in my mind for me to remember the way he'd let his head fall against the headrest as I sped down 299. His sneakers, the bottoms of his sweatpants, would be soaked with dew. I'd bring him a glass of water, insist he wrap a towel around his shoulders against a chill. He would sink into the couch, pressing the glass to his forehead, and say, "I haven't told you about my father, have I?"

I would shake my head. Except for some basics—a father, mother, younger brother and sister, all of them plagued by disease and disaster—I didn't know anything about his family. He never spoke of them. By the time I had met him, so much of Roger's life had already happened that his family had seemed distant, of little consequence.

Roger would drain the water and pass me the empty glass with a "Thank you." Before I had the chance to return the glass to the kitchen, he would start talking. "My father was an alcoholic. Where and when I grew up, that term did not have much currency. A man who enjoyed his bottle too much was either a drunk if it took over his life and caused him to make a fool of himself in public, or none of your damned business if the worst you noticed was that his cheeks were a little redder than they should be, or that his breath was a tad fierce. Father was one of the none-of-your-damned-business alcoholics, a designation that was not hurt by the fact that he also owned the town's undersized Sears and half-a-dozen houses. Oh yes, my dear, I knew money before I met Joanne. Father liked his bottle, but it never interfered with his business responsibilities, so it was his concern. That he would beat my brother, sister, and me when he was in his cups was nobody's concern but ours.

"You knew, when he was drunk, that someone was going to feel his fist before too long. In that way, he was almost comfortingly predictable. His drinking, which had remained at a more-or-less constant rate throughout the long work day—he started before seven and returned home for dinner at six—would take a sharp jump while we ate, two or three more glasses of Jack Daniel's by the time Mother was passing around the dessert plate. Something would happen—once, I fumbled his dessert onto the floor; another time, my brother, Rick, scraped his chair on the floor; still another, my sister, Elizabeth, laughed too hard and sprayed the milk she had been drinking across the table. If the offending party was close enough, Father's hand would lash out and catch us where he could, the jaw, the cheek, the ear. He did not believe in pulling his punches. If we were sitting too far away, he would push himself back from the table—and we knew, the second we heard his chair stutter across the floor, we knew what was on the way. He would rise, and God help you if you snickered at the way he needed to grab hold of the table to keep himself from pitching over. Even before he was on his feet, he was talking. 'Boy,' he would say, or, 'Girl,' 'what in the name of the Almighty Lord God, the good and most merciful Jehovah, have you done?'

"He had wanted to be a preacher, you see, that had been his secret, childhood desire, which had been squashed by his father, who told him in no uncertain terms where his future as the only son of the town's richest man lay. Father's business duties kept him too busy to become a deacon, which I assume the church was grateful for, but we were there in the front row every Sunday, and the walk back home was inevitably given over to Father disparaging the day's sermon, and offering his own in its stead. To give the man his due, he knew his Bible. He tended to express that knowledge, however, as a series of questions to whichever one of us he was preparing to unleash his fists on. The fourth commandment—he was obsessed with Honoring Thy Father and Mother. No matter what we did, or he thought we did, it all came back to that commandment. His hands were the instruments of God's justice, you see."

"What about your mother? What was she doing while he was terrorizing you?"

"Minding her own business. Clearing the table. Doing the dishes. She and Father had made their peace a long time ago; he did not raise his hand to her. Until we reached the age of seven, we were under her protection, unless we'd committed some particularly egregious trespass, in which case, she was the one who turned us over to Father. Once we had achieved the age of reason, however, we were his. It was bad—it was every bit as bad as you can imagine, and worse, besides."

Roger reached up and fingered the bridge of his nose. "Have you ever wondered who did this?"

What do you do with that? What do you do with hurt that's festered for half a century? For five mornings running, I heard variations on the same tale: the time Father gave Elizabeth a black eye for having given him a Look; the time Rick lost one of his front teeth for an offense Roger still couldn't identify; the time Roger fled out the front door rather than face another beating—in return for which, his father had the town police arrest his son and treat him to a night in jail for his insolence, after which he got the beating. From a vague backdrop, Roger's childhood and adolescence leapt into sharp focus. I don't know if anyone's ever told you anything like this, but when they do, you wind up re-evaluating everything you know about them. Roger would talk until dawn was pouring into the apartment, when he'd finally let me lead him to bed. I would lie beside him, listening for his breathing to change, to deepen, and then I would sleep, too, as best I could.

• • •

After a week off from school, Roger decided to return to his classes. I tried to argue him out of it. Instead of teaching his students *Great Expectations*, he should be talking to a psychiatrist. "You require the services of a psychoanalyst when you do not understand what is the matter with you," he said. "I understand what is the matter with me. My son is dead and I am grieving for him. What I need is a distraction to occupy me while I do what Freud calls the work of mourning." I didn't pursue the argument, didn't tell him there was more to it than that. He was grieving, yes, but he was guilty, too. The last thing his only son had heard him say was that he was nothing and they were no longer father and son.

When the reports started to come in—about Roger not being prepared for class, thinking they were reading *Bleak House* when it was *Little Dorrit;* or delivering the same lecture for three classes in a row; or not showing up for class because he was in his office trying to pull his thoughts together on a book he'd taught for the last thirty-five years; or standing for long stretches of time in front of his students without saying anything—I wasn't exactly surprised. That's not true. I was surprised at the extent of Roger's collapse. I'd expected him to have some kind of difficulty teaching; there was no way he could be the kind of teacher he usually was. Roger at half-speed was still better than ninety-five percent of the people in that department, and I thought that it would be worth him fumbling around a little bit if it helped him in the long run. A lot of people, when they're having a hard time, they let it all hang out at home, in private, but when they go out in public, to work, they pull themselves together, you know? With Roger it was the opposite. With me, he would rally himself; with his students, he went to pieces.

While this was happening, we held Ted's memorial service. The service was my idea. Joanne held one in the city, but neither of us wanted to make the trip. You just knew it was going to be a chance for Joanne to grandstand, to present herself as the bereft but dutiful mother, while Roger would be the father who, the last time he'd seen his son, had been fighting with him. No way. Roger was going through enough, already; I had no intention of letting him walk into that. God only knows what they would have thought of me. Joanne didn't press the matter. I'm sure she was more than happy to have the spotlight to herself. Since we hadn't attended her service, we had to have one of our own. I thought it would be therapeutic, help Roger reconnect with Ted. At first, Roger wasn't interested. We had spent a Saturday driving down to the cemetery in Westchester where Ted's ashes had been buried—in Joanne's family plot, of course; Roger hadn't contested her decision. There was no headstone yet, only a strip of bare earth and a tiny American flag. On the drive, we had stopped at a mall so Roger could run into a sporting goods store. When we found Ted's grave, he removed the baseball he'd bought from his coat pocket and set it at the head of the grave. That was enough for him, Roger said. "It isn't for me," I said, "I need something more formal," which wasn't exactly true. He needed it—and if he did, so did I. We bickered about it for a week, at the end of which Roger gave in. I went to talk to the minister at the Dutch Reformed Church on Founders. I was too preoccupied with what I was going to say to the minister to pay much attention to Belvedere House. Ted's service was scheduled for the following Saturday.

I don't want to relive that hour. While it wasn't the worst thing that happened after Ted died—not by a long shot—it may have been the most painful. I sat watching him try to deliver Ted's eulogy, up at the front of the church in the new black suit I'd taken him out to buy two days before. Almost from the moment he began, with his account of how Ted hadn't wanted to read when he was a boy, but Roger had made him, he'd insisted, because he'd known how important it would be to his son—and I could see him struggling not to cry and failing, I was thinking, *Don't do it, honey, it's too much. That's okay. Sit down and this can be over and I won't do anything like this again, I swear.* When he tried to recite that Houseman poem...Once the service was over, I tried to get him back to the apartment as quickly as I could, but that was more difficult than it sounds. Despite everything, Roger insisted on staying at the church to greet and talk to the people who'd attended the service. He had that sense of obligation. I stood by his side throughout, watching the looks on people's faces as they realized they'd have to say something to Roger before they could leave. A number snuck out while he was in conversation with Benedict, who must have spent a good ten minutes trying to console Roger by explaining *Four Quartets* to him. Finally, I succeeded in guiding him from the church to the car. I drove. As we were buckling our seatbelts, Roger said, "I believe those who came found the service quite moving." He leaned over and kissed me on the cheek. "Thank you, dear." I swear, it was like the punchline to some awful joke. I pulled out of the parking lot and headed for home. As we passed Belvedere House, Roger turned to look at it. I half-expected him to say something, offer another quotation, but he was silent.

That night, Roger went to bed fairly early—the service had done that much for him, anyway, tired him out—while I sat up watching TV. If the afternoon had exhausted Roger, it had left me wired, on edge. There was a *Twilight Zone* celebration on the Sci Fi Channel, hour after hour of black and white weirdness framed by Rod Serling's laconic pronouncements. I switched between that and the cooking channel, a succession of would-be eccentric chefs taking you through the world's cuisines a half-hour at a time. Every now and again, I'd stand up to use the bathroom or rake through the refrigerator. I wasn't especially hungry; it was seeing all that food.

As I was leaning over with the refrigerator door open, trying to decide if I really wanted to open the tub of veggie dip and the bag of baby carrots, I heard Roger say, "And when you die, may you know fitting torment." At the same time, I realized someone was standing behind me. I hadn't heard any footsteps; I'd been too distracted by my memory. I was just aware of someone there, the way you are sometimes—like when you know there's a student standing outside your office. Of course I assumed it was Roger. I said, "Midnight snack, anyone?" and, when he didn't reply, stood up and turned around.

The kitchen was dark. The whole apartment was dark. For a second or two, my eyes were dazzled by the refrigerator's light and all I could see was a great white blotch on top of a great black blotch. I blinked, and the blotches started to break apart and resolve into a more coherent picture—and I saw the figure standing behind me. Even with the refrigerator light shining on it, it was dark, but it was tall, taller than Roger. My heart jumped and so did I, back into the fridge. Its contents clattered and crashed. A blast of cold—ice cold, much colder than the fridge—blew over me. I put one hand over my mouth. For an instant—not a second, less time than that—I saw this black shape, and then my vision cleared and it was gone.

I ran straight for the bedroom. I didn't close the refrigerator door behind me, and I certainly didn't stop to turn off the TV. No, I threw myself into bed beside Roger and huddled as close to him as I could. I didn't move from that spot for the rest of the night. I didn't say anything to Roger, either, even when he complained about the fridge having been left open all night. In the morning, with sunlight pouring in through the windows, what had been absolutely real a few hours before seemed much less substantial. The dark shape I'd seen standing behind me appeared the product of too little sleep and too much *Twilight Zone* than it did—well, of what? A supernatural experience? A ghostly visitation?

Frightening as that momentary encounter was, I worked to put it out of my mind. Together with what I'd seen when I'd lost the baby, it didn't seem to say too much good about the state of my mental health, and that was a truly terrifying prospect. It wasn't till later, when things at Belvedere House had slid from bad to worse, that I recalled it.

• • •

The week following Ted's memorial service brought a call from Steven asking if he could talk to me about Roger. There had been some complaints from a few of Roger's students, and Steven wanted to speak with me to get a sense of how Roger was doing. "What complaints?" I asked him, and he told me. As I listened to him try to phrase the students' grievances in as non-confrontational a way as possible—you know Steven—I saw Roger standing in front of the church. When he asked me how Roger was managing, I said, "He hasn't seemed that bad to me—all things considered—but I think he's been keeping a lot to himself. You're probably right that most of the students just resent having to work—but the rest may be onto something."

"I see," Steven said, and his voice told you he was already dreading the prospect of confronting Roger. He said, "I have a meeting with Roger scheduled this afternoon to discuss these complaints; I'm sure we'll be able to resolve this, then. Thanks for your help."

They had their meeting, but it didn't solve anything. Roger told me about it over dinner. He was angry, the most inflamed I'd seen him since Ted's death. "Apparently, some of my students are unhappy with me," he said.

"Oh?"

"They feel I am being derelict in my responsibilities. A number of them have complained to the Chair."

"Really?"

Roger nodded. "He asked if he could speak with me this afternoon—if he could 'schedule a meeting' with me. It used to be, if the Chair wanted to talk to you, she came to your office and talked to you. 'Schedule a meeting.'"

"What'd Steven say?"

"Not much of any consequence," Roger said. "I swear, that man could be a lawyer, he parses his words so. There are students who feel I have been neglecting to give them my full attention; they claim I've been repeating myself, that I don't know what novel the class is supposed to be reading; that I have missed class."

"Well," I said, "for the sake of argument, is there anything to their accusations?"

"Nothing whatsoever," Roger said. "I grant I occasionally repeat a point made in a previous class in order to establish a connection between what I said then and what I am saying now. And, from time to time, I have devoted a certain portion of my lecture to a novel other than the one currently under consideration, but that has been solely in the interest of establishing a link between that other text and the present one. As for missing class: if I have failed to be present for one or two classes here and there, it has been because I had become absorbed in trying to settle a problem raised by the novel we were reading, and time escaped me."

"Honey," I said, "you have been under a lot of stress since Ted died."

"Which means what?" Roger asked. "That you believe these charges? You were my student. You know first hand what I am like in front of a class. Did you find me irresponsible?"

"You know how much I respect you," I said. "You know you're the best professor that department—that school has. There's no question. But you've suffered a terrible loss, and that's bound to affect you. There's nothing wrong with that."

Roger wouldn't have any of it. Although he'd admitted that all the student charges were essentially true, he couldn't see that. Steven had floated the possibility of Roger taking a few weeks off—the rest of the semester, if he wanted—which Roger had declined with his full measure of scorn. As far as he was concerned, the matter was closed; although he resented what he perceived as my questioning him. We ate dinner that night in silence, and spent the rest of the night and the next morning that way, too. Roger left for school earlier than usual—making a passive-aggressive point.

Once he was at SUNY, though, it was more of the same. The students were filing into Steven's office two and three at a time, now. One tried to approach Roger directly, at the end of class, about the two papers she'd submitted that he still hadn't returned, and he lost it. He spent ten minutes going up one side of her and down the other. He didn't mention this to me. I heard it from Steven, who called me after the student's mother, understandably furious, had called him and reamed him out for half an hour. He'd tried to locate Roger—as had the student's mother before him—but Roger was nowhere to be found. After castigating the student, he'd walked out of the building headed for parts unknown. (No doubt, he'd returned to Belvedere House.) "I'm afraid Roger's behavior is becoming a bit of a problem," Steven said. I could picture him wincing at having to be so direct.

"I don't know what to tell you," I said. "I tried talking to him about it, and it didn't go over too well. I think he knows he's in trouble; he just doesn't know what to do about it."

"Well," Steven said, "this student's mother was going to call the Dean, next. I may have talked her out of it; if not, Roger could have a lot more to deal with." Actually, Steven hadn't talked the woman out of anything. After I hung up, the phone rang again and it was the Dean, looking for Roger. She was not happy. She said she expected

Professor Croydon in her office at eight-thirty tomorrow morning. I said I'd tell him, and she hung up. When he returned home that afternoon, Roger didn't breathe a word of the day's events. I kept waiting for him to confess, to offer his take on the morning, however distorted by self-justification, but nothing—not a word. I tried to wait him out, but finally, as we were getting ready for bed, I cracked and told him the Dean was expecting him in her office first thing in the morning.

"Can't," he said. "I teach then."

"I think she's arranged for someone to cover it for you."

"Has she?" Roger's cheeks flushed.

"That's what she told me," I said. "Is there anything you want to say to me?"

"No," Roger said, and that was that. I was so angry with him. I mean, I was his wife. I was the one he was supposed to talk to about things like this. But no—ever since I'd suggested his students might have a point, I'd become a member of the opposition. Fine. If this was the way he wanted things, this was the way things would be. Let the Dean try talking to him.

She did, but not in her office. Roger didn't keep their appointment. He went to his class and ordered the adjunct Steven had found to cover it out. It didn't take long for the Dean to learn what he'd done. She was waiting for him outside the room at the end of class. I don't know what Frances said to him, but you can bet she didn't pull any punches. Roger wasn't cowed. Things turned ugly pretty much immediately.

The call from the President's office took longer than I expected. One of the adjuncts I was friendly with sent me an e-mail about Roger and the Dean. I read it while I was still at Penrose, and was positive I'd find a message from someone higher-up in the Administration waiting for me on the answering machine when I got home. There wasn't, which made me nervous. I knew the Dean well enough to be sure there was no way she was going to let Roger's behavior to his student—and to her—go unpunished. Roger might have a bookshelf full of books and articles, but that only buys you so much. Needless to say, Roger didn't tell me anything about his confrontation with the Dean. I didn't tell him about the e-mail I'd received. We sat watching *The News Hour*, filling the time before bed with idle chatter. What a pair, right?

His behavior was more and more a mystery. I knew he was motivated by pride—Roger ranked his teaching equal with his scholarship, and to come right out and say that he was falling down on the job was an affront to decades of accomplishment. I knew that fear was driving him, too. He'd already had so much taken away from him, starting with his parents and continuing through Ted. The prospect of his career joining his list of losses must have been terrifying. I could understand how the combination of ego and anxiety would cause him to reject Steven's approach. I could even understand how it would cause him to reject mine. I didn't like it, but I understood it. What I couldn't understand was what he thought he was doing with the Dean. Roger was very conscious of position, which grew out of his sense of his own in the department and on campus. Whatever he thought of the Administration and its representatives in private, in public he always did his best to stay on good terms with them. For him to ignore a meeting with the Dean, and then to argue with her in public—especially someone as full of herself as Frances—it went against everything he'd done previously. It was a deliberate slap in the face, an invitation to disaster.

In retrospect, I think that's exactly what he was doing. Here was Roger's fatalism in action. He knew that things were bad. How much he knew, how bad he thought they were, isn't important. What is is that he recognized their badness, and decided that there was nothing he could do about it. He was on a downward spiral. Everything he'd struggled against for the whole of his adult life—all the world's evil— had finally caught up with him. There was no fighting it. His only option was to see it through to the bitter end. He was smart enough to recognize the self-fulfilling-prophecy aspect of what he was doing, but it was another case of Roger not seeing what he didn't want to.

Do I have to add that, underneath it all, he was punishing himself for Ted?

All of which makes it that much more remarkable that the President was able to talk Roger into taking a leave of absence before things got any worse. She waited out the weekend to contact Roger. At the end of his office hours on Monday, she called him herself and asked him if he'd mind joining her for lunch. He agreed. He must have taken this as the moment he'd been waiting for, the end of the line, the walk up to the guillotine. Having the President of the college fire him would have satisfied his pride; that it would be done over lunch would have soothed his anxiety.

I don't know what Carley said to him up there on the tenth floor. Roger wouldn't tell me. He was waiting for me when I opened the door that afternoon, with a big bouquet of mixed flowers already in a vase on the kitchen table. He took me in his arms, kissed me like he hadn't in weeks, and said, "I had a talk with the President today." Immediately, I tensed. I'd wondered how being fired would affect Roger's pension, if we'd have to rely on my meager paycheck. He felt me stiffen. He said, "It's all right, everything is all right. I've decided to take a leave of absence, effective immediately."

"You have?"

"Yes."

"What happened?" I wasn't a hundred percent sure this wasn't a strange joke, or a set-up for something else, a kind of loyalty test.

"Suffice it to say, I saw the error of my ways."

"Really?"

"Really. Now," he said, "in celebration of my decision—and the newfound freedom attendant upon it—I am taking you to dinner."

There were thirty essays weighting my bag, not to mention four chapters of *The House of the Seven Gables* I'd assigned my class that I should at least look over. I left the bag at the door and we finally had our dinner at the Canal House. What a night. I don't know if you've been to the Canal House—it's right on Main Street in Cooper Falls. It costs an arm and a leg and another arm and leg besides. But it's worth it. Roger and I both ordered seven course meals, and they were amazing. And it was all served in this old house. We were in one of the upstairs rooms, at a table next to a window. The room had a fireplace, crackling away. Faintly, you could hear other people in other rooms, voices murmuring, silverware clinking on plates, chairs scraping the floor. Roger—Roger was suddenly his old self again. It was as if he'd been carrying a tremendous weight—a sack full of boulders—for the last two months, and he'd put it down at last. He joked with the waitress, the server who brought us our courses, the wine steward. We talked like we'd used to, trading thoughts and arguing—gently—about books we were reading and teaching. I could feel myself relaxing, so much I realized I hadn't been aware how tense I had become. Roger tipped generously, and after dinner was done—concluded: you don't just finish that kind of meal, you bring it to a conclusion—we walked up Main Street to the falls. Standing looking at all that water foaming white in the moonlight, I could believe that the worst was over, that we'd come near the precipice but saved ourselves from going over it. That night—well, suffice it to say, the night ended well, too.

• • •

There was about a month after that that was almost the honeymoon we'd never taken. We ate out a lot, took day trips, even went away to Martha's Vineyard for a long weekend. I walked around in a daze. My students' grades improved as I read their essays through my new, rose-colored glasses. I gave out more A's that semester than I ever had. Roger was better. He was still sad over Ted's death, but it was a calmer sadness. One night, we talked over maybe trying to have another child. Neither one of us was ready, yet, but at least we could discuss it. That month—it was like a pause, you know? Even then, I felt that way, that this was only an interlude. "As of this moment, I am no longer your father; you are no longer my son": the curse was never as far from me as I would have liked, or the image of those faces hissing in their doorways. I assumed we'd settle into a more normal routine. When I remember that time, those four weeks, I wonder if there was something I could have done. Maybe I should've suggested we go away for a while, spend the next six months or a year driving cross-country—or go to Europe. Roger had lots of friends in London. We could have rented a flat and he could have shown me all the Dickens sites. I could have looked up the places Hawthorne visited when he was in London. Someplace—something that would have taken us—him—away from Huguenot, from that house.

I think that, then I think, *No, there was nothing I could have done*. Roger—we—had been granted a reprieve, but it was temporary. Here I am calling him the fatalist, right? I don't know. After the fact, it's hard to believe that things could have turned out any other way than they did. Roger was who he was. It's like—one semester, I took Old English, to fulfill the development of English requirement for the Master's. I wrote my final paper on *Beowulf*—because let's face it, when you're studying Anglo-Saxon, there's not a whole lot else to write on. Anyway, I became really interested in the word "weird." Its roots are in the Anglo-Saxon "wyrd," which most translators render as "fate," and which isn't completely accurate. I did all this research, cracked open old dictionaries you had to blow the dust off, and I discovered that what "wyrd" actually means is something like "the way things had to be because that's the way they are." It's kind of hard to wrap your mind around, at first. If things hadn't been meant to be the way they are, then they would have been different. Since they are the way they are, that must be the way they were intended to be. Talk about circular logic, I know. But I think they were on to something, on to how, when you look back over your life, the events in it can seem oddly inevitable, as if there really are Fates. I know Aristotle said character is fate, but that amounts to pretty much the same thing, doesn't it? Who can escape who they are?

During that month we had, Roger slept better than he had since hearing that Ted had died. Even on the nights he was awake late, he was calmer. He'd sit up in bed beside me, reading. No more late night walks; instead, Roger took up jogging. His doctors had been telling him he needed to start exercising on a regular basis, and he decided this was the time to follow their advice. Every morning at five, Roger set out on a run that took him from the apartment, up to campus, and back again. By the time he returned, I'd have dragged myself out of bed and started the coffee, and we'd sit at the kitchen table and have breakfast together.

Sometimes, Roger varied the route he took to or from the college. Once he'd crossed the bridge over the Svartkill, he'd turn right on Water Street and push up the steep hill, there. Or he'd turn left, onto Founders, loop around to 32, and follow that into town. At first, he did so for the sake of variety, to look at some different scenery. He took other routes, too. Over breakfast, I'd ask him where he'd gone and he'd narrate his run: past Pete's Corner Pub, only recently emptied from the previous night, its doors open to air the place out; past the bus station, full of early morning commuters to the City; or past the quiet neighborhoods around the college, nodding at the occasional fellow-jogger. If he was feeling especially ambitious, he kept going past SUNY to Dunkin' Donuts.

The bad thing about his runs was that they left Roger alone with his thoughts. As far as I'm concerned, the great thing about exercise is the excuse it gives you to hamster-out, leave your brain behind as you make your wheel go round and round. Roger couldn't do that. Some mornings, he'd spend breakfast telling me about an idea he'd had for an article. Others, he'd talk politics. His opinion of the President had never really changed. He was one of the only people I knew who cut Bush no post-9/11 slack. A lot of conversation focused on the War on Terror, especially Afghanistan. "This administration has no understanding of anything," he said. "They think of a place like Afghanistan as the setting for a *Rambo* movie. Do they understand that the West has been involved in that country since Dickens's day? Oh yes, the first war between a Western power and the Afghans was started in 1838, by the British. It dragged on for four years. I looked into it because I thought I might write an article about its effects on Dickens's novels of the time. The British were concerned about Russian influence on the country that bordered their Indian holdings, so they invaded and tried to replace the emir of Afghanistan with a puppet. It did not work; they suffered heavy losses and, in the end, negotiated with the same man whose ouster had been the aim of their incursion." He shook his head. "Nor is the subsequent history of Western involvement any more cause for optimism. Ask the Soviets. But Bush and his cronies think that their laser-guided bombs and unmanned surveillance drones will make things different for us. They won't. Eventually, these kinds of things come down to negotiation, to people talking to other people. Given this crew's communication skills, such does not bode well."

I wasn't sure how to respond. I mean, 9/11 had felt like the beginning of a war to me. What else were we supposed to have done?

The first time Roger told me he'd run along Founders, past Belvedere House, I looked up from my bagel. Since Ted's memorial service, we hadn't returned to Founders. I thought his sight of the house that morning was the first he'd seen it in months. I was expecting—well, I wasn't expecting anything—I was just surprised, and a little concerned about the effect encountering the place might have on him. I asked, "How was it?"

"How was what?"

"The house," I said, "seeing it again."

He hesitated, running the tape of the morning's run in his head. He said, "It was fine."

"Are you sure?"

"Yes," he said, turning to me. "Belvedere House will always stir memories in me, darling; how could it not? I lived the majority of my life under its roof. It is my house of memories, you might say. Some of them are pleasant; more, I fear, are not. But you needn't worry about my past overwhelming me. I can stand my own history." He smiled, and I smiled, too, because that was what I'd been worried about.

(I tried not to remember that huge vacant space, those faces. I almost succeeded, too.)

• • •

I'm not sure exactly when Roger began to vary the course of his run less. It must have been a week, maybe two, after the end of that good month. A couple of days in a row, when I asked him which way he'd taken today, he said, "Oh, the usual." I assumed that meant he'd headed straight up Main Street to the traffic light at Manheim and turned right there. I'm sure he knew I would think this way. Why he didn't want to tell me he was running past his former house on his way into and out of town—when I finally figured it out and asked him about it, Roger claimed he hadn't thought it worth mentioning. "You didn't think I'd want to know that you were running past the place you used to live with your ex-wife and dead son, twice a day, seven days a week?" I said. "Especially when there are plenty of other routes you could have been taking? You didn't find your own behavior in any way unusual?"

"Not in the slightest," Roger said. He was lying, of course, but by that point things had gone so far down the road to ruin that to hear he'd lied to me a couple of months before—or misled me, whatever— to hear that was of academic interest, at best, the kind of information you'd want to hold onto for later, after the train wreck you were part of was over and you were trying to understand what had gone wrong. Like now.

So there was Roger, in his sweats and sneakers and the sweatband I told him he didn't need but that fit his picture of a jogger, his feet pounding the pavement, the house where his relationship with his son had grown, blossomed, faded, and died looming to his right. Belvedere House with its stone first storey and wooden second, third, and attic storeys, its host of windows, its double front doors, its broad lawn dotted with the occasional tree. It sat there and drew his attention to it irresistibly, his own personal black hole, bending all his thoughts in its direction. Every window was a movie screen playing a different scene from his thirty-three years there. Do I have to say all of them were of him and Ted? On his and Joanne's bedroom window—the one that looked out on Frenchman's Mountain—he watched himself walk back and forth across the bedroom, singing Victorian lullabies to the infant Ted to soothe him back to sleep. On the kitchen window, which faced the south lawn, he saw himself sitting down beside a ten-year-old Ted at the kitchen table to explain why the Huguenots had fled France. On the basement windows, he looked at himself and Ted trying to build a basic solar panel for Ted's eighth grade science project. Other windows showed him and Ted throwing the ubiquitous baseball, after all these years, his hand still remembered the slap of the ball as it smacked into his glove, his arm, the pleasant ache of throwing fastball after fastball, his eyes, squinting against the morning sunlight. Then Roger was past the house, on his way to Route 32 and the college. The memories trailed along with him for a while, dissipating the further he went.

When Roger started going out for walks again, he presented it to me as an extension of his exercising. Once he was back from his run and breakfasted, he'd shower, shave, and sit down either to read or write. He was rereading *Bleak House* for the I-don't-know-how-many-eth time. While out on his runs, he said, he'd been struck by an idea for a new article on The Ghost's Walk in that novel. Roger worked straight through to the early afternoon—one or two—when he broke for lunch and a walk. "I need to unwind myself," was how he explained it, "mind and body." Of course I remembered those nights he'd spent out after Ted's death—but this was different. For one thing, it was during the day; for another, after having sat in front of the computer for five or six hours, it was no surprise that Roger would want to stretch his legs, have a change of scene. Most afternoons, I wasn't even home. If I wasn't teaching at Penrose, I was in their library, doing research for an article on Hawthorne, Dickinson, and Puritan guilt. "An afternoon stroll will complement my morning run," Roger said, which he meant one way and I took another.

His walks led him all over the place, but there weren't many that didn't include the house. Moving at a slower pace, Roger could linger over the memories he'd revisited that morning. He could recall Ted's weight in his arms, the smell of talcum powder, the floorboards creaking as he paced them. He could see Ted's fifth grade social studies textbook open on the kitchen table, a portrait of Cardinal Richelieu on the lower right hand corner of the right hand page, and he could smell the sweet Juicy Fruit gum Ted was chewing loudly, a sure sign Joanne had bored him. He could remember standing beside Ted at the cluttered basement workbench while Ted sawed the end off a piece of

plywood, the saw dropping a steady stream of almost-fragrant sawdust as it rasped back and forth. Near the house and its memories, Ted
didn't seem so far off, so irretrievably lost.

• • •

What surprises me most about Roger's decision to move back into
Belvedere House is that it took him so long to come to it. The idea
occurred to him early on—his third run past the house, it flickered
across his mind. With each new encounter—especially after his memories started playing out on it again—returning to the house appeared
less ridiculous, less masochistic, and more attractive. He couldn't
imagine Joanne truly wanted to hold onto it. She had always been
one of those people who doesn't like to dwell on what was. Roger
had sufficient funds to purchase her share of Belvedere House if she
would be willing to part with it. He'd lost some money when the dot
com bubble burst, but he'd recovered it in relatively short order and
made more on top of that. ("The benefits of a Republican financial
advisor," he said.) He was sure he'd be able to convince Joanne to
sell. It seemed increasingly important—urgent, even—that he take
possession of the place again. He called his lawyer and instructed him
to contact Joanne's lawyer and start talking.

I was caught completely off-guard—shocked, really. We were
lying in bed one Saturday afternoon and Roger said, "I've got something to tell you."

"What is it?" I asked. I thought he was going to say that he
wanted to order-out for pizza, which he'd been trying to cut back on
for his cholesterol.

Instead, he said, "We're moving."

I thought he was joking. I said, "Okay, we're moving. Where are
we moving to? I vote for Hawaii."

"Belvedere House."

"Right. As if Joanne would ever sell her share to you."

"She already has," he said.

"What?" I sat up.

He was serious. "I had my lawyer contact hers about buying her
out. She was amenable. The lawyers negotiated a price. I mailed a
check to her three days ago. Yesterday, Dr. Sullivan received her one
month's notice."

That was it. The whole thing was a *fait accompli*. I was not happy. I said, "What makes you think I want to move?"

"Oh please, Veronica," Roger said. "How often have you complained about our lack of space? This apartment was too small for you on your own. With two of us sharing it, it's positively cramped."

The apartment was too small. When I'd moved in, I hadn't cared. Actually, its size had been one of its charms. Living room, kitchen, bedroom, and bathroom: I was like Emily Dickinson with my tiny, ordered place. I'd had to be inventive, make maximum use of the space I had, but I could look out my living room window onto a garden—Tom and Jack, the landlords, kept this enormous flower garden in the backyard—and beyond the garden was the river, with farmland on the other shore. There is something to be said for living somewhere nice; the aesthetics of place are underrated. After Roger moved in, though, what had been too little room to begin with shrank to the point of no return. He put most of his stuff in storage, but even so, every square inch of the apartment was piled high with books, CDs, and videotapes, not to mention Roger's clothes, which had a habit of displacing mine onto the bed and couch. If we'd had our baby, there would have been no way we could've stayed there.

All the same, who wants to move into the house your husband lived most of his last marriage in? That was the first thing I thought of, not Ted, but Joanne. Roger intended to take me to her house. Hers, because she'd decorated it. She'd picked the furniture, the wallpaper, the drapes, the color scheme, everything. Living there, I'd be surrounded by a hundred little reminders of her and her starched personality. I was more insecure than I should have been, I know. It's—you can stand the thought that the person you're with now was with someone before you, as long as you don't have to confront that fact daily. I said, "Okay, fair enough. The apartment is too small. Why there? Why couldn't we move someplace else?"

"Because," Roger said, "for the amount I paid Joanne, we couldn't get one-half the house."

He made it all sound so reasonable, which is why, although I debated the matter with him for the rest of the day and well into the night, in the end, I agreed. I can't lie: the prospect of having all that room was very attractive. I mean, the house had its own library, for God's sake. If Roger wanted this as badly as he did, then I figured he'd be willing to let me redecorate, which he was. Late that night, I said yes. Roger was delighted, as happy as I'd seen him. We made love, went to sleep, and, the next morning, started packing.

That afternoon—I was emptying one of the bookshelves into the last cardboard box I'd had stored under my bed. Roger had gone out to the liquor store in Joppenburgh for more. I lowered a stack of books into the box—they were all Theory, Kristeva's *Powers of Horror* on top. Very funny. I stood up, and the air was full of the smell of blood. Thick, copper—it was so strong I gagged. I coughed, went to turn on the fan, and I was walking across an open space towards an enormous face framed by a doorway with a cracked lintel. To either side of it were equally huge faces in their own doorways. The face opened its mouth, and its tongue, pink and wet, uncoiled down its chin and slapped onto the floor. The tongue wriggled and flopped like a fish out of water. I took a step back, through air full of Roger's words, fluttering around me like moths: "disown" and "blood" and "failure" and "anything." The oversized tongue squirmed on the floor. I took another step back. *This is not happening*, I said to myself. I said it out loud: "This is not happening." Blood reeked in my mouth. I shouted, "This is not happening!"

I was alone in my living room. For a second, the blood smell hung around me, then that was gone, as well. I sat down and did not raise myself up until Roger was opening the door, a stack of flattened boxes cradled in his arms. "Sitting down on the job?" he said.

"Just taking a break."

I know, I know: Why didn't I say anything? What was I supposed to say? I had a recurrence of a hallucination I had when I miscarried? Because that was what I was sure had happened. That it might have been anything more was ridiculous. If it hadn't come from what were obviously the troubled depths of my psyche, then why had it stopped when I'd told it to? (Never mind that I'd had to repeat myself.) With the prospect of taking up residence in the very house that had figured in my fantasy to begin with, wasn't it only natural for that fantasy to offer a repeat performance? Wouldn't it have been more strange if the day had passed without me seeing anything?

I realize how lame this sounds—I think I did then, too. You wouldn't guess—you'd assume that, if even one of the incidents I've described happened to you, you'd be at the psychiatrist's pronto. Maybe some people would be. It's—once everything's over and done, and you're sitting turning events over in your mind, doubt wastes no time in letting itself be heard. Was that really as bad as you're making it out to be? Aren't you being just a little bit melodramatic? You don't count on the inertia of your personality. That, and the more time passes, the more absurd the whole thing seems. You feel embarrassed, even ashamed.

All of which is to say that, I returned to packing books, and if the specter of that coppery stench haunted my nostrils, I opened a window.

Dr. Sullivan and her family moved within the week. Having thrown them out, Roger tried to make it up by returning their entire security deposit. He couldn't understand why they were so cold to him when he went around to hand them the check. "They have their own house, now," he said.

As did we. I remember my first walk through it. This was—it must have been two days after Dr. Sullivan had left. Roger had been over that same afternoon, and all of the next day, besides, and he'd been urging me to come with him. I had a small mountain of papers to grade. I was teaching a couple of summer courses the first summer session at Huguenot, and I was on a tight schedule. I sat at the kitchen table reading essays on "The Fall of the House of Usher" while Roger came and went and came back again, taking box after box of books with him. I was a little worried he would overexert himself. I got through my essays as quickly as I could, and when I'd entered the last grade in my grade book, I stood, stretched, and went out to see my new house.

You might expect that, on the drive over, I'd have yet another flashback to the hollow house of my vision, hear Roger's curse one more time. At the very least, you'd assume I'd be nervous. None of which would be right. I suppose it was because I hadn't really connected the house of my vision with the actual brick-and-mortar structure. As I turned from Springgrown onto Main, what I was remembering was the first time Roger and I had made love in the house. It had been our third day together. That afternoon, I'd met him after his two o'clock Victorian Lit class; by the time we were back at his office, I was ready to do it with him on his desk. No, he said, not here. (That was for later.) Instead, we drove down to the house. We'd barely closed the front door, and half our clothes were off. Roger led me upstairs, to the bedroom—but there was no way I was going to do anything with him on Joanne's bed. Talk about your complete turn-offs. I led him up one more floor, to his office, and the pull-out couch; although we didn't manage to unfold it. I was so—so ready, so turned on. It was like when you're first starting to explore sex, to experiment, and you feel drunk on it. He—we fit together perfectly, better than anyone else I'd been with. I was floating on the pleasure, riding the waves. As I climaxed, I threw my head back and looked out the window, at the sky blue and pale and perfect, and I had never seen anything so beautiful.

I pulled up into the driveway, parked behind Roger's car, and walked up to the front door. Roger was waiting for me. He bowed, sweeping his hand to one side, and I entered the house.

It was big. I hadn't appreciated how many rooms there were, how much the house contained. As I went from the front landing to the front parlor, from the front parlor to the dining room, from the dining room to the kitchen—Roger gushing away beside me like the world's worst tour guide—I was intensely aware of the space around me. I could almost feel it, this slight tickling at the ends of my nerves. I had expected to notice all of Joanne's touches, which I did, but I hadn't been prepared for the way the house itself would feel. I'd never been in a house where I was so conscious of the architecture, of the structure surrounding me above and below and to either side. This wasn't my first time in Belvedere House, but it was the first time I'd been—sensitive to it like this. The roof of my mouth tingled. I kept licking my lips, as if I could almost taste something. I didn't mention any of this to Roger. What would I have said? "Boy, this house feels weird"? He would have chalked it up to my knowing it was our house, now, no doubt backed up by some quotation or another from Freud—and who could have argued with him?

That sensation of the house at the tips of my nerves persisted. It moderated a bit in the days that followed, as we transferred the majority of the apartment's contents, leaving the bed and a few changes of clothes. Roger did the lion's share of the work while I was in class, traveling back and forth to the house. When I was done for the day, I'd help for an hour or two. The apartment was more overstuffed than I'd realized. We didn't unpack immediately. The entire house had to be repainted—Roger had hired a couple of graduate students to help him—then there were new carpets and furniture to be delivered. It was a heady experience, standing in the front parlor and saying that we should cart off the fraying Oriental rug in the middle of the floor and replace it with a room-sized carpet in light blue. And those paintings looked dated and dull. Suppose we hung mirrors, instead? The furniture's too dark, too much dark wood—what about something lighter? Joanne's taste was so conservative and timid, it was almost a parody of itself. I wanted to shake things up, make the house lighter, friendlier, hipper. Roger accompanied me as I went from room to room, filling a legal pad with notes that would be turned into reality within weeks. We made a couple of big day trips to IKEA, a lot more little trips to Home Depot, and ordered all kinds of things online. Redecorating a house that size—reconceiving it—was more work than I'd anticipated. I used a lot of mirrors—as if the rooms weren't big enough already—and tended towards the simpler.

That was the first time the change in my own financial situation—the difference marrying Roger had made—really came clear to me. I hadn't considered myself poor. I was. I bought all my clothes second-hand and had barely enough money to cover my bills and keep food in the fridge. Going out to the diner was an extravagance I saved for major occasions. But so what? I was a graduate student. I was supposed to be penniless. After Roger and I got together, I hadn't noticed that much of a change. I mean, we split the bills, which was nice, and we could afford to eat out at the better restaurants, or go to the movies whenever we wanted—also nice—but, all things considered, we lived a relatively plain life together. Maybe that would've changed if we'd had the baby. We would have had to move, no doubt about it, not to mention had to buy a ton of stuff. Now, being able to say, "A nice dining room set here," or, "A love seat and an easy chair there," and have Roger say, "Yes, of course," and have the things I'd called for appear—it was a pretty heady experience. I didn't exactly think of myself as rich, but I did understand I was sitting on a lot more money than I'd appreciated.

For what seemed like the longest time, the house was in a state of transition, rooms full of stacks of unopened boxes, furniture coming and going standing in the halls, drop cloths and cans of paint migrating from room to room, floor to floor. We slept at the apartment, on the bed we'd take apart and move when we were ready to leave the apartment behind. We could have bought a new bed—maybe we should have, in keeping with the spirit of new beginnings—but a lot had happened in that bed. I had bought it when I moved into the apartment. It was a queen-sized, really too big for the bedroom, but it was like a symbol of freedom, you know? Roger and I had slept in it when he came to stay with me. We'd made our child there. By taking it with us—talk about symbols. I thought it would be a way of showing that our life together was continuing in this new place. It was like transplanting your favorite rose bush.

Then, almost overnight, the house was no longer in-between. There were still cabinets to be put up and filled, a recliner and big-screen TV that were on back-order, but the house had passed the point of no return. Instead of looking like a bunch of rowdy kids had run wild through it, doing their best to ruin Joanne's carefully wrought effects, the house had become something else. All the choices I'd made cohered, and Belvedere House was no longer the epitome of old money trying to remind you of itself—discreetly, of course—now the house was the kind of place you could feel comfortable in, relax in. There was still a contrast between its exterior and interior, which startled more than one person who visited us and which I wasn't sure how to soften—or if I wanted to—but I didn't lose too much time worrying about it.

The real contrast—the one that forced itself on me—was between the way the house's interior looked and the way it felt—still felt. My awareness of it, that sense of it just beyond the edges of my nerves, so that when Roger ran his hand along a wall, my skin would prickle, continued. I would stand in the second floor hallway, its newly exposed hardwood floors catching the morning light and sharing it with the cream walls, and I could taste the way the sun felt on the wood, the plaster. One afternoon, there was a brief thunderstorm that pounded the house, and I could feel the rain thrumming on the roof, the walls, like the world's biggest shower set on high. All of which was weird, but not entirely unpleasant. What wasn't so nice was the sensation that there was more to the house than I was seeing.

At all sorts of places throughout the house I would stop, sure that I'd passed a door I hadn't remembered, and when I'd turn around, there would be no door. Even so, I would be half sure one was there—or had been a moment ago. I made a real effort to stay on top of the cleaning—Roger wanted to hire somebody to do it, but I was still enough of a socialist to find such an idea abhorrent—and I can't tell you how many times I was sure I'd washed more windows than the kitchen or the living room had. I tried to keep count, but I always seemed to lose track about halfway through. It was strange, but not so

much I felt I had to tell Roger. Or maybe I should say, not so strange
I didn't think he'd have an answer for it I could already guess myself.

. . .

There was one room in the house Roger refused to let me touch,
and—you guessed it—that was Ted's. Not the third-floor room he'd
moved into when he became a teenager—oh no, Roger was only too
happy to have me turn that into a combination study-guest room. The
room he insisted must be left alone was the one Ted had lived in as a
child. I can't say I didn't understand—after all, I was bringing my bed
with me—but in the expression on Roger's face when I suggested that
Ted's room would make a nice place for the stationary bike he said he
wanted to buy, I had my first real inkling of the reason behind Roger's
desire to return to Belvedere House. A couple of weeks later, when
Roger walked into the living room and handed me a box of photos
of Ted, all of them from his time in the Army, and said he wondered
if there might be a place for these, I remembered how his eyes had
narrowed, his mouth tightened, at my idea for changing—disturbing,
I'm sure he would have said—Ted's childhood room.

I spent a while staring at those more recent photos of Ted after
Roger wandered back up to his office. There were formal portraits,
head and chest shots of Ted in his dress uniform staring intently into
the camera, the flag draped behind him. I'm sure I must have passed
them—or ones very much like them—during previous visits to the
house. If so, I hadn't noticed them, and Roger hadn't ever pointed
them out to me. The only picture of Ted he kept and seemed to care
for was the one of him in his little league uniform that looked down
from a bookcase in the office at school. He had a couple of frayed and
faded baby pictures tucked away in his wallet, but that was, so far as I
knew, the extent of his photographs of his son. When he'd moved in
with me, he hadn't brought any pictures of Ted with him—he hadn't
moved any more into his office, either. All of these photographs—
there were a couple dozen. Four of the formal portraits, Ted at various
stages in his career, each one framed; and eighteen or twenty smaller
pictures, casual shots of Ted and his friends, of him training, of him
next to Hummers and helicopters, each one of these framed, as well.
Roger had wrapped every photo in a plastic bag that he'd carefully
taped shut, then placed them in a heavy cardboard box he'd taped

tightly closed. He had sliced the box open with an X-ACTO knife before bringing it to me, but he'd left the individual pictures in their plastic envelopes. I unsealed them carefully, picking at a piece of tape until I'd loosened one edge, then sliding my thumb underneath and gently easing the rest of it off. Once I'd parted all the tape, I unfolded the plastic bag and slid the photo from it. It took me an hour and a half to unwrap the box. If I hadn't felt the need to be so elaborately careful, I could have had the pictures out in five minutes, but it was like I was an archaeologist, uncovering my husband's ancient memories, and the situation demanded a certain formality.

When I had the last photo out, I spread them all on the living room floor. Here was Ted's adult life in shorthand. That portrait in the upper-left-hand corner must have been taken not too long after he'd enlisted. That was definitely the face of an eighteen-year-old, skin in the last phases of its battle with acne, mouth struggling to appear serious, eyes wide, as if they couldn't believe Ted was actually in the Army, for God's sake. The uniform—it fit him all right, but at the same time looked too big, you know? By the time you reached the second portrait—across the floor in the upper-right-hand corner— the uniform was a better fit. The skin was clearer, the mouth more secure, and the eyes said yes, Ted was in the Army. Ted's face hadn't yet thrown off the last traces of his adolescence. It was long and thin and waiting to fill out, which it started to do in the third portrait, on the lower-left-hand corner. Probably the most dramatic difference between any two of the pictures was between the second and third. In the second, he's still a kid. You could be polite about it and call him a young man, but it's clear that, whatever combination of factors it is that makes you an adult, it hasn't happened to Ted. In the third portrait, he's grown up. His skin has left its acne far behind and is tanned. His mouth has gained enough confidence to relax. His eyes are—reserved, the lids lowered just a little, as if keeping something back. Maybe joining Special Forces had made the change in him, or maybe it had been his first serious relationship. Gene Ortiz told me that Ted had had a long and tortured affair with a woman who worked in town. She was a teacher, I think. She was also married. Can you believe it? Maybe that's why he was so mad at Roger.

By the time you arrived at the last portrait of Ted, in the low-er-right-hand corner, you were looking at the man who had stood outside the apartment at three in the morning, yelling at his father.

Of course, his face was calm here. Lines had cut themselves into his skin, at the corners of his eyes and mouth, hints of aging, and across the bridge of his nose, a hint of something more violent. The scar was the souvenir of a knife fight, Gene said. "A knife fight?" I said, but he claimed that was all he could tell me.

In amongst the four portraits, I placed the twenty or so smaller pictures of Ted, doing my best to arrange them chronologically. Judging from the photographic record, Ted had had a lot of friends. More than half the shots were of Ted with groups of smiling or laughing soldiers. There was also a picture of Ted lying on his bunk, reading. *Bleak House*. Who'd have thought? I picked that picture up, turned it over, and slid open the back of the frame. There was writing on the picture's other side, a broad scrawl. "This Dickens guy is all right," Ted had written, "although I'll probably retire before I get done with this." I closed the frame, returned that photo to its place in the sequence, and selected another. All the pictures sported brief comments from Ted, even the portraits. If I'd felt like an archaeologist staring at a wall of hieroglyphs, I'd suddenly been handed a Rosetta stone. A couple of dozen sentences hardly constituted an autobiography, but they were something.

There was one picture in particular that caught my attention, and that was because it was so different from all the others. It wasn't framed, just tucked inside an envelope whose postmark was Fort Bragg; the date was this past March, right after Ted had been killed. The photo showed Ted not in his uniform—in fact, I didn't recognize it was Ted—the only reason I thought it might be was because it was in with all these other pictures of him. The man I saw had a heavy, dark beard and was wearing a turban, a heavy brown coat, loose tan pants, and high boots. He was sitting cross-legged, a machine gun on the ground in front of him. The landscape around him was bare, arid. He was reading; I squinted and saw that it was the same copy of *Bleak House* Ted had been holding open on his bunk; although the book looked as if it had traveled quite a bit since then. I turned the photo over, and read, "Even here, I can't escape this guy." I assumed "here" was somewhere in Afghanistan. I meant to ask Roger about the picture, what Ted was doing dressed up like an Afghan, but it slipped my mind.

I contemplated hanging all the photos together, maybe arranging the portraits in a row on top and setting the smaller shots beneath them. In the end, I decided to spread them throughout the house. I thought of it as a way of incorporating Ted's memory into our daily lives, of welcoming him home, so to speak. I hoped that they might relieve my hyper-awareness of the house, of its unseen dimensions. Roger didn't say anything to me about my decision, but I saw him every now and again, stopped in front of a wall, noticing the photo I'd hung there. Why shouldn't Ted be part of our new home?

• • •

I wish I could say that our move into Belvedere House was good for Roger. But, right from the start, being surrounded by that house took its toll on him. He did his best to appear happy, which I think he was, but it was a strained happiness. He wore a smile like a soldier wears a uniform, because it's required. If you tried to call him on it, he'd deny he was anything other than perfectly content. From time to time, though, you'd catch a glimpse of him underneath the mask, itching to tear it off and let himself breathe. Returning here had been his idea, and he felt he had to put a brave face on it.

About a week after we'd finished moving in, we were sitting together in the living room, reading. I was on the couch, Roger was enjoying the recliner that had finally arrived the day before. The stereo was on low, Miles Davis's *Kind of Blue*. It wasn't late—ten-thirty at the most—but it felt like the middle of the night. You know how that is sometimes. You were up early; you had a busy day; it's a quiet night; and time seems to stretch out, to elasticate like taffy. You read for what you're sure must be hours, and the clock hands advance fifteen minutes. You have to leave the TV off. Switch it on, and the effect is ruined.

Anyway, there I was on the couch, reading this novel, *Bliss*, that one of my students had recommended to me, and little by little I became aware of the house around me. I was never unaware of it, but most of the time, it was a background sensation, like the sound of cars passing by on the street—you hear them, but they don't really register. This night—it was as though an enormous vehicle were moving slowly down the road, shaking the house, vibrating the air with its passing—something so big and loud it forces itself to your attention. There was that familiar feeling of space, but amplified, as if the rooms were fuller, held more within themselves. The house seemed *deeper*. From my spot on the living room couch, I could feel the house going off in all directions. Cold—suddenly, the mercury was in freefall. I was wearing a t-shirt and sweatpants, and all at once, freezing cold was pouring over me. My breath appeared in a white cloud. The cold was streaming out of the mirrors, the walls, the windows—I could almost see it eddying around the room. Along with the drop in temperature came a smell, a charcoal odor of meat left on the grill way too long, blood boiled away, fat melted, flesh carbonized. The air filled with tiny flakes, like snow, only black. Around me, the house drifted, as if I were on a cruise ship that had gone rudderless, something massive floating freely, rising and falling with the swell of the ocean. I was sure that, if I looked out the windows, I'd see the landscape drifting by. Charcoal flakes swirled about me, riding the cold. I—once, when I was a senior in high school and in my pot-smoking phase, someone gave me a bag of bad weed. I don't know what was wrong with it, but the way it made me feel—completely disoriented, as if there were something wrong with everything around me, something I could be aware of but not put my finger on—that, and dizzy to the point of nausea—that's the closest comparison I can come up with for this experience.

This was insane. I stood up, caught myself from falling over, and said, "What the hell is going on?"

Roger's face was white as the proverbial sheet, whiter, even. He had dropped his book and was gripping the arms of the recliner as if he were an astronaut and it the rocket rushing him into orbit. His eyes were focused on a scene whose reflection on his face—it was the look of someone seeing something at the limit of his ability to process. I said, "Roger!" Nothing. Pushing through the cold, I half-staggered over to him. I shoved his shoulder. "Roger!" He started, his eyes fluttering. He opened his mouth. I said, "Roger."

The air was clear. The black flakes had melted out of it, the charred stench dissipated. It was still cold, but the cold no longer was streaming into the room.

"I'm fine," Roger said, his voice's shakiness betraying him.

"Don't lie to me," I said, "you're not fine, and neither am I. What the hell just happened?"

"What do you mean?" he asked.

"Just now—I saw—I smelled—I felt like—like I don't know what—like the house was moving in all sorts of strange ways. It looked like you were—like something was happening to you, too."

I could see him trying to decide what to say, even as he was processing my words. He settled on, "Why, I was only having a little nap with my eyes open. That's all."

"Then why were your hands clutching this chair like you were afraid it was going to throw you off?"

His cheeks flushed, and I knew I was right. I added, "What was it? Some kind of mini-stroke?" which was completely unfair. Roger was very worried about the possibility of something happening to his mind as he grew older, stroke, Alzheimer's, senility. To suggest that his worst fear might have come true was hitting below the belt. I didn't care. I was frightened and I was annoyed. He was lying to me, trying to hide something, the way he'd been keeping things from me this past semester, to the point of ruin. If I stepped on his toes now, I wasn't inclined to feel too badly about doing so.

The mini-stroke remark did the trick. The flush on his cheeks went from embarrassment to anger, and he snapped, "No, I did not suffer a TIA, although I'm happy to note it's the first explanation that occurred to you."

"So tell me what happened," I said. "Look—we were both just in the middle of something very strange. I saw—these flakes, like snow, only black—like bits of charcoal—and I smelled burning, like overdone meat. I felt—the entire house felt like it was drifting through space."

Roger shook his head. He took a breath. He said, "All right. I was rereading chapter 35 of *Bleak House*—that's the chapter where Esther discovers her bout with smallpox has scarred her face. From the corner of my eye, I saw something on the window over there," he pointed, "across from me. The window appeared to—to shimmer— for the barest of instants, you understand, and only from the corner of my eye. When I looked directly at it, the window was as still and as solid as those to either side of it. I would have dismissed it as a trick of my eyes, and returned to Esther, except that I noticed a second peculiarity. In the windows to the right and left of that one, I could see the interior of the living room reflected. There you were, curled on the couch, and there was the stereo, with the kitchen door beyond it. The middle window, however, where I should have seen myself, was a blank. It was as if the windowpanes had been painted black. I could not understand how this could be, what combination of factors should rob the window of its reflection."

He took a second, deeper breath. "This was unusual, to be sure, but intriguing. As I sat there considering the problem of the window, trying to estimate what combination of the angle of the room's lights and my angle of vision would be necessary to produce such an effect, I became aware of something else. There was a presence on the other side of that window, someone staring in at me as I was staring out. While not an everyday occurrence, this sensation was not unprecedented. There have been instances where I've known there was a student waiting outside my office. Even at the possibility that a stranger was gazing in at us, I was neither especially worried or threatened. I assumed it to be a late-night walker whose curiosity had been piqued by the sight of the lighted windows. Honestly, I thought that, once the peeping-Tom realized he had been discovered and I was peeping at *him*, he would beat a hasty retreat.

"The longer I stared at the window, I noticed that I could in fact distinguish something within it. Not our secret admirer's face, no—this was so faint as to be all but impossible to see, faint and small, as if I were seeing it from across a great distance. There was a kind of opening, an archway, which gave onto a long corridor. In that corridor, there was a figure—it was too far and too dark for me to discern much about it except that it was holding its hands out to either side, stumbling forward—its left hand trailing along a wall, its right suspended in space. The entire scene—it was so distant, so hard to see I'm not positive I saw it correctly—if I saw anything at all. I squinted, trying to bring it into focus, and, as I watched the figure lurching along, my heart was moved by a tremendous pity mixed with a tremendous dread. I can not say whence the twin emotions had their origin, but their descent was immediate and overpowering. I could not move. I could only sit staring through the presence on the other side of the window at this distant figure, whom I believe were one and the same, although I am not sure why. It felt as if hours dragged by—hours of pity and dread—before you shook me free. For which I am most grateful." He smiled tightly.

"My God, Roger," I said. "What just happened?"

He shook his head. "I cannot say. Simultaneous hallucinations?"

"Did that feel like a hallucination to you?"

"Not having hallucinated a great deal, I am hardly an expert in the varieties of such experiences," he said, "but no, no it did not. I would very much like it to have been one."

"Me, too."

"The thought that it might not have been I find—unnerving."

"Yeah," I said, "it scares the crap out of me."

I wanted to discuss whatever you'd call had happened to us, but I had a hard time finding the right words—adequate words. I knew the house's history—not as thoroughly as Roger, but well-enough to know there was nothing in it to explain both of us—how would you describe it? Being touched by the paranormal? You see what I mean? Some things you go through, and the only way to approach them is in words that sound so ridiculous they basically shut you up. I can't imagine how you can write about this kind of stuff. I'd think the problem of language alone would be insurmountable.

Despite this, despite the sheer absurdity that assaulted us when we opened our mouths to speak, we did our best to talk about the possible causes for what I christened Our Mutual Weirdness. At one point, I started shaking and couldn't stop, the way you do when the flu overtakes you. Roger came over to me and held me until the fit passed, which must have been at least ten minutes. He remained pale for the rest of our discussion, as if he'd lost a pint of blood.

We threw out things like radon almost immediately. Neither of us knew that much about it, but we were reasonably sure its effects did not include incredibly vivid hallucinations. Roger wondered if we'd shared some manner of psychic encounter, but the details didn't seem to support that, either. (Or, not exactly—I explained my awareness of the house.) I leaned toward the ghostly, which Roger didn't like but agreed appeared the more likely answer. Nothing about the house's past, though—nothing we knew of—suggested a former inhabitant hanging around.

• • •

Roger had told me the house's pedigree late one night—it was the night I agreed to move in there. We were lying in bed, and I made some kind of remark. I can't remember what it was, but in answer, Roger related the house's history. It was, he said, "rather mundane." He said, "The house is one of the original dwellings built by the Huguenots when they settled here. A fellow named Jean Michel lived in it with his family. The house he raised was decidedly more modest than what stands there now. Like the other buildings on Founders Street, it was built of fieldstone, and occupied roughly the space of what is now the front parlor and hallway." He might have been delivering the voice-over for a PBS special on historic houses. He went on, "What you might call the house proper did not appear for another one hundred and fifty years, when Michel's great-great-grandson, Roderick Michel Sears, decided to renovate the ancestral home to something more in keeping with his status as the town's richest man. He brought in a small army of workers, and what had been another in a series of stone houses became the biggest and grandest house in the area. Since its construction, the house had been known as the Michel house; following Sears's transformation, it became the Sears House; although one local wit dubbed it the Taj Michel.

"That's the extent of the place's history, really. Thomas Belvedere summered there in 1953; there's evidence he started his 'Dark Feast' paintings during his stay. When the last owner, a woman named Nancy Milon, died in a nursing home in Florida in 1958, there were no relatives who wanted to move into the house, which was already falling into disrepair. The Huguenot Historical Society made a move to purchase it for a museum, but this fell through for reasons I don't know. The house was subdivided into ten apartments and rented to students at the college; this was the sixties in Huguenot, so you can be sure its walls witnessed their fair share of surreal experiences. By the time Joanne and I arrived in town, the place was in decay. Its upkeep was a constant and formidable task, and since it was being rented to students, the owners didn't trouble themselves over it much. We bought the place for a song, and a fairly cheap tune at that. In all our renovations and repairs, however, we failed to turn up anything out of the ordinary, no secret passages, no corpses sealed up in the walls, no Indian burial ground in the basement."

How strange is it that we didn't think of Ted right away? Well, that I didn't. Despite my inability to relegate Roger's cursing Ted to the past, not once did it occur to me that the night's strangeness might be the result of him pronouncing, "Let our blood no longer be true."

* * *

We went up to bed not long after deciding we weren't going to figure out what had happened to us right away. Sitting in the living room, all that space around us, I felt exposed, terribly visible and vulnerable, and

I'm pretty sure Roger did, too. In bed, huddled under the covers next to Roger, wasn't much better. Sleep kept its distance, and while I was lying awake with nothing but my thoughts and the sound of Roger's snoring to distract me, there was the house around me. Not like I had in the living room—this was more the normal sensation of it I had—the normal abnormal, as opposed to the terrifying abnormal—the awareness of it at the ends of my nerves, as if I'd been outside in the freezing cold and just stepped into a hot room. Except now, I knew that feeling as one end of a scale that reached I didn't know how far: at least into the uncomfortable—the profoundly uncomfortable—and possibly well beyond. I didn't expect I'd sleep before dawn, if at all, but as I lay feeling the house around me, I seemed to flow out into it, and then it was late the next morning.

Do you know what's truly bizarre in all this? When I woke up the next morning, I was—not happy, exactly—it was more that I was relieved. For a long time, I'd been—well, you might say concerned about my mental well-being. After all, ask any doctor what the diagnosis is for visions so real you can walk around in them, and you're going to get some form of psychosis. That, or a brain tumor. Now—now, the same thing had happened, and it had happened to someone else, as well. Okay, Roger's and my experiences hadn't been exactly the same, but you see what I mean. For as troubling as the prospect of such things' reality was, there was comfort in the thought that my mind was in better shape than I'd feared.

In the days that followed, Roger dug in the village's archives in search of any clues to the Mutual Weirdness. (I was busy finishing my summer classes.) He turned up next to nothing, and what he found was tenuous at best. According to the goings-on-in-town column of *The Huguenot Trumpet*—basically a glorified gossip column that had a surprisingly long run, (most of the nineteenth century)—a couple of the workers Roderick Sears brought in for the expansion of the house into its present form were of "mysterious origin," given, the columnist wrote, "to strange manners and practices." What those manners and practices were, the writer didn't specify, but the description sounded to me like a bored columnist trying to inject some life into his otherwise boring report by appealing to American xenophobia. Out of curiosity, I wondered who those guys had been, what work they'd done on the house, but we couldn't find out. The columnist probably invented them.

The only other piece of possibly relevant information Roger found was in one of Thomas Belvedere's letters. Two years after his stay in the house, Belvedere wrote about the "unusual" sensations he'd experienced while living in it. He didn't go into any detail as to the nature of these sensations—although he said they were "not unconducive to a certain kind of inspiration"—in that letter or any other. Roger went so far as to call the curator of special collections at Stanford, where Belvedere's papers are, to ask her to check. She did, and found nothing. By this time, I'd turned in my final grades, so I joined Roger in consulting Belvedere's paintings, especially the "Dark Feast" series, which he began during his stay at the house, and completed shortly after. Have you seen them? I've never been that crazy about Belvedere—too much a Jackson Pollock-wannabe—but I studied those four paintings like they were the ceiling of the Sistine Chapel. I didn't like them any better when I was done, but there was one, the second, that was interesting. The background is a series of black and royal blue squares, done in a kind of checkerboard effect. On top of that, Belvedere painted the silhouette of a house in lots of wavy white and yellow lines. Inside the house, so to speak, there are all these loops and swirls in dark green and purple. Belvedere arranged the background, the checkerboard, and the silhouette to suggest windows. The outline of the house wasn't an exact match to ours. There were enough angles missing and added that I could understand how no one had made the connection between the painting and the house. (No one had; I checked.) It was the house, though. Looking at it spread out across the pages of the library book on Belvedere, I had no doubt that this was my house. That wavy outline, the absent and extra windows and angles—they weren't exactly how the house felt to me, but they were like it, if that makes any sense. After about a day and a half of studying that painting, staring at it until it was burned onto the backs of my eyes, I had no doubt whatsoever that Thomas Belvedere had undergone something similar—parallel—to our experiences when he'd stayed here.

Of course, since I didn't have anything more than the painting and that line in his letter, my conviction wasn't much use. I e-mailed Belvedere's biographer, hoping that she might know something. Maybe there was a letter that wasn't in the archive, or someone had mentioned something in an interview. No luck. I went so far as to write to Belvedere's widow—she's still alive, ninety-four years old and living in Provincetown. She replied right away, but only to say that she was done answering questions about her late husband, and if I wanted to know anything about him, I should contact his biographer.

So there I was, with what seemed like reasonably good evidence that at least one other person had undergone a strange experience in the house, and nothing to do about it. I had this picture of Thomas and Viola Belvedere that I'd photocopied from his biography. It wasn't very big—about the size of a standard photo. Sometime during the first few days of my research, I'd taped it to one side of the computer screen. More and more of the time I was supposed to be devoting to following the leads I'd found, I spent staring at that picture, as if the answer I was searching for was encoded in its black-and-white depths. The photo had been taken in the spring of 1955, about a year after Belvedere's summer in the house. He and Viola were at a reception at Princeton. I don't know if you've seen a picture of Belvedere. He was medium-tall, skinny-running-to-fat, which you noticed in his stomach, straining his shirt-fronts long before the rest of his body caught up with it. For most of his life, he affected a long mustache—not quite a handlebar, but heading in that direction—and a crewcut. Not a good combination, if you ask me, but I think it was his attempt to add distinction to what was otherwise a plain face. Viola was much more interesting looking, these strong features—dark eyes, Roman nose, full lips, sharp chin. On its own, any one part of her face would have been too much; together, they held each other in balance. She was ten years older than her husband; although in this picture, him wearing a dark suit with a narrow tie that looks as if it's slowly strangling him, her in a black and white dress that looks as if it had been shipped directly from *The Dick Van Dyke Show*, you wouldn't guess there was more than a year between them either way.

I wondered about contacting some of the other people who'd stayed in the house—the students who'd rented it in the sixties— but the farthest I got was an awkward call to Dr. Sullivan. I couldn't figure out how to find out what I wanted to know. I mean, you can't just come out and ask someone if they had a supernatural experience, can you? You could, but they'd think you were some kind of nut. I spent about ten minutes asking if she or anyone else in her family had noticed anything strange while they were in the house, anything unusual, anything out of the ordinary. She kept saying no, no, nothing in the slightest, until she lost her patience and demanded to know what was going on. Radon gas, I said. It was the first thing that came to mind. We haven't been feeling well lately, I said, and we're concerned it might be due to radon. And wouldn't it be just my luck that she should know something about radon poisoning? I had to invent a whole history of additional, phony symptoms for Roger and me. By the end of our conversation, she was urging both of us to have full check-ups. I didn't like lying to her, but at least I was able to rule out radon as the cause for the Weirdness.

* * *

While I was busy with all this—and believe me, no Ph.D. student writing her dissertation worked this hard; for about two weeks, this was all I did, all day—while I was up to my elbows in the facts of Thomas Belvedere's life and studies of Abstract Expressionism, Roger was pursuing other interests. For the first week, he'd taken the lead in researching the house, but once I became involved in a serious way, he withdrew, gradually, then all at once. I didn't notice. That's not true. I noticed; I didn't attach any significance to it. He tended to run through things much more quickly than I did. Obviously, he'd taken his researches as far as he could. He had his own projects, which I assumed he'd returned to. If I hadn't been so busy with studies of the house as a structural manifestation of the feminine archetype, I probably would have paid more attention to the oversized envelopes that had started arriving in the mail for him, or I would have ventured up to the third floor to ask him what he was doing in his office for hours and hours and hours.

And if I'm being honest, more than my work kept me surrounded by the library's tall bookcases. Ever since the Mutual Weirdness, the house had felt—contingent. It was as if the invisible house, the one that hovered at the edges of my senses, had drawn closer. Not a lot closer, but sufficient to make the walls around me, the floor beneath, seem more tenuous. I would sit on the library's couch, poring over Belvedere's biography, already festooned with post-it notes in half a dozen colors, for the fiftieth time, trying to squeeze additional meaning out of details long since wrung dry, and for all my concentration—almost because of it—I would feel the house—I want to say shimmering, as if it were an enormous soap-bubble. I would be positive that, were I to put my feet on the floor, the entire house would burst, revealing—I wasn't sure what. Maybe nothing. You know how it is when you're alone. The strangest ideas seize hold of you and refuse to let go. So I left Roger to his own devices, which was a mistake.

Because it wasn't only that he was spending more and more of each day in his office—that happened when he was absorbed in an article or book—and who was I to talk about that, spending fourteen pretty-much-uninterrupted hours in the second floor library, all my material on Belvedere spread out on the floor around the computer desk. No, it was that, when I saw Roger, when he brought lunch or dinner to me, which he did most days, or if he waited for me to come to bed, which he did less and less, he seemed more stressed— more strained—than ever. His smiles were painted on. He'd jump if I tried to put my arms around him from behind. If I placed my hand on his, or his arm—you know, one of those gestures you make to your spouse—it was like touching a high voltage wire. You could practically smell the ozone. In the days after the Mutual Weirdness, I chalked up the change to that experience. I hadn't been affected that way, true, but I wasn't as much a dyed-in-the-wool rationalist as Roger, and anyway, here I was burying myself in all these books, so maybe I'd been more affected than I realized.

With each day that went by, however, Roger seemed worse. On a couple of occasions, I asked him flat-out what was wrong, only to have him shake his head and retreat out of the library. On a couple more—once in the library and once in the kitchen—he started to say something to me, only to break off after barely a sentence. During that second week, when I was in the thick of my research, I kept promising myself that I was going to do something about this—shift in Roger. I wasn't going to sit on my hands the way I had while he'd crashed and burned at school. I just needed to finish this article. Maybe I should have left, escaped, instead of sequestering myself each day in the very heart of peril. I'd like to say it was because I didn't want to abandon Roger, which isn't untrue. I knew he'd never agree to move from the house, no matter how unhappy being there was making him. But strange as it sounds, leaving didn't seem like an option to me, either. I'm not sure I can explain it, but it was like, the very same feeling that should have sent me screaming out the front door kept me exactly where I was.

That second week, there was one moment. I was curled up on the couch, plodding through this essay by Derrida that had sounded relevant when I'd read about it in another article, but had turned into the written equivalent of trying to walk down a path that's completely overgrown. No, it wasn't about Belvedere. It was on Antonin Artaud. I was tangled in a typical sentence, rereading it over and over in an attempt to force some meaning from it—and frustrated to the point of wanting to toss the pages aside and be done with them. It didn't help that it was late, about eleven, and I'd been at this nonstop since seven a.m. I had tried to take notes, but my writing had gone from sentences to words to question marks. As I was adding another question mark to the list, I noticed a figure standing in the door. I thought it was Roger, and my heart gave a little leap at the possibility that he had come to talk to me at last.

You guessed it: when I looked up, the doorway was empty. I wasn't especially freaked out. I thought I'd seen Roger and I hadn't, that was all. What gradually got to me, though, was wondering why, as I remembered what hadn't been there, I'd imagined Roger so much taller than he was? That, and something else—the figure in the doorway had been dark, as if it had been standing in shadow. Yes, I recalled that night in my apartment when I'd seen someone behind me. This had been briefer, and even less certain than my old kitchen at three a.m., but as I compared the experiences—and my chances of finishing Derrida decreased dramatically—they were similar enough to make me very nervous. The house was quiet. I could hear Roger pacing upstairs, even a pair of late-night walkers talking as they passed on the street. Underneath that quiet—or beside it—my sense of the house, at the border of my skin. Caught up in the silence and the skin was something else. Not a feeling, not an awareness of whatever had or hadn't been in the doorway—it was more the lack of awareness, a kind of positive lack, an active absence. It was enough to make me wish I could stay in the library for the rest of the night, instead of yielding myself to the danger of walking out the door and down the hall to the bedroom. I did not want to pass through the space that shadowy form had occupied. I delayed as long as I could, flipping through the introduction to the Derrida, consulting the index, but in the end, I went. I wasn't happy about it, but I left, flinching as I crossed the threshold. The hallway was dim. As I padded up it, I heard something, so faint as to be almost lost in the slide of my socks over the floor. I stopped, listening. Nothing. I waited, but whatever it was had stopped. I hurried to the bathroom. I hadn't heard words, had I? "Blood," "torment," "anything." No.

• • •

By the end of two weeks of research, it was pretty clear to me that the mysteries of Thomas Belvedere were going to remain unsolved. I hung on for another day, finishing a couple of articles I'd started, searching online when a new idea occurred to me, but that was as much me not wanting to have given up too soon as anything. It had been pretty clear by the end of week one that we weren't going to learn anything more than we already had. You hope, though; you hope that somewhere in the midst of all this information are the clues that you alone will notice and assemble. The mark of a scholar, right?

In looking for those non-existent clues, however, I'd been neglecting the very obvious signs that Roger's troubles were worsening. As I was reading the final article I'd copied—it was one by Harlow, on Belvedere and this H. P. Lovecraft story, "The Dreams in the Witch House"—as I was returning stacks of books to the libraries at SUNY and Penrose, finally getting myself out of the house, Roger's behavior was sliding from bad to worse. He wasn't preparing any meals. He was ordering breakfast from one of the diners and going to pick it up, lunch and dinner from Chinese and Italian restaurants and having it delivered. Once the food arrived, he carried his portion up to his office, knocking on the library door on his way past and calling that whatever meal it was was waiting for me in the kitchen. His jogging schedule had become erratic, his walking even more so. Mostly, he left his office to use the bathroom, fetch meals, and go to bed—which he didn't do until early in the morning. He was back at his office before I was awake. One night, he either slept upstairs or worked straight through till morning. I was trying to give him the benefit of the doubt—that was what I told myself—maybe he'd become obsessed with an exciting idea. What I was doing, of course, was delaying the inevitable. I was afraid of what was going to happen when I confronted Roger. I was afraid he was going to need serious psychiatric help, and I didn't have the faintest idea how to convince him to seek it out, or, if he refused, to insure he received it. Of all the possible complications I'd worried about when we got together, Roger losing his mind had not been among them, and trying to deal with it was overwhelming.

How very nineteenth century. Granted, it was usually the woman who was insane and living upstairs—*The Madwoman in the Attic*, right? When the man was out of his mind—well, no attics for him.

When Roger showed me what he'd been doing in his office, it didn't help matters any. The day after I returned the last book on Belvedere to the library and filed my notes away for future use, Roger asked me if I would join him on the third floor. I was at the kitchen table, eating a late breakfast and leafing through the latest issue of *The New Yorker*. He was freshly showered—his hair was still wet—and he had on a clean pair of jeans and a blue and orange SUNY Huguenot sweatshirt. "What is it?" I asked him.

"Come up to my office and we can discuss it there," he said, and before I could ask him why we couldn't talk about it here, where I had half an omelet sitting on my plate, he walked out of the kitchen. I heard the stairs creak as he started up them.

I must have sat there for five, maybe ten minutes. I wanted to finish my breakfast, and I wasn't sure I wanted to go up to Roger's office. Tension spilled from him like heat from a sunlamp. I wasn't worried about him becoming violent or anything. I knew him well-enough to be sure that wasn't in him, and besides, I'd beaten him at arm-wrestling enough to know that, if it came down to a fight, I could kick his ass. It was—all of a sudden, that office became—whatever had been going on with Roger this past week was going to be reflected in that room, and I couldn't decide if I wanted to see that. I washed and dried my dishes, then stood looking out the kitchen windows. There was a woman walking along Founders Street with her baby—she had the baby in one of those sport strollers, you know, the kind with the big wheels. She was wearing a maroon tracksuit and white sneakers; her hair was pulled back by a maroon and white headband. She was too far away for me to be able to tell for sure, but I thought she looked around my age. I couldn't see the baby. I looked down, and saw that, without realizing it, I'd put my hands over my belly. I watched the woman push the stroller past the Dutch Reformed Church, then around the bend that leads to Addie and Harlow's place. When she was out of sight, I left the kitchen and climbed the stairs.

On my way up to the third floor, along walls Roger and his students had painted pale yellow, past pictures of Ted I'd hung up the stairways, the mirrors at the top of the second floor stairs and the bottom of the third floor stairs, I was acutely aware of places where the house felt—less dense, as if, were I to smash a hammer through them, I would find, not wood and wires, pipes, but darkness, an opening into I couldn't say what. For a moment, there was almost something there—as if something were pressed against the other side of the wall, listening to me pass. I imagined Roger's face, enormous as I'd seen it that day in my apartment; I pictured those oversized features slowly bleeding onto the plaster. The vision of the house I'd first had when I miscarried seemed less psychological symbol and more…I wasn't sure what—diagram, maybe.

Outside the door to Roger's office, which was closed over but not shut, I paused, cleared my throat, and called, "Roger?"

"Come in," he called back.

I pushed open the door. Roger was standing a few paces in front of me, his head down, his hands clasped behind his back. He must have been holding that pose for some time, since I hadn't heard anything from the office as I'd approached it. He'd probably been that way for the last ten minutes. *How theatrical*, I thought, which was always true of Roger. He loved those kinds of gestures. I was so concerned with him that it took a minute for what he'd done to his office to register.

The office wasn't especially large. Our bedroom was about twice its size, the living room four or five times bigger. When we'd moved into the house, he'd set it up exactly as it had been before he'd left, and it had always been very full. To your right, as you entered, was his desk, which was fairly modest and held his computer. In the middle of the room, there was a large, heavy oak table where he would lay out whatever materials he required for his latest undertaking. This table had its own chair, an old kitchen leftover that creaked and swayed and threatened to collapse under you. He liked to sit at the table and make extensive notes—really, they were more rough drafts. To your left, there was a couch where Roger could sit and read—it folded out into a bed, and was where—well, you've heard that part of the story already, haven't you? The room was ringed with floor-to-ceiling bookcases, most of which were stuffed with the lifetime of material on Dickens Roger had collected, including first editions of most of his novels. Directly across from the doorway was a window that looked out on the back lawn. There wasn't much wall space. Over his desk, Roger had hung an oversized bulletin board that was layered with pictures and postcards, the majority of them of Dickens and his friends. He'd taped a few posters and flyers to the bookcase shelves, pretty much all of which had to do with him: lectures that he'd given, conferences he'd been the keynote speaker at, books he'd written. I suppose he was entitled.

All that had been changed. Everything was still in the same place—as far as I could tell—but now every last inch of the office had been covered in maps. I recognized their subject immediately. How could I not? In the past years, we'd all seen Afghanistan's broken oval enough times on the news and in print to know its outline. Hanging to the left of the window was an enormous map that completely obscured the bookcase it was taped to. It was some kind of National Geographic special that displayed not only the country's topography and settlements, but the sites of all the battles in the recent U.S. war. The country was colored desert-brown, outlined in a white line and, around that, a yellow line. All the surrounding countries were white, blank spaces. Roger had written on the map. I couldn't read the words from the doorway, but I could see that they clustered next to Kabul, which he'd circled in black magic marker. No, it wasn't a circle; it was a spiral whose tail descended into the city.

There were other maps of the country—other kinds of maps— hanging from the rest of the bookcases like elaborate paper drapes. None was as big as the map across from me. A few were a couple of feet wide, but most looked as if they'd been photocopied from textbooks. There was another map of Afghanistan's geography, which was next to one of those maps that show height and depth in gradations—what do you call them? Mercator maps? One color-coded map revealed the country's average rainfall amounts; another, the type and distribution of its principle crops; a third estimated its population density. A largish map broke the place down into its various tribes and ethnicities; a larger map than that marked the ebb and flow of its historical borders. A cluster of smaller maps showed the country's margins at specific historical moments. Some maps were satellite photos with borders superimposed; others looked like they'd been drawn by British cartographers during the heyday of the Empire.

Mixed in with the outlines of Afghanistan were other pieces of paper, which I recognized as maps, too, though I couldn't tell of what. There was the same variety to them, the same mix of different reference points, of new and old. Then I saw the word "Kabul" at the top of one. Every last one of these maps was covered in Roger's handwriting, in three or four different colors of ink. He'd put stickers on some of the maps—those little round ones they use for the prices at flea markets and church fairs—which he used to anchor pieces of thread connecting one map to another. Two or three Post-It notes dangled from each map of Kabul, and more filled what little space remained on the bookcases.

That wasn't all. The table in the center of the room was heaped with books, most of them with "Afghanistan" in their titles; though a few were called things like *The Modern Army* and *Special Forces: A History*. Sandwiched in between the books were manila folders stuffed with papers. A half-dozen ragged legal pads competed with stacks of oversized color photos—the ones I could see were of the streets of a city I assumed was Kabul.

I couldn't take it all in. I haven't mentioned his desk, or the books stacked on the couch. I said, "Roger."

He raised his head and said, "No doubt you're wondering what all this is about." He didn't look incredibly insane.

I nodded.

"I have been doing a little research of my own—"

"So I see."

"—and I believe I know what happened to us three weeks ago."

"All right," I said.

"Aren't you going to ask me what I think?"

I didn't need to. The moment I'd recognized the enormous map hanging across from me, I'd known. I said, "It's Ted, isn't it? You think Ted is haunting us."

Roger smiled. "You always were my brightest student. I wouldn't use the word haunting, as it connotes something more sinister than what we are experiencing. I prefer to say that Ted is trying to reach out to us."

"What makes you so sure?"

"There appears little doubt that Our Mutual Weirdness, to use your phrase, was supernatural. I have considered all the natural explanations and found every last one wanting. Given its supernatural character, the question of its origin confronts us. The house itself is the most obvious culprit; however, my investigations into its history convinced me that it was a dead-end in fairly short order, and I am correct in assuming your more extensive research confirms such a conclusion, am I not?"

"There's nothing glaringly obvious."

"Once the house is eliminated from consideration, our focus must shift to those who underwent the Weirdness. I cannot think of anything in your short life that would account for such occurrences, which leaves us with me. What is there in my life that fits the supernatural explanation? Only one thing: Ted."

He delivered his argument the same way he did his case for a particular interpretation of a passage. I said, "And you think Ted is... reaching out to us."

"That's right."

"Why?"

Quick as a bird flashing past a window, a look that mingled pain with something else—fear?—crossed Roger's face. "Why sweetie," he said, "I'm his father. Why wouldn't he want to contact me?"

Here it was, so soon. "Well," I said, "the last time you two spoke, you disowned him."

He flinched. "I did at that."

I didn't say anything.

"It was a mistake," Roger said at last. "I spoke in anger."

Do you know, that was the first time we'd mentioned his disowning Ted? Let alone him admitting it had been wrong. Under different circumstances, this would have been an important occasion. As it was, it was still significant, but that significance was overshadowed by its context. I said, "You were angry. Maybe Ted saw that, too. But you never took those words back. As far as Ted knew, you no longer considered him your son. I'm not trying to be mean, but why would he think anything had changed? How would he know to make the attempt to get through to you—us?"

Frowning, Roger said, "Ted and I have unfinished business."

"Okay," I said, "I guess you do. But I don't—at least, I don't think I do. Why should I be involved in this? How is my feeling the house moving around me Ted trying to communicate with me?"

"Though I am not certain, you understand, I believe your sensation of the house to be a side-effect of Ted's effort to establish contact with me."

"Then why did I notice it the moment I set foot in here?"

"Because," Roger said, "Ted has been struggling to reach me since that time—since before it, most likely. You crossed into the house at the moment he succeeded—the moment he began to succeed, I should say. The house itself may have played some role in helping his effort; its long association with him—with us—may have assisted him in focusing his energies. After all, you didn't notice these feelings on any of the previous times you were in the house, did you? As I recall, you didn't mention it during our rendezvous here."

"No," I admitted. "Why all the maps?"

"Everything you see here," Roger said, "is part of my attempt to understand Ted's death. If I am to reach out to where he is, then it is imperative for me to understand as much about the circumstances of his—his leaving this life as is possible."

"Where do you think he is? Is he still in Afghanistan?"

Roger shook his head. "I can't say for sure; although Kabul is significant as Ted's—call it his entry point to the hereafter. While I am hardly an expert in these matters, it is my guess that Ted currently inhabits what the Tibetan Buddhists call the bardo, a kind of ante-chamber to life. From this space, one is supposed to move away from the illusions of this world towards eternity; it is possible, however, for a soul in that state to look back the other way, to the life departed."

"Tibetan Buddhists?"

"These last weeks," Roger said, "I've acquainted myself with a great many religious traditions, in hopes that one of them might offer some clues to our situation. The Southern Baptistry of my parents and siblings speaks little to the possibility of ghosts and the ghostly. There may be warnings and encouragement from souls in heaven, or regret and temptation from souls in hell, but little else. As a rule, the more fundamentalist-leaning sects of Christianity appear to have little room for whatever is not spelled out in the Bible. The Catholics, Episcopalians, and Lutherans are somewhat more open when it comes to such matters, but they warn of demons masquerading as the dear departed. Generally speaking, Christian traditions grow very nervous at the hint of anything that suggests death may be more—or less, I suppose—than the carrots and sticks they hold out to and threaten their followers with. The failure of the faith most familiar to me to tell me where my son is sent me searching for what other peoples have had to say, which led me to the Tibetan Buddhists."

The bardo sounded analogous to Purgatory, but now wasn't the time for an extended theological debate. Instead, I said, "All right. Ted is in the bardo trying to contact you so the two of you can finish your unfinished business—so you can be reconciled and he can be at peace, I assume. What do we know about it? Is there any way we can help him?"

"I'm not sure," Roger said. "By immersing myself in the particulars of Ted's passing, I hope to become as receptive to him as possible—to put myself on his wavelength, so to speak. I can't say it has succeeded as yet, but I have only been at this for a short time. I believe that much of the work must be done from the other side, by the soul in question. We are on Ted's timetable."

"Huh," I said, or grunted. Really, what else was there to say? I wandered over to the futon, crowded with teetering stacks of books, and carefully sat down on the edge of it. Roger was watching me expectantly—waiting, I knew, for me to speak and render some kind of judgment on what he'd told me, the whole, mad explanation. Which I couldn't do. Rationally speaking, of course it was insane, but we were already at some distance from what was rational. If Roger was delusional, then I was encouraging him in the worst way just by having this conversation with him, entertaining his fantasy instead of insisting he speak to a psychiatrist. If he wasn't delusional—look, I understand that idea may seem delusional in and of itself, but I'd been at the center of the house's strangeness since I'd set foot in it. I couldn't say whether Roger's explanation was in any way accurate, but at least it acknowledged what I'd been experiencing. Was it so bad for Roger to want to talk to his son, to make up with him? I mean, given everything, wasn't it natural? People grieved in strange ways. How was what Roger was doing here different from a person who goes to church every day in hopes of a message from their loved one?

He was still waiting. I said, "What's next? Do we hire a medium? Conduct a séance?"

He exhaled; his shoulders relaxed. "No, I'm afraid it's more of the same. More research; more waiting until something happens."

"What is going to happen?"

"Ted will find a way to contact me."

"And?"

"Presumably, he will be able to move off into the bardo—to be at peace."

That was pretty much that. As I stood to leave the room, Roger surprised me by walking over and catching me in a long hug. "Thank you," he said. "I have evaded this conversation longer than I should have. I was afraid that you would not understand—to be frank, I was afraid that you would think I had descended into raving lunacy. I've wondered the same thing, myself, at certain moments. I appreciate the act of faith this requires on your part, and I am grateful."

• • •

I'm not sure Roger would have been quite so grateful if he'd known I went to speak to a psychiatrist myself three days later; although, since it didn't lead to anything, he might have been. I saw Dr. Hawkins, the psychiatrist my ob-gyn had recommended after the miscarriage. Her office is on Founders, in that red brick house beside the old graveyard. Yes, I noticed that, too. How appropriate, right? The funny thing is, she had a copy of one of Belvedere's paintings hanging in her tiny waiting room; this one called *Night Passage*. It's a small canvas, maybe a foot by a foot-and-a-half. Belvedere worked on it, on and off, for something like twelve years, from a couple of months after his stay in our house until he abandoned the piece in the mid-sixties. The critics I'd read regarded it as a five-fingered exercise, a diversion from more serious projects. It is unlike any of his other paintings; I actually like it a lot. There's none of the straining after effect you encounter in his major pieces. It reminds me of a cross between cubism and Looney Tunes. The subject of the painting is a black-and-yellow funnel, a stylized tornado, which begins in the lower-left-hand corner and curves up and across an off-white background, growing broader on the way. The funnel is presented in cross-section, as if to give the illusion you're looking down into it, but Belvedere laid on the paint so thickly that it compromises the effect. Surrounding the funnel, passing inside and out, are a series of bright, almost pastel figures that look kind of like the forms you encounter on totem poles, kind of like characters from a children's book. There's one that resembles an eagle or hawk, another that might be a fisherman, something that could be the big bad wolf. It's obvious they're members of Belvedere's personal pantheon—it is to me—but no one's bothered trying to determine their identities. I speculated a bit on them while I sat in the waiting room, wondering if I were betraying Roger.

Scratch that. I knew I was betraying him by coming here. It was a question of degree, I—it was something I felt I had to do, an option I had to explore. Going in, I had a decent idea what the psychiatrist's verdict would be—though I told myself she might surprise me.

She didn't. She's tall, Dr. Hawkins, and skinny, so much so that all her joints protrude. Her hands and feet are enormous. I felt like a little kid shaking an adult's hand when she came out to greet me. She wears her hair in a braid that hangs down her back, and these cat's-eye glasses that you know she thinks are trendy but that make her look like the mother on a fifties TV show. She had on a dull red, shapeless dress with a long necklace of black beads—to balance the braid, I guess. From almost the moment we sat down in her office and she opened her mouth, I knew I wasn't going to learn anything new. But it was like, Oh well, I'm here; I might as well talk to her. She kept insisting I call her Yvonne, to put me at ease—which it didn't. When I go to see a professional, I'm going to see them as a professional. I don't want my doctor to be my friend. I want her to be my doctor. It's the same with my students. I'm not "Veronica" to them; I'm "Professor Croydon"; "Ms. Croydon" if they're sticklers about the Ph.D.

Anyway, I sat in one of Dr. Hawkins's chairs, which wasn't half as comfortable as you'd expect a chair in a psychiatrist's office to be, and gave her the *Reader's Digest* version of what I've been telling you. My husband thinks the son he disowned is trying to speak to him from beyond the grave. I was paying by the hour. She heard the crucial information, asking occasional questions along the way, and when I said, "That's about it," she said, "I see," and started writing on a legal pad she had balanced on her knee. She wrote for about five minutes, filling one page and going on to another. Finally, still looking at the legal pad, she said, "Without talking to your husband myself, I can only speculate on his psychological state. It's important you understand that at the outset. What I'm offering is speculation. Informed, yes, but speculation all the same. Your husband—Roger has suffered a significant psychic trauma in the death of his son. Losing a child always wounds a parent, no matter how old the child, no matter how poor the relationship. Additionally, in this case, there were complicating factors. Roger had been ambivalent about Ted, natural enough given what you've told me of their history, but uncomfortable for a parent nonetheless. Rather than resolving itself as Ted grew older, Roger's ambivalence towards him increased—fed, I suspect, by his own lingering issues with his father—until their confrontation at the apartment allowed years of pent-up emotion to vent itself in anger and actual violence, climaxing in what you call Roger's cursing Ted. However satisfying such a release may have been in the short term—and I imagine it was very gratifying for your husband to be able to let these feelings out—in the long term, it left Roger in an even more uncomfortable psychic state. And then Ted, the object of decades of conflicting emotions, was killed. That death is like a great, black magnet. It drew all those difficult feelings down into itself and will not release them, thus significantly complicating any attempts by Roger to resolve them. How is this sounding to you? Are you with me?" she asked, looking up.

"So far," I said.

"Roger needs to find a way to come to terms with his feelings about Ted, because although Ted is dead, Roger's relationship with him is not. As you can appreciate, this is an intolerable situation. It must be addressed, and the sooner, the better. Roger could have done so positively, through conversation with you, or a therapist, an option he has not chosen. He could have done so negatively, through use of alcohol or recreational drugs, an option he also has not chosen, thankfully. He could have sought a creative outlet for his needs, writing down his memories of Ted, or writing letters to him, techniques I employ sometimes in these kinds of situations. Roger hasn't exactly chosen this course of action, but the one he has selected is related to it. He has invented a scenario that will allow him to meet his needs more directly, namely, the haunting. Tellingly, he has created a situation in which Ted is haunting him—Ted is the one who requires their reconciliation. That Roger has projected his own deepest wishes onto the ghost of his son suggests that, even in so private a fantasy as this one, Roger remains unable to face his past actions, and, I believe, his continuing feelings, fully."

"All right," I said. "Roger's living out this fantasy." I felt like adding, "Duh," but didn't. "So what's going to happen?"

Dr. Hawkins held up her hands. "That I can't say for sure. Please keep in mind, this is all hypothetical."

"I understand that," I said. "I'm asking for your opinion."

"It's unlikely that Roger will be able to come out of his fantasy on his own. Unlikely to the point of impossible, I would say. From what you've described to me of the changes in his office, he's already invested too much of himself in the scenario he's invented for him to be able to disengage from it without professional help."

"What if he doesn't want that help?"

"The fantasy will continue. It could persist for a considerable time, depending on how well Roger is able to accommodate it to his continued failure to communicate with Ted. Over time, such a failure could lead to depression—in fact, I'd say that's almost certain. It could lead to that self-destructive behavior I mentioned, to alcohol or drugs. Veronica," she said, "I know how difficult this is to hear, but without some form of intervention, your husband is not going to get better. There is no good end to this for him. Time is of the essence. The mind is like any other organ: the sooner you catch and attend to a problem, the easier it is for it to heal."

That was the end of our consultation. As I was writing the check, though, I said, "What would you say if I told you I thought there might be something to Roger's fantasy?"

"What do you mean?"

I tore off the check and handed it to her. "That maybe Roger *is* being haunted."

While she filled out my receipt, Dr. Hawkins was silent, but I could practically hear her composing her reply. Handing me the receipt, she said, "I would say that you were caught up in your husband's invention, possibly due to your own guilt at perceiving yourself as the cause of Roger and Ted's last fight. I would stress to you that Roger's fantasy is that. I would repeat to you that this situation cannot turn out well, and I would urge you to seek counseling for yourself immediately. Would you like to schedule another appointment?"

"No thanks," I said, folding the receipt and sliding it into my purse.

"Are you sure?"

"No," I said.

"Veronica," Dr. Hawkins said, "I don't want you to misinterpret this, but the dead are fearsome. I'm not talking about floating white sheets. I'm talking about the losses that score themselves on us. They are greedy. They are always hungry. They will take whatever you have to give them and it won't be enough. It will never be enough. I lost my sister to leukemia twenty years ago and it still grieves me. You cannot make the dead happy. You cannot achieve any kind of mystical understanding with them. Those things are the province of movies and bad self-help books. I'm sorry to speak in metaphors, but I hope my point is plain enough. You have to leave the dead to themselves, and attend to your life."

"And when the dead won't let you do that?" I asked.

"That's why we have therapy," she said.

That and a hundred and fifty bucks an hour, I thought on the walk home. With the exception of her remarks about the dead at the very end there, Dr. Hawkins hadn't said anything very surprising or interesting. I mean, you hardly needed an MD to connect the scenario Roger had described to his need to resolve his own, no-doubt-still-conflicted emotions. Nor did it require much subtlety of thought to recognize the role my guilt must be playing in my actions. When you came right down to it, you didn't have to have a higher degree to assert that the dead are implacable; though this was an interesting enough idea for me to give Dr. Hawkins credit for it. I know, I know. If I was so unhappy with her, why did I bother? Why did I sit through the entire session? Mostly, it was so I could tell myself I had given this option its full chance. Depending on what was going to happen next, I didn't want to think, "Oh, if only I'd talked to someone about everything." Now, I had spoken with a professional, found her advice pretty useless, and could move on.

Understand, I didn't doubt the importance of either Roger's or my guilt in what was occurring. I just didn't think that was all there was to it. Having brooded on Roger's version of events for the last three days, I still wasn't sure what my opinion of it was. It made sense, but only if you were willing to accept its premises, which I wasn't certain I was. After all, it was possible to the point of probable that Thomas Belvedere had undergone something during the summer he'd lived in the house. Granted, it was a dead-end as far as specific information went, but that didn't rule it out completely. Who knew what had happened in the house over the years—the decades? It had been an apartment house for college students, for crying out tears, in the sixties. And who was Roger to say there was nothing in my life to explain what we'd been going through? I'd lost a child, too. Who was to say it wasn't that spirit trying to speak to us? Given everything that had passed between him and Roger—between him and me—Ted did make a certain sense, more than that lost child and more than the house. Yet I couldn't shake the conviction that Roger's explanation was radically incomplete, that at the very root of things he'd missed something important. I wouldn't say I shared Dr. Hawkins's pessimism about the dead, not exactly, but—there was Roger staring into space, saying, "You are an embarrassment and a disgrace." "I disown you; I cast you from me."

Of course, it never occurred to me that Roger's account might sound incomplete because he was deliberately leaving something out—but I'm getting ahead of myself.

My walk had brought me to the very edge of the house's lawn. I stopped there and stood gazing up at the huge structure I was already thinking of as home, this enormous space where some of my life's most important moments had taken place. Not many, granted, and certainly not as many as for Roger, to be sure, but enough that I was connected to it, too. Uncomfortably so. Standing there watching the late afternoon sky, a riot of white clouds and bronze sunlight, reflected in the house's windows, I thought of Roger, jogging or walking past, pausing here to let his gaze wander, until he was seeing not only the physical house, but the temporal one, the structure where his memories of Ted lived.

A car passed behind me, honked its horn. I jumped and looked around. It was Lamar, the minister at the Dutch Reformed Church, in his Saturn. I returned his wave and watched him continue down the street to his residence beside the church. Fortunately, it was too far away for him to ask me what I was doing, because I didn't have a good response. Fantasizing about my husband's fantasizing? I wondered if Dr. Hawkins would drive past the house on her way home, and what she'd think of me standing here staring up at it: if she'd leap out of her car and try to administer on-the-spot emergency therapy. What's that joke? Insanity doesn't run in our family—it gallops? I went inside.

Moving around the kitchen, though, opening the fridge to see what if anything we could have for dinner, which wasn't much, mostly cartons of half-eaten fried rice and orange chicken—I swear, the Chinese take-out place must've had our pictures on their "customers-of-the-year" wall—anyway, even as I was trying to determine if we had the ingredients for a red curry, I was thinking of Roger. You've seen the house's kitchen, haven't you? It's all windows, makes it ten degrees colder than the rest of the place, especially in the winter. From the counter, I could look out across the lawn to where I'd been standing five minutes earlier. Roger had left the house for only one of his walks during the last three weeks—the first or second night after I'd joined him researching the Mutual Weirdness. He'd been gone for hours, wandering the nighttime streets of the town. I could almost picture him standing where I just had. There would have been no moon, no light on inside except for a small lamp in the library. The house would have been in shadow—in places, its edges hard to find. In a way it never had before, the house would have seemed larger to him tonight, as if all that shadow had added to its bulk, made it more massive. Roger would have jammed his hands in his pockets and blown his breath out in a half-whistle—one of the things he did when he was particularly annoyed, a hold-over from the childhood where he hadn't dared express his feelings openly. To think that this place, of all places, should have become foreign to him, the house that he had restored with his own hands, the site of his best scholarship, the location of his family, of his son, of Ted.

The red curry momentarily forgotten, I stood staring out at the lawn. Every last window in that kitchen had gone from late-afternoon sunlight to middle-of-the-night darkness. I've always had a vivid imagination, though, so I took what I was seeing as no cause for distress. I blinked and went to return to my cooking. The windows remained black, the kitchen dark. Startled, I looked up. The kitchen was surrounded by night. To my left, the dining room, to my right, the laundry room, glowed with sunlight. Between them, the kitchen surveyed moonless dark. Shadows flooded the yard. Overhead, stars dotted the sky. Holding onto the countertop, I shut my eyes and counted ten as slowly as I could. When I opened them, blackness continued to press in on me. I made a noise—half a laugh, half something else, a whimper or moan. I could not be seeing this. This had to be left over from my imagination of Roger. Unless it were some kind of drug flashback, which was unlikely, since the worst thing I'd ever done was pot and pot didn't give you flashbacks, did it? Or unless this was the first sign of a psychotic break. But if you thought you were having a psychotic break, didn't that mean you weren't? If the scene outside was a hallucination, it was a remarkably detailed one. The grass looked shorter, as if it had just been mown. The trees were late-October bare. The stars seemed different, off, rearranged into new groupings. Any fascination I might have felt was rapidly replaced by fear. I wasn't behind this; it was emanating from the same place that had produced all the other weirdness. I could feel the space on the other side of the windows, as if the house had gained another, huge room. The hair on my arms stood straight up. My mouth went dry. I let go of the countertop and walked over to the windows. I know. Why didn't I run into one of the other rooms, escape to where the sun was still shining? As I drew closer to them, I could feel cold pouring off the windows, freezing the air. This wasn't the cold you felt in the kitchen in winter. This was the kind of cold you read about in places like Antarctica, cold that burns the air free of everything but itself. Shivering, I raised my right hand and touched one of the windowpanes. It was even colder than I'd thought, so cold it rushed through me like an electric shock. I cried out, jerking my hand back—

And the scene outside vanished, replaced by late afternoon as if a giant slide projector had advanced a picture. Fingertips stinging the way they do when you scald them under the tap, I stared out over the lawn that wanted mowing, the trees heavy with leaves, the sun blazing as it sank towards the mountains, too bright after such heavy dark, the details it highlighted almost grotesque. In the space between me and the windows, the air was bitterly frigid, although the cold was running out of it like water draining from a tub. I stepped away from that fading chill. My leg struck a chair. I sat down on it.

There were footsteps in the hallway, then Roger calling, "Honey? Is everything all right?" A moment later, he hurried into the kitchen. "I thought I heard—" He caught sight of me sitting by the windows and rushed over. "What is it?"

I gestured at the windows. "Out there."

"The yard?" Roger said. "What about it? Did you see someone out there?" He was halfway to his feet.

"No," I said. "It wasn't—it changed."

"Changed? The yard? How?"

I exhaled. I could do this if I took the experience a little at a time. "It got dark."

"Dark."

"Like nighttime," I said. "It was night—night and cold."

"You looked out the window and the lawn was dark."

"Not just dark," I said. "I looked out there and it was the middle of the night. The grass, the trees, were different. Like I was seeing another time of year, fall, maybe, or winter. The stars were—I could see the stars and they weren't right. They were in different patterns. I could feel it, too—like another room. I went to the windows and touched them," I held up my right hand, showing Roger my fingertips red and raw. "It was freezing. That was when you heard me scream."

Roger took my hand in his. "Good Lord," he said. "What happened next?"

"It disappeared," I said. "Everything went back to normal."

Leaning over, Roger raised my hand and gently kissed my fingertips. His lips burned ever-so-slightly, but I smiled weakly at the sentiment. Between kisses, he said, "Poor, poor dear."

I didn't say anything.

"Did you feel," Roger started to ask, stopped. "That is, could you tell—"

"Was it Ted?" I completed his question. "I couldn't tell. There was just the sense that what was outside the house was also part of it. Not everything outside, only what I was seeing." Roger frowned—not an angry frown, but a concentration of his brows that made me ask, "What? What is it?"

"Nothing," he said, then added, "Not nothing. I'm wondering about the timing of this."

"The timing?"

"Yes," he said. "What you saw lasted how long?"

"A couple of minutes—if that."

"Then I was already on my way downstairs when it began. I paused at the office door because I thought I might jot down one last idea, before deciding it could use a little more time to ripen. As I was descending the stairs to see about dinner, the kitchen underwent a change that I missed at most by seconds."

"You think this was intended for you," I said.

"The coincidence is striking. The kitchen was my destination."

I wouldn't have used as strong a word as "striking," but it was worth noting. I asked, "So what was the point?"

"Why communicate with me in such a manner?"

"Yeah," I said. "Why not rattle a photograph, or turn the TV on to a baseball game? Wouldn't either of those have been more direct? What's the message here?"

Roger shook his head. "I can't say. Given that your vision was interrupted, perhaps there was more to come that would have explained what you saw. It could be you were seeing the place Ted is."

"The bardo?"

"It's possible."

"Is that what it looks like?"

"There aren't any photographs of it."

"Well, I hope not," I said. "If it's cold enough to freeze the windows like that, how cold would it be for anyone walking around in it?"

"All the more reason to help Ted depart it."

No argument there. Roger stayed in the kitchen and helped me prepare the red curry and some jasmine rice. We ate a mostly silent dinner. Roger was disappointed to have missed the latest weirdness. You didn't have to be especially observant to read it in the half-hearted way he picked at his meal. He was never a huge fan of Thai food, but he usually made a better effort than this. Maybe he was thinking about the scene I'd described to him. I was.

• • •

I wasn't interested in debating Roger's explanation, because I was still processing the experience, but I wasn't inclined to agree with him, either. If anything, Roger's account only underlined my feeling that there was more going on here than he recognized or was willing to recognize—underlined, and put in all caps and bold, besides. None of what we'd been involved with so far was what you'd expect from the situation Roger had come up with. Not that there's a guidebook for this stuff, but—look, when I was little, my grandma, my mother's mother, told me a story. She was watching me and we got to talking about ghosts. I don't remember what started the conversation, probably a story she told me. Grandma was a great one for stories, all the classics, and a whole book full of strange ones that I only ever heard from her. "The Boy Who Cheated the Sun"; "The Mirror's Dilemma"; "Veronica and the Hungry House." Obviously, she made up that last one for me. I think she invented them all. They were great, crazy. It's a shame she never wrote them down. She would have made a fortune.

Anyway, after some story or another, I declared to Grandma that I, for one, did not believe in ghosts. She looked at me very seriously and asked me why I'd want to say a thing like that. Because ghosts were stupid, I said. After telling me not to call anything stupid, it wasn't a nice word, Grandma said that she believed in ghosts, which was kind of a shock. I was at the age where I was trying to figure out what was real in the stories I heard, and, in general, Grandma was pretty straightforward. She didn't say anything about Santa or the Easter Bunny, but I learned from her that the Tooth Fairy was Mom and Dad's generosity, and that leprechauns were festive decorations for St. Patrick's. So when she threw the weight of her opinion behind ghosts, they immediately gained substance.

I wasn't willing to let it go at that, though; I asked her, "How come you believe in ghosts, Grandma? Did you ever see one?"

She shook her head up and down. "Oh yes," she said, "I did." That admission alone was almost enough to make me wet my pants. I didn't want to ask any more—what I'd learned already would be enough to give me nightmares for years—but I couldn't help myself. In for a penny and all that. "What did the ghost look like?" I asked.

"Oh, I shouldn't be telling you this," she said. "What will your mother say? Let's play a game, instead."

"No," I said, stamping my foot. "I want to hear what the ghost looked like."

"Temper," Grandma said, waving her finger, then, "I don't want to scare you."

We were way past that, but I said, "I'm not scared, really. Tell me."

"Please."

"Please."

"All right." I'm sure she must have known how scared I was. I think she realized that if she didn't tell me something definite, my imagination would run amok. She said, "When I was a girl your age, I was very close to my grandma, too. My daddy had gone to heaven, and Grandma Jane—that's what I called her—came over a lot to help us. We were great pals. And then, when I was a bit older, Grandma Jane got very sick and she went up to heaven, too."

"You mean she died?"

"Yes, darling, she died. I was very unhappy when she did, and I'm afraid I acted like a very bad girl for a little while."

Grandma bad was an oxymoron. I asked, "What did you do?"

"I wouldn't do what my mommy told me," she said, "and I would slam doors and run around the house and not say, 'Please,' or 'Thank you.' I was not very nice at all.

"One day," she went on, "I was an especially bad girl, so bad that I was sent to my room with no dinner. I screamed and I yelled and I jumped up and down on my bed and threw my toys all over the place."

"Grandma," I said.

"I know," she said. "There was a picture of Grandma Jane on my bureau, in front of the mirror. It was a picture from when she was a young woman. It was very old, and it was in a heavy frame made out of a metal called pewter, which looked like silver. While I was misbehaving, that picture started to shake—just a little at first, and then a lot. The picture shook and danced on my bureau and it made an awful racket as it did."

"What did you do?"

"I screamed," Grandma said, and laughed, which I thought was strange. "I screamed and sat down right there on my bed and watched that picture shake and fall over—bang!—on the bureau.

"And that was when I saw her. I looked in my mirror, and there was my grandma, standing behind me wearing her favorite dress. She was not happy. One look at her face, and I could see how upset she was with me. I turned around to her—"

"And?" I breathed.

"There was no one there. She'd only come for a moment, to tell me to pull up my socks and start behaving. From that day on, I was a much better girl."

"Did you ever see your grandma again?" I asked.

"No," she said. "She was the only ghost I ever saw, but see her I did. Your Great-aunt Eleanor—that's Grandma's younger sister—she said she saw Grandma Jane several times. I don't want you to worry though, darling. You're not going to see any ghosts."

"You did," I said.

"Yes, but I was being very bad. You're a good girl."

"Was Great-aunt Eleanor bad?"

Grandma smiled. "Your Great-aunt Eleanor was a lot of things. Don't worry about her."

That was that. Until everything with Roger, I'd never been part of anything even remotely supernatural, much less felt or seen a ghost. At Penrose, I had known a couple of people who told strange stories. There was this one girl from Long Island who talked about a haunted campground. All the counselors were supposed to have killed the campers while they slept. But you heard those when we were sitting around at two a.m. drinking and trying to freak each other out. Even that story, though—it was pretty straightforward. Apparently, there was a spot on the road leading out to the former camp where, if you drove past early in the morning, your car would stall. You had to be there at something like quarter-to-five, which, of course, was the time local legend had assigned to the massacre. No matter what you did, your car would not restart for a solid ten minutes, which was how long it had taken the counselors to slaughter every last kid. If you stepped out of your car to check the engine, you'd notice that your doors were covered in the undersized handprints of children. No one stayed out of their car to see what came next.

I never really believed the story. The handprints were a nice touch, but when I asked the girl who told it if it was true—this was a couple of days later, when our respective hangovers had long since subsided—she got very offended and walked away from me, which I took as a tacit confession she'd invented the whole thing. I was at a couple more parties where she repeated it, and the specifics remained pretty consistent, but I'd already written it off as fabrication. Later, I wasn't so sure, and wondered if she'd walked away because she was insulted at my questioning her honesty. I don't always put things in the nicest way.

The point I'm trying to make is—you could say these stories, and a few more besides, are like templates. Most ghost stories you hear fall into one of these two categories: either a single, relatively unambiguous sighting and/or occurrence, or a repeated action. The picture dances and Grandma sees her grandmother giving her that look, "Shape up," or the one hundredth car stalls at the exact same spot and time and little handprints decorate it. I know it sounds contradictory to talk about the paranormal having rules, or tendencies. But you don't run into people telling the kind of story that Roger and I were in.

We had a series of events that didn't fit the available models of supernatural experience. There was one more thing, however, and that was my grandmother's connecting the apparition of a ghost to how good or bad you were. Yes, I know it was a ploy to insure I behaved myself—and boy, did it work; no kid walked straighter and narrower than I did—at the same time, Grandma's story appeared to give the connection some weight. And here was Roger, who by his own admission had done a bad thing, had rejected his only son. Maybe it was all the Hawthorne I'd assimilated, but I was increasingly convinced that what we were undergoing was the end result of Roger's—Hawthorne would have called it his sin, and I didn't know that that word didn't fit. Roger's words—his curse had broken something—I don't know how to phrase it—they'd knocked things out of alignment, seriously out of alignment, and now we were paying the price for it. He had asked for blood to drink, and it would only be so long before it was served up for him, steaming hot in a glass with a jagged edge.

I realize this sounds like so much magical thinking. I'm sure that's what Dr. Hawkins would have diagnosed. Later that night, after we'd put away the dishes and gone through to the living room to watch TV, I laughed at the thought that here I was, back from my trip to the psychiatrist's, not only supporting Roger's ideas, but adding fuel to the fire. What else could I do? Even if I had been a good enough liar to fool Roger—which I wasn't—how had there been enough time for me to recover from what I'd seen outside the kitchen windows and invent a compelling lie? If I'd thought there was any substance to Dr. Hawkins's analysis, I guess I would have made the attempt. Telling him was proof that I had chosen to go along with him, no matter where we were headed.

• • •

The next week I spent in a state of high expectation. Not only did the house still tingle there at the edge of my skin, ever-ready to race from whisper to roar; now, it threatened to open to another space, to a place I could see. For three or four days, I was catching things out of the corners of my eyes—standing off to one side or the other, climbing a staircase, flashing past a window. I jumped every time, and, naturally, when I whipped my head around to look at them, there was nothing there. I kept Roger updated, but these apparitions owed their existence more to stress than the supernatural, since they wavered in and out of existence without any change in my sensation of the house.

As for Roger, his project had entered a new phase. He had cleared every last book, every last paper from the table in the center of his office, and was in the process of constructing a scale model of the neighborhood in Kabul where Ted had been killed. He studied his maps of the city for a solid day before trying to reproduce them from memory, first on a legal pad, then, when he was confident he'd memorized the layout, on the tabletop in colored chalk. The streets were yellow, the positions of various buildings orange, blue, and green, the spot where Ted died red, a red circle. Having copied the map to his satisfaction, Roger started filling in the divisions on the table with plastic buildings he'd special-ordered from a war-gaming site. The majority of them were one or two stories high, plain, dun-colored buildings most of which, Roger said, were residential. The exception was a three-storey structure that Roger said had been a movie theater before the Taliban had come to power and banned everything. "This is the place," Roger said, tapping the toy theater with a pen. His reading glasses perched on top of his head. "This is the spot from which the reports agree the rocket-propelled grenade was launched." Once he'd placed the final building, plus a row of tiny plastic trees he'd bought from another online site, I thought he was finished. There wasn't much to say. He'd been thorough and exact.

At the end of the week, when I wasn't leaping at every shadow anymore, a small, heavy package arrived for Roger via UPS. I signed for it, and brought it up to the office. When he saw the return address—Chicago—he said, "Finally!"

"What is it?" I asked. He wouldn't tell me. "You'll have to see," was the best I could get.

The package was a heavy cardboard box in which thirteen small figures had been carefully packed, individually bubblewrapped and then slotted into a styrofoam frame. Roger removed all the figures from the frame before unwrapping them, deliberately picking off the pieces of tape that sealed them into their plastic cocoons. What he uncovered were lead soldiers, each one no more than two inches high. They looked Afghan, like mujahidin. Each one was in his own pose, this one at attention, this one relaxed, this one with his gun ready to fire. They'd been painted with a remarkable attention to detail. No two were the same. Their coats and pants were faded, their tiny faces sunburned, their beards full. I couldn't tell for sure, but if I squinted, it looked as if there was writing on some of their guns.

There was only one figure that wasn't a fighter, a model of an old man wearing a striped red and yellow robe. His hair and beard were white. I knew this was the man who'd run out to Ted's patrol, with whom Ted had been trying to talk when the RPG had found them both.

"Aren't they something?" Roger said. "There's a fellow in Chicago, and this is what he does for a living. You fill out an extensive questionnaire, and then he procures the appropriate models and paints them to your specifications. He has clients all over the world, as far away as Japan." He picked up one of the figures and studied it. "What care," he said. He did that with each of the models, held it up for inspection and pronounced it acceptable. The old man came last. As Roger examined it, his lip curled.

Once he was satisfied with his purchase, Roger began placing the fighters on the table, arranging them first in a ragged line up the center of his scale-model street. "There had been rumors of Taliban holdouts at work in the city, possibly planning an attack on Karzai. Ted and his fellows were sent out to investigate."

I was confused. "Wait a minute," I said. "Aren't these guys," I pointed to the mujahidin, "the Taliban?"

"This is Ted's patrol."

"Are you sure?"

"Yes. They were Special Forces, which means they tried to live in-country like the men they were supposed to be fighting with. Call it anthropological warfare. They grew beards, wore turbans, local dress. This was supposed to allow them greater freedom of movement."

"Oh. Okay." I remembered the photo of Ted in Afghan dress, reading Dickens. "Go on."

"They moved like this, close enough to hear each other's voices, but sufficiently spread-out to minimize the chances of more than one of them being hit at once." At the end of the street was the square, the movie theater to its left. Roger studied the figures, then started picking them up and transferring them to the open space. "They came to this square," he said, "and they proceeded into it. Had they suspected danger, they would have been more cautious, kept closer to the cover of the buildings. As it was, they knew of no reason not to walk straight across; although where the street emptied into the square, one man lingered. He might have seen something. From his spot, he might have been able to catch the movement at the top of the movie theater—he was scanning the space in front of him, the tops of the buildings as well as their windows and doors, and he might have been able to raise the alarm had it not been for the distraction of this man." Roger set the model of the old man down on the right-hand side of the square, at the entrance to an alley. "He comes running out, waving his hands and yelling," Roger slid the figure across the table. "Instantly, all eyes are on him—and all guns, too." He gave each of the soldiers a quarter-turn, so that they were facing the old man. His hand moved to the third soldier in line. "Ted approached him." Roger slid the model toward the figure of the old man, until they were practically touching. He'd positioned them inside the red circle he'd drawn on the table. "His gun was at the ready, but it is my impression he did not judge the man especially threatening, or he would have maintained his position in the line. The man was as dangerous as any sacrificial animal is. While Ted attempted to converse with him, the attack began."

Roger pointed at the roof of the movie theater. "Its opening salvo was the rocket-propelled grenade, fired from here." He traced a line in the air from the theater roof to the figures of Ted and the old man. His finger hovered above them, then knocked them over. They clunked on the table. "This attack was followed by machine gun fire from several positions. Here," he touched a building beside the theater, "here," one across from it, "and here," a building between those two, opposite the place where the soldiers entered the square. "Obviously, the plan was to establish overlapping fields of fire, creating a killing zone. However, the assailants made a fatal error. Rather than positioning themselves on the rooftops of these buildings, like their friend with the RPG, they chose to fire from street-level, out of windows. I presume these men must have thought these stations would work to their advantage; they did not. Their positions significantly reduced each shooter's choice of targets and field of fire. While initially they succeeded in wounding two of the patrol," Roger touched a pair of figures near the line's center, "both were still able to use their weapons. The troops dropped to the ground, with the exception of this fellow," Roger pointed to the figure at the entrance to the square, "who had identified the theater roof as the source of the RPG and was firing upon it. He killed that assailant almost immediately. The others took longer."

Roger's face was distant and drawn. "I've not yet established the precise order of events for the remainder of the battle. I am also unsure of the exact number of attackers. Five men were killed: the one who fired the RPG; one in each of these positions," Roger gestured to the buildings on either side of the square, "and two here," the remaining building. "But there may have been others who fled when they saw that their plan to assassinate an entire American patrol had gone awry. From the moment the grenade is launched, the fight lasts approximately sixteen minutes. It ends when two of the soldiers throw hand grenades at the last attackers, the two in the same spot. Anywhere from one to two minutes after that, the reinforcements the patrol had summoned at the beginning of the firefight arrive. They will spend the rest of the night going through every building in the immediate vicinity, taking away half a dozen men for questioning. Their interrogations will prove fruitless. No one will know anything.

"As for Ted," Roger's gaze strayed to the red circle and the figures tipped over inside it. "During the first few moments of the attack, one of Ted's fellows crawls over to where he lies. He checks for a pulse, breathing, and finds neither. Subsequent examination by the Medical Examiner will conclude that Ted's death was instantaneous. All indications are that he never knew what happened to him. Nor did the man who ran out to him, the Judas goat." Roger's voice hardened. "That man makes me crave the existence of the hell of my childhood, for no other reason than that there be a place of sufficient and unending torture for him. No family came forth to claim him. He was buried in a pauper's grave. I would have been happy had he been left where he was, food for dogs."

My ears were practically ringing from the stutter of machine guns, my eyes and nose stinging from the pungent gunpowder and charred flesh. I couldn't help noticing the figure Roger had selected to represent Ted. It wasn't the fighter standing at attention, or the one holding his gun casually. To stand in for his son, he had chosen a figure in a firing stance, its legs spread, its gun held up to its cheek. If you scrutinized its face—which I did, later, after Roger went down to order dinner and I said I had to use the bathroom—if you looked closely, you could see that the figure was sighting down the barrel of its gun, one eye closed, its brow lowered in concentration. Maybe the choice had been accidental, but when I thought about the care Roger had taken unsealing each soldier and positioning it on the table, I knew it hadn't. I could imagine Dr. Hawkins's diagnosis of his selection—of the whole set-up. Scanning her legal pad, she would say, "It's an obvious attempt by Roger to bring the circumstances of Ted's death under his control by reducing them to a size he can handle and distancing them through his use of the models. The figure Roger has picked to be Ted is ambiguous. It is dynamic, performing an action we associate with soldiers. It is also aggressive, hostile. Roger's selection of it reflects his own continued ambivalence about his relationship with Ted; the figure's aiming at him suggests Roger taking aim at himself, putting himself, so to speak, in the crosshairs." "You are a stranger to me." I replaced the soldier inside the red circle, next to the old man, the generic Afghan, and went downstairs to join Roger.

• • •

Everything Roger was doing in his office—the research, the maps, now the model—you couldn't say any of it was making him happier, or more relaxed. Just the opposite: he was radioactive with stress; if there'd been a Geiger counter for tension, his readings would have bounced the needles right off the scale. Whatever room he was in, the air crackled. It must have been exhausting, to be wound that tight all the time. I couldn't understand how he kept going. I mean, they say your body can adjust to anything, but Good Lord. You would have thought that letting me in on what he was up to, sharing his ideas about Ted with me—and more importantly, me not laughing at him, me listening sympathetically, treating him seriously—you would have thought that would have taken the edge off his stress, dulled it, but no such luck. I was more and more sure that, for all his apparent openness, there was something Roger was keeping back from me. In the days after he showed me the model, I asked him about it on a couple of occasions. "Honey," I said, "is there anything you haven't told me?" Each time, he gave the same answer, "No, nothing." If I persisted, pressed the matter, he turned defensive, snapped, "I believe I have answered your question," which, needless to say, only made my hunch stronger.

If working in his office didn't alleviate his stress, what it allowed Roger was a way to focus that tension, direct this superabundance of nervous energy at a single point, knowing Ted's death as thoroughly as possible. It was dangerous, because Ted's death lay thick in the midst of volatile emotions Roger had yet to work through. Admitting his mistake in disowning Ted had been an important first step, but it had opened the door on a storehouse full of guilt, regret, and anger. By playing his attention over those feelings, he risked sending the whole structure up in flames.

All the same, the long hours Roger spent laboring over who in Ted's patrol had taken aim at which of their attackers, what the order of their assailants' deaths had been, what the effects of a rocket-propelled grenade on the human body were—they made Roger seem together, coherent. The benefits of obsession, I suppose. I thought that, when he finally confronted Ted's death head-on, as the irreplaceable loss it was, that coherence would help him to do what he had called his work of mourning. Maybe Dr. Hawkins had been wrong. Maybe some good could come out of his time in his office.

There was one, relatively minor improvement in Roger's behavior—he started coming to bed at night. He didn't sleep when I did.

Every night, I drifted off to the steady sound of him turning the pages of whatever book he was reading. Awake or asleep, it was nice to have him there beside me. I tried not to make a big deal out of it, the first night I returned from the bathroom to find him sitting there, his book propped on his knees; I climbed into bed, leaned over and gave him a quick kiss, and picked up my own book from its place on my nightstand. Actually, I was more surprised the following night, when I entered the room and there he was, again. I couldn't help myself, "Roger," I said, "you're here."

"Yes," he said.

I wanted to ask, "Why?" but didn't think that would come out right, so I settled for "Good," and left it at that. When he was waiting for me the third night, and then the fourth, I understood that something had changed. He had decided that this was where he should be at this time, here with me. I didn't realize how happy this made me until about a week had passed. Finding Roger reading yet again, the half-glasses he'd bought at the pharmacy balanced on the end of his nose, his hair a mess—he let it go at least a month after it needed cut; before Ted had died, I used to tease him about developing crazy professor hair—my heart lifted, the way it does sometimes when happiness catches you unawares. For an instant, every detail of the scene in front of me was almost painfully clear: the lines on Roger's forehead, his wedding ring gold against his skin, the book he was reading, the edges of its cover worn a lighter shade of red, the places on the sheet where Roger weighted it taut, the yellow light of the reading lamp casting shadows across his face, his chest, the bed. It wasn't just that I remembered how much I loved him. I realized that love was even deeper than I'd known, not in spite of all the madness of recent days, but—almost because of it. The feeling was surprising, a little bit overwhelming, and in the grip of it, I did something I hadn't done in ages. I pulled my nightgown over my head, pushed down my panties, and walked over to Roger. He didn't complain when I took the book from his hands and placed it on his nightstand. He was already removing his glasses. We made love for the first time in weeks, and it was like rediscovering this person you knew years ago.

Can I tell you something crazy? I thought I might get pregnant. In fact, I hoped it. The timing was right. We weren't using any protection. Yes, given the situation, how could I have considered such a move, let alone risked it? While everything was happening, and for a short time after—when we were suddenly making up for lost time, making love the way we had when we'd first gotten together: doing it in the living room first thing in the morning, the kitchen after lunch, the third-floor stairs on the way to dinner; testing the beds in the guestrooms, the desk in the library, random chairs throughout the house; doing things that would have made the guy who wrote the *Kama Sutra* blush—I was filled with such hope. All at once, our problems, the black cloud we'd been living under since Ted had been killed, seemed more manageable. The bad things—Roger's disowning Ted, his heart attack, the miscarriage, Ted's death, whatever it was that was happening to us, this haunting—I was sure that if I were to have a baby, it would balance all of that, tip the scales in the other direction, even. The weirdness pressing in on me—if I were pregnant, full of life, I thought I'd be able to push back, send good energy streaming out along the very same channels that poured strangeness on me. Roger didn't ask what we were doing. If he didn't know the ultimate purpose of our lovemaking, that didn't stop him from participating enthusiastically. And he must have realized there was at least a chance something could happen. How different, finally to want to get pregnant.

Obviously, I didn't. I'd never believed those people who tell you that it isn't that easy to conceive a child. I guess all the safe-sex lectures in high school and college really did the trick. I'd become pregnant before without any difficulty, which had seemed to bear out the warnings of those teachers trying to hide their embarrassment as they talked about condoms and spermicidal lubricant. After my period showed up on time, though, that pregnancy seemed more of a fluke than I'd appreciated. Opening the door to the bathroom closet for a maxi-pad, I was disappointed. Funny how, after years of avoiding and fearing pregnancy like it was the plague, your attitude can change so quickly and completely. But my disappointment, sharp enough to blur my eyes with tears, was mixed with the tiniest drop of relief. Things were—at that point, I wasn't sure what they were.

• • •

At about three the morning my period arrived, I'd come out of a deep sleep to the sight of Roger sitting on the edge of the bed, his back to me. The room was dark—his reading lamp was off—but the windows admitted enough light for me to see that there was something different about him. The way he was sitting, the position of his shoulders, head—there was something odd about it. From being ready to turn over and slip back into sleep, I took a step in the other direction, not completely awake yet, but less asleep. I was about to speak, ask him what was going on, when he stood. For a moment, he remained there by the side of the bed, swaying slightly, and I understood. He was sleepwalking. Sleepstanding right then, but you know what I mean. Now I was awake. I raised myself up on an elbow. Roger turned to the door and walked out of it. I didn't know what to do. I'd never dealt with anyone sleepwalking. You weren't supposed to wake them, were you? That was supposed to drive them insane. Or was that an old wives' tale? From the hall, I heard Roger walking towards the third-floor stairs. I decided I better follow him. I wasn't sure how well sleepwalkers did on stairs.

When I leaned my head out into the hall, there was no one there. The third-floor stairs hadn't sounded their chorus of creaks, so it was as if Roger had walked right out of the house. *Don't be ridiculous,* I told myself, *he went into a room, that's all. Maybe he had to use the bathroom.*

The bathroom was empty, and anyway, his footsteps had sounded as if they were taking him further down the hall. I checked the guest room on the other side of the bathroom, then crossed the hall and peered in the library. Empty, both of them. That left two rooms, the remaining guest room, next to the library, and Ted's old room. I didn't bother with the other guest room. This wasn't a horror movie; there was no need to draw out the suspense. I found Roger standing in the middle of Ted's room, gazing at a blank wall. I paused at the doorway, watching him watching bare space. His face was slack, almost confused-looking. His lips were moving—he was speaking, his voice too low for me to hear. It was unnerving—it was downright creepy to see him there and not there, you know? When he was finished studying whatever he'd seen there, he did an about-face and headed for the door, still murmuring. I retreated into the hall, expecting him to turn left and return to our room. Instead, he turned right, to the third-floor stairs, which he began to climb with no apparent difficulty. I followed half a dozen steps behind. He reached the third floor and walked along it to his office. I don't know what I thought I'd see when I reached the door—Roger holding the figure for Ted in his hand, something like that. I didn't expect to confront Roger. His eyes were dull, his lips moving. I yelped, stepped back. No, he wasn't waiting for me. He was looking at something on the wall next to the doorway, something hung at roughly my height. Once I'd started breathing again, I tried to recall what occupied that space. I could have squeezed past Roger and seen for myself, but I didn't know if I could do so without waking him, which I was still nervous about doing. I didn't think it would drive him insane—any more so—but I wasn't feeling especially lucky. From where I was, I could see the maps draping the bookcases opposite me. Visualizing the place Roger was staring at, all I could bring to mind were more maps.

We must have held our respective positions for a half-hour, for-ty-five minutes, Roger totally absorbed in whatever was in front of him, me, now that the adrenaline rush had subsided, struggling to stay awake. All the while, he kept murmuring, a steady stream of sound that never grew loud enough for me to separate into sense. A couple of times I almost fell asleep. My lids grew heavy; my eyes closed; for half a second, I dozed; then my head tilted forward and I jolted awake. I should have gone back to bed. Roger appeared in no immediate danger of harming himself—he'd proved he could handle the stairs—and there would be plenty of time during the day for me to discover what had so fascinated his sleepwalking self. But I was concerned—I was curious, and my curiosity wouldn't let me return to the comfort of bed just yet. Watching Roger in this state—it was like I'd been given a window into his psyche, or—what it really was, was as if his unconscious had stepped out to take a walk around. In the process, the house—the rooms in the house had gone from rooms to symbols—everything had acquired a new level of meaning.

Finally, when the sky outside was starting to lighten, Roger left his office and returned to bed. Within seconds of his head sinking into his pillow, he was breathing deeply. I saw him safely to bed, then dashed back up the stairs. Inside the office, I fumbled for the light switch. Blinking against the sudden glare, I approached the spot where Roger had been standing. The wall beside the door was papered in maps, in eight smaller maps—each one about the size of a piece of printer paper—taped together at the edges to form a larger map. The individual maps showed streets, buildings, even trees, and were full of Roger's handwriting, of notes made in the typical assortment of differ-ent-colored inks, and of other writing, what looked like mathematical symbols, pi over delta, that kind of thing. It was a map of the square in Kabul. There was the same red circle Roger had drawn on the table, taking up almost all of one of the smaller maps and ringed by more notes than were on any of the other maps. This was what Roger had been staring at; although, as I came closer, I saw something else—something shiny inside the red circle. I drew closer. It was a mirror, a small, rectangular mirror like you find in men's toiletries bags, for shaving. It had been glued to the center of the red circle, so that, in looking into the circle, you were looking at yourself. There was no writing next to the mirror, no writing at all inside the circle, only white space and then the fall into that silvery plane. Uneasy, I stared at it. I didn't know what this was, but it was more than the effort to comprehend the circumstances of Ted's death. What more, though, I couldn't say, and it didn't take much longer than five minutes in front of this…diagram for me to know that I could stay there for another hour and I wouldn't be any closer to understanding the significance of what I was seeing than I was now. If I wanted to know what this meant, I would have to ask Roger.

Which was what I did that morning, forcing myself to crawl out of bed after him a few hours later. I waited until we were seated at the kitchen table with our coffee and cereal, and before Roger could open the day's *Times*, I said, "You know, you were sleepwalking last night." I was too tired to lead up to it with small talk.

Roger said, "I beg your pardon?"

"Sleepwalking," I said, "about three this morning."

"No," Roger said, setting the paper down.

"Yes," I said. "You woke me up getting out of bed. First you went into Ted's old room, then you went upstairs to the office. Then you came down and went back to bed."

"You followed me."

"I wanted to make sure you didn't hurt yourself."

"Why didn't you wake me?"

"Because," I said, "I heard you're not supposed to do that."

"Isn't that a myth?"

"I didn't want to take a chance."

"What did I do?"

"You stared. In Ted's room, you stared at the wall. In the office, you spent about an hour looking at that map by the door—the one with the mirror on it."

Roger said, "Hmmph."

"Do you remember any of it?"

"Not a thing."

"I took a look at that map myself," I said, "after you were asleep. Honey, what is that?"

Roger took a mouthful of cereal. "That map," he said after he swallowed, "is my attempt to bring together and coordinate the information I have gathered on Ted's death—every last piece of it. I've tried to connect all related facts with one another."

"And the symbols—the math?"

"In addition to understanding the event historically—narratively, as it were—I've also tried to comprehend it mathematically, to know the various angles of fire, the velocities of the weapons employed, the energy released. It's another means of apprehending the situation."

"Okay," I said. "What's the mirror for?"

He must have known I'd ask about that, but he blushed anyway. "I don't know."

"What do you mean?"

"I mean that setting that mirror on the map was an action I felt compelled to perform, but for reasons that remain unclear to me."

Now it was my turn to say, "Hmmph." I asked, "Where did you find it?"

"In a box of Ted's things," Roger said. "On his fourteenth birthday, I gave him a shaving kit. He'd been shaving with an electric razor for a few months by then, but I fancied I was upholding something of a Croydon family tradition. When I reached fourteen, my father presented me with a shaving mug and brush, which he told me his father had done for him on his fourteenth birthday. It was one of the few kindnesses the old man did me. In keeping with the tradition, I presented Ted with a kit that contained a mug, brush, soap cake, razor and pack of razor blades, and a travel mirror. He was less than enthusiastic about the gift. He perked up when I said I had one more thing for him, and followed me into the bathroom, but his face fell when I told him I was going to teach him to use the kit I'd given him.

"To put it mildly, that was a mistake. Ted refused to hold the razor properly, so in the process of scraping it across his neck and chin he opened dozens of cuts, some of them quite deep. There was blood everywhere, all over his shirt, the counter, the mug, the mirror. I ruined one of Joanne's good hand towels stanching the flow. When the worst was past, Ted stalked out of the bathroom, leaving me to wipe the spatter from the counter, the mug, the mirror. I placed the kit in his room, but he made a point of using the electric razor for the rest of his time in the house.

"I discovered my old gift when I went searching for the photographs of Ted. To be honest, I'm not sure how it came to be in my possession. I brought it to the house because," Roger's voice wavered, "because it had touched him, once. I kept the kit in one of the desk drawers in my office. Every now and again, I'd take it out, turn the mug over in my hands, run the brush over my palm, play sunlight off the mirror." He shrugged. "Almost the moment I started work on this particular map, I knew the mirror would go in its center. Having presented itself to me, the notion would not be denied. On the one hand, having something of Ted's included in what I was constructing seemed somehow appropriate. On the other, I was concerned that I was indulging in a kind of fetishism. My concerns aside, into the center it went.

"So much for the mirror," Roger said. "Well?"

"I don't know," I said. "If you hadn't been staring at it while you were asleep, I would have said it was no big deal."

He crossed his arms. "Since I was—"

"Since you were, I still don't know. You were in Ted's room first, and you spent a long time on the wall in there, too. Don't get me wrong. I think there's something to this. I think maybe spending so much time on Ted's death is taking its toll on you."

"It is necessary. If Ted is to exit the bardo—"

"I understand," I said. "I understand why you're doing it. All I'm saying is that doing it so much may be more than you can handle."

That was all there was to the conversation. Roger said he would have to consider the matter, and we finished breakfast in silence. Once he was done, it was upstairs for a shower, and the third floor after that.

• • •

So when I felt my period later that day, and realized I wasn't pregnant—up till then, I'd been in this kind of in-between state, not sure if I was or wasn't. I hadn't gone so far as to buy a home-test, because I didn't want to jinx anything and I thought it would be nice for Roger and me to go for it together, but I had found the baby name book I'd bought for my previous pregnancy and flipped through it. I'd thought about a nursery, too. There were plenty of rooms going unused in the house. The guest room closest to ours, on the other side of the bathroom, seemed like it would make a good choice. We could paint it pale green, put down a new rug, get a rocking chair—one of those gliders. Pregnancy was still a series of largely disconnected images for me, like pictures in a magazine, and when I understood that that was all it was going to be—the home-test would remain unbought; the baby name book unread; the guest room undecorated—disappointment stabbed me. I climbed the stairs to the second-floor bathroom—I'd been reading in the front parlor—with tears hot in my eyes. By the time I was opening the bathroom closet, my cheeks were wet. In the midst of that sadness, however, that sharp regret at opportunity missed, there was relief—which at the time felt like such a betrayal, yet another act of treason, as if I were admitting that I hadn't really wanted this, that I wasn't totally committed to it. For a second, my sense of my own—unworthiness, I guess, forced a series of sobs out of me.

I knew, though, I knew that wasn't it. Had I been pregnant, I would have given it everything I had. But Roger—things with Roger were worrisome. The sleepwalking, of course; the mirror didn't thrill me, either; and both of those occurred against the background of the Mutual Weirdness, which we seemed no closer to understanding— and which seemed less mutual and increasingly focused on yours truly. They say that if you wait until life is perfect to have kids, you'll never do it. Fair enough, but a child deserved better than this.

• • •

For a week and a half, not a night went by without me waking up at three a.m.—it was always the same time—to Roger seated on the edge of the bed. Then he was up on his feet and away. His journeys—that was how I thought of them—had two parts. The first took him to some place in the house—and once outside it—related to Ted. Granted, that was pretty much the entire building, but there were spots where the associations were especially strong. Ted's childhood room, obviously, but the third floor, too, where he'd moved as a teenager—we climbed there a couple of times. The living room was a favorite, as well. I think because it was where they had watched baseball together. Wherever the first half of his sleepwalking led Roger, the second half concluded in the same place, his office, him standing in front of that map—to

which he added fresh notes every day—gazing into Ted's old mirror.
Some nights, he made his rounds in a little under forty minutes. Once,
he didn't wander back to bed until the sun had risen and daylight was
pouring through the windows. I rose with him every night, driven by
the combination of concern and curiosity; although, as he successfully
navigated the house, the concern pretty much dropped away, while
the curiosity deepened with each new destination.

A few hours later, I would spend breakfast narrating his previous night's perambulations to him. It got to the point he no longer
waited for me to raise the subject. While I was pouring my coffee,
he'd say, "So, where did my nocturnal odyssey lead last night?" You
could hear the attempt at good humor in his voice—and I did my
best to respond in kind—but immediately underneath it you heard
the anxiety. However cavalier he wanted to appear, Roger was worried
by his sleepwalking. Not worried enough to take my advice and ease
up on his time in the office. (I didn't even bother suggesting he see
a doctor.) Every other day or so, a new envelope or package would
arrive. I swear, the things you can find on eBay. There were eight-by-
ten photos of the square in Kabul that linked up side to side to form
a panoramic view of it. Roger hung them right around the office so
that, standing in the middle of the room, it was as if you were looking
through a window in it out at the square. There was a packet of brown
dirt that a man in Maine swore came from Kabul. Roger carefully
scissored one end off and poured the dirt up and down the streets of
the tabletop model in a fine stream, saving most of it for the square.
There was a tiny box that held a fragment of scorched metal swaddled
in a cotton cloth. I asked Roger what it was. He said, "A piece of a
rocket-propelled grenade."

"Like the one that killed Ted?"

"As far as I've been able to ascertain," Roger said, examining the
fragment, "yes, it's an exact match. The RPG-7."

That was when I decided we were getting out of that house, if
not for good, then at least for a week or two. Accompanying Roger
on his sleepwalking tours had taken its toll. After three nights, I was
exhausted; by a week, I was dead on my feet; at a week and a half, I
was the living dead. Maybe that was why the sight of him holding that
little piece of metal as if it were a relic—well, I didn't know whether
to shriek with laughter or sob my eyes out.

• • •

Something else had happened, earlier that same day. Along with Roger's latest package, the mailman had brought a letter for me. Roger left it, along with the bills and the circulars, on the kitchen table, where I found it when I went to see what I could scrounge for lunch. There was no return address; although the postmark was Provincetown, MA. The handwriting was frail and spiky, an old person's script. I thought I should recognize it, but it wasn't until I slid my thumb under the flap, eased the envelope open, and slid the folded sheets out that I learned why. The letter was from Viola Belvedere.

Sitting at the kitchen table, seven sheets of fine paper that felt like onionskin in my hand, my heart started to pound. Viola's writing covered both sides of each sheet from top to bottom, running right out to the edges of the paper. The letter was dated four days ago. My head was throbbing. I put the pages down, and went to the fridge for a glass of iced-tea. I drank half of it staring out the kitchen window, flashing back to the afternoon the window had frosted over. I looked at the kitchen table, where the pages lay, one on top of the other, the envelope beneath them. My heart wouldn't stop pounding. I wasn't sure what I expected from Viola, but it wasn't idle chatter.

Headache worse, I resumed my seat at the table. The room—it was as if the kitchen had shrunk two sizes around me, and the rest of the house with it, as if everything wanted to see what Viola had to say. I swore I could see more out of the corners of my eyes than I had five minutes ago; the kitchen's contents crowded my vision. I raised my head, and all was as it should be.

I focused on the top sheet. "Dear Mrs. Croydon," I read. "You wrote to me some time past asking about the summer my late husband spent in what is now your house. At the time, I gave your inquiry a cursory glance. To be frank, I did not give it even that. I have grown tired of carrying the burden of my husband's fame. However much it has benefited me, I have more than repaid that debt through years of answering letter after letter from anyone with an interest in Thomas's work. Far too often, my diligence has been repaid by descriptions of myself, my motives, and my effect on my husband's work that border on slander. I read everything that is written about him, you understand. Those who have not slandered me have been like vampires, returning again and again to drain information from me. The long and short of it is, I now refer all questions about Thomas's life to Professor Rice. While her biography of him makes several errors of interpretation, it is faithful to the facts of his and our lives. The professor tells me it improves her standing if I pass along the queries that come to me, so I do.

"You are not interested in my relationship with Professor Rice, I understand; you are wondering why I have changed my mind and written to you, after all. It may be that, despite my protests to the contrary, I miss my work on behalf of Thomas. He was the center of attention for so long, it was nice to have people asking me what I thought, especially scholars. But I do not think this is the case. I have no plans to answer any of the four or five dozen other letters I have received in the last few months; I have been happy to forward all of them to the professor. Your letter has nagged at me. It has resisted my efforts to dismiss it, so I have picked up my pen in hopes that a reply will satisfy it.

"I assume you have consulted Professor Rice's biography of Thomas. You know that the summer of 1953 was a difficult time for us. Thomas had not been easy in our marriage, and once our twins were born, his uneasiness increased. My cousin and her daughter moved in to help us with the babies, which made Thomas even more unhappy. His discontent was sharpened by the correspondence that had sprung up between him and an odd painter living in Greenwich Village. This man, Rudolph de Castries, contacted Thomas because he had seen one of Thomas's paintings hanging in a gallery in SoHo. I cannot recall which gallery it was. He wrote a long and admiring letter to Thomas. Thomas, who did not know de Castries's work, responded with a long letter of his own. Soon, Thomas was writing to de Castries and de Castries to him several times a week. They exchanged theories about painting, opinions of other artists, and gossip. I find men are much worse gossips than women, don't you?

"As they grew closer, our relations grew steadily more strained. I do not know if you have any children yourself, Mrs. Croydon, but if you do, you know how all-consuming their demands on you can be. My cousin and her daughter were a great help in looking after the twins, but neither of them had a very high opinion of Thomas, and they were not shy in sharing their views. Rather than sitting in the attic all hours of the day and night painting paintings no one could understand, he should be out working a proper job to support us.

They would not say anything directly to Thomas, but they were adept at delivering their assessments whenever he was within earshot. I cringed when they did; at the same time, I did not stop them, because they were giving voice to sentiments I shared, at least in part.

"Thomas and I fought. Ours had always been a contentious love, but this was different. We argued fiercely and often. The last straw was a letter from de Castries I found on the dresser. This was strange, since Thomas never left his correspondence lying around. It was all filed safely away. Only later did I realize I had been intended to find it. The long and short of the letter was de Castries urging Thomas to follow his inclinations and leave me and the twins. As they had agreed, an artist could not be shackled to a family. Great art demanded a creator who was absolutely free to give himself to it, without distractions. From everything Thomas had written him about me, I would forever stand in the way of his achievements. And so on. I was devastated, and wasted no time flying up the attic to give Thomas the confrontation he so desperately wanted. The end result was him taking the suitcase he already had packed out the front door with him. He took the train from our home in Princeton into Manhattan, changing there for a train to Huguenot. De Castries had secured a room for him at what is now your house. I believe its owner was an acquaintance of his. She may have bought one of his paintings.

"Thomas stayed there for the entire summer. When I had seen him slide the suitcase out from under our bed, I had understood he intended to leave, but I had not realized for how long. I expected him back within a week, unable to stop missing me and the babies. After two weeks, I grew frantic. My cousin's declaration that another woman likely was involved did nothing to help. At last, a month after he'd left, Thomas sent a postcard informing me where he was and that he was well. I was relieved. I was also furious. I did not reply. Another postcard followed a week later. I did not answer that one, either. Next came a letter. A second arrived in four days, and a third three days after that. At first, the letters were angry, full of self-justification. Their tone quickly moderated. By summer's end, Thomas was writing me every other day or so, letters full of love and longing. He included little sketches of the house he was staying in, the views from its windows, the village he walked around in. I did not reply to any of it.

"Finally, he wrote saying that he was coming home the next Thursday. I was not there to meet him, although I sent my cousin and her daughter home the weekend before. When he knocked on the door, I opened it. He looked thinner. I had one question for him: 'Was it worth it?'

"'No,' he said.

"Satisfied, I let him in. I will not say that was the end of our troubles. He had a terrible temper, and no patience with the children. But it was the only time he left. After that summer, there were no more letters from Rudolph de Castries. A year or two later, I read of his death in the *Times*. From alcohol poisoning, I believe. Thomas's fortunes had improved by then. The 'Dark Feast' series had sold for more money than we had hoped. There were articles about him in *Time* and *Life*. Enough commissions came in to keep us comfortable.

"In the professor's biography, everything I have written so far is summarized in a few sentences. 'By June of 1953,' she writes, 'the stresses of Thomas and Viola's marriage had reached the point of crisis. After one fight too many, Thomas left, his destination the village of Huguenot in New York's Hudson Valley. A friend had arranged for him to stay at an old house there. During this time, the idea for the "Dark Feast" paintings came to him. When he returned to Princeton that September, he had already completed dozens of sketches, several studies in crayon and watercolor, and at least one canvas.' She makes no mention of Rudolph de Castries. I told her about his role in what happened, but as you may know, some of Thomas's papers were lost during the transit to Stanford. I suspect they are sitting in a collector's vault, accumulating value. Among the missing material were Thomas's letters from de Castries. Professor Rice contacted de Castries's biographer, but it appears he kept none of his correspondence. Since she was unable to substantiate my claim that Thomas had been in touch with de Castries with physical evidence, the professor chose to omit it. Apparently, memories are no good unless accompanied by documentation.

"I was sufficiently annoyed not to tell her that Thomas and I had spoken about that summer in 1970, the year before his death. I had no proof of that conversation, either, no tape recording or home movie, so what was the point? Really, it was pique. For the first few years after Thomas had left, I did not want to hear that summer referred to. He understood this from the start. Once or twice he let something slip out, but the look he received was enough to correct that error. As time passed, however, my curiosity grew. I could not credit that Thomas had left because he wanted to paint. He had been able to paint while he was with me. I assumed that my cousin had been correct and a woman had been involved. For a time, my suspicions fastened on the owner of the house in which he'd stayed. She was a good decade older than Thomas, but very attractive. I saw her picture in *Life*. In that same article, however, I learned that she had been in Europe that year, and my fears quieted. Later still, I decided there must have been someone else. I didn't know whom. It could have been someone who'd come to one of his shows. It could have been someone local he'd met pumping gas, or at the supermarket. There was a teachers' college in Huguenot; it could have been a student. Whoever she was, perhaps Thomas had planned to leave me for her and their affair had not worked out. Perhaps it had been intended to be only an affair.

"After the doctors discovered the cancer in Thomas's large intestine, I decided to ask him. I was not sure how my worst fear's being confirmed would affect me. But I could not stand the prospect of not knowing. I did not want Thomas to carry the secret of that summer to the grave with him. I would like to believe in an afterlife, but I do not. That Christmas, the right moment presented itself. The twins had gone out to visit my sister and her children. Thomas and I had the house to ourselves. I made him a whiskey sour and poured myself a large sherry, then carried them through to where he was sitting in front of the fire in the living room. By then, he was always cold. He was surprised to see the drink, but not ungrateful. We toasted the holiday. We did not say it was our last. I said I had something I wanted to ask him. I cannot imagine he had any idea what it was. It was about the summer he'd left, I said. I wanted to know if there had been another woman.

"He did not hesitate. 'No,' he said.

"In that case, what had he been doing? He smiled and said that he had been painting. The moment he had walked out the front door, he had known he would be back, so he had thrown himself into his work. He had the run of a large house. He set up easels in several of the rooms. He left pads of paper in others. When he grew tired of one idea, he moved on to another. A lot of it was junk that he had thrown out, but it had allowed him to break through to a new style. I asked him if he was sure there hadn't been a woman in the picture, so to speak. Maybe some of the canvases he'd discarded had been of her. 'Absolutely not,' he said.

"That should have been enough. It was such a relief to hear him say that there had been no one else. There was one more thing I wanted to know. 'What about Rudolph de Castries?' I asked. I had wondered why, after the two of them had been so close, Thomas had had no communication with him whatsoever once he'd returned from that summer. As you may guess, I had not been unhappy with this. Receiving a letter from him caused Thomas to withdraw from me and the babies. To be honest, after Thomas began living with us again, I had been determined to tear up any letter from Rudolph de Castries that might arrive. None had.

"At the mention of de Castries's name, Thomas grew extremely agitated. 'I had rather you not mention that man,' he said. I asked him why not. He stared at the fire for so long I assumed he was refusing to answer. I was standing to carry our empty glasses to the sink when Thomas said, 'Rudolph de Castries had a lot of ideas.'

"Yes, I said, I remembered his ideas.

"'Not that,' Thomas said, 'that was the least of it. He was a geometrist.'

"I thought this a strange word and said so. 'Do you mean he was a mathematician?' I asked.

"'Of a kind,' Thomas said. 'He had ideas about painting, about art, that were not good. At first, they excited me, because I thought I saw in them a way towards achieving something new in my work. He made pronouncements that I took as metaphors, as maxims for the artist to live and work by. They were more than that.'

"What did he mean? He shook his head. 'De Castries thought painting could accomplish much more than any one realizes. For that reason, he did not like to refer to it as painting. Sometimes he called it, "the gateway," and other times, "the quickening." His favorite term for it was "the birth canal." His uncle,' he said, and stopped.

"What about his uncle?

"'Never mind his uncle,' Thomas said. 'His uncle had some bad ideas, and he passed them on to Rudolph, who improved on them in certain ways.'

"'Did you meet him?' I asked.

"'Rudolph?' Thomas said. 'No. He was supposed to come up and spend the weekend with me, but he didn't.'

"'Did you write to him while you were at that house?'

"'For a time. Then things happened that caused me to lose faith in his idea of painting. Or rather, things happened that gave me too much faith in his ideas. Either way, I decided I had had enough of Rudolph. I wrote and told him so. There was a brief, unpleasant exchange, and I did not hear from him again.' Thomas turned his eyes from the fire to me. 'Are you thinking of buying the house I stayed in?'

"His question caught me by surprise. Although we were quite well-off by then, and no doubt could have afforded that house had we been so inclined, the thought had never crossed my mind. Why should I want to purchase the house my husband had spent his summer away from me and his children in? I said as much to Thomas, and he relaxed. 'Good, good,' he said.

"I asked him what was wrong with that house. He said, 'I fear I may have left it in worse condition than when I moved in.' This seemed ridiculous to me. Surely any damage he might have done the place would have been repaired long since. 'What damage could be,' he said.

"That was the last we spoke of that summer. Shortly thereafter, Thomas's cancer worsened, and there were more immediate things to think about than the events of seventeen years prior. In the years since my husband's death, I have reflected on our conversation that Christmas night. I am not sure how much of what Thomas said I truly understood. About ten years after we laid Thomas to rest, I became very interested in Rudolph de Castries. I spent a good deal of time in the Princeton library. Much has been written about his painting. His is the kind of work predicated on elaborate theories that academics so love. He wrote a book whose title I cannot remember. It was either Greek or Latin, and meant something like the magic of places or the magic of houses. It is dreadfully written. I will not bother expounding its contents.

"I presume you are interested in writing about Thomas's time in your house, perhaps an article for a local magazine. I have told you what I know, which I realize is not much. Thomas did not keep a diary. He said his art was all the journal he required. If your interest is more academic, then I would suggest you consider the use my husband made of Rudolph de Castries's theories. Everything I know about de Castries convinces me he was unsavory, even for an artist. Perhaps this is the real reason I did not tell Professor Rice about our Christmas conversation. As far as I know, no one has noticed the connection before now. Nonetheless, it is there. Rudolph de Castries had some influence on my husband."

Viola's letter concluded, "I wish I could explain why, after more than three decades, the memory of Thomas's final words about his summer away make me reach for my sweater. No doubt you will dismiss my reaction as an old woman's hysteria. It is not. I will not offer further assistance, as I have told you all I know. I wish you well in your endeavors."

Once I came to the end of Viola's letter, I went back to the beginning and read it a second time, then a third. The fourth and fifth reads were more skims. Far away, my headache was pounding. Here was Viola Belvedere writing—what? Was she confirming my beliefs about her husband's summer here? Or was I reading too much into her letter? I scanned it again, especially their last conversation on the subject. This de Castries seemed worth checking out. I folded the letter and replaced it in its envelope.

• • •

I was on my way up to the library to Google Rudolph de Castries when Roger met me at the top of the stairs to ask if I would come to his office; he had something to show me. Watching him bending over, maneuvering the fragment so that it wouldn't smudge the circle, I had to leave the room, immediately. I know, I know. After everything I'd been through in the last few weeks, to freak out over Roger's latest online purchase? You never know what your own limits are, I guess. I mean, look: their possible supernatural implications aside, Roger's activities in the office were pure desire, untrammeled by rational thought. However intrigued by them I was, I recognized that. In general, though, he was so systematic about everything it made what he was doing seem more rational—more believable. In the expression on his face as he straightened up and surveyed the model, I saw through all the research, all the model-building and mapmaking, to the heart of the matter, to my husband's raw need, to the wound of his son's death that continued to bleed deep inside him.

Mumbling something about dinner, I ran out of the office, down the stairs to the second floor, and along the hall to the stairs to the first floor. Halfway down, a tidal wave of dizziness swept over me. I thought I was about to tip over the banister. I sat down, holding onto the banister as the house swung around me. Blackness swarmed the edges of my vision. Black spots blinked in front of my eyes like messages in Morse code. I didn't lose consciousness, not exactly, but everything around me receded, as if I were at one end of a long, dark tunnel and what had been around me was at the other. I slumped back on the stairs, swooning—how Victorian, right? It wasn't as scary as I would have expected. In fact, it was surprisingly peaceful, this floating in a calm, lightless place.

In the midst of that sudden disconnect from the outside world, I was aware of the house. Rooms side by side and one on top of the other; walls inside and out; floors and ceilings; windows and doors. The sensation was no more intense than normal, but with nothing to distract me from it, I could notice that some parts of it were no longer the same. The change wasn't dramatic. With a few, notable exceptions, my connection to Belvedere House occurred at the lowest level of my perception—what I was feeling now was occurring at the lowest level of that lowest level. In places, the house was becoming thinner. I'm not talking about termites here, or dry rot; I mean the house's space was failing, losing its integrity. Not at the places you would have expected, either. Ted's childhood room was fine, but both ends of the second floor hallway weren't. At those spots—beyond them—even more faintly, more subtly, I felt movement, as if enormous things were shifting out there, swinging into position. The house was being reshaped—reconfigured—in ways I didn't understand, and that frightened me. From other parts of the house, what seemed like long tunnels stretched away so far I couldn't tell where they ended. They were empty, these tunnels, so empty, it was like they were made out of emptiness. *What travels through these?* I wondered, and any remaining peace I might have felt evaporated, replaced by out and out fear. I no longer wanted to be in my swoon. For that matter, I no longer wanted to be in this house. I struggled to bring myself back to consciousness, to heave myself back from wherever I was, but the swoon held me tight. I felt those empty tunnels going on and on and on, out into cold and dark. I felt them reaching to places that weren't even places, places there aren't words to describe. There was no one there—no thing—but the prospect that there would be fueled my terror.

From far away, I heard something—a voice, saying my name. For a moment, I was sure it was coming from one of those distant not-places, and I swear my heart stopped. I saw huge copies of Roger's face mouthing my name. My thoughts jumbled, *Oh my God*, and, *They know my name*, and, *Stop, why won't this stop?* before I realized that the voice was from someplace else, from above where I was lying on the stairs. In an instant, the world rushed back around me, Roger along with it, bending over me and saying, "Veronica? Honey, can you hear me? Veronica?"

Trying to sit up, I said, "I'm all right. I'm fine."

Roger slid his arm behind my back and helped me up. "You left in a bit of a hurry," he said. "I was on my way to lend a hand with dinner and I came upon you, collapsed here. What happened?"

"I swooned," I said.

"Why?" Roger said. "What brought this on?"

Talk about your moment of truth. What was I supposed to say? That the sight of him holding his mail-order relic had made the obsessive, wish-fulfillment nature of his work in his office painfully clear to me, and that was why I'd run out, into—what? Funny—there had been a time when I could, and would, have been that bluntly honest with him, during the first days of our relationship. We used to say these devastating things to one another, but it was okay, because we didn't really know each other that well, so we weren't aware of how terrible some of what we said was—and since we knew we were in this state of mutual ignorance, we didn't take offense. Now, it was harder to be so direct—especially about the project that occupied Roger's days and nights. Knowing each other better gave us less room to offend. As for telling him about what I'd experienced while I was out of it—that would only convince him that what he was doing was working.

Yes, wasn't it? It does seem the slightest bit contradictory, doesn't it? Here I am reducing Roger's work to desperate longing; meanwhile, I'm having these paranormal experiences. Yet each experience strengthened my conviction that Roger didn't understand what was happening to us—to me. Not that I did. I simply recognized that the situation went beyond Roger's account of it. After what had just washed over me, my need to escape the house was as great as it had ever been. So, I lied to him. I looked into his face, full of concern, and said, "It's—I'm exhausted, Roger. I need a break."

The arm supporting me tensed. "What do you mean?"

"I mean that I've been up every night with you roaming the house, and it's taken its toll. I can't function like this."

"There's no need for you to get up with me—"

"Give me a break," I said. "What else am I going to do? What would you do, if positions were reversed?"

"What are you suggesting, then?"

"A few days away. Addie told me this week's renters for the Cape House canceled at the last minute. It's too late for them to advertise it. If I call them now, we can get it." I could see the resistance gathering in his eyes, so I hurried on. "I'm not saying we have to stay for the full week, just for a couple of days—so I can catch my breath, recharge my batteries. We won't be there long enough for it to make any difference to your plans. But honey, I really need this."

"What makes you so certain I won't continue to sleepwalk at the Cape?" he asked.

"It's worth a try," I said.

His face was a study in conflicting emotions. He jabbed his teeth into his lip. "All right. Let's go to the Cape."

Had he not found me semiconscious on the stairs, I'm sure Roger would have turned down my request. At best, he would have insisted I go. I might have, too. I'm not certain I would have been able to decide if it was more important for me to be there with him, or for at least one of us to get out of the house for a few days. As it was, he saw me weak and defenseless and went along with me—which I normally would have found pathetic and repellent—but we were racing through brand new territory at a hundred miles an hour, and if weak and defenseless was what it took for us to pull off at the next exit, then so be it. The moment Roger agreed to a few days on the Cape, I struggled to my feet, lurched down the stairs, half-supported by Roger, and called Addie on the phone in the hall. She was so thrilled to have someone to take the house that she offered it to us at a discount. Could we drive out tomorrow? I asked, and Addie said yes, that would be fine. Great, I said, we'd drop off the check in the morning, on our way to the Thruway.

That was what we did. Rudolph de Castries and his crazy theories could wait. I packed a few days' supply of clothes and toiletries for Roger and me. By eight o'clock the next morning we were speeding up I-87.

• • •

First, though—first came the night's sleepwalking. Roger had worked the rest of that afternoon and through the night. By the time he came to bed, it was past midnight. I had wondered how the prospect of his imminent departure would affect his sleepwalking. Either he'd be so relieved, I thought, that he'd sleep like a baby, or he'd be off on his longest journey yet. As it turned out, neither of those guesses was correct. Once I'd seen him safely to the top of the third-floor stairs—force of habit—I was tempted to cut my observations short and return to bed, myself. I would have, if I hadn't realized that, tonight, Roger's constant murmur was louder than usual, and growing louder still as he neared his office. I heard him saying, "A knife, a by-God knife," and ran up after him.

He was holding his usual position, in front of his homemade map. Although the rest of his face was slack, his lips were moving furiously, almost spitting his words. His voice was angry, choked with emotion. "Words," he said. "What good are words. Curses? Don't make me laugh. Fucking motherfucker. So what. Where's the power in that? How could you hurt anyone with that? Not him. Not him at all. Take it as a compliment, most likely. Words with meaning. Sharp. Razored. Barbed, tipped with slow-acting poison. That's what you need. Not too long, or you'll lose him. Never had much of an attention span. Dyslexia, right. Not too short, or he'll brush it off. Have to hit him hard and fast. Drive it in deep, twist it, leave it stuck in his gut.

"Always wanted to be taken seriously. Wanted to amount to something. Wanted approval. Want want want. Wanted to do what he wanted to do. Wanted what he thought was important. Wanted what he hadn't earned. Want. That's where you go.

"Get his attention. The best part of you ran down your mother's leg. No, the best part of you dribbled down your mother's leg. Better. Wait. Boy, the best part of you dribbled down your mother's leg. *He* used to say that to me. Oldie but goodie.

"Move quickly. Get to the point. Points, pitchfork. Pitchfork him. Reading. Reading writing rithmetic. Just reading. I have always been disappointed in you. No. Isn't your problem. Your fault. You have always been a disappointment to me. Better. Say it all. From your inability to read even a single book when you were a child, to the self-indulgence of your adolescence, to the blind surrender to authority that you call a career. Careful!" Roger sucked in his breath. "Too long. Yes? Depends. What's next?

"Keep it short. You are an embarrassment and a disgrace. Good, good. Boy, the best part of you dribbled down your mother's leg. You have always been a disappointment to me, from your inability to read even a single book when you were a child, to the self-indulgence of your adolescence, to the blind surrender to authority that you call a career. You are an embarrassment and a disgrace. Yes. More?

"So much more. Nothing. Your life has been nothing. It is nothing. It will always be nothing. Okay. Get to the point. I disown you. Too short. Not enough weight. I am no longer your father; you are no longer my son. Almost. Time. As of this moment, I am no longer your father; you are no longer my son. Wait. I disown you; I cast you from me. All right. Leave it there? No no. Balance is off. A knife. Needs proper balance. Your life has been nothing; it is nothing; it will always be nothing. As of this moment, I am no longer your father; you are no longer my son. I disown you; I cast you out. Let all bonds between us be sundered; let our blood no longer be true. Yes. Enough?

"Almost. Big finish. Die. Death. When you die. And when you die. What? And when you die, may you know fitting torment. May you not escape your failure. Nice. Something to conclude? You are a stranger to me. Good day. Sir. Yes. Add the sir. Ha. Good touch."

Roger repeated the eleven sentences of his curse once, twice, three times. They didn't become any easier to hear. After the third repetition, he fell silent, and I thought this was it for the night. It was enough, believe me.

Then he spoke again, in a stage whisper that seemed too loud for the movement of his lips. To be honest, it sounded as if it came as much from the walls of the house as it did his mouth. "You know what you are asking," the whisper said. After a pause, it continued, "Much is required. What do you offer?" The words fluttered through the darkness around me. "Blood," the whisper said. "Pain." Bloodpain, bloodpain, bloodpain, the words echoed down the hall. The hair on the back of my neck was standing straight up. I wrapped my arms around myself. My heart was pounding high in my chest, almost at the base of my throat. The house, usually quiet during Roger's sleepwalk, was awake; that was what it felt like, awake and watching. Roger's mouth moved, and the whisper said, "Sweet—but not enough."

Suddenly, Roger's voice was back. "Anything," he said hoarsely. "Anything—take whatever you need. Whatever you need. Anything."

INTERLUDE

STANDING AT THE RAILING

"And?" my wife asked.

"That was all she told me," I said. "More or less. She said the story was taking longer than she'd anticipated, and this was as good a place to stop as any. Then she headed off to bed."

We were seated around the picnic table on the Cape House's back lawn, together with Leigh, who had roused herself in time to join us for the lunch Ann had prepared. Robbie, whom I had fed his meal of pureed beef and carrots and dessert of liquid pears first, was toddling around the grass still stiff and crackling from winter, each step an adventure. The sun was streaming light; in the lee of the house, the air was warm enough for us to require only sweaters to sit outside. Addie and Harlow had left early, to visit friends in Hyannis, as had Veronica, who had been up and on her way out to Provincetown when Ann, Robbie, and I were making our way downstairs. "I have an appointment," she had said, "I won't be back for dinner." Over breakfast, Ann had asked me what had kept me up so late. I told her in two blocks interrupted by Robbie's morning nap, and punctuated by his babbling and occasional outbursts. When Leigh put in her appearance, I was concluding the recounting to whose secrecy I had sworn Ann, and which Leigh agreed not to disclose in return for me catching her up and then finishing.

"That's the most ridiculous thing I've ever heard," Leigh said.

"What is?" I asked.

"The whole thing—all of it. She really expects you to believe this,

145

just swallow it, hook, line, and sinker? Please—she's obviously making her story up as she goes along."

Robbie had picked up a pinecone and was bringing it towards his mouth. "Robbie," I called, "put that down, please." He ignored me, closing his lips on it. I leapt up from the bench, crossed the yard to him in two strides, and removed the pinecone from his mouth. Startled, he looked up at me. "When Daddy tells you to put something down, you put it down," I said, tossing the pinecone into the trees. He immediately burst into tears.

Ann hurried over to him. "He's just a baby," she said, picking Robbie up.

"He needs to learn to do what I tell him."

Ann didn't reply.

"Don't you think it's crazy?" Leigh asked as the three of us returned to the table. "Honestly, how could Veronica think she could get away with something like this?"

She appealed to Ann, who had seated herself with Robbie on her lap.

"I don't know," Ann said.

"She acts as if she's telling the truth," I said. "As if she believes her own story, anyway."

"Ghosts? Visions? Curses?" Leigh said.

I shrugged. "It could be."

"Oh, you're only saying that because you write this stuff."

Stung, I did not answer; although I felt my cheeks redden. Robbie saved me by overturning Ann's water. "Robbie!" I said.

He rubbed the puddle he'd created with both his hands, spreading it across the table. I said, "Robbie!"

"It's fine," Ann said, reaching for her napkin.

"No, it's not. He needs to listen to me."

"For God's sake," Ann said, "how old do you think he is?"

"Okay," Leigh said, standing up and circling around to Ann and Robbie, who held out his wet hands to her. "That's lovely sweetie; very nice. What a brilliant boy you are." She caught him under the arms and hoisted him up. "Why don't you and Auntie Leigh go inside and see what messes we can make in there, and maybe Mommy and Daddy can go for a walk on the beach."

"That's all right," I started.

"Go," Leigh said, waving her arm at the car. Robbie copied

her. "For heaven's sake. We'll be fine for an hour, won't we?" Robbie grinned at her, and Ann and I laughed.

I looked across the table at my wife. "Do you want to?"

"Maybe it would be a good idea."

Leaving the remains of lunch for Leigh to attend to, we drove the mile or so to the nearest beach, Newcomb Hollow. Robbie's eyes started to fill with tears when he realized his mother was leaving, but Leigh distracted him by bouncing him on her hip and singing a nonsense song. Except for a van whose red exterior had been weather-beaten to dull lava, the beach's parking lot was empty, the ocean breeze swirling sand over the cracked asphalt. We parked next to the van and made our way down the shifting slope to the beach. The tide was in, the Atlantic sending in long, white rollers that hit the sand with a boom. Ann and I hadn't spoken since we'd stood up from the table. She struck off to the right, and I followed her.

She was angry, I knew, at the way I'd spoken to Robbie. I wasn't particularly happy about my tone, either. In the abstract, I understood that he wasn't even a year old, that most if not all of what he did was in exploration of the world he was trying to know, that there was no need to take any of it as personally as I usually did. In reality, I could not seem to control the frustration that rose in me whenever Robbie failed to listen to me, which led me to responses far out of proportion to whatever my son was doing. For some years, I'd known I had inherited my late father's quick temper, but avoiding situations that would provoke it had been relatively easy, and, when such moments could not be evaded, they remained infrequent enough for me either to control my response or walk away from them. Indeed, in the English department, I had a reputation as easy-going, tolerant, even light-hearted. Having a child had changed everything, had placed me on the receiving end of more stress and tension than I had known—since I had been a child myself, and fearful of my father's sharp tongue, the sudden storms of his displeasure. If I thought I understood those rages better than I ever had, it was too small a benefit for the price of repeating my upbringing with Robbie.

I caught Ann's hand. "I'm sorry."

She said, "He's just a baby."

"I know; I know that."

"You can't yell at him about everything."

"It's just—he doesn't listen to anything I say to him. You tell him something, and he does it right away."

"Not always."

"More than he does with me. I could count on one hand the number of times he's done what I asked him."

"That isn't true."

"It feels like it."

Ann stopped walking and, to my surprise, hugged me. "You're his daddy," she said. "He knows that."

Hand in hand, we walked on, silent. The wind tugged at Ann's hair, played with its curls, and I remembered our first trip here, both of us fresh from recent relationships soured, the long walks we'd taken on this beach, sometimes with Leigh, sometimes with Harlow, sometimes with each other. Once, we'd been accompanied by a dog, a red-gold Lab who had appeared from nowhere, frolicked around us while we walked, then raced away down the beach until he was out of sight.

"What are you thinking about?" I asked.

"Veronica's story."

"Oh."

"Do you believe her?"

I hesitated, said, "I think so. She believes what she's saying; I'm sure of that. If you could have been there, heard her. She was completely submerged in the story she was telling. But," I added, "Leigh's comment about me accepting Veronica's story because of what I write touched a nerve. Maybe I'm too willing to take what she's saying at face value."

"What other choice do you have? You can't spend every second doubting every word that comes out of her mouth."

"No, I can't."

"Are you planning on staying up with her, tonight?"

"If she returns before it's too late. I'm pretty shattered."

"Why don't you take a nap when we get back to the house?"

"Really?"

"Leigh and I can look after Robbie."

I laughed. "How sad to think that sleep now occupies the same place in my life sex once held."

"You can't blame this on Robbie. You kept yourself up."

"Yes, yes, guilty as charged."

"As long as that's all you're guilty of."

"Honey," I said, "what are you implying?"

"Nothing," Ann said. "But Veronica's attractive, and she's already lured one member of the English department away from his wife—"

"You have nothing to worry about."

"Good."

When we got back to the Cape House, I went upstairs for a two-hour nap. My dreams were vivid in the way that daytime dreams are. Most of them centered on Belvedere House, and even asleep, I was not surprised at this. In one, I was at a huge party, like the department parties I'd attended, only much bigger, as if the entire college had been invited. Dressed in a black suit I knew with dream-certainty had belonged to his father, Roger Croydon shook my hand and told me that the shrimp-dip was wonderful, and his liver wasn't bad, either. This gave way to another dream I could not recall, which yielded in turn to a long scenario in which I was searching Belvedere House's rooms for Robbie, whom I could hear somewhere nearby, crying, but whom I could not locate. As the dream went on, Robbie's cries grew more frantic, my search more panicked, until finally I swam up out of sleep.

True to her word, Veronica did not make dinner; although Addie and Harlow did; nor was she back in the hours thereafter, while we tidied up and bathed Robbie. She did not walk in the side door until ten, by which time Robbie was long since in his porta-crib and everyone else had gone upstairs for the night. "Are you going to wait up?" Ann had asked me.

"Just for a little while," I'd answered. I had thought I might read—interestingly enough, *The Complete Ghost Stories of Charles Dickens*—but I could not keep my attention sufficiently focused on the page in front of me to make any headway through it, so I abandoned nineteenth century prose in favor of twenty-first century images and turned on the TV. The second half of *The Innocents* was showing, and while it was not my favorite film, it passed the time until I heard the side door open well-enough.

"I wondered if you'd wait up for me," Veronica said when she walked into the living room. She was dressed in a dark purple pantsuit with a black blouse.

"Anything for a good story," I said.

"You really want to hear the rest?"

"Of course."

"It's just—"

"You're regretting having told me the first part."

Veronica considered my statement. "Actually, I was asking myself if I was today. Hang on a minute." She retreated to the kitchen. I heard the cupboard open, then the refrigerator. The clink of glass on glass told me she was removing the mostly full bottle of Pinot Grigio from the top shelf; the pock of the cork being pried loose confirmed my supposition. She reappeared with a glass of wine in one hand, the open bottle in the other, and her jacket folded over the arm with the glass. She indicated the empty water glass on the coffee table in front of me and held up the bottle. "Want some?"

"No, thanks."

"More for me." She placed the bottle on the coffee table, transferred her glass to her free hand, and placed her jacket on the arm of the couch before settling herself onto it. She eased off her shoes, and curled her legs up beside her. "I swear," she said, tasting the wine, "I've done more drinking the last day than I have—than I have in a while."

I waited for her to pick up the thread of last night's narrative, wondering if she'd spring up and decide another shower was in order.

"Do you know where I was today?" Veronica asked. "No, you don't. How could you? I was in P-town. I spent the day with Viola Belvedere."

"Thomas Belvedere's Viola?"

"She's her own person, but yes, his widow."

"I thought she didn't talk to anyone."

"She doesn't. It's taken me a year to convince her to speak to me."

"What did you talk about?"

"What do you think?"

"Thomas's summer in the house."

"You win the prize. We talked about a lot of other things, too."

"That's quite a coup."

"Her house has this absolutely magnificent view of the ocean, these three huge windows that frame the sea and sky like paintings. I could have stared out of them for hours, lost myself in the view. Except—"

"Yes?"

"Talking to you last night, telling you everything I did—it stirred up my memory. I was kind of annoyed. I mean, here I was, interviewing this woman who doesn't do interviews, and in her beautiful house, besides, and I couldn't stop thinking about my story."

"But you were there—"

"Because of the house, I know. I just—I hadn't planned on everything being so immediate. Here I am, drinking Earl Grey out of a china teacup that's so expensive I can feel it, listening to Viola Belvedere talk about Willem de Kooning making a pass at her, and all I can think about is the drive Roger and I made back from the Cape."

"Back from the Cape?"

Veronica nodded. "Things hadn't gone the way I'd hoped. There were a few, nice moments, but overall, the trip was worse than a disaster. We didn't escape anything, not by a long shot.

"So there we were, driving west on 90, the Berkshires raising themselves around us. We hadn't spoken in hours. Déjà vu. I was— overcome, I guess that's the right word, by one of those memories that arrives from nowhere and completely absorbs you, so that for the two or three seconds it takes to play in your mind's eye, you relive it. I was sixteen, with my mother and father on what was to be our last family trip, to Mystic, Connecticut. It was September—Labor Day weekend. I was still at the age where the prospect of spending three minutes, let alone three days, with my parents made me ill, but I'd always wanted to see Mystic, and if I brought my Discman and a couple of thick books with me, there was a good chance they'd take the hint and leave me in peace. I was right. As long as I was present for breakfast, lunch, and dinner—and as long as I returned to the hotel room by ten—my parents were content to allow me to roam Mystic myself. Mostly, this meant I found a coffee and ice cream shop overlooking the Sound and sat drinking successive cups of cappuccino and plodding through *Moby Dick*. Melville had seemed appropriate to bring to a former seaport, you know? I hadn't read him, so I had no idea he was such a titanic windbag. Suffice to say, it didn't take me long to find out. I learned more about cetology than I ever would have dreamed existed. It was like, okay, I get it: everything in the world can be related to whales.

"There was one exception to my parents' laissez-faire attitude, and that was Saturday afternoon. My father wanted to go on a whale watch, and he wanted my mother and me to come with him. He insisted, which was pretty rare. Talk about life imitating art. I resented the interruption of my personal time, but I was curious to see the creatures that had so captured Melville's imagination they'd become a way of understanding the world for him. Mom was the one who really didn't want to go. She wasn't much of a swimmer, and the prospect of being out in two or three hundred feet of water as enormous animals cavorted around her was not her idea of a good time. She and Dad argued about it over breakfast Saturday morning. Why couldn't he take me and she'd browse the shops until we returned? That was fine with me, but he was adamant. We were going to do this as a family, he said, his face turning not red but gray as he grew more agitated—a forecast of the heart attack that would, in three months' time, carry him first to the hospital, then the cemetery. My mother gave in, and it was settled.

"They offered free Dramamine on the whale-watch boat. Mom took two, which made her extremely tired. For most of the trip out, she sat in her chair, smiling absently, eyes glassy, lids gradually lowering over them. By the time we reached the whales, she was snoring quietly. Dad wanted to wake her, but I convinced him to let her be. I was sure she'd prefer to open her eyes and find herself back at the pier. Who knows? She probably took two pills for exactly this effect.

"That left my father and me to watch the whales, which wasn't the worst of situations. Dad and I got along all right—not great, but not that bad, either. Maybe that was because he didn't pretend he understood me—unlike Mom, who never missed a chance to tell me she knew exactly what I was going through. When she was my age, she'd had an experience that wasn't even remotely similar to mine but that qualified her as an expert on whatever my difficulty was. The point of these stories seemed less to offer me any real advice than to allow her to relive selected moments of her youth, as if she needed to reassure herself that she'd had one. Dad didn't bother with stories he knew I didn't want to hear. If I came to him with a problem—which was basically never, but hypothetically speaking—he listened to whatever was bothering me, asked a couple of questions to clarify matters, then delivered a pronouncement. Your best friend's talking about you behind your back? Get a new best friend. His solutions were always direct and completely unworkable.

"The funny thing is, buried under the layers of my mother's ever-expanding autobiography was usually an insight I could use. I just had to be the princess and the pea. I had to be able to feel that tiny sphere through all those mattresses. What I appreciated about

Dad was more a matter of style. He listened; he asked questions; he told you what he thought. End of story. When you're a teenager—at least, when I was, the last thing I wanted was for my parents to identify with me. I wanted them to respect who I was, which was, of course, completely different from either of them, let me do what I wanted to, and provide food, shelter, and cash as needed. Neither of them lived up to that ideal—not even close. What it boiled down to was, Dad was slightly less annoying than Mom.

"There the two of us were, standing at the railing as the ship rode up and down surprisingly choppy waters. Dad had positioned himself at the railing almost the second we'd boarded the ship. He'd looked over to where Mom and I were sitting and gestured to either side of him, eyebrows raised, but I'd shook my head and so had Mom. He'd shrugged and returned to watching the harbor. As the boat had made its way out into the ocean, he'd stayed where he was, the wind catching his hair—he wore it in a bad comb-over—and tugging it up over his head like a pennant. I'd paid more attention to him than I'd intended. I'd brought *Moby Dick*, only to find that a few minutes of reading on the high seas made my head ache and my stomach feel like it might like to send my lunch up for a second look. I'd forgotten my Discman in the car, so that left people-watching as a way to kill time. Most everyone else was seated, staring off at the sea. A few hurried in the direction of the bathrooms, their faces distinctly green, their mouths unstable. Fewer still stood at the rails—mostly young couples wrapped around one another, laughing in each other's ears, and my father. Hands clutching the rails, back straight, he looked more vibrant than I was accustomed to. He didn't remind me of Captain Ahab—God forbid, right? He didn't remind me of a ship's captain, or even an officer. What he made me think of was an old sailor, the kind of guy new sailors—new officers, too—were told to listen to, because he'd already forgotten more about the sea than they'd ever learn. It was strange, seeing him that way, strange and kind of nice.

"The ship slowed, and the guide's voice crackled over the speakers, announcing that they'd sighted a family of humpbacks ahead to our right at about two o'clock. Everyone rushed over to the rail. Dad was perfectly placed. Leaving Mom asleep in her chair, I pushed my way through the crowd until I was next to him. He put his right arm around my shoulders and pointed with his left hand. 'There they are,' he said, 'there.' Fifty, sixty yards away, what looked like the back of an enormous snake curled under the waves. To its right, a flat tail like the leaf of some huge, exotic tree raised itself above the water before sliding straight down into it. To the left, a long, white-gray lozenge—a flipper—waved lazily. There were eight whales altogether, six adults and two calves, and for the next forty minutes, we watched them and I think they watched us, too. The guide's voice droned on throughout, listing this or that feature that identified this or that whale. Every time he'd say, 'Directly in front of us, you'll see a whale with a large dark patch in the center of her tail. We call her Spot,' Dad's hand would shoot out, his finger drawing a straight line to it. 'Do you see it?' he'd say, and I did. Under normal circumstances, I would have found such a display completely intolerable, but these circumstances were not normal. I couldn't distinguish any of the marks the guide referred to, while Dad was able to do so before the guy had completed his sentence. My father's face was—it was like, he was completely there, completely involved in what was happening right in front of him, not distracted by anything.

"Towards the end of our time out there, one of the whales disappeared from view. The ship, which had been rolling up and down on the waves, surged higher. Eyes blazing, Dad looked at me. 'Did you feel that?' he asked. 'That whale swam beneath us.'

"Pure terror raced up my back. I couldn't tell exactly how long any of the humpbacks was—I couldn't see that much of them through the water—but I thought our ship was longer, bigger. What would happen if one of them decided to surface beneath us? Would they do that? If they did, would they capsize the boat?

"A second and third whale dove. I held my breath. The ship rose and fell, rose and fell, rose—and rose—and fell, rose—and rose—and fell. I wrapped my arms around Dad, who, to his credit, didn't laugh. 'Could they tip us over?' I asked into his shirt.

"'I don't know,' he said. 'I doubt it. If one of them decided to surface beneath us, he could probably make the ship tip to one side a bit, but I doubt they're big enough to do more than that. If all of them were to try together, I guess they could give us a bath, but whales don't do things like that.'

"'You're sure?'

"'Reasonably,' he said. 'They wouldn't run these cruises if there was a strong chance of the whales drowning everyone on board. Besides, you know how to swim.'

"That was Dad, full of comfort. I held onto him until we were in sight of the harbor, when I carefully disengaged myself. Do you know, I never asked him what the deal was with him and whale watching? Or maybe it was with him and the ocean, or him and ships. I thought about it three months later, when he was in intensive care at Penrose, tethered to all these machines designed to keep him here with us. Looking at him lying in the hospital bed, his skin pale and saggy, his eyes unfocused, I remembered him standing at the railing on the whale-watch ship, his hands firm on the rail, his head alert as he scanned the ocean. It was like two different people—to tell the truth, it was like three different people. There was the father I knew; that man on the ship—who had been, I was sure, who my father wanted to be, whom he saw himself as in his best moments—and this man dying in front of me—who he didn't want to be, a man overwhelmed by his traitor heart. During one of his lucid moments, I sat beside him and asked him if he remembered our trip to Mystic, the whale watch we'd went on. He nodded—he wasn't speaking much by then—and squeezed my hand. Before I could say any more, thank him for comforting me when I was freaking out, ask him what had been so important about all of us going to see those whales, he was asleep. The next time he was awake, I'd forgotten the question.

"I tried to ask my mom about it, after the funeral, but I couldn't figure out how to phrase what I wanted to know, and she stared at me like I had two heads. So who knows?

"That's not the point, though. That's not what returned to me so vividly as Roger drove us west through the Berkshires. What took hold of me was the memory of being on the ocean, riding the swells up and down, then feeling the water leap up that extra bit. Being on the ocean is already unnerving—for me, at least. You think, *The water here's a hundred feet deep*, or two hundred feet, or three hundred, and at first that's just a number. Two hundred feet? How much is that? I could walk that in like, a minute—less, even. Then you think about the buildings you're used to, your house, your friends' houses, school, the mall, and you realize that two hundred feet of water would cover them with room to spare. There are a couple of tall buildings in Poughkeepsie—a couple of the dorms at Penrose are pretty tall—but I'm not sure they'd rise above that depth of water. Maybe the top one or two floors would, but I doubt it. You think about standing at the foot of one of those buildings and looking up, and you imagine that's all water. At the bottom of two hundred feet of ocean, it would be completely dark. Pitch black and cold, not to mention the whole crushing-water-pressure thing. I don't know what the ocean floor looks like. I picture bare rocks and the occasional shipwreck, but it's not important. What is, is that feeling of depth, that you in your little boat are floating over tremendous darkness and cold. I guess I have more in common with my mother than I'd thought.

"And the whales—this is where they live. This is their home, their habitat. This incredibly alien environment, and they're swimming around in it. I don't know if they dive all the way to the ocean floor—I guess it depends on where they are—but they can go down pretty deep if they want to. I know whales are supposed to be all cute and cuddly—at least majestic—and I'm all for saving them, don't get me wrong, but after that first one swam under the boat, any sentimental feelings I had were washed away by a wave of pure fright. These things are gigantic. They're powerful. They roam around this absolutely incredible place—loathe Melville though I do, I have no problem understanding why he made God a whale—because that's what *Moby Dick* is about, isn't it? What's funny is—do you know, apparently, whales used to be land animals? This is millions of years ago I'm talking about. The evidence is there in their skeletons. The bones in their flippers look like enormous hands. They have tiny, vestigial leg bones. Obviously, they breathe air. That kind of stuff. At some point in the far distant past, they exchanged sun and sky for dark and saltwater. What made them do that? What catastrophe chased them from the surface of the earth?"

Veronica finished her glass of wine, poured another. "That isn't enough, I know. You want to hear what happened while we were on the Cape, what triggered that memory."

"I do," I said. "I want to hear everything."

"You will."

PART 2

MALEDICTION

Roger wasn't happy (Veronica said)—almost the moment he agreed to come with me to the Cape, regret twisted his mouth. As he drove us up the Thruway and out the Mass Pike, he was silent. I knew he was trying, which in this instance meant not letting any one of the dozen complaints at the tip of his tongue escape. It meant keeping the car pointed east. I was so relieved to be on our way someplace else—to be crossing the Hudson, Albany a distant cluster of buildings to our left; to be in among the Berkshires, speeding along between old, rounded mountains; to be stopping at a rest area for a Big Mac, for God's sake—I was so relieved, not to mention nervous that Roger might take it on himself to abandon our plan and turn the car around, that I was willing to sit for almost three hundred miles in silence, whatever NPR station the radio could pick up chattering in the background.

That wasn't all I was nervous about, either. Roger's—what do you call it? His speech? His dramatic monologue? It was playing on repeat somewhere not too far from the front of my brain. I couldn't not think about it. I was trying not to worry about it—too much, anyway, especially the change in his voice at the end. Not that the stuff before that was terribly pleasant, but at least that made sense. Even without the weird voice that had sounded so hollow, so full of the space inside the house, I would have preferred not to have eavesdropped on Roger's composition process. Yes, from the moment I'd heard him deliver those words to Ted—inflict them on him, is the way I really think of it—I'd known that my husband contained depths I hadn't suspected, pits full of black, bubbling resentment, anger. I'd continued to think of his words as spontaneous, however, which was not unreasonable. After more than three decades in the classroom, Roger was a master of the extemporaneous speech. So long as I could think of Roger's words as a heat-of-the-moment kind of thing, I could live with it. Maybe not as well as I would have liked, but I could deal. To think that it had been this premeditated was unsettling, to say the least. Who wants to think that the person they love has it in them to intend such damage to someone else—to their child, for crying out tears—that they could plan it out so methodically? The image that kept occurring to me was of Roger, dressed not in his blue short-sleeved shirt and chinos, but in furs, sitting not in the driver's seat of a Jetta, but in a cave lit by a smoky fire. He's holding a piece of bone in his left hand, a sharpened stone in his right. As he repeats last night's monologue, he scrapes the stone across the bone, shaping it into a weapon, a knife suitable for driving into his son's soft belly. I did my best not to dwell on it.

• • •

Instead, I tried to think about the house we were going to. Although Addie had shown me pictures of the Cape House, and I'd told her I'd have to come out to it, I never had. I'd been to the Cape once, when I was nineteen. I drove out to Provincetown with the guy I was seeing at the time. We were on the verge of breaking up. The trip was one of those things you do when both of you know what's coming but are trying to resist it, one of those epic, empty gestures. On our way there, we got lost—the guy claimed he knew a shortcut that became a longcut, and by the time we arrived in P-town, the sun was on its way down and our tempers were frayed. We walked Commerce Street for an hour, then had an unpleasant dinner at the Lobster Pot. He had seen his first drag queen and been freaked out. I accused him of being intolerant. We spent our meal bickering over whether he was. Our conversation on the ride home alternated between further bickering and half-hearted attempts to plan our return trip, when we had more time and could rent a motel room. It was sad—sad and frustrating, because I could see this was a beautiful place, and I couldn't enjoy it.

Roger's associations with the Cape were more positive. He and Joanne had vacationed here several years in a row, after they were first married. They missed a year when Joanne was pregnant with Ted. When they inquired about renting their old apartment for the following summer, they learned that the artist who'd taken their place had already put down a deposit for the following year. Roger called about a couple of other rentals, but that was the year everything had been booked in advance. If the Cape wasn't available—which meant about a half-dozen apartments in P-town—they'd have to look elsewhere. Joanne's hairdresser suggested the South Jersey Shore, and that was how they found the spot they'd be vacationing in for the next half-dozen years, until they decided to take Ted to Disney World.

The Cape, for Roger, was P-town. It was occasional walks on the beach, but mostly lunches, dinners, and cocktail parties with friends. It was visiting gallery after gallery, sometimes accompanied by the artist whose work was on display, sometimes purchasing a painting for Joanne to hang in one of the house's guest rooms. It was going to hear critics and writers from *The New York Review of Books* and the *Sunday Times Book Review*. "We might as well have been in Manhattan," Roger said, which I'm sure is why Joanne enjoyed it. She taught him how to eat lobster. Is it any surprise that she had a knack for cracking open shells and digging out meat?

I don't think Roger and Joanne were ever at the Cape at the same time as Addie and Harlow. By the time the Howards started vacationing here, Roger and Joanne had moved on to the Jersey Shore. They returned to the Cape a handful of times, but only for long weekends. Friends of Joanne's rented a house in Hyannis, and they invited her and Roger to visit them. Neither Roger nor Joanne had been to the Cape House, before or after their split, and I have to admit, I was happy about that. If you're going to be with someone who was married before and lived in the same place you're living in now—especially someone who had along marriage—then you have to accept that pretty much anywhere the two of you go, the two of them went first, and probably second, third, and fourth, besides. You tell yourself that it doesn't matter whom he was with before; it's a question of who's there now. You let him talk about what the two of them did here or there in the past, because that's part of his life and you want to know about his life. You tell yourself that you're making new, better memories in these places, that you're claiming them for the two of you, now. It's the price you pay—and if it seems like you keep paying it, what can you do?

But it means that, when you discover something the two of them didn't do together, whatever it is, right off the bat, it's even sweeter.

One time, back when we were sharing the apartment—pre-confrontation with Ted—I convinced Roger that we should go mini-golfing. He hadn't been with Joanne. She wasn't interested in it. The night turned into kind of a joke. Roger is fiercely competitive, even about things like mini-golf, which, I'm afraid, he was terrible at. He kept hitting the ball too hard, ricocheting it off the obstacles, bouncing it onto the other greens. The worse he played, the angrier he got; the angrier he got, the worse he played. To make matters worse, mini-golf is one of the few sports in which I excel. To put it mildly, I was kicking his ass. On top of this, when we were about halfway through the course, it started raining, a sudden, torrential thunderstorm—I mean, there was hail coming down, these pea-sized ice pellets that really stung, not to mention absolutely soaking rain and lightning striking all around us—us with our metal clubs. The entire course cleared in about two seconds, except for—you guessed it—Roger, who refused to leave until the game was completed. First I'm screaming at him to get out of the rain, doesn't he realize how dangerous this is, then I'm playing, too. It was like, Well, fine, if you want to electrocute yourself, then I'll electrocute myself, too. How do you like that? There the two of us were, water streaming into our eyes, hair and clothes plastered to our bodies, shivering madly, and would we stop the game? Not till the last hole, and, for the record, I won. On the ride home, Roger was so furious he refused to talk to me. When I stopped at the diner and ran in for two hot chocolates to go, he wouldn't drink his—so I did, which made his mouth fall open first in astonishment, then laughter. What a night.

The point is, for as soaked as we were—for as much danger as we'd been in—for all that my plan for a pleasant hour or two had gone horribly off-track—for all of that and more besides, that night was ours. We didn't have to share it any way, shape, or form with Joanne. I'm sure there are more of those nights than I realize. I know there are ones that are less melodramatic. After that experience, Roger refused to play mini-golf with me again. But if I treasure our meal at the Canal House, I treasure that game, too, because it was ours.

I was hoping we'd make more of those memories at the Cape House, which I guess we did; although most of what happened—well, Joanne would be welcome to it, let's put it that way. The drive—can I just say I love the drive out here? I love how, as you get closer to the Cape itself, the trees are all shorter—from the wind off the ocean, I suppose—and through them you can see cranberry bogs every now and again, and then you're at the Bourne Bridge, crossing over the channel, and if it's a sunny day, the water below dazzles. The bridge—funny, how sometimes landscapes can be so blatantly symbolic—once you're over it, I'm always surprised at how long it takes you to get out here. You think, I'm here, I'm on the Cape, and you forget that you still have to drive all the way out to the elbow and keep going. It's all right, though. In places, you can see the ocean, or the bay, and you can smell the salt water. You see these houses with weatherworn shingles, whose yards are basically sand—there's sand everywhere, the farther out you drive. I know, I know. You drove here, too, you saw all of this, already. I suppose Route 6 isn't all that different from any other local highway. There are the same restaurants, stores, strip malls—except that, out here, all the restaurants advertise fresh seafood, and the stores sell Cape Cod hats and t-shirts and knickknacks, and the strip malls are just a little less tacky. Yes, I'm romanticizing. When it comes to this place, I'm a total tourist. To anyone who lives here, I'm sure there are plenty of places on 6 that make them cringe. But the sight of all of it was enough to make Roger's monologue, and my image of him scraping the sharp edge of a rock up a piece of bone, recede. Did I mention there's a mini-golf course? Have you seen it?

We passed the mini-golf course, and Roger, whose last words had been uttered when we'd stopped for an early lunch two hours before, said, "No."

It took me a moment to realize he'd spoken. I'd been lost in the scenery. I said, "I beg your pardon?"

"I saw you gazing fondly at that miniature golf course," he said.

"What? I wasn't—" I was confused, until I understood he was trying to be funny. "Oh come on," I said, "one game."

"Never."

"I'll let you win."

"My dear," Roger said, "I do not require anyone to 'let' me win. I am fully capable of winning on my own."

"That's not what I remember."

"My march to victory the last time we played was interrupted by the weather."

"Seems to me it was more of a crawl than a march."

"The insolence of youth. Golf isn't a natural sport, anyway."

"Oh? What sport is?"

"Baseball."

"Baseball?"

"Baseball," Roger said. "It is the noblest game."

"Right. That's why they've found all those pre-historic baseball sites, because it's part of our DNA."

"Exactly. Our ancestors used to play their Neanderthal cousins. It is the true reason for the disappearance of the Neanderthal: poor pitching and catching skills. They were murder with the bat, though, when they could see past their tremendous brows." He lowered his, and stuck out his jaw.

I laughed. "Is this your new career? Baseball anthropologist?"

Roger nodded. "I am the only one of my kind. I follow the course of the world's greatest game up and down history's corridors. I consider the Trojan War, where mighty Achilles struck out noble Hector in the bottom of the seventh with three men on and two out. I reconstruct Charles Martel's homerun against the Moors. I map the trajectory of the pop-fly Alexander Hamilton caught, for which Aaron Burr shot him."

"Wait a minute," I said. "I thought you Dickensians played cricket."

"Perish the thought," Roger said. "Cricket is only a ruse invented to hide our proficiency at baseball."

"Which is why half the world plays it."

"It was a successful invention."

That was how it was the rest of the way to Wellfleet and Addie and Harlow's, this weird banter about baseball and world history that included Roger's abbreviated account of Dickens's career as a short-stop. It was funny. He improvised a few stanzas of "Cheney at the Bat." It was light, his effort at resuming conversation, but not about anything important. By the time we were turning off 6, we were discussing dinner plans. I wanted to go into P-town, to the Lobster Pot. Roger wanted to order in from Gutsy Bender's. Have I mentioned what a fan of junk food that man was? If it came in a disposable container and doubled your cholesterol, Roger adored it.

●●●

First, though, was the Cape House. Do I have to tell you what a relief this place was, after Belvedere House? Sure, it isn't nearly as impressive on the outside, but when impressive means Chock Full of Weirdness, plain is just fine. We'd arrived at the perfect time. The house was glowing with early afternoon light. We brought our bags up to the master bedroom, then explored the rest of the place. Roger was impressed. He didn't say anything, but I could read it on his face, which made me happy—happier, since I was already pretty pleased at the thought of us way out here, almost at the end of the Cape. To be honest, the house could have looked like anything, inside and out, as long as it let us escape. That it was so nice was a bonus.

For dinner, we settled on driving into Wellfleet, where we had drinks and dinner at the Bomb Shelter. Have you been there? They seated us on the front porch, so we could eat looking out on the bay. There was enough of a breeze to keep the air free of mosquitoes, and we had a leisurely meal while the sun dipped down to the water, painting the sky gaudy behind it. Our conversation continued light. Being on the Cape reminded me of *The Bostonians*, which Roger didn't care for and which led us to a mild debate about the virtues of Henry James. Roger condemned him for striving too hard for subtlety; I defended his effort to get at the nuances of perception. The argument was a far cry from those we'd had in the early days. Those had been the verbal equivalent of full-scale combat; this was more of a chess match. After dinner, we walked across the road to the beach, where we took off our shoes and socks—well, Roger did; I was wearing sandals—and went for a barefoot stroll.

The walk lasted longer than I expected. We weren't back at the house till twenty to midnight. I switched on the TV, and, in the process of searching for *The Tonight Show*, clicked on a black-and-white film that made Roger leap forward and say, "Stop here!" The local public television station was showing David Lean's version of *Oliver Twist*. I had stumbled onto it close enough to the beginning to allow us to watch the rest. Roger was delighted. There have been plenty of adaptations of Dickens, some better than others—although there's no version of a Dickens novel that's half as bad as that version of *The Scarlet Letter* Demi Moore did a few years ago; I'm just saying—there have been a lot of Dickens movies, but this one had all kinds of personal significance for him. Not only was it a brilliant work by a brilliant director, he'd first seen the film as a grad student leaning towards Dickens, but unsure about following that inclination. *Oliver Twist* had been playing in a revival in a local theater. Roger went to see it, loved it, and felt like he'd been given a sign to pursue his desire. Of course, it didn't hurt that he had a chance to work with a leading Victorianist, either. Running across it was a reminder of a happier time. Between watching the movie and raiding the kitchen cupboards for snacks when it was done, we were up until after two.

That night, I couldn't sleep. I lay awake beside Roger, waiting to see if he would continue sleepwalking. Although I hoped the new location would be enough to keep him in bed, I wasn't counting on it. Nor was I confident in his ability to navigate unfamiliar terrain. If he did rise, I didn't know if he'd have a speech to deliver, either the same one as last night or something new, even more damning. The night was warm. We'd left the bedroom windows up. I listened to the ocean breeze rustling the trees. I did my best not to look at the clock, whose red numbers showed that what had felt like at least a half-hour had been five minutes. I should've switched on the light and sat up reading, but I was afraid to do anything that would disturb Roger. I wasn't sure what his sleepwalking here would signify. That I'd been wrong about leaving the house, I guess. When he stirred—at three, a glance at the clock confirmed—I held my breath, wondering which direction he'd head, if I could catch him before he tripped down the stairs, if I could stand hearing what he'd have to say. But his stirring was no more than him turning over in his sleep, after which he was still again. Despite the relief that rushed through me—if nothing else, I'd finally be able to get a decent night's sleep—my eyes didn't close for another half-hour. I wanted to be sure that Roger's schedule hadn't been thrown off, and he'd be up for his nightly walk a little later. Now that I seemed able to draw a line between his sleepwalking and Belvedere House, I needed to figure out what that meant. Granted, the line was dotted. Roger would have to sleep peacefully every night we were here before I could make it a solid one. This night—he had insisted on driving today—we hadn't discussed it; he'd just kept driving and, when I'd asked him if he was okay, had nodded his head—the point is, his failure to leave the bed tonight could have had as much to do with exhaustion as anything.

• • •

My relief at the prospect of a full night's sleep had been premature. For the rest of our time at the Cape House—we stayed from Tuesday to Saturday—I kept myself up until three every night. I slept in later than usual—most mornings it was ten or ten-thirty before I dragged myself downstairs—but I knew that Roger had maintained his waking time of six, and I was reluctant to leave him alone with his thoughts for too long. He'd brought his copy of *Our Mutual Friend*, which he said he hadn't read straight through for several years and which he claimed he spent the hours before I woke rereading. Every morning I found him on the big couch in the living room, the novel open in his hands. You could chalk it up to paranoia on my part—although, what is it they say? Just because you're paranoid doesn't mean they're not out to get you? Seriously—there was no point to us traveling all this distance only to have Roger sit brooding about Ted. I couldn't control Roger's thoughts, but I could give him other things to think about. Who knows? Maybe I could've slept until noon every day and Roger would have been fine. But I was more afraid than I wanted to admit that, the one morning I indulged myself and stayed in bed, I'd come down to find Roger in the midst of laying out another tabletop model. For that reason, I was coffeed, showered, and out the door with him by eleven at the latest.

We spent a lot of time at the beach. It was our first stop after leaving the house each day. We took an hour to walk up and down it, past families whose parents lay out in the sun tanning or reading a novel while their children ran back and forth to the ocean, sloshing plastic pails of water for the sandcastles they were building. We passed couples young and old—their children future gleams or past memories—reclining on beach chairs, studying the ocean out of sunglasses. We met other walkers, some of them with dogs that raced around the sand, kicking it up in gritty sprays, then dashed into the waves for a quick swim before trotting out, shaking themselves off, and starting the whole thing over again. We exchanged nods and hellos with solitary fishermen, their poles dug into the sand like spears, the lines running taut and barely visible to the waves.

Whether we walked at high tide or low or whatever they call it in-between, we were accompanied by the sound of the waves, the noise the ocean makes as it dissolves itself onto the land, which I sometimes imagined as the old man of the sea clearing his throat: harrumph. It's a sound that can be loud one minute—so much it startles you—and soft—almost intimate—the next. I would try to figure out the rhythm of it, but although I was sure I could hear a pattern to the waves, I couldn't formalize it. A constant breeze blew in with the waves, and that made even the hottest days—we had one overcast day while we were there—more bearable.

Depending on what time we arrived at the beach, we would step over pieces of driftwood, clumps of black seaweed jumping with sand-fleas, fragments of crabs that the gulls had made meals of. The gulls themselves came and went overhead, sometimes hovering in the wind, the way they do, so that they look like kites, hanging there. Between their cries, floating bright and ragged on the air, and the hiss of the ocean as it fell back into itself—and the smell, that saltwater smell that you can miss, until the wind shifts and there it is, as full and rich in your nostrils as the sight of the ocean blue to the horizon—it was like a recipe for the complete beach experience. In a setting like that, the events of the last almost-year, from Roger's curse to Ted's death to all the weirdness—well, you couldn't escape them, but it was easier to tell yourself that they were in the past and have a chance of believing it.

Once our walk was done, we were off someplace else, which usually meant Provincetown, although on the Friday I convinced Roger to drive down to Wood's Hole so we could take the ferry to Martha's Vineyard. We'd spent a long weekend on the Vineyard at the beginning of spring—I think I mentioned it last night. We had gone there that month after Roger agreed to the leave of absence. It had happy memories for us, which was why I told Roger I wanted to see it again. As it turned out—

That's rushing ahead. First came our excursions into P-town. I insisted we do all the touristy things, like climbing the Pilgrim Monument. Roger had never done that. Can you believe it? He'd vacationed here for years in a row. He couldn't avoid seeing the monument—I mean, there's nothing half as tall around—but it was like those New Yorkers who live all their lives in sight of the Statue of Liberty and don't ever visit it. I couldn't believe Joanne hadn't wanted to climb it. True, she's hardly athletic, but you would think her blood would have glowed even bluer at the prospect of a Pilgrim Monument. Oh well, that left it for us. Roger raced up the stairs—all that walking and jogging—I struggled to keep up and quickly fell behind. When I reached the top, he was standing with his back to me, surveying P-town spread out below him, its streets full of cars, its harbor full of boats, the bay shining in the afternoon sun. I was reminded of how he gazed down at his model of the street in Kabul, and what I had tried to leave three hundred miles away was right beside us again.

Sometimes before we played tourists, sometimes after, we had lunch. Actually, it was pretty much always before. The day we climbed the Pilgrim Monument was the only time we ate after, which was a mistake. By the time we walked out of there, my legs were shaking, I was so hungry. We lunched at a different restaurant each day, the same with dinner. I ate a lot of seafood, a lot of fish, a lot of shrimp, some lobster. Roger stuck with chicken and occasionally steak, which I could not understand. Here we were, right beside the ocean—in some case, literally dining on top of it. If you're not going to eat fish here, then where? How much fresher do you want, right? He refused to discuss it: he ordered what he ordered and that was that.

Lunch finished, off we went to tourist. I had it half in mind to look up Viola Belvedere, then, but her phone number's unlisted, and although I asked about her at every gallery we stopped in, no one knew who she was. I wasn't especially disappointed. I would address her letter once we were back in Huguenot. Still, P-town isn't that big, and it was strange to think that, as we strolled its streets, we could have been passing in front of her house. She could have been an old woman we stepped off the sidewalk to walk around. We contented ourselves with more normal touristing, after which it was time for a snack, which tended to be the same thing every day, a double scoop of Ben & Jerry's. Do you know that, before we got together, Roger had never had Ben & Jerry's? For introducing him to that alone, he should have married me.

Cones in hand, we strolled P-town, window-shopping Commerce Street—ducking into a store if something caught our eye—or wandering the rest of the place. Every other house in P-town seems to be a B&B, doesn't it? We'd turn from this street to that, the day's heat melting the different flavors of our ice creams into new blends, banana-chocolate-chunk-chocolate-fudge-brownie, and depending on where we were, Roger would gesture at a house and, between licks of his ice-cream cone, tell me that it was where he'd spent an evening arguing the merits of Rossetti's painting with the art critic for the *Village Voice*.

Our ice creams done, the last piece of cone crunched, sticky fingers wiped with soggy napkins, we made our way back to Commerce Street for more window-shopping. We spent this part of our day

browsing the aisles of Marine Salvage. After considering the assortment at the front of the store—the windchimes, the surplus airline
flatware, the rubber lobsters, the keychains—we'd drift further in, to
the racks of clothes. They have all those military uniforms there, you
know? Most of them aren't American. They're from Russia, Germany,
and Britain. I can't imagine how they got it all. We tried some of it on,
the hats and helmets, mostly. Roger was more convincing as an officer
in the Russian navy than you would have thought. I wanted to buy
him the hat, but he refused. In the midst of the uniforms, there's other
stuff, too, canteens in leather pouches and shovels that fold up into
themselves. While Roger moved on to the back of the store, I raked
through boxes of the canteens and shovels.

· · ·

Our second night there, I found a gas mask—with post-9/11 concerns about bio- and chemical-terrorism, no longer a quaint antique.
I turned it over in my hands, but couldn't bring myself to put my
face into it, even for fun. It was too claustrophobic. The light played
across its empty eyepieces, and I thought of Ted. I didn't know if
he'd had to wear one of these in Afghanistan. I didn't think so, but
he'd probably had to train with one, because as a member of Special
Forces he would've had to be prepared for everything. They look so
alien, gas masks. You may tell yourself they're shaped like the faces of
elephants, but no elephant ever looked like these things. They're the
cubist nightmare of an elephant. People put them on and become
different. In a back room in my mind, Roger said, "I disown you; I
cast you from me." The mask was made from a rubbery material—
maybe it was rubber—that was warm and soft to the touch. It felt
uncomfortably close to skin, as if I were holding someone's face. I
dropped the gas mask on top of a pile of gray German helmets and
hurried off to find Roger.

When we returned to Marine Salvage the following day, however,
I lingered at the front of the store only long enough to convince myself
I didn't intend to head straight back to that stack of gray helmets. I
hadn't given the mask much thought—not that I had let myself be
aware of, anyway. A couple of times later that evening, I'd recalled
the feel of its material with a little shudder, but that was hardly worth
mentioning. It wasn't until we were walking up Commerce once again

that I was seized by this compulsion to rush into the store and find the gas mask. It was the kind of change in your internal weather that catches you by surprise and before you know what's happening has turned you in a new direction. I tried to resist it, forcing myself to stand at a bin full of brightly colored plastic telescopes, but it swept me into the store with hurricane force. As a rule, I'm not a compulsive person. Prior to everything I've been telling you about, I could practically count on one hand the number of times I'd been overtaken by this kind of impulse. Lately, though, it seemed I'd been acting increasingly at the behest of motives that were unclear to me. My recent attempt at getting pregnant had been a relatively benign manifestation of this trend, my need to escape Belvedere House another example. This, though: Why should I be possessed by the urge to see a surplus gas mask, to hold it in my hands again? If the force of my compulsion was frightening, its object was bizarre enough to take the edge off my fear. I found the pile of helmets, the same height as yesterday, but no gas mask. I pawed through the helmets, which tumbled and rolled against one another, colliding with a dull, plastic crack. I thrust my hand into the midst of them, and felt the mask's snout in my palm. Clearing away helmets with my other hand, I freed the gas mask, holding it up to the light.

And do you know what? The moment it was in my hands, the same weirdness I'd experienced last night at the thing's appearance—accompanied by the revulsion I'd felt at touching it—overcame me, and, almost as soon as I had it out, I was dropping it back in with the helmets and heading to the front of the store as quickly as I could. My feet carried me outside at just under a run. Roger was another ten minutes picking through racks of t-shirts, plenty of time for me to ask myself what was going on. I had no idea. When Roger emerged onto the street, I told him I was ready for dinner and asked how he felt about returning to Wellfleet to try Aesop's Tables. "What," he asked, "no Lobster Pot?"

"We ate there last night."

"True, but I believe I heard you say that you would not need to dine anyplace else, now."

"Can we just go?" I said. All at once, it was too much effort to keep up the light and witty banter. I wanted out of Provincetown, away from Marine Salvage and its gas mask, and that was that.

"Of course we can," Roger said. "Sweetie, what's wrong?"

"Nothing," I said, "low blood sugar, I guess." Because, really, how could I tell him I'd been freaked out by surplus military equipment?

The gas mask was at the forefront of my thoughts during the ride to Wellfleet and our meal at Aesop's Tables. Have you eaten there? Isn't it good? It reminds me a little of the Canal House, mostly because they're both old houses—I think I read that Aesop's used to belong to a sea-captain, or something like that. We were seated in the back room, and the first thing I did was order a glass of white wine. Between the wine and the meal that followed, I relaxed enough for casual conversation not to take a concerted effort. After we'd paid the check, we went for a walk, toward the bay. There was a house for sale, this big white colonial thing that was a B&B. Roger paused. "What do you think?" he asked, "Should we take it, relocate here, abandon academia for the lives of innkeepers?" His tone was light as ever, but an undercurrent of seriousness startled me out of my gas mask meditations. I opened my mouth to say something that would prolong his musing. What came out was, "And leave Belvedere House?"

I meant to ask him if he was serious, but my words ran away from my intentions. Roger turned to me, and I could see that he'd taken my question as a reproach, that implied in it he'd heard, "And abandon your son—again?" I said, "Roger," trying to add that that wasn't what I'd meant, but he sighed and said, "You're right, of course. There are responsibilities at home—I have duties that cannot be shirked. It was only the moment's whim."

I swear, I could have kicked myself. Why couldn't I have said, "Yes"? How complicated is that? All the way back to the car, I kept trying to think of ways to revive the subject, but by the time Roger was unlocking my door, the moment had passed. Frustrated as I was by my inability to say the right thing—or my ability to say exactly the wrong thing—I felt a faint stir of hope. The jury was out on the long-term effects of my strategy of separating us from Belvedere House, but in the short-term, Roger's sleepwalking had abated and he was joking about moving up here. Yes, I could be clutching at straws, but these seemed good signs.

I, on the other hand, was obsessed with army gear. As I lay awake on sleep-walking watch that night, it occurred to me that while coming to the Cape might have been a good idea for Roger, the change of scenery hadn't worked any wonders for me. Yes, I couldn't sense the house anymore. The feeling had steadily drained away the further we'd driven. But I was uncomfortably aware of where the sensation had been. It was like when an especially deep cut is healing, and it itches deep under your skin, where you can't scratch it. If those feelings had receded, they'd been replaced by other things, by my fixation on this gas mask.

Roger breathing steadily, the house quiet, I pictured the mask, the flat disks of its eyes, the round canister dangling below them, the assortment of straps at its rear. It was olive green, except for the straps, which were black. Despite what I'm sure must have been the dozens of people who'd handled it, its lenses were clean enough for you to see yourself reflected in them. I lay in bed listening to the ocean breeze rustling the trees, trying to understand the urge that had driven me back inside Marine Salvage. I knew that the gas mask reminded me of Ted, but you have to admit, it's a pretty strange object to fixate on. A camouflage jacket, a regimental patch, even the kind of knife he'd carried—any of the things I'd seen in the photos of Ted I'd hung around the house would have made more sense. Branches whispered. Roger snorted once, twice, made a sound that might have been a word, might have been a cough, and resumed his sleep. I was near the edges of unconsciousness, myself, and probably would have slipped across the border had it not been for the gas mask, which I knew was waiting on the other side. What role it was going to play, I wasn't sure, only that it wouldn't be pleasant. The anticipation of encountering it in a place where I had even less control than I did in the waking world kept me on this side of sleep.

Three o'clock came and went. Roger stirred, but only to turn over. Fatigue and unease were waging a battle in me, fatigue pulling my eyelids down, unease pushing them back up. It wasn't going to be long until unease gave in and left me to my nightmares, which I was almost tired enough to accept as the cost of sleep. Then, in one of those intuitive leaps that are so sudden you're halfway to accepting them before you've thought about whether they make any sense in the first place, I realized that I had fixated on the mask because that was what Ted looked like, now. Not literally—it was more a kind of analogue for the changes death had made to him. He had become something like this—something other. Even as the more rational part of my brain was throwing up its hands and saying, "Wait a minute! How do you know this? Since when have you had any contact with Ted?" I was back in the land of the completely awake, chased from sleep by the conviction that this grotesque mask was like a shadow cast by Ted's true face.

However irrational—a-rational—that belief was, I was immediately and totally convinced of it. Dawn was paling the sky. I pushed myself out of bed and went downstairs, where I made a bitterly strong pot of coffee that I drank while watching an old John Wayne movie on PBS, *Red River*.

By the time the credits were rolling, the sun had crested the horizon and was shouting light into the house. From the kitchen, I heard a mug thunk on the counter, the coffee pot rattle. Roger must have come down while I was engrossed in the end of the movie and made straight for the caffeine. Upstairs, the bathroom door closed. I sat up on the couch. For the briefest of instants, that feeling I had in Belvedere House, that almost-sensation I thought I'd left in another state, flickered on like a candle teased into flame just long enough to be blown out. There was—it was different from what I experienced in the other house. There was no awareness of the Cape House as such. To be honest, there wasn't much of anything except—except in the kitchen, where I could sense—nothing, really—it was as if I could tell that someone had been there, but wasn't anymore. I stood, and walked into the dining room, expecting to see a steaming cup of coffee sitting beside the coffee maker.

The counter was bare. I heard Roger's feet padding down the stairs, and decided that this was the day we were going back to Martha's Vineyard. Obviously, the Cape House was not remote enough to let us escape the weirdness that had invaded our lives in Huguenot. We'd never made any good memories here, so there was nothing in place to keep the bad stuff out. The Vineyard, though—from one end to the other, the island was crowded with echoes of the four days we'd spent there seeing the sights, shopping the shops, sampling the restaurants. To my sleep-deprived, over-caffeinated brain, it seemed like a haven, one I was prepared to spend the rest of our vacation on if it offered me peace. By the time Roger reached the bottom of the stairs, my arguments were ready. He took some convincing. Coffee in hand, he heard my request that we drive to Wood's Hole this morning so that we could take the ferry to the Vineyard in time for lunch. When I was finished, he said, "Why go to Martha's Vineyard? We've barely arrived here."

"We have," I said, "but we're not going to be here for very long, and how often are we this close to the Vineyard?" I was talking too fast; I couldn't help myself.

"But we've just been, the other month."

"I know, and wasn't it wonderful?"

"Yes, but—"

"Then doesn't it make sense for us to go back there?" It didn't—not really. We had been recently enough, and there was plenty to do around us, for Roger to have an argument, but I didn't let him realize that. The debate wasn't done—hadn't gone much further than what I've told you—and I was hustling him back upstairs, telling him he had a half-hour to be showered, shaved, dressed, and ready to go. To speed things up, I would use the downstairs shower. All the way down Route 6, Roger questioned why we were doing this, not angrily, but in the tone of someone who finds himself carried along by forces beyond his control. I answered him with variations on the same response. We'd had such a great time on the Vineyard before, how could we not visit it when it was so near?

• • •

Once we'd arrived in Wood's Hole, Roger had accepted that, impromptu as it was, this was how we were going to be spending the rest of our day. Should the Vineyard feel more congenial, I wasn't sure how I was going to convince him to stay there tonight. I could try to delay us enough that we'd miss the last ferry, but that would be an uphill fight. Roger was one of those people who knows where you have to be when, and plots out the shortest route there and when you'll have to leave if you want to arrive ten minutes early. I could fake illness, but if I didn't time it properly that could land me on the ferry even sooner. I might have more luck telling him I wanted to spend the night there and that was that. Especially if the B&B we'd stayed in the last time had a vacancy, I might be able to pass it off as more romantic impulsiveness.

The B&B, when we came to it, was booked solid, but by then the only thing that could have kept me on that island was a major storm cutting off ferry service, and even then, I probably would have insisted we hire an intrepid fisherman to get us away from here as quickly as possible, whatever the risks. Needless to say, the day had not turned out as I'd planned.

• • •

While we were waiting to board the ferry, a heavy fog rolled in off the water. One minute, Roger and I were gazing out over the harbor; the next, it was gone, whited out. Daytime fog is strange, different from the fog you encounter at night. Maybe it's the conditioning of hundreds of horror movies, but nighttime fog is inherently creepy. It makes what you see even darker, more threatening, and of course it's the perfect substance to write all your fears onto. But—because of those same movies—it's like a special effect, you know? You half-expect your headlights to pick out a massive vat of dry-ice steaming off to one side of the road. Daytime fog is grayer than the nighttime stuff; although I guess that's because of the time it's out. It does the same thing: fades what's near, obscures what's far, but to a different effect. Daytime fog turns what's around you into a giant stage set, setting off what you can see as so many props, reducing the rest to folds of gray backdrop. Standing in this kind of fog—especially when it's as thick as this stuff was; I swear, this may have been the thickest fog I've ever been in—I always feel like I'm seeing through to how the world really is, although I'm not sure what that state is. All the world's a stage? Sort of, but not really.

The fog filled the distance to the Vineyard. We were out of sight of the mainland while we were still in the harbor, and we didn't see the island until we were docking at it. In between, we hardly seemed to be going anywhere. If you paid attention, you could feel the ship moving up and down on the water; if you stood outside, a strong wind fluttered your hair and tugged at your clothes; if you looked over the side, you saw the sea foaming away from the hull—but it all seemed curiously static. Gulls came and went out of the fog, as if pieces of it had broken off, swooping in to keep pace with the ferry, then veering away. A few passengers stood at the rail and threw food to them. Our previous trip, the day had been overcast and dim but clear. We'd watched the mainland sink into the ocean behind, the Vineyard rise from the water ahead. Roger and I had sat on deck, squinting out across the pewter waves at the various boats sharing the ocean with us, sailboats with their sails up and full of wind, speedboats skipping over the waves, trawlers chugging out to their fishing grounds. Now, we sat in the galley, nursing cups of coffee.

Despite the fog, I was relieved to be on our way somewhere

safe—relieved and excited, enough so that I could've done without any more coffee. I let Roger buy me a cup because there was no harm in being sure, and because it gave him something to do. Since we'd climbed the ramp up to the ferry, he hadn't spoken. I asked him what was on his mind, he said, "Nothing," and I couldn't decide if nothing meant nothing, or something masquerading as nothing.

When the captain announced that we'd be docking shortly, Roger and I abandoned our table and returned to the deck, where we stood straining to see anything. Through the soles of my shoes, I felt the ferry slowing, even as I heard its engine changing pitch. There were dark shapes to the side—poles, pilings, the pier. With a last lurch that had me grabbing for the rail, the ferry came to a halt and we were at Martha's Vineyard. The fog was heavier here. Crossing the gangplank to the pier, I couldn't see the water slapping the pilings below, while the pier itself dissolved into grayness a short distance ahead of us. I had been sure I'd have no trouble finding my way around the island once we arrived—on our last trip, I'd had the lay of the land by the end of our first day there, and I could still visualize the Vineyard's towns and roads and how they intersected. But the fog confused everything.

You know how it is in dense fog. You can't see any landmarks, all the distances are off—longer or shorter than they should be. The end of the pier seemed to take forever to reach. For a moment, I was afraid I was leading us in the wrong direction. When we reached the road and found a bus letting out passengers, we hurried on board without asking the driver his destination. I hoped it was Oak Bluffs, which was where we'd spent most of our previous visit and which is the next town over from where the ferry docks. Even if the bus was headed in the opposite direction, I didn't care. The road loops around the island. We'd get where we were going.

We lucked out. Oak Bluffs was the next stop. In town, the fog was slightly less dense. Looking up Main Street was like looking through sheets of gauze hung one behind the other. The closest shops and restaurants were reasonably clear; the ones a little farther away were washed out, like a painting someone had smeared a brush full of white across; the buildings beyond that were faint geometry. Roger wanted to have lunch. I wanted to ride the carousel.

Do you know about the carousel? I'm pretty sure it's on the national register of historic landmarks or something. We'd discovered it on our last trip. I'd read about it in a guidebook. I hadn't realized how elaborate it was, with all the hand-carved and -painted horses, and the arm they lower so you can grab for the brass ring as you swing by. I'd never done that before, never been on a carousel that had one of those long cartridges full of hand-sized rings. To be honest, I hadn't known they existed. I hadn't gotten the brass ring. There were these kids, teenagers, who could slide out four or five rings at a time. Video game reflexes, right? One of them got the ring almost every time, except for when a tourist who shouted in Spanish took it. I didn't care. I mean, I would have liked to find out what prize the brass ring brought you, but being on the carousel was enough. I'd dragged Roger to it at least once a day for the four days we were on the Vineyard, except for Saturday, when I went twice.

Yes, I am a big fan of carousels. My dad used to take me on them at every opportunity. Like every little girl, I'd wanted a pony, which there was no way for my parents to afford. Apparently, I was pretty insistent. Not only did I ask for a pony for my birthday, Christmas, and Easter—in the months between, I'd draw elaborate pictures of me and my pony-to-be that I'd magnet to the refrigerator. I invented lengthy adventures for the two of us that I'd spend all of dinner narrating to my parents. I asked my mom to make me a list of everything I'd have to do to insure Santa brought me a pony this December. (Which, may I say, she took full advantage of, year after year.) I was a girl on a mission. That my pony continuously failed to appear did nothing to diminish my resolve. For a while, I think my parents were worried about me. To compensate for my lack of a flesh-and-blood pony, they bought me all kinds of toy ones, from tiny porcelain horses to a stuffed animal that was practically big enough to ride. With the amount of money they spent on fake ponies, I'm sure they could have afforded a real one.

Anyway, the other thing Mom and Dad did was find carousels for me to ride and then let me stay on them till I was so dizzy I almost fell off my wooden horse. Mostly, this meant visiting all the county fairs within a two-hour radius of our house, but they also took me to theme parks like Great Adventure and the Great Escape. I have to give them credit. I can't imagine it was any fun for them to drive two, two and a half, sometimes three hours so I could ride a wooden horse into nausea. The benefits of being an only child, I guess. And you know that, as soon as my stomach had settled, I was ready for another thirty or forty circuits. I wouldn't say I outgrew my pony obsession so much as other things occupied my attention. Every now and again, if circumstances allowed, I would indulge it, go horseback riding, or spend the day at the races in Saratoga—or ride the carousel on Martha's Vineyard.

When we'd first walked into the big barnlike building that houses the carousel, I'd been delighted. Roger had been amused by my enthusiasm; then a bit befuddled by my insistence that we return the following day; then more than a little annoyed when I compared him accompanying me to this carousel to my father taking me to past ones. I thought it was funny; he could be prickly about things like that. So much for Freud.

Roger's experience with carousels had been limited. His parents hadn't taken him to any when he was a child. Joanne hadn't liked them—there's a shock; although, with that face, she'd have fit right in. Ted had wanted rides with more action, roller coasters, bumper cars—apparently, he and Roger had never missed a chance to drive undersized cars into one another. How's that for blatant symbolism? If Roger didn't fully appreciate the carousel, he was willing to stand holding my jacket as I rode a wooden horse up and down to the strains of calliope music. On the car ride down from Wellfleet earlier that morning, he had said, "I assume we will be returning to the carousel," and do you know, with everything that was going on, my fixation on the gas mask, I had forgotten about it?

• • •

The carousel was in full-spin as we entered the building, the horses climbing their poles; the riders holding those poles, or the reins if they trusted their balance, or nothing at all if they were trying to be daring; the air vibrating with the shrieks of teenagers and one small child protesting his parents' decision to take him on this scary contraption, all laid over a merry pipe-organ melody. Considering the weather, the line was shorter than I expected. When the carousel slowed to a stop and its riders dismounted, I was in the next group to be admitted. There was this one horse I was looking for, a white horse stretched out in full gallop, his head lowered, his mouth open as if panting with the effort of keeping ahead of everyone else. His mane was real hair—at least, it felt real when I ran my hand over it, which I did, the way you might greet a real horse. His tail was the same. The detail was remarkable. Each and every muscle, the edges of his hooves, even his teeth had been carved with a thoroughness that itself was a relic of a bygone era. His saddle and reins were purple and gold, freshly painted. As I swung myself up onto him, I pulled my hair out of the ponytail I'd threaded it into during the drive to Wood's Hole and shook it loose. I looked for Roger, who waved when he saw me searching for him. I waved back.

A few last-minute stragglers hurried through the gate and up onto the carousel. My horse was on the outer rim. Its companion on the inner rim was almost identical, a white horse in full gallop, except that it was tossing its head to its left, towards its mate. There was a girl seated on it, six or seven at a guess, wearing a jean-jacket and jeans, her hair long and red. She was like a snapshot of myself at that age. I'd had the same outfit, although my jacket had had a pair of large, cartoonish daisies sewn onto its shoulders. She was staring straight ahead, with this deadly serious expression on her face. I knew what she was thinking. When I used to sit waiting for the carousel to heave forward, I'd put myself behind the starting gate at one of the big races, the Kentucky Derby, the Belmont, the Preakness. I would gaze at the next horse on the carousel, trying to see beyond it, to a dirt track and a bandstand full of excited racing fans wearing their Sunday best. As the calliope started, I would strain to hear the starting buzzer. I never maintained the illusion for very long, but when it worked, I saw the gates burst open, felt my horse leap out onto the track, his hooves spraying dirt. That was what the girl beside me was after, so I didn't say hello to her, which I would have if she'd been snapping her gum, or playing with her horse's reins.

Instead, I contented myself with studying the carousel, survey-ing the other horses—none of which was as nice as mine; although there were a pair of roans ahead that were all right. The inside of the ride—that enormous cylinder that sits at the center of the carousel and houses the engine; I don't know what it's called, the hub?—it was decorated with mirrors. They were long, rectangular, framed with what was supposed to be gold. It was hard to see yourself in them— the building was full of pale light let in by the windows at the tops of its walls; to supplement that, whoever was in charge had switched on the lights; and the combined glare made the mirrors look as if they were full of fog. I could see the girl next to me in it, but I wasn't much more than a blur behind her. Behind me—

I couldn't say what I saw reflected there, because the moment I jerked my head around to look for its original, the carousel came to life. The pipe organ blared, the ring of horses surged forward. My nerves flared, and the carousel was at the edge of my skin, close—closer than Belvedere House usually was. I was so surprised, so caught off-guard, I had to grab my horse's mounting pole to keep from tumbling off. I glanced back across to the mirror, but all it showed now were the red-headed girl and me, reduced to Impressionist approximations by the light washing across the air. My awareness of the carousel stuttered, stopped. I righted myself, releasing the pole so I could take the reins. I had been startled by the shape looming over my reflection, but I was tired, very tired, and so prone to seeing things. There was no reason for my heart to be hammering, my palms slick on the reins. No doubt, all the coffee I'd drunk was making me jumpy. Here was the arm that dispensed the rings being lowered into place; I could make a try on this swing past. Standing in the stirrups, I angled to the left, raised my arm, and—

And almost fell off the horse as my balance deserted me. I was perched on my horse as it climbed its pole, hand outstretched to seize at the end of the arm. Then it was if the carousel sped up. I lurched back and to the left, the carousel's floor tilting up to meet me, the ring arm impossibly high. The hand I'd extended flailed. My right hand grabbed for the pole as the horse descended it. I caught the pole and hauled myself up to it. There was time for me to think, *What the hell was that?* then the carousel spun even faster. The ride was gaining speed, but I was feeling that gain ten times as much as I should. I had all I could do to hold on to the pole and keep from flying off into space. I was the only one experiencing this. To my right, the red-haired girl crouched forward on her horse, her gaze never wavering from the fantasy unfolding before her. In front of and behind us, other riders laughed and mugged for companions' cameras and took rings from the arm. To my left, the interior of the carousel hall and its contents had become a luminous smear. The calliope music piped far away, as if it were playing from the next building over. Beneath me, I heard a steady snickering, as some part of the ride's undercarriage dragged around the floor. The ring arm sped past. Caught by the wind of the carousel's spin, my hair streamed out behind me. I stole a glance to my rear, to be sure no one was there. That no one was wasn't reassuring. I was sure I had just missed someone standing there, holding his ruined fingers up to the ends of my hair. Ted? Who else? I wanted to look again, but that first glance had brought the gallon of coffee I'd drunk churning to the back of my throat, and I had a good idea what a second look would cause. So I closed my eyes as the ring arm sped past for the who-knew-how-many-eth time and tried not to feel fingers fluttering the air behind me. *Panic attack*, I thought, *you must be having a panic attack*. I concentrated on trying to bring my heart, straining in my chest as if it were trying to tear itself free, down to mere heart attack level. *Calm*, I told myself, *breathe*. I opened my eyes. The red-haired girl's hair rode the wind like a banner. The ring arm sped past. Beneath me, the carousel snickered around its circuit. Everything beyond the carousel was a pale smudge. *Calm*, I thought. *Breathe*.

I looked at the red-haired girl, who had yet to break her stare. Whatever scenario she was racing through, she was maintaining the illusion much longer than I'd ever been able to. With her hair blown back by the wind, I could see the earring clinging to her left ear, a silver horse, standing with its head down, grazing. It wasn't big, and it looked like a clip-on, which was strange. These days, it seems like most girls have their ears pierced when they're about three days old. At the sight of that earring, I felt a stab of nostalgia so sharp it cut through my nausea and panic, for my own pair of silver horse earrings. They had been a present from Grandma for my First Communion. They were clip-on, slightly too big for my ears, but I put them on the moment I realized what they were, discarding the gold crosses my parents had given me earlier at the breakfast table. These horses had been galloping, their manes and tails rippling, their hooves close together as they drew their legs in. Until my ears were pierced, those earrings had been my favorite. I kept them at the top of my jewelry box, in their own drawer, and polished them every time I wore them. After my ears were pierced, I tried to have the horse earrings converted, but the jeweler botched the job. The right one fell out the first time I wore them, to the mall with my friends, and despite my dad's best efforts, it was lost.

Pipe organs thundered, I jumped, and everything was normal again, the calliope, the inside of the building, the carousel—which was slowing, as the ride wound down. The ring arm swept past, and I reached up and took the ring from the end of it. It was plain, gray, oddly reassuring. On impulse, I leaned over to the red-haired girl and held it out to her. "Would you like this?"

Eyes full of annoyance, she said, "What for?" packing her question with all the scorn seven years old could muster.

Face already reddening, I shrugged. "I don't know." My hand wavered, withdrew.

Rolling her eyes, the girl blew her hair through pursed lips. The gesture surprised me. Not because I didn't understand it—I did. It compressed about half a dozen meanings into itself, including, "I am not a baby," and, "You are an adult and therefore incapable of doing anything right." What startled me was that this had been my gesture, the one I took pride in having invented, developed, and perfected. For a moment, I almost said, "Who taught you that?" but I caught myself before my mouth was more than half-open. No doubt, the roll-of-the-eyes and weary sigh had been combined long before hours of practice brought me to them. No doubt, kids would be employing them when people were living on Mars. "Sorry," I said to the girl, who was already dismounting her horse as the carousel eased to a stop. She didn't reply, didn't even spare me a second glance as she leapt off the carousel and joined the crowd exiting the ride.

I hurried to catch up. Whatever I'd just been through sent a thrill of vertigo through me as I stepped down. I staggered and would have fallen, but an old woman caught my arm. "Steady," she said.

"Thanks," I said, bracing myself against her. "All that motion. I guess it got to me."

"It does, honey," she said. "It does at that."

The exit to the carousel lets you circle around to join the line for another spin, or continue out of the building. Roger was waiting for me, which meant one time on the horse was going to have to be enough for me—as you can guess, not a problem. Hanging at the exit was a large plastic bucket with "RINGS" stenciled on it. As you passed, you dropped your losing ring into it. You know, I still don't know what prize the bronze ring gets you. I considered slipping my plain gray ring into my purse. I had kept the last ring I'd taken during our previous visit, as a souvenir—but I didn't want or need a reminder of this particular ride. I held the ring over the bucket and let it fall.

A small hand caught it. I looked up in time to see the back of the red-haired girl's denim jacket as she fled the building with her prize.

A man bumped into me from behind. I apologized and moved to join Roger. "What was that about?" he asked, nodding after the girl.

"I have no idea," I said. "I offered her the ring on the carousel and she didn't want it."

"Strange are the ways of children."

• • •

We walked out into the fog. Roger wanted lunch, and despite the fact that the word alone made my stomach squeeze, I agreed. We made our way up Main Street to the Oak Bluffs Bistro—basically, a diner trying to pass itself off as more upmarket than its vinyl-seated booths and fake-wood tabletops confessed. Its plastic-coated menu did what it could to bolster the illusion, christening generic diner fare with idiosyncratic names intended to convince you that you were ordering something more exciting than the cheeseburger platter Roger selected, or my scrambled eggs and toast. When the waiter had left with our order, Roger said, "So. Was the carousel all that you remembered?"

I wanted to say, "All that, and a lot more besides." Instead, I asked, "Couldn't you tell?"

"No," Roger said. "I fear I was distracted."

"What do you mean?"

"Just as the ride was beginning, I heard someone call my name, twice. Not 'Roger,' but 'Roger Croydon,' so I assumed it was someone I knew. After all, how many Roger Croydons can there be? More than one, apparently, for I spent the next few minutes searching through the crowd for a familiar face, and found none. I was certain whoever had called to me was standing across the room. The voice sounded rather distant. In a space of that size, however, with everyone talking and the carousel's music playing, who can say for sure? The consequence was, I was occupied for the length of your ride. I did see you stumble on the way off, but that young woman caught you."

"Young woman? She looked pretty old to me."

"Why, she couldn't have been more than twenty, twenty-one."

"Roger," I said, "she had a good ten years on you, minimum."

"Which qualifies her as very old, I am pleased to note. I assure you, my dear, she was a few years younger than you, which, I believe, makes her practically a child."

"The voice you heard," I said, "did it sound familiar?"

"Not particularly," Roger said, "although, as I've said, the acoustics of that building distort everything."

"Could you tell if it was male or female? Young or old?"

Roger smiled. "Why all this interest in crossed wires?"

"Could you?" My heart was racing again.

He shook his head. "If pressed, I might say that the voice was that of a young man, but I would in no way stand by that answer. It could as easily have been an old man, a young woman, an old woman. Why?"

"But you think it sounded like a young man?"

"Yes."

"And you didn't recognize it?"

"Yes, yes, a thousand times yes," Roger said, his exasperation only partially mock. "Is this some type of joke I'm supposed to have gotten by now?"

"It's not a joke," I said. "I don't know what—"

"Ted," Roger said, his eyes widening. "Oh my dear Lord, you think that was Ted calling to me. Why? Why were you asking if I saw you on the carousel? What happened there? Tell me," he said, his voice strident.

"Calm down," I said. "I'll tell you about the carousel, just calm down."

Our waiter had returned with Roger's Coke and my tea with lemon. He placed Roger's glass in front of him, fumbled with my cup and saucer. I reached up to help him, glancing at his face as I did. The next instant, I was on the other side of the booth, hands pressed over my eyes, screaming at the top of my lungs. Far away—I had to get as far away from him as I could. I scrambled on the seat, trying to push myself further into the corner. One of my feet slipped, connected with the waiter's knee. I heard him shout, the clatter and crash of the tray, tea-cup, saucer, spoon, and teapot as they slipped from his hands onto the table and floor. A wave of boiling water rolled off the table onto my leg, flaring fireworks of agony along it. "Veronica!" Roger said, reaching across the table for my hands. I slapped at him furiously, keeping my eyes squeezed shut. Something touched my leg. I kicked at it, hit nothing. All the while, I kept screaming, screaming my throat raw. Roger struggled to grab my shoulders, wrists, hands, anything, saying, "Veronica!" over and over, as if my name were some kind of magic charm. I fought him as if he were the devil himself, slapping and scratching and punching as I tried to compress myself into the smallest space possible.

You've probably guessed I saw Ted. You can understand how confronting my dead stepson would have been frightening, even terrifying—how I would have jumped, shrieked, tried to get away from him—but you can't understand the intensity of my reaction, the hysteria. You've also figured out that, whatever I saw, Roger didn't. When I threw myself screaming to the other side of my seat, he immediately looked at the waiter. All he saw was a skinny seventeen-year-old whose olive skin was a roadmap of acne. I saw Ted, yes, as he had been and as he'd become. It happened so fast I want to use one of those cliché phrases like "in the blink of an eye," except even that seems too long. In film—in a movie reel, there are—what?—twenty-two frames a second? Something like that. Well, this happened in the space of maybe three frames.

Imagine the camera is focused on me as I lift my eyes to the waiter. Now freeze the film as you see what I see. The first frame shows Ted's face above the waiter's black t-shirt. It looks pretty much the same as it did the one and only time I met him, the way it does in the portraits hung around Belvedere House. The long, horsey features, the scar across the bridge of the nose, the eyelids slightly lowered. The skin is tanned, but gray underneath. It's an expressionless face: I want to say it's the face of a corpse; only, somehow, it's blanker—an active, as opposed to a passive, nothing written on it. Bad enough, you would think.

Advance a frame. That empty face has been replaced by—by something I can't describe. You remember I said the gas mask was an analogue for what Ted looked like now? Here was the original staring at me. Can you imagine something so—alien, so terrible, that the briefest glance at it overloads your brain? You can't, can you, because whatever you can visualize, you can find some way to accommodate, to deal with it. What I saw in that single frame was so far removed from my frame of reference that I can't completely remember it—even at the time, I couldn't see all of it, because I didn't understand what I was looking at. The eyes—the eyes were round and flat—oversized—like a pair of lenses that the skin around had been stretched to hold. They might have been glass. Roger and I were reflected in them. There were no lids. I saw that, too. The eyes were trapped open. The skin around them was—it was—I don't know—I think braided is the word I want.

No, that isn't right. It was more—it was moving, okay? Not all of it, but parts, as if it were crawling over itself. The color—it was pale, like white with a blue light playing over it. There was black, too—black underneath the pale. That's the best I can do. The rest—the rest was worse, so bad it's starting to warp the frame showing it. You can see its center bubbling and thinning, as if someone were holding a match underneath it. Whatever the frame showed has already been distorted beyond recognition.

Flip ahead a frame, and you have a picture that looks as if it's been triple-exposed. There's the waiter's face, then there's Ted's human face, while behind the two of them, Ted's other face shows just enough of itself to freeze your blood. Roll forward one more frame, and you're back to the waiter's attempt to hide his boredom with his job. Too late, though: the damage has been done, my rational mind has blinked off, every last one of its fuses blown by whatever it was that burned a hole in that second frame. Older reflexes, the kind that would have sent you scrambling away from the saber-toothed tiger, took over, putting as much space as possible between me and the horror that had shown itself. Believe me, if we hadn't been seated at a booth—if we'd been at a table or the counter—I would have been out of that restaurant and halfway to the dock before the waiter had finished setting my tea on the table.

As it was, though, we were in a booth, and escape was impossible. Roger continued to try to catch hold of me until, fed up with being slapped and punched, he seized his glass of Coke and dashed its contents into my still-screaming face. Cold soda and ice cubes splashed my hands, face, neck. Coke sloshed in my mouth and I coughed. Ice cubes slipped under the neck of my blouse and ran freezing down my back. While I was coughing, Roger reached over to the booth behind us, grabbed the water glasses of the couple sitting there, and threw them over me, as well. Ice cubes rained like hail. Rusty-tasting water washed the Coke out of my mouth. For the second time that day, I came back to myself, though not in time to prevent Roger tossing a last glass of water at me. My hair and clothes dripping, my throat ragged, I opened my eyes to a chaotic scene. The booth's table and seats were wet, dotted with ice cubes sliding slowly towards the table's edge to join their fellows in the massive puddle on the floor. Plastic cups rolled on the table, clicking against the broken remains of my teacup and saucer. Roger stood at the end of my seat, empty cup in hand, watching me with one eye, searching for more cups of water with the other. Of course everyone in the diner was looking at us—at me, some with expressions of concern, a few with amusement or contempt, most with blunt curiosity. A youngish man with a beard and glasses had left wherever he was sitting to offer his assistance. He was about three feet behind Roger. The waiter was nowhere to be found; having limped off, I presume, to ice the leg I'd kicked. I held up a hand to Roger, saying, "Okay, okay. It's all right. It's all right."

Except it wasn't okay; it wasn't all right. It was anything but. Still holding my hand up, I leaned forward. Roger took my hand and helped me out of the booth. Ice cubes fell from me in droves, tinkling on the floor, as I stood. The rest of the diner continued watching me, waiting to see how whatever drama they'd found themselves unexpected spectators to was going to conclude. My nerves were jumping—my whole body was. What I'd undergone on the carousel had been disorienting. This had been pure shock, as if all of me, body, mind, and soul, had suffered a violent blow. Standing beside Roger as he asked me what had happened, I started shivering uncontrollably. Roger said, "Poor dear. All that cold water," and put his arm around me, drawing me to his warm—and dry—chest. Maybe the gallon of ice water that had been poured on me did have something to do with me shaking, but I doubt it. From the corner of my eye, I could see a man approaching, his belly straining his black t-shirt, his name tag declaring his rank assistant manager. I had no desire to stand there explaining the last five minutes to him. In the distance, I heard a siren, and knew that either the police or EMTs—or both—would be walking through the front door imminently. I had even less desire to deal with them; although my left leg was throbbing where the hot water had spilled on it. Slipping out from under Roger's arm, I said, "I can't do this," and fled the restaurant, pushing past the startled assistant manager on my way to the door.

* * *

I never asked Roger how he explained my screaming and kicking to that man, or to the police and/or EMTs—assuming they showed up, which I didn't ask him about, either. Walking rapidly, I went right out of the diner and up the street. Through the fog, I saw a clothes store three storefronts along. I turned in at it. The salesgirl reading the magazine behind the counter was college-age. When she saw me standing in the doorway, soaked and still shivering, she started, then left her place and hurried over to me. She was wearing a saffron pant-suit; her hair was piled on top of her head. "Oh my God," she said, "what happened to you?"

"Kids," I said. "A couple of kids ran into me—spilled their drinks all over me."

"And you need something to change into."

I nodded.

"No problem." She led me to a rack of blouses, which she sorted through until she came up with a white linen thing she held up for my inspection. "How's this?"

The part of my mind that decided such matters was still shorted out. The blouse was plain. I said, "Fine."

"Good." Holding the blouse, the salesgirl walked across the store to a rack of skirts. With her free hand, she selected a denim skirt. "What do you think?"

"Great."

"Great," she said. "There are changing rooms at the back of the store—but maybe you'd like to use the bathroom first, to clean up?"

"Yes."

"We're really not supposed to do this," the girl said, "my manager would flip if she ever found out, but look at you," she ran her gaze up and down me, and for the first time saw my leg, which already looked pretty bad. The skin was bright red and angry; clear blisters had raised themselves from it. Her eyes widened and she said, "Oh my God. Your leg."

"Yes," I said. "Coffee—one of the kids was carrying a cup of hot coffee."

The salesgirl's brows lowered. How many kids run around with cups of hot coffee? She said, "Do you need a doctor? Because I can—"

"I don't need a doctor," I said, forcing a smile onto my face. "It looks worse than it is."

"Well, aloe cream, then. There's a drugstore next door. Once you're finished in here, you should stop in there and get a bottle of aloe cream. I had a wicked sunburn last year, and my boyfriend used that stuff on it, and it completely cooled it down."

"Thanks. I will."

"Aloe cream. It's green, and comes in a clear plastic bottle."

"Green," I said.

"Uh huh." She nodded.

"Is the bathroom—"

"Oh my God, right," she said, "I'm so sorry. This way."

I followed her through a door at the store's rear, down a short corridor. "Thanks," I said when we reached the bathroom.

"Do you want to take the clothes in with you, and try them on in here?" the salesgirl asked. "I'm really not supposed to do this, either, but, in for a penny, in for a pound, right?"

"That's right," I said, taking the blouse and skirt from her. I had no idea what she was talking about. "I'll be a couple of minutes."

With the bathroom door closed and locked, I stood staring at the wall. The new clothes were in my hands, but trying them on seemed an impossibly elaborate task. I could see myself in the small mirror hung above the sink, hair wet and bedraggled, makeup smeared, skin drawn taut and pale. I looked like I'd seen a ghost, all right. *One step at a time*, I told myself, and hung the new clothes on the doorknob. I stripped off the wet clothes, and dried myself with about half the roll of paper towel mounted beside the sink. When I was reasonably dry, I washed my face and cleaned the ruined makeup off it. My hair was still damp, and sticky in places from the Coke, but the rest of me was dry and clean enough for me to reach for the new clothes.

They fit, which, considering the girl hadn't asked me my size, was pretty impressive. Or, it should have been. Buttoning the blouse, sliding the zipper up the side of the skirt, it was as if I were watching someone else performing these actions. I recognized that both blouse and skirt were well-made and only slightly overpriced, but this registered with me in the same way as the white walls of the bathroom, as one more thing to notice.

What was occupying my thoughts was keeping myself together, which was becoming more difficult with each passing moment. When I'd run out of the diner, I'd been driven and guided by instinct more than the consciousness Roger had splashed back into existence. That consciousness was a patchwork affair, a jury-rigged jumble of memory and idea barely up to the challenge of answering the salesgirl's questions, let alone of dealing in any way, shape, or form with what I'd seen. Really, I was doing what I could not to recall that face, because I had no doubt the mere memory of it would be more than sufficient to reduce my improvised self to rubble. Did I mention that I hadn't looked directly at the salesgirl once? I was terrified that I'd see Ted's face—his faces—staring back at me from above her jacket. I'm sure she took it as one more piece of the strangeness that was me.

There was a knock on the door. The salesgirl's muffled voice called, "Is everything okay in there?" I glanced at my watch. I couldn't say for sure, but I thought I'd been in that bathroom for something like half an hour. I unlocked the door and, eyes lowered, said, "Sorry. It took me a while to clean up."

"No problem," the girl said. "What do you think?"

I almost asked, "About what?" before I understood she was talking about the clothes. "I'm not sure," I said. I pointed to the mirror over the sink. "That's the only mirror."

"Oh, sure, right," she said. "Come back out front." I picked up my wet clothes and hurried after her. She stopped beside a full-length mirror and gestured to it. "Here you go."

As if my behavior hadn't been odd enough, when I stepped in front of the mirror, I kept my gaze to one side. I was afraid of seeing something other than myself staring back at me. I don't know why I even bothered. The salesgirl couldn't help but notice, but she spared me any questions. I guess she was used to dealing with eccentricity. I waited what seemed a reasonable time, then said, "This'll do," which was about the truest thing I could say.

"Are you sure," she asked, "because if you're not—"

"It's fine," I said, "honestly."

Once I'd paid for the new clothes and placed my old ones in a plastic bag, I ducked out of that store and into the drugstore next to it, where I picked up some aloe cream for my leg, as well as a Martha's Vineyard baseball cap and a pair of cheap sunglasses. Suitably disguised—I hoped—I left the drugstore at a stroll, trying to pretend I wasn't that woman who'd been screaming her head off a few doors down. I had no idea where Roger was: if he was still in the diner, trying to account for my actions and settle the damages; or if he had finished there and was searching for me. If all else failed, we would meet at the dock, but I didn't spend much time worrying over it.

Movement was my concern, not staying anywhere long enough to allow any further weirdness to envelop me. Although doing so aggravated my leg to no end, I walked up the street. I almost welcomed the pain as a distraction. Eyes on the sidewalk, I concentrated on avoiding seeing more than the feet and legs of the people I passed.

Once, the fog unveiled a pair of army boots below green camouflage pants, and in my panic, I looked up—but the man I saw wasn't Ted. I hurried past him.

Inside, I was trying to keep on the move, as well, concentrating on not remembering what had held me in its gaze in the diner, those glass eyes torturing the skin around them. I was close to some great expression of emotion—screaming, crying, even laughing. Holding back that one memory set a host of others free, and I walked out of the street into memory—out of one memory, into another—

—*The tile of the hospital room floor is cold on my cheek; I look up at Roger's hospital bed, looming mountainously high above me; another round of cramps grabs me like a great hand squeezing my insides out; warm blood that smells like pennies spills down my thighs*—

—*I enter Belvedere House's living room, which smells faintly of the lemon cleaner Dr. Sullivan and her family used in their final cleanup; the blinds are drawn, and glow white with the early afternoon sun; my arms, legs, neck—my whole body prickles, as if I've walked through an enormous cobweb—only I can feel the strands running off in all directions*—

—*Roger's face is a map of purple bruises; dried blood crusts the corners of his mouth; the faint odor of pepper spray clings to him; through swollen lips, he says, "I cast you from me"; spittle flecks his unshaven chin as he says, "May you not escape your failure"; each word bursts against my eardrums like thunder*—

—*His thumb and forefinger dimpling as they close on the lead soldier, Roger places it inside the space bordered by plastic buildings, third in line, just outside the circumference of the red chalk circle flaking on the tabletop; the light overhead and the light through the window send two tiny shadows out from the figure's base; the plastic pungence of bubblewrap stings my nostrils; Roger's hand hovers over the soldier; he exhales*—

—*The kettle whistles, I fill the white mug, watching the boiling water darken as the odor of instant coffee lifts into the air; the red numbers of the kitchen's clock radio read 4:15; the black coffee singes my lips as I stare out the apartment window into the early-morning dark where Roger walks*—

—*Grandma looks at me over her half-glasses and says, "Poor bunny; my poor, poor bunny. We must stay awake and see evil done just a little longer"; her voice sounds as if it is full of dirt, and she reeks of pine trees*—

I shook my head—my grandmother had never said that to me. Ahead, the fog curled around a street sign. I turned right and followed the new street as shops gave way to houses. First a couple of contemporary places, studies in bland luxury, then a row of pastel A-frames, their eaves, doors, and shutters carved into lacy patterns like the icing on a cake. When the street I was on joined another, I saw more A-frames vanishing into the fog in all directions. I had found the gingerbread houses.

• • •

Do you know them? There are literally hundreds of houses that look like something from a children's story, all painted bright, cheery colors, all sporting intricate carving that does make them resemble enormous confections. Prior to our last trip here, I'd never heard of them. Roger had known about them, but not seen them. When the two of us found them—it was after my first ride on the carousel, and seeing house after house with its ornate decoration gave me the momentary illusion I'd fallen into one of the books I'd reread so obsessively as a girl, *Little Women*, or *The Wizard of Oz*. I had been delighted, Roger less so—he'd said, "It all seems so...New England Yankee," which I guess it was.

Now, wrapped in fog, the houses were less cheerful. I passed one whose front garden was full of white roses, their heads bobbing ever so slightly in a breeze I couldn't feel. I passed another whose front porch displayed a couple of wicker chairs, one of which held what I thought was an oversized burlap sack until it said, "Hello," and resolved itself into an old woman. I passed a house whose shutters were closed, its paint flaking off in large patches, its front yard bare. One after another, the houses appeared, variations on an architectural theme. Where previously the repetition had charmed me, today it seemed decadent, obsessive.

The street I was walking t-junctioned the road around the park where the old Methodist revivals had been held. I don't know the history in any depth—really, all I can tell you is that, during the latter half of the nineteenth century, this part of the island had been the site of Methodist revivals, some of them attended by thousands. At what I assume was the height of the revival craze, the Methodists had built this gigantic metal pavilion in the park across from me. It's enormous—I'm talking circus big top, here; it seats something like five hundred people—with open sides and stained-glass windows set high up in it. Even with the fog, I could see it lifting itself in the near distance, a huge presence, which, for reasons I didn't understand, had been painted black. It's like some kind of avant-garde cathedral. The gingerbread houses sprung up on the ground surrounding the site. I'm not sure what connection, if any, there was between the two. Probably none.

I crossed into the park. The ground dips in the middle, which makes the pavilion appear even taller as you approach. I was alone—although the fog hung pretty dense in and among the grass and trees—and when I climbed the far slope to the pavilion and looked into it, I saw that it was empty. The fog had found its way inside the metal tent, pooling at various points throughout. Even so, it was less thick in there. I could see rows of seats fanning up and out from the altar, amphitheater-style.

My leg felt as if someone had poured gasoline on it and added a match. I needed to stop walking, if only for ten minutes, and get the aloe cream on. Inside the tent, I'd at least be able to see anything coming towards me. The fire in my leg raging, I walked into the pavilion and all the way along one of the aisles to the altar. Once I was seated, I retrieved the bottle of aloe. When I slid my skirt up, I saw that the skin on top of my leg was crimson, crowded with blisters that oozed clear fluid. I squeezed a green stream of the aloe up and down the burn, gently spreading it across the angry skin, wincing and catching my breath as new agony bit my nerves. I followed that coat of aloe with a second one, by which time the first was starting to work, cooling my leg. Talk about blessed relief. When you're hurt like that, your whole body contracts around the wound. As the cream dulled the pain, it was as if all of me relaxed away from it. I wouldn't have minded a couple of gin and tonics to help the process along, but I was reasonably sure a Methodist tent was the last place you'd find a bar. Finished tending my leg, I replaced the bottle of aloe in its bag, wiping my hand clean on the blouse in there. I left my skirt up, letting cool air flow over it.

I'm not sure how much of my decision to enter and then to remain in the pavilion owed itself to the place's religious past. Yes, it had been site of prayer services, but I had no idea if it still was. Had I read that it was used for more secular activities these days, for concerts, lectures, readings? Maybe. I didn't know if Methodists con-secrated these kinds of places, the way Catholics do when they build a church. I didn't know if such a thing would make the least difference to Ted—because while I was at or near the center of a continuing supernatural experience, it wasn't the supernatural you heard about at Sunday mass. To be honest—this is going to sound strange—what drew me to the pavilion and kept me there was that it reminded me of Belvedere House. Yes, the very place I'd been trying to escape. The resemblance was hard to pin down. Mostly, it lay in the way the two buildings gave this profound feeling of occupying space. Sitting on the altar, I felt—not safer, no, not protected—I felt calm, as if I didn't have to keep struggling so hard to keep myself functioning—as if I could catch my breath.

Wispy patches of fog congregated in the aisles, hovered over seats, drifted across the floor in front of me. Small clouds meandered around the inside of the roof, tinted by the weak light pushing through the stained-glass windows up there. The clouds almost seemed to circle the roof, which reminded me of the carousel I'd been on an hour ago. An hour. God, it might have been a month. The memory of the carousel brought with it the sensation of the ride spinning ever faster as I tried to maintain my seat on my horse. I put my hands out to either side of me to steady myself. Obviously, what I'd been through on the carousel was connected to the diner and therefore to everything else. In coming to the Vineyard, we—I hadn't gotten away from anything. In the space of sixty minutes, the island had gone from a haven to something approaching a trap. The feeling I'd had ever since this weirdness had erupted into our lives, the suspicion that there was more to it than Roger was letting on—that it was in some way sinister—had been confirmed. Ted was actively hostile, if not outright malevolent.

What I couldn't understand was, why me? Yes, I was the woman his father had left his mother for—I was sure that Ted wouldn't have seen that their marriage had been over for years before I came on the scene—but that was Roger's decision, not mine. He'd had the fight with Roger at the apartment, but that was hardly my fault. I'd been the one who pleaded the two of them out of anything more than a stern lecture by the judge. I'd called on September 11 to find out if Ted was okay. He was the one who'd hung up on me. Since his death, I'd put Roger's photos of Ted throughout the house. I'd left Ted's childhood room alone. I was not the one to blame, here. You couldn't say that Roger had been unaffected by Ted's death—not if you'd seen his office; not if you'd trailed around the house after him in the wee small hours of the morning—but everything he'd underwent had flowed from the inside out, from the guilt and regret choking his psyche. What I had been through came the opposite route, from the outside in, and it made no sense.

Even if I'd misinterpreted Ted's actions, which I was sure I hadn't but which was possible, he was dangerous. Another look at his face—his true face, which I was still not-remembering—a second glimpse might be more than my mind could recover from. I had thought that distance was the answer, that in leaving Belvedere House behind, we'd leave Ted with it. When I'm wrong, I'm wrong. Whatever role the house had played in all of this, it was glaringly obvious that Ted wasn't tied to it. Almost the opposite—the farther away from it we went, the more dramatic his actions became. I could elect to follow Roger's lead, let Ted complete whatever plan he'd set in motion—but there was enough wrong with that course of action for me not to consider it seriously. I was pretty sure that Ted's plan was not focused on sentimental reconciliation. Given the amount of attention I'd received already, there seemed a distinct possibility that I was intended to suffer. Again, I could be mistaken. Roger might be Ted's intended target, but so far I was the one taking the fire, and there was a real possibility of me winding up as collateral damage.

Talking about all of this in this way—it makes it sound as if I were sitting there on the altar, calmly weighing my options, which was anything but the case. It was more tides—tidal waves of emotion rising and falling within me. Resentment gave way to confusion, which gave way to fear. If we couldn't escape Ted, then we had no choice but to return to Huguenot and deal with him. We—I, because I knew Roger wouldn't take part in anything that might jeopardize his fantasy. And dealing with Ted, how was I going to do that? Hire an exorcist? I didn't think you could hire one—it's not as if they advertise in the yellow pages—and didn't they deal with demons? It was my impression that the Church tried to be less Medieval about these sorts of things, and any request for an exorcism on my part was more likely to be met with a recommendation for counseling. I didn't think I'd have any more luck with other denominations. The ones that would take you seriously would be the same ones you wouldn't have any faith in. You could picture some variety of the televangelist stomping through Belvedere House in his powder-blue suit, one hand clutching

his Bible, the other raised, his face red and sweating as he called out
for the unclean spirit to depart in the name of Jesus, which he would
pronounce, "Jeeeee—zuss," as if it were the correct answer to the big
question at the end of a game show. No thank you. I would prefer
not to.

That left trying to address the root cause of the problem, namely,
Roger's curse. It was like some kind of Freudian nightmare, the
all-powerful father condemns the rebellious son and his words are
so powerful they follow the son into the afterlife. There's this Kafka
story—the title slips my mind, but it's about a young man whose
father tells him what a failure he is and passes a death-sentence on
him, so the son goes and drowns himself in the river. We seemed to be
dealing with the Hollywood version of that story, suitably expanded
and adapted for an American audience. I still had trouble with the
idea that a few words spoken in anger could have such profound consequences, so physical—metaphysical an effect. I mean, words don't
mean anything, isn't that what we believe these days? They're just a
self-contained, self-referential sign-system. You're a writer, maybe you
think differently, but I doubt you believe language has magic power.

There was more fog inside the pavilion. It rolled down the stairs,
flowed in among the seats, pooled along the floor in front of the altar.
The interior of the tent was becoming less distinct. I heard the words
of the curse tumbling one after the other. If there was a secret to
understanding what was going on, it had to lie in the time between
when the cops had dragged Roger and Ted out into the early-morning
dark and when I'd seen them later that day.

I could picture Roger sitting in the holding cell at the Huguenot
police station. His eyes still burn from the pepper spray. He's given up
fighting the tears that wash down his face; although he continues to
wipe his running nose every few minutes with a wad of toilet paper. It's
been less than an hour since he and Ted were brought in, processed,
and locked across the holding area from one another—but enough
time has passed that he should have calmed down. He hasn't. His
heart still pounds as if the cell doors might spring open any moment
and set him and Ted loose for round two. With each breath he inhales,
pain stabs his right side. He knows Ted has bruised or broken ribs
there, but he's so high on adrenaline he doesn't care—his only concern
is that he did some damage of his own. If Ted broke two of his ribs, he
hopes he broke four of Ted's. His left hip and the left side of his back

feel as if a sledgehammer pounded them, a sharp surface pain laid over a deeper ache—pretty much his entire body feels as if someone's taken a meat tenderizer to it with great enthusiasm.

Roger doesn't care, which is only partially due to the adrenaline. Most of his lack of caring is due to anger. He is enveloped in it. He has been angry before—with Ted, especially. All those previous occasions, however, every last one of them, have been different. No matter how angry Roger has felt, he's always restrained himself, always been careful to release just enough to make his displeasure known, and contained the rest. He's bottled it, the way his father told him to when he was eight years old, as if his anger were some kind of volatile gas frothing inside a glass jug. If Roger's life were a house, then the rooms marked "TED" are full of shelves, and those shelves are crowded with glass bottles stoppered against their own contents. This time, however, at the very moment Roger was trying to contain his anger, when he attempted to close the door on Ted and his grandstanding, he failed. Ted forced the door open, stepped inside, and Roger, whose hand had been poised over the latest bottle's neck, threw the cork away.

Twenty years of anger rose up in Roger in a mushroom cloud. This was anger unlike any he'd known before, and by God did it feel good. What a relief, finally, to be able to surrender to it, not to have to pretend that it's all right, Ted had his reasons, no doubt he was at fault, too—his rage swept over and through him, annihilating everything in its path, spilling out the tips of his fingers, the top of his head. When he holds his hands up in front of him, he can almost see it flickering there, a white-hot flame that dances and leaps from his skin and does not consume it. The marvelous thing about this anger is that it doesn't go away. It doesn't subside and leave him feeling empty and ashamed. With two decades of fuel stacked up, it could burn for a long time, and with this newest offense—this showing up at the front door at three in the morning, heaping abuse not only on him, but on his wife—Ted's stepmother—calling her a slut—and then raising his hand to him, to his father, who never, never, *never* lifted his hand to deliver any of the blows his son so richly deserved, not once—with this outrage, the flame streaming from Roger might burn for as long as he has left to live.

• • •

It was so hot, I could feel it, across the distance of months and miles. I had imagined Roger's activities plenty of times in the past—it's something I'm pretty good at. Maybe that means I should be a writer, too. It's hard to convey how vivid all this was—how real. I'd pictured detailed scenes before, but however elaborate they'd been, however absorbed in them I'd become, they were still internal; I was still watching them with my mind's eye. This—it was as if I were standing in the cell with Roger. I could smell the pepper spray clinging to him, the dried sweat underneath it. I could smell the pungent industrial cleaner that had been used to scrub down the cell, the reek of urine beneath that. I could hear Roger's labored breathing, the scrape of his sneakers on the floor. His thoughts—it wasn't that I could hear them, but—I knew what was burning in his mind, as if I could read the words written on him. I wasn't all the way there with him—the altar was solid and cool beneath me—but this was not your garden-variety daydream.

• • •

Whatever self-satisfaction Roger feels in embracing his anger—and he luxuriates in it; he rolls around in it; he dives deep beneath its surface and surfaces grinning—it's not enough. After they were shut in their separate cells, he and Ted continued to hurl abuse at each other, but it was of the four-letter variety, too familiar to be more than a placeholder for their sentiments. This hadn't stopped either of them from stringing those curse words together in varied and even inventive combinations—until one of the police officers leaned his head in and told them that if the two of them didn't knock it off, he was going to pepper spray them again, which shut them up. Staring across the corridor at Ted, who's lying down on his cell's metal bunk, his back to Roger, Roger hears the echo of their insults and thinks that those aren't really curses. They're simply words we've been told are inappropriate, so that saying or hearing them gives a small charge. They don't carry any weight, those words, they don't do anything more than momentarily offend the sensibilities. Let's face it, when was the last time anyone was really and truly offended by someone swearing? Certainly Ted's stream of obscenities has rolled off Roger's back, as he assumes his torrent of abuse rolled off Ted's. None of it hurt Ted, and right now, that's what Roger wants more than anything. That is what his anger requires, for him to wound his son in such a way that Ted won't be able to shrug it off.

If he were stronger, Roger might be able to count on breaking Ted's jaw. That would teach him to show up at his father's door at three in the morning, shooting off his mouth. He knows he doesn't have the strength, though, which makes his anger burn all the hotter. Physically speaking, in whatever terms you want—strength, speed, skill—Ted has the edge, for which Roger has suffered the consequences. The way things stand now, he is the one who'll take away the scars of their meeting, and this is intolerable.

Which brings Roger back to the curse, to words with meaning. If there's one area where Roger's superiority to Ted remains unchallenged, it's words. He can put together a lethal sentence as quickly and efficiently as Ted strips, cleans, and assembles his M4. God knows there's enough raw material lying around for him to use—although he has to be careful. If he speaks for too long, Ted's eyes will glaze over and he'll have lost him; or Ted will start in with his own list of complaints; or he'll laugh and walk away. What Roger has in mind must be delivered economically and forcefully. He has to hit Ted hard and fast, has to drive the knife in deep, twist it, and leave Ted to extract it from his bloody gut.

Roger's words from his last sleepwalk sounded in my ears. "Words with meaning. Sharp. Razored. Barbed, tipped with slow-acting poison. That's what you need." The image I'd had of him as we drove up to the Cape, the picture of Roger as some kind of caveman carving a crude knife, returned with even greater detail. He'd use a sharpened rock to shape the piece of bone in his hand into sharpness, then something finer—a needle of some kind, maybe bone, as well—to scratch symbols, the same figures tattooed up and down his arms, across his face, into it. Not only is he going to hurt Ted physically, he's going to wound his spirit, his soul, whatever you want to call it.

When he's finished, when he's sure that those eight sentences, those one hundred twenty-three words, are enough, are sufficient, Roger recites them quietly, his eyes closed. He's testing his weapon. Those first four sentences, they're the stab, the sharp blow in just above the navel. Wait a moment, then the next four, which are the twisting, first to the right, then the left, leaning on the grip with each twist. He can see Ted's eyes widening with shock. He can feel the hot blood running out over his fingers. Impatient for the moment to come, he's tempted to utter his sentences—his curse—then and there, to have as much time as possible to enjoy the spectacle of Ted's agony. He opens his mouth, hesitates. He can hear people moving around on the other side of the door to the holding area. How would it look if he started to deliver his carefully crafted condemnation, only to have it interrupted by some crewcut moron telling him to keep it down? He'd be ridiculous, a laughing-stock, and that he cannot risk. The right moment will present itself, he thinks, be patient.

With as much devotion as any monk praying the rosary, Roger repeats the curse to himself. That white-hot flame pours from the tips of his fingers, the top of his head. He sits turning the knife over and over in his fiery hands, the fire hardening the weapon, making it shine. Dawn breaks, sending red-gold light through the holding area's small, high windows. The air glows, the way it does when the sun puts in its first appearance, and Roger's heart leaps in anticipation. As it does, he feels a pain—a new pain—burst in his chest and race out along his left arm. The words of the curse tumble from his mind, scattered by a new thought: heart attack. That's impossible, he thinks, and, as if in response, the pain sags.

Good, he thinks, retrieving the curse, and then the pain announces itself a second time. It's as if a cinderblock has slammed against his chest. He gasps as the suddenness, the intensity of the pain pushes the cell away from him. He concentrates on the words, the one hundred twenty-three words, the eight sentences. While his left arm throbs and his chest presses in, Roger deliberately recites the curse, stubbornly ignoring the voice in his head telling him to call for help, for God's sake, there's a cop outside the door, the fire station is next door, they have an ambulance, call for help. "Not in front of the boy," he whispers through teeth soldered together by pain. He doesn't want to appear weak in front of Ted, doesn't want him to know he's scored such a substantial victory.

Sweat stands out on Roger's forehead. His teeth loosen and rattle as chill after chill runs through him. He clings to the curse, repeating it so quickly it's no longer separate words, just one long mass of sound punctuated by gasps as the pain drops a second cinderblock on him. If his eyes weren't already moist from the pepper spray, tears would have been squeezed out of them. As it is, his eyes send hot trails down his cheeks. The curse has lost much of its sense, has become half-words held together by almost words. Roger gazes up at the ceiling, panting, looks back down—

And sees something. His heart is in too much pain to jump, his lungs too tight to draw in breath, but his eyes widen. There, in the corner of his cell below the high window streaming light, where the shadows have retreated—there, he sees what might be another shadow, except that it seems thicker, denser. Through his tear-smeared vision, he has the impression of an eye, a great eye like a dark mirror. There's more, something like thick coils stacked one on top of the other. He has the sensation of vastness. He isn't seeing all of this—he can't see all of it. If the cinderblocks weren't crushing his chest, if his arm didn't feel as if it were caught in a vise, he would be terrified. The only fear the pain will allow, however, is of the distant, intellectual variety, the I-must-be-afraid-because-I-should-be-afraid kind that has no practical effect. Roger continues to recite the curse—the string of sound it's become. He stares at the thing in the shadows. It's as if the shadows are a kind of window—no, it's as if the thing itself is the window.

• • •

I saw it, too, saw and felt it. All over my body, my nerve endings flared, my skin shrieked, as if a blast of arctic air had poured over me. My leg trumpeted new pain. Even as I gripped the edge of the altar, digging both hands into it to reassure myself that this was not real—vision or hallucination, it was not happening—I was aware of the thing across the cell, felt its coils scraping against one another, as if my nerves ran out to it. Up to that point, I had viewed what was playing out in front of me as a kind of mind-movie, my unusually vivid imagination of a possible past. What I was experiencing now was no memory—it was present. It wasn't that I'd gone back in time—it was more that to see this thing in the past was to see it in the present, if that makes any sense. I'd thought that I was beyond being afraid—that my capacity for fear had been exhausted, tapped out—but terror jolted me. I no longer wanted this vision. Whatever insights it promised, I could live without. I stood—

And was standing in the cell. The pavilion had vanished. Frantic, I looked around. There was Ted in the cell across the hall, lying with his back to me. There was the door to the police station. "Help!" I screamed. "Help me!"

Nothing happened. Ted didn't leap off his bunk. No cop rushed through the door. I turned to Roger and reached out my hand to him. My fingers pressed against his shoulder, but he gave no sign he felt the contact. "Roger!" I shouted. "Roger!" He didn't hear me. He continued to stare at the shape in the shadows, one hand pressed to his chest. "Ted!" I shouted, "Ted! Can you hear me?" Ted stirred. I screamed his name again. He didn't respond.

All the while, there was the thing in the corner, watching me. When it was clear that neither Ted nor Roger could hear or see me—that, for all practical purposes, I was a ghost—I turned to look at it. In the act of turning, as I saw the thing out of the corner of my eye, I had a momentary impression of crazy geometry, impossible angles—and then it was gone, replaced by the great eye.

· · ·

The thing speaks, its voice a whisper that seems to well up inside Roger, from someplace down deep in him, past the pain squatting on his chest. It isn't his voice—isn't any voice he's ever heard—but it's maddeningly familiar. I heard it crawling around the cell walls, and recognized it as the voice that had issued from Roger during his last sleepwalk at Belvedere House. It says, "You know what you are asking."

Roger understands it's talking about the curse. He nods. When this brings no response, he says, "Yes." If Ted hears him, he gives no sign.

"Much is required," the voice says. "What do you offer?"

"What is it you want?" Roger has to force each syllable out.

"Blood," the whisper says. "Pain."

"This," Roger says, raising his right hand from its place over his struggling heart, "here—you want pain, take it."

The voice inhales with what could be pleasure. The heavy coils shift with a sound like concrete scraping on concrete. The eye bobs ever so slightly. "Sweet," the voice sighs, "but not enough."

Black spots dance at the edge of Roger's vision. His head is light. He thinks, What am I doing? My son—what am I doing? What is all this? Despite the pain wracking his body, the distant fear at the thing on the other side of the cell, the anger is there to answer in its voice like the roar of a burning house. "Retribution," it says. Roger nods, yes, of course, and says, "Anything—take whatever you need. Whatever you need."

The door to the holding area clangs open, more light floods in ahead of the police officer bringing Roger and Ted their nominal breakfasts. In an instant, the shadows, and what they held, are gone, washed away by sunlight.

• • •

There I was, back under the pavilion, standing in front of the altar. When I saw the fog hanging heavy before me, the rows of seats barely visible through it, my legs almost deserted me. I thought I was going over on my ass, then I caught myself. My knees would not stop shaking, so I stood in place and concentrated on maintaining my balance. Although I had escaped the vision, I wasn't free of it. I knew what happened next—it was there in my memory, a parting gift from the thing in the shadows. I had had enough of this story, of all of it—to say I was sick of it was an understatement—but even as I was gauging how nauseated it made me, I was watching this particular chapter play itself out.

• • •

With the shadows' departure, the pain in Roger's chest leaves, as well. He hasn't realized how hard he's been bracing himself against it until it isn't there. Then it's like yanking away a support from a sagging wall. He collapses onto his bunk. The police officer, who's given Ted his cup of instant coffee and shrinkwrapped donut, turns in time to see Roger slump backwards. "Hey," he says, "you okay in there?" Roger doesn't answer, so the cop says, "Hey—hey grandpa. You all right?"

The "grandpa" does the trick, spurring Roger up onto his elbows. "I am fine, thank you," he says. His mouth is dry. Behind the cop, Ted doesn't look at him.

Roger accepts the undersized cup of bitter coffee and the donut that's already started to melt in the cop's hand, smearing chocolate across its plastic wrapper. As he eats the kind of breakfast he hasn't enjoyed since he was an undergraduate, he stares over at Ted, who has finished his meal and is seated on his bunk, gazing up at the ceiling, very deliberately ignoring his father. Roger is aware of the space in his chest that the pain occupied. He can't believe it's actually gone, and he entertains the momentary thought that it didn't vanish, it crescendoed, stopping his heart, and what he's living now is some kind of last-minute fantasy his brain has conjured to protect itself from its own incipient end. A fantasy that includes chocolate all over my fingers? he thinks.

Wiping his hands on his bunk, he realizes what the voice he heard reminded him of: the house—he has the crazy notion that if the house could talk, that's what it would sound like. How bizarre. Already, he's writing off the thing in the shadows as a delusion brought on by the agony overloading his system, by his need for revenge. Of course, he doesn't think of what he has planned for Ted—he reviews the one hundred twenty-three words; yes, he still has them all—he doesn't see it as revenge. He tells himself it's justice, just desserts held back for years, for decades too long. His sudden brush with his mortality has not put things into perspective for Roger. If anything, it's sharpened his desire to wound Ted, to hurt him while he still can.

All through the morning that follows, Roger keeps his words, his weapon, close to him and waits for the opportunity to present itself. It isn't there when the cop returns to take him and Ted—handcuffed—from the holding cell through the station to the village hall and the courtroom. It isn't there when I stand up and deliver my defense of father and son. It isn't there while the judge lectures him and Ted. By the time Roger is walking with me out into the parking lot, he's starting to wonder if the moment is going to come at all, if maybe it showed itself and he missed it.

He and I are halfway to the car when he sees Ted walking towards him. Ted, whose face, he's pleased to note, shows a few bruises itself, and whose anger has eased into something else, into what might be grudging respect. Ted's guard is down. He is perfectly vulnerable. Roger pretends he doesn't notice him and continues toward the car. He feels Ted's hand grip his shoulder. He hears Ted say, "Wait," in that tone Roger still recognizes, the one that means, Okay, I screwed up. His chance is here. Roger says, "Take your hand off me," in a voice intended to stun Ted, a voice so harsh it almost surprises him. Ted's hand flies off Roger, who drives his weapon home.

My legs calm enough for me to risk moving, I took three halting steps to the altar and leaned against it. I looked toward the entrances to the pavilion—where the entrances were supposed to be. In the fog, they were little more than white patches in a sea of whiteness.

• • •

For the fifteen or twenty seconds Roger takes to speak, the three of us stand there as if we're having some kind of civilized discussion. Anyone watching us might think Roger is commenting on the weather—well, maybe not, since he's looking away from Ted as he talks to him—but any onlooker would in no way suspect what's being unleashed. To get at the emotional register of what Roger is doing, you have to reconfigure the scene. You have to picture it all in terms of actions. When Ted grasps Roger's arm, Roger's free hand catches Ted's arm. The knife—that piece of sharpened bone, etched around with strange symbols—is in Roger's hand before either Ted or I can react. I'm raising my arm, opening my mouth to protest, when Roger stabs me in the belly, in the place where what could be our child floats in darkness. Even as I feel the knife, icicle cold, Roger has withdrawn it and turned it on himself, driving its bloody point into his chest, off-center so as to miss the breastbone. His grip on Ted slackens as he grunts with the pain, but there's no danger of Ted escaping. He's frozen with disbelief. As Roger tears the knife from himself, he pivots, pulling Ted to him while he brings the knife in and up. Ted's reflexes finally kick in, but it's too late. The knife is in him, Roger putting all his weight behind it and twisting it, first to the right, then the left, then releasing it. One hand fumbling for the blade buried in his gut, the other clutching Roger's arm, Ted drops to his knees. He never looks at Roger as he topples to the side. Swaying like a drunk, Roger gazes down at his son, a triumphant smile writing itself on his face—and collapses, falling in on himself like a building that's been demolished. This leaves me to lower myself to the ground carefully, and lay my head down. From above, the three of us make up the sides of a bloody triangle.

• • •

I know, I know. Described this way, it's like the climax to an Elizabethan revenge tragedy. Oceans of blood, everybody dies, all you need is for Fortinbras to walk in and clean things up. In some ways, though, an over-the-top scenario like this gets at what was really happening in the parking lot that morning better than repeating what Roger said. At the risk of sounding perverse, I almost wish that my blood-soaked scene had been what happened. Right from the start, all of us would have understood what was going on—assuming any of us survived, that is.

What I saw in the fog was—you want a word like revelation for it. Most of it was subtle, a matter of degrees of understanding. Obviously, Roger had been angry at Ted—I hadn't appreciated the extent of that anger. It was hard not to think about those stories he'd told me about his childhood, those anecdotes so full of rage. Roger hadn't traveled all that far from that bitter little boy. That was why he'd shared those memories with me—he'd been trying to account for his actions to himself. However successful he'd been at putting his pact with the thing in the shadows out of his mind in the short term, in the long term, he'd been unable to escape it. He'd been trying to explain why he'd done what he'd done to all of us, to Ted, to me, to himself. He'd been trying to explain why he'd given our child away.

Because he had. In promising the thing that disclosed itself to him in his cell whatever it wanted, he'd allowed it to rip my womb open. My hand strayed over my belly. I didn't require any supernatural agency to be back in that hospital room, the floor cold against my cheek, my nostrils full of the smell of blood. The fog inside the pavilion had thickened, to the point the roof was lost above me, the entrances obscured. Really, the only thing I could see clearly was the first couple of rows of chairs in front of me, and even they were looking kind of faint. Fog had crept onto the altar with me, was eddying around my hips, spilling itself over the edge of the altar down to the floor in gray slow-motion. The feeling I'd had during my vision of Roger's deal with the thing in the corner had subsided, but my nerves still prickled. Fog flowed over my legs, climbed my chest and arms. The rows of chairs were vague rectangles. I had no desire to stay there, but I had even less to wander around. There was the practical concern of not being able to see where I was going, and the less practical one of what I might meet. What am I talking about? Given the circumstances, worrying about what was lurking in the fog was every bit as practical as worrying about tripping up the stairs.

Of course, whatever might be prowling the fog could also find its way to me, if I remained in one place. Hadn't I wanted to keep on the move? Well, yes, I had, but movement now seemed impossible. I was paralyzed—not literally, it was more that moving—that the idea of moving was too much, you know? I realized, yes, that if something lunged at me out of the fog, I would play the terrified heroine and run screaming up the aisle, no doubt falling several times on the way. Until that happened, however, until Ted or whatever that thing in Roger's cell had been found me, I was incapable of rousing myself from my spot on the altar. No matter that the chairs had been wiped away. No matter that, when I held my hands up, they looked washed-out, spectral. I closed my eyes for relief from all the whiteness. For a moment, it was as if I were back in Belvedere House. Not that there was any strange sensation, no. What I felt was much less tangible than that. It was a—sureness that, were I to open my eyes, I'd be looking out the living room windows onto Founders Street.

When the hand closed on my arm, I wasn't surprised. I'd expected to be, but what I thought was, *Of course*. Then Roger's voice said, "Veronica."

• • •

I opened my eyes, and there he was, one hand clasped on my arm to prevent me running away from him again. I could see him clearly. The fog was much less thick than it had seemed. His face was a study in concern, eyebrows slightly raised, eyes searching, lips open. "Honey," he said, "are you all right?"

In all fairness, what else could he have said? All the same, I nearly burst out laughing. The man who had made a pact with I-didn't-know-what, had traded the life of one child so he could have revenge on the other, had condemned that other child to some variety of hell—this man, to whom I was married, was asking me if I was all right? He added, "Everything is fine, now, honey. I'm here, and everything is fine," and it was almost too much to bear. The sight of him standing there, inclined slightly toward me—I wasn't frightened of him—maybe I should have been, but I was more frightened for him—for us.

That, and angry, deeply, deeply angry. My left arm, the one he wasn't holding, thrummed, and it was all I could do to keep it from leaping out and hitting him. I don't mean like I had in the diner, those frantic, convulsive slaps. I mean a roundhouse that would've snapped his head back. The accelerated course in sheer terror that had held me in its grip since the diner—since the carousel ride—was incinerated by the phosphorous burn that surged through me. The desire to hit him not once, but over and over again, to punch him, slap him, kick him, to bruise and break and bloody him, swept over me. I wanted to shout at him, tell him what a complete idiot he'd been, ask him if he had any idea what he'd done, what his little stunt in the cell had cost us, was costing us? At the very least, I wanted to tell him to take his damned hand off me.

"Veronica?" Roger said, and I knew I wasn't going to yell at him, wasn't going to hit him. Part of it was the concern I heard in his voice; part of it was that I needed him to help me get off this island. I said, "I'm here, Roger."

"Thank God," he said, releasing my arm so he could take me into a hug. I submitted, even managed to pat his back. "I was so worried," he said as he held me. "One minute, we were talking, the next, you were gone. I didn't know what had happened. I searched up and down that street for you. I went in every store. No one could tell me where you'd gone. I remembered the cottages, how much you'd admired them, and decided to check them. I almost ignored this place. Even when I looked in it, I could barely see you, with the fog."

"You found me."

"Are you all right?" Roger asked, holding me at arm's length and surveying me. "These aren't the same clothes—"

"I bought new ones," I said. "The others were soaked."

"Honey—you must understand—I did that—I had to—"

"It's fine, Roger. Let's get out of here."

• • •

We did. Within the hour, my great escape to Martha's Vineyard was at an end, and we were on the ferry back to Wood's Hole. On our way to the bus stop, we passed a plain, two-storey house, white with black trim, set at the other end of a brick walk bordered by bright yellow and purple wildflowers. Something about it tickled my memory, but I was more interested in departing the island as quickly as possible than in lingering over quaint houses. Roger was the one to stop. "What is it?" I said. "What's wrong?"

"Nothing," he said. "Don't you recognize where we are?"

"No," I said, then I did. "Oh." This was the B&B we'd stayed in during our last, happier visit.

"Shall we see if they have a room?"

"What?" I turned to him. He wasn't joking—given the day's events, he couldn't have been thinking very clearly, but he was serious. If I said I wanted to stay here tonight, he was willing. My schemes for remaining on the island recurred to me, and for the second time that afternoon, black laughter bubbled at the back of my throat. Roger would stay here tonight because he thought there was a chance he would encounter Ted. He hadn't said a word about it to me during our walk out of the pavilion, through the maze of gingerbread houses, and back toward the bus stop, but you could practically see the idea floating over his skull. Although he didn't know the specifics of what I'd been through, he had no doubt it was connected to Ted.

Fortunately for me, the sign at the near end of the front walk was hung with a NO VACANCY sign. I pointed this out to Roger, whose face fell, only to pick up almost immediately as he said, "If you'd like to stay someplace else—"

"I wouldn't," I said. "I'd like to go home—to Wellfleet."

There were maybe two seconds during which I watched Roger debate with himself. Was it worth insisting that we stay here? I was ready to go home without him if it came to that. I had my own car keys, and I was the one with the keys to the Cape House. Let him stay on the island as long as he liked. At the end of the two seconds, he grinned apologetically and said, "Of course."

• • •

As the ferry was pulling away from the Vineyard, Roger gazed at the island—or the spot where the island was; the fog lay as heavy as before—and murmured too quietly for me to hear. We were back in the galley, a cup of tea in front of me, a can of Coke in front of him.

"What?" I asked.

"Just thinking," he said, "remembering a few lines from Tennyson."

"Oh?" I hate Tennyson. Talk about a gorgeous poet with no mind.

"Yes, the end of 'Ulysses.' I assume you've read it."

"I'm familiar with it."

"At the very end, when the aged Ulysses is trying to rally his followers for one final sail into the unknown, he holds out hope of what they might encounter on their voyage. He says,

"'It may be the gulfs will wash us down;

"'It may be we shall touch the Happy Isles,

"'And see the great Achilles, whom we knew.'"

Roger shrugged. "That's all."

That wasn't all. It was a code, and it wasn't very hard to break. Roger was afraid we'd just set sail from the Happy Isle, that we were leaving great Achilles wandering the mist. He was asking for reassurance, for me to reach across the table, grasp his hand, and tell him that it was all right. Instead, I said, "I can't understand how you can stand Tennyson. My God. Talk about sound and fury, signifying nothing."

Whatever Roger's other concerns, he was not about to let such a blatant attack on one of his favorite poets go unanswered. I had counted on this. I wanted an argument. We occupied ourselves with a fairly heated one for the remainder of the boat ride, Roger summoning examples of Tennyson's depth and brilliance, me countering that they were shallow and contrived. What a relief, to have an outlet for the hostility churning inside me. I didn't really want to argue with him about Tennyson—so he liked a lousy poet, so what?—I wanted to argue about what he'd done in that holding cell. Only, I didn't want to argue with him about that. What I mean is, however mad at him I was, however much pleasure it would have provided to scream at him in the short term, in the long term, I needed to talk to Roger about what he'd done, which I wouldn't be able to if we fought about it now. So instead, we debated the merits and defects of a second-rate poet.

• • •

The argument was pretty much over by the time we were driving up 6 to Wellfleet. Roger had lapsed into silent outrage, which was fine by me. My anger temporarily appeased, I had a mostly quiet ride to turn over what had happened on the Vineyard. I thought about the shape I'd glimpsed in the carousel mirror. Ted, yes—he'd been the cause of whatever I'd been through on the carousel, that—disorientation. Why, though? For that matter, why had he shown himself to me at the diner? (Not that I was thinking about what I'd seen, no.) To scare me? Mission accomplished, in spades. Certainly, the day's events might mean nothing more than their effects on me; although they seemed a bit elaborate if fright were Ted's only goal. What about the thing in Roger's cell? The thing whose voice had seemed to come from some-place deep within him, and which was so reminiscent of the house, the thing that had offered to fulfill his curse in exchange for, what had it said? "Blood and pain."

We were almost at the Orleans traffic circle. I told Roger to turn off into Orleans. "What for?" he asked.

"I want to stop at the liquor store."

He grunted, and steered to the right.

At the liquor store, I bought a bottle of red wine, two bottles of single-malt Scotch, and a bottle of soda water. Scotch was Roger's drink, not mine: too medicine-y. If I planned to talk to him, I was going to need to loosen his tongue, and I figured a couple of Scotch-and-sodas, on top of the wine we'd drink with dinner, would help him along.

For the remainder of the drive to Wellfleet, the thing in the corner occupied me. The moment I'd seen it in my—what was I going to call that experience? A vision? A vision of the most intense kind. The instant I'd noticed it among the shadows, my nerves had jolted. Did this mean the thing was the house? Or was it like the house—or the house like it? It seemed too much of a stretch for it not to be connected to the house, so—was it the source of the weirdness we'd been through? Where had it come from? I had a momentary image of a group of the college students who'd rented the house in the sixties playing with a Ouija board, opening a door that should have been kept closed, throwing a switch that shouldn't have been thrown.

No. There was Thomas Belvedere and his "Dark Feast" paintings, which I was more certain than ever recorded the strangeness he'd undergone during his summer in the house. Viola Belvedere's letter hinted as much. Whatever was wrong with the house reached back at least to him, and possibly beyond—which, when you came right down to it, wasn't anything I didn't already know. When you're facing these kinds of problems, though, any sense you can find in them feels like a victory.

The house had been—haunted? Off? Let's say off. The house had been off for at least a half century. Not everyone who lived there had experienced anything. Dr. Sullivan and her family hadn't reported a single out of the usual occurrence. For that matter, neither had Roger, Joanne, and Ted for the decades they'd lived there. Did that mean the house was intermittently off? That it was following some kind of occult schedule, a giant alarm clock, set to ring every fifty years—which begged the question, who'd set it?

The turnoff for the Cape House was ahead. Roger took the driveway faster than usual—his way of showing he was still annoyed—slaloming up and around it, gravel pinging off the car. When I didn't respond, he must have taken it as my way of saying I could play this game, too, but honestly, I was thinking about the house. As he brought the car to a stop, I turned to him and said, "There are steaks in the fridge. Do you feel like grilling them?"

"I suppose I could," Roger said, doing his best to feign disinterest. He couldn't fool me, though. I saw the secret thrill that ran through him at the mention of the word "grill." If there's one gender stereotype I abide by, it's this: allow a man to apply fire to raw meat, and he'll be happy as a clam. It must make guys feel like great strong hunters, roasting the mastodon steaks over the campfire. Talk about atavism.

While Roger poured fresh charcoal onto the grill and soaked it in lighter fluid—it didn't matter that the charcoal was the pre-soaked kind; Roger wasn't satisfied unless there was a distinct chance of him burning his eyebrows off—while he started the grill and prepared the steaks, rubbing them with a combination of cracked pepper, dry mustard, and crushed garlic, I set the table and threw together a salad. The salad done, I opened the bottle of red wine and poured a sizable glass of it for Roger, a more modest portion for myself. I wanted a bigger glass—I would have been happy to skip the meal and go directly to the alcohol—but I needed my head reasonably clear. I passed Roger's wine to him when he came back inside in search of the fork and tongs. He took it outside, where he rested it on the backyard table beside the plate with the steaks while he waited for the towering inferno to subside and the coals to heat.

I brought my glass through to the living room, where I stood looking out the front windows at the cemetery. The wine was strong, sharp, and it snapped your tongue as it went down. What you'd call an acquired taste, I guess, although I appreciated its roughness. You had a house that was malignant—or that had a malignancy. Could houses get sick? Not literally—I'm talking more metaphorically—metaphysically, even. Could a house turn against itself? Or could it attract the notice of some kind of—disease? Tumor? The thing in the corner had asked for blood and pain. How much pain had the house seen while Roger and Joanne—and Ted—had lived there? Nothing out of the ordinary, at first. Roger and Joanne's marriage had known the normal peaks and valleys, as had their relationship with Ted. But then things had started to sour. Joanne had her affair with the anthropology professor. Ted submerged into teenage angst and rebellion. Roger grew isolated from the two of them. All the relationships under that roof had decayed. None of it unusual—lots of families endure much worse—except that here, in Belvedere House, it had fed something, what might have been the house itself, or might have been hanging around the house like a dog lurking under the table, hoping for scraps.

I drank more of the wine—gulped it—and my eyes stung. I walked back into the kitchen, where I could watch Roger, glass in one hand, turning the steaks over on the grill. He splashed some of his wine over the meat; fire jumped to taste it. Why would this thing reveal itself to Roger? Because he had stumbled onto something that promised it a meal to make what it had been dining on so far seem like—it would be like going from eating dog-food to a seven-course meal at the Canal House. Yes, I mean the curse. Roger had—he'd signed Ted over to the thing. I didn't know if he'd known that's what he was doing—however much he wanted revenge on Ted, I wasn't sure it went all this way, to wanting to consign him to a pocket hell. Did this mean the thing had my child, as well? How could I know? I had no doubt the miscarriage had been part of the price Roger had paid for cursing Ted, but without the malediction being extended to cover that child, could the thing take it, as well? Hard to imagine that what had been little more than a collection of cells could have satisfied this thing's appetite, but who knew?

Roger jabbed the fork into one of the steaks and held it up for inspection. Almost, but not quite. He returned it to the grill and, as he did, caught me looking at him. He raised his glass—his attempt at a cease-fire, if not an apology—and without thinking, I repeated the gesture, which brought a smile from him. My glass was already empty. I hadn't been aware of finishing it. If I didn't take it easy, I was going to be asleep before the end of the meal. I rinsed it and settled on water for the time being.

I knew how much of what I was thinking was supposition, and

of the craziest kind. It made sense, though. It gathered what had happened and arranged it into a coherent pattern. During my conversation with Dr. Hawkins, she'd said, "We're all continuously trying to invent a narrative that will account for our lives." At the time, her statement had struck me as one more platitude, but in the weeks since, it had stuck with me. It's at the root of psychoanalysis, isn't it? Instead of calling it "the talking cure," we should call it "the storytelling cure." Dickens tries to come to terms with his childhood traumas, his adult ambivalences, by writing about them over and over. Hawthorne tries to clarify his Puritan legacy to himself in story after story. Whenever something happens to you—something too much—you create a story to deal with it, to define if not contain it. I had done exactly that—it's just, where most people's stories are written by Anne Tyler, mine was by Anne Rice.

Not that it was a perfect story. There were all kinds of things it couldn't account for—or hadn't yet, if I wanted to be optimistic. A lot—enough of what I'd been through didn't fit my explanation especially well. Ted revealing himself at the Vineyard diner—okay, I could believe that had been done to torment me. My sensations inside Belvedere House, though, my view of that nighttime landscape outside the kitchen window? Granted, they'd been strange, confusing. I supposed you could say they'd caused me sufficient discomfort to provide the thing in the corner a snack, but that didn't seem their intention—if they'd had an intention, if they hadn't been random occurrences. I didn't need my story to explain Roger's sleepwalking—I'd already known he had guilt to spare. It didn't explain the strange map he stared at during the second part of each sleepwalk, that combination of geography, history, and physics with Ted's old shaving mirror winking at its center.

Most importantly, the narrative I'd arrived at didn't tell me why I should be the one having all the weirdness visited on her, while Roger got off scot-free. There was no doubt that, on some level, he was horrified at what he'd done. He'd have to be. Maybe that was enough for the thing. Although you would have thought that letting Roger see what he'd done to Ted would have increased his suffering that much more, made the thing's meal that much richer. Yes, there was the vision Roger claimed to have had of the figure wandering the corridor—the figure he himself had assumed was Ted. That was pretty bad, I supposed, but nothing like my up-close-and-personal view of Ted. Was this the thing's way of rewarding Roger for having pronounced the curse? It seemed unlikely, to say the least.

• • •

The sliding door rasped, and Roger said, "Dinner is served." I went to the fridge for the salad, tossing my water in the sink on the way. Roger poured me a fresh glass of wine when I sat down. I raised it and said, "To Tennyson."

Roger smirked and said, "To the impudence of youth."

He'd grilled the steaks medium, a little rarer than I liked, a little more done than he did. Despite that, they were tasty, and the salad was a crisp, green complement to them. As we ate, we made small talk about the Cape House. Roger finished his second glass of wine. I poured him number three. A flush was already creeping up his cheeks. "What about you?" he asked, pointing at my glass, still mostly full, with his fork.

"Don't worry about me."

By dinner's end, Roger had drunk four and a half glasses of wine to my two. His face was rosy, but his speech was clear and coherent. He was desperate to ask me about the Vineyard, but had decided it was better to wait. I'm sure he was afraid of provoking another freak-out, and no Coke at hand. We cleared the table, washed and dried the dishes, filling the air with more mindless chatter, and I reached to the top of the fridge for the bag containing the two bottles of Glenkinchie. Roger hadn't known I'd bought them, and his eyes widened as I withdrew first one, then the other. "What's this?" he asked, unable not to smile as he held the bottles up for inspection. "I thought you didn't care for Scotch?"

"After the day I've had," I said, "I need something with more fortitude than wine. I was hoping you could make the drinks?"

"With pleasure. Do we have any soda water?"

"In the fridge."

"Excellent," Roger said. "You've thought of everything."

Well, not everything, I thought while he searched for a pair of suitable glasses. *I still don't know why your son is giving me the all-out, special-effects extravaganza, while the worst thing you have to worry about is thinking you hear someone call your name inside a crowded building.* Roger uncorked the Scotch, twisted the cap off the soda water, and combined the two, favoring the liquor over the soda—to help me talk, I realized. Oh, irony. He passed me my drink, bubbles pushing their way through the honey-colored liquid, and said, "To what shall we drink?"

"We've already saluted Tennyson," I said, "any other poets you'd like to recognize?"

"Very funny."

I considered proposing a toast to the honesty that was essential to the success of our marriage, but I didn't think I could manage it without tipping my hand too early. Roger solved the problem by saying, "To a fine meal, expertly prepared all around." I tasted the drink. It was as astringent as ever—with the soda water added, it was like medicine-flavored soda. Nevertheless, I smiled as if the thirty dollars a bottle had been worth it.

"Shall we retire outside?" Roger asked. "I don't believe the mosquitoes are particularly bad as yet."

"That's fine," I said. "Why don't you grab the Scotch, and I'll take the soda, to save us having to come inside every five minutes."

"Inspired thinking." Roger grabbed the bottle by the neck and led the way out to the backyard table.

The evening was pleasant, the sun at the treetops, about to begin its final plunge, the air warm and smelling faintly of the ocean. We deposited the bottles on the picnic table and seated ourselves at it. Roger inhaled and said, "I have to admit, I love the sea air. There's something so invigorating about it, don't you think?"

"Mmm."

He drank from his glass. Here it comes, I thought. He said, "Before—just now, when I asked you about your selection of the Glenkinchie, you made reference to the day's events."

"I did."

"Yes. I don't want you to feel pressured in any way by what I'm going to ask you. If you don't want to speak about what you went through on the Vineyard—if you aren't ready, if you're never ready—there's absolutely no need for you to do so. However, should you—"

"I saw Ted."

Roger breathed in sharply. My words hung between us, almost visible. "You saw him?"

"Yes."

"Where? On the carousel? The diner?"

"Both. I had a glimpse of him standing behind me on the carousel—in one of the mirrors—and I saw him face-to-face in the diner. It was only for a second—less—but it was Ted."

"My God," Roger said. "I knew—I was certain something—that you'd seen." He finished his drink and poured a second from the Scotch bottle alone. When he'd drunk half of that, he coughed, and said, "Judging from your reaction to him, I take it the encounter was not pleasant."

"It wasn't."

"Can you talk about it?"

"He's—" I paused. "He's bad, Roger."

"What do you mean?"

"Ted is—he's different—changed."

"How so?"

"I can't describe it. I can't even remember it. I don't want to remember it. He isn't—he isn't something you could look at. I'm sorry—I don't know how to describe him."

"I don't understand. Is he disfigured? Is it his injuries?"

"No, not exactly—I mean, he's been injured—I'm pretty sure that's why he looks like—"

"Like what?"

"Like nothing human."

"Nothing—are you sure it was Ted?"

"Yes—I saw his—I saw what he used to look like first, then I saw him as he is now." I was struggling not to confront the memory head-on—even as I was realizing that part of it had already—not faded, exactly; it was more as if part of it hadn't taken, as if my mind hadn't been equipped to hold onto everything I'd seen—which didn't mean that what was left wasn't enough to start me screaming all over again.

"As he is now," Roger said. He was being deliberately obtuse.

"His eyes are glass," I said. "Glass, or something like glass. He can't close them. The skin around them is—stretched, tortured. He's being tortured—he's in torment." I swallowed some of my drink.

"No," Roger said.

"Yes."

"No, I am sorry, I understand you have undergone some type of disturbing experience today, but that was not Ted you saw. You are mistaken." His lips were trembling.

"Roger—"

"I need a walk," he said, springing up from his seat. He took the bottle of Scotch, ignored the soda water, and set off away from me at a brisk pace. My own glass still in hand, I stood and gave chase.

• • •

He circled the house and started up the driveway, almost falling when his foot struck a clump of sand that gave beneath him. Arms flailing, he caught himself in time and continued his trek. At the end of the driveway, he halted, turning his head from side to side long enough for me almost to catch up to him, then turned left into the cemetery. I called, "Roger—Roger, wait." His head jerked at the sound of his name, but he continued walking. He strode straight through the cemetery. When he reached the far side of it, he turned right and started walking around it. Like some kind of idiot, I followed him the entire time, despite the fact that, after one circuit of the graves, the burn on my leg was shouting with pain. I should have sat and waited for him, but I was afraid he'd leave the graveyard, head into the woods surrounding it, and I wouldn't be able to find him. We circled that cemetery three times, until Roger stopped, panting, and turned to wait for me. "That wasn't Ted," he said when I was standing next to him. "Not my boy."

"It's the curse," I said, breathing a bit heavily myself. "It's what you said to him the last time you saw him."

"What?"

"In the parking lot in front of Village Hall," I said, "you cursed Ted. You disowned him, remember? 'I disown you; I cast you from me.'"

"Don't be absurd," Roger said, but something flickered across his eyes.

"You cursed him," I said, "and it worked." Understanding rushed through me. "That's why he isn't haunting you—not directly. You cut your ties with him—you cut him off completely. He can't reach you—not like he can reach me—because you shut the door on him."

"This is ridiculous," Roger said. "Are you quite through?"

"Roger," I said, "I know what happened in the cell. I know about the deal you made."

Fear, shame, and anger hovered over Roger's face, already

scarlet from the combination of alcohol and his circuits of the cemetery. "Deal?"

"With the thing in the corner. The eye in the shadows."

"I'm afraid I don't know what you're referring to."

"It offered to make the curse you had come up with for Ted real, to make it work."

"Really?" Roger said. He tried to smile. The effect was hideous.

"You asked it what it wanted. It told you, 'Blood and pain.'"

He flinched at those three words, and any lingering doubts I might have had about what I'd seen were put to rest. He said, "So you're saying I made a pact with the devil during my time in the holding cell?"

"You made a deal with something," I said. "I don't know what."

"I see. And did I sign this agreement in blood, promise away my immortal soul?"

"You offered it the heart attack that had already started. That wasn't enough, so you offered it whatever else it wanted—anything, including the child I was carrying. Which it took. You offered it Ted for its amusement."

"Is that what this is about? You blame me for the miscarriage?"

"That isn't the point, Roger."

"Oh, I should say it is. It's obvious your losing the baby affected you more deeply than I was aware, in response to which you've invented a scenario that paints me as responsible for it. I had no idea you had been so traumatized."

"This isn't about me," I said. "It's about you in that jail cell trading away whatever it took for you to have your revenge."

"I had no idea your resentment of me ran this deep."

"Come off it," I said. "Are you telling me you didn't spend hours and hours coming up with that curse?"

"I planned my rebuke to Ted, yes. I was angry. This gave me a way to channel that anger. Should I not have been angry at him for showing up at our doorstep at three in the morning to yell at his father? Should I have thanked him for attacking me?"

"What about your heart attack? When did that begin?"

"I became convinced that I was in fact undergoing a heart attack during the time it took me to walk away from Ted to the car that following day."

"That was the first of it? There was nothing before?"

"I had some indication while I was in my cell, I admit, but I understand that's not uncommon."

"And what did you see while you were in the middle of your 'indication'?"

"Honestly," Roger said, "this is too much. I am not to blame here. I am not the villain. I'm trying to help Ted. If I had wanted to condemn him to some manner of eternal torment, why would I be working so hard to help him escape it?"

"Guilt," I said. "At some point—I don't know when; maybe when Ted was killed, maybe before, maybe after—you realized what you'd done and regretted it. Given the chance to make amends, you leapt at it."

"You've certainly thought this through. I presume my guilt is what has kept me from revealing any of this to you previously."

"Guilt and doubt. I'm guessing you've convinced yourself it was a hallucination brought on by the stress of what felt like a heart attack. Because if it were true, if you did strike a bargain with something to curse your son—well, what does that say about you?"

"How have you arrived at this—this story? Is it my sleepwalking? Have you decided that a change in my nightly routine must indicate a troubled conscience?"

"I saw it."

"What? What do you mean?"

"After I saw Ted—after I ran out of the restaurant, I ended up at the pavilion, where you found me. While I was there, I had—I had a vision. I saw you that night in the cell. I saw you start to have a heart attack, and I watched that thing—the eye—appear to you. It was right after sunrise."

Roger drank directly from the bottle this time, a slug that would have done any undergraduate proud. He wiped his lips with the back of his hand. "This is incredible. Let me see if I understand the situation. You undergo an obviously traumatic experience as we are eating—I refuse to believe that you saw Ted, but whatever it was, it was sufficiently severe to propel you out the front door and through the streets of Oak Bluffs. During this time—while you are in this state, you have a 'vision,' which portrays me as a villain and which you immediately accept at face value. Not once, from what you've indicated so far, does it occur to you that your vision might be less than accurate, that under the stress of the moment you would be as prone to invention as anyone."

"Why, Roger? Why would I make up something like this?"

"As I've said, it's obvious you hold me responsible for the miscarriage. Perhaps you believe my confrontation with Ted at the apartment placed too great a strain on you. Since we've returned to the house, you've suffered a couple of disturbing incidents. It's no secret you're under stress, Veronica. Why else are we here? Have you forgotten your collapse on the stairs? Apparently you've been closer to the breaking point than I was aware. Earlier today, you—you reached that point, and in its aftermath, put together a scenario that combines the events of the last few months into a coherent whole."

"So you can accept that your dead son is calling out to you from the bardo—you can even accept that he's reached out to me—but what I saw in the pavilion is a hallucination."

"It isn't true."

"I walked around in it. I was there. I tried to get out of it and I couldn't. I saw you on your bunk; I saw the thing in the corner—I felt it. The same way I can feel the house, I could feel it."

"Funny. I remember a great deal about the hours I spent in that cell—it being my first experience with incarceration—yet I don't recall seeing you there."

"I wasn't there—I mean, it was like I was invisible."

"I see. Or, I didn't, which I gather you would say proves your very point."

"All right. There's nothing I can say to convince you I saw this."

"I've no doubt you saw it. It simply did not happen."

"Same difference. I can't convince you, which is ironic, because why should I have to convince you of something you've done? Forget that. There's something you can do to show me I'm wrong."

"Which is?"

"Lift the curse. Rescind it; take it back; say you never meant it."

"I have expressed my regret at my words to Ted."

"That isn't the same thing as renouncing your words. You know that."

"Don't be ridiculous."

"If it's ridiculous, what's the big deal? Lift the curse."

"This is rapidly moving from the ridiculous to the offensive."

"Oh?"

"You cannot be serious."

"And yet I am."

"I do not need to humor you. You come to me with these baseless accusations—you accuse me of—what you accuse me of would be monstrous if it weren't so absurd."

"You're stalling," I said. "I'm your wife. Indulge me. If this'll help me with all the stress I've been under, shouldn't you do it immediately?"

"You're mocking me."

"Not at all. I'm giving you the chance to prove me wrong—I'm asking you to. All you have to do is break the curse. Take Ted back. Say you're father and son again. Lift his banishment."

Roger glared at me. His knuckles were white around the Scotch bottle. I was surprised it didn't break in his grip. He licked his lips. "No," he said, "no."

"No what?"

"I will not, as you put it, lift the curse. There was no curse. There were only words, spoken in anger—great anger, yes, but only words. To say that they meant any more than they did would be dishonest— and though I regret having expressed myself so harshly, I do not regret the emotion that prompted me to do so. My feelings were completely justified—however incensed he may have been by receiving the wedding announcement you sent, Ted had no business behaving the way he did. If I didn't raise him well enough to know that, common decency should have told him. Ted brought my words on himself."

"What about the thing in the cell? Did he bring that on himself?"

"There was no thing in the cell. There was only me and my anger."

"Why do you think he hasn't appeared to you? Why do you think I've been at the center of this?"

"You forget, I saw Ted through the living room window. And I believe you were correct when you implied that the voice I heard in the carousel hall was his. I'm sorry, but you are hardly the center of these events. Close to it, perhaps, but not as close as I am."

"Your sleepwalking?"

Roger swallowed. "I do not know why I have been sleepwalking," he said, holding up a hand to forestall my answer. "If I were the victim of a guilty conscience, as I'm sure you would suggest, why would that conscience have left me alone once we departed the house? Is it on vacation, too? No doubt there is some psychological cause. I am not above admitting the effect—the considerable effect Ted's death has had on me. That, combined with returning to the house in which I raised him, is likely the root of my nightly excursions."

"You don't believe that. I don't know what you believe, but that isn't it."

"Once again, you're mistaken."

I had run out of arguments. I stood there as Roger said, "It seems that this trip has done you more harm than good. I fear to open another can of worms, but I believe it would be best for you if we returned home sooner rather than later. Tomorrow?"

We could have stayed a couple more days—we had paid for the house—but, really, what was the point? "Whatever you want," I said, and turned and walked back to the house.

• • •

Roger didn't follow. In fact he didn't return to the house until almost midnight. I spent the hours between staring at the TV. PBS was showing a biography of Emily Dickinson I'd wanted to see for a while. Of course, it had to play when I had next to no interest in it. The conversation—confrontation with Roger was front and center in my mind. You know how it is after an argument. You replay it, listening to the other person's accusations and denials again and again, formulating the perfect response to them. That's what I do, anyway, what I did for hour after hour as nineteenth-century photographs were replaced by talking heads, who in turn gave way to footage of contemporary Amherst and its surroundings. I was so preoccupied with Roger's words—with his attempt to discount everything I'd had to say, to blame it all on my buried resentment toward him over the miscarriage—that I didn't hear most of what the documentary had to say. I recognized the rhythms of Dickinson's poetry at certain points, well-worn lines like, "Because I could not stop for Death," but the rest was a distant ebb and flow of sound.

I was angry with Roger. Not as angry as I'd been in the pavilion— that had been the fury that comes with revelation, with discovering that your husband has done something stupid and terrible that's caused the two of you tremendous pain and difficulty. The anger now was a slow burn at being lied to when you both know you've got him dead to rights. It was anger at him trying to change the subject, shift the blame for what he'd done onto me. It was complemented by another anger, this one directed inwards, because he'd almost succeeded. Not really—I knew what I'd seen, felt, on the Vineyard, all of it—but he'd managed to sow sufficient doubt for me to have to weed it out of my thoughts. Maybe I had resented him for the miscarriage, for not being available to take care of me while it was happening, and afterward— for having fought with Ted—maybe I had held the stress of watching the two of them trash the apartment secretly responsible for my losing the baby. What about the curse, though? I hadn't imagined that. What about Roger's sleepwalking, or his office, for crying out tears? If it was all in my head, why wouldn't he just lift the curse? In the morning, we would return to Belvedere House and whatever awaited us there. Do I have to add I had no doubt it was going to be bad? If blood and pain had started this, then the odds looked pretty good for blood and pain being necessary to end it.

On the TV, the actress who'd been chosen to read Dickinson's poetry said,

"Doom is the house without a door-
"'Tis entered from the sun-
"And then the ladder's thrown away,
"Because escape-is done—"

Change "sun" to "son" I thought, *and you've got that right.*

● ● ●

Roger didn't speak to me when he came in—still playing the part of the aggrieved innocent—he headed up to bed and was fast asleep by the time I decided to join him an hour later. I don't know what I was expecting that night. After everything I'd been through earlier in the day, not to mention the creeping weirdness of the days before, you would have thought I was entitled to a break. What I deserved, however, had very little to do with what actually happened to me. That had been one of the lessons of this whole drama. The more I was subject to, it seemed, the more not only could but would happen. So when *Charlie Rose* had been replaced by a film, *The Haunting*, and I decided to go upstairs because I was too tired to follow the plot, I anticipated—I don't know, Ted putting in another appearance in all his tortured glory, maybe letting me see him for longer this time, maybe reaching out and touching me with a hand wrapped in razor wire. Essentially alone in the house, the voices from the TV somehow small and echoing at the same time, I wasn't especially nervous, nor was I as I climbed into bed. I wasn't beyond fear; I wouldn't say that—every time I'd thought I was as frightened as I could be, I'd learned there was worse to come. It was more a case of being too worn out to be afraid of being afraid, if that makes sense. My mind was in better shape than it had been immediately after the wrecking ball that was Ted's true appearance had crashed into it. The various angers that had inhabited me had done a lot to repair the surface, prop up walls, repair holes, throw a tarp over the roof. Having my thoughts struck and repaired had evicted a lot of lesser concerns, like worrying about worrying. They'd return soon enough, no doubt, once the walls had been reinforced and the windows replaced, but for the time being, I was unconcerned—almost ready—for whatever the next stage of strangeness was to be.

Naturally, nothing happened. The night was quiet and peaceful. I fell asleep pretty much the second my head hit the pillow, and slept a dreamless six hours, until the sound of Roger packing wakened me. I sat up in bed and he said, "Did I wake you? I'm sorry. I thought we should get an early start." You know, I was so well-rested, so happy at being well-rested, that I bit off the nasty reply at the tip of my tongue, threw back the covers, and went downstairs for breakfast.

• • •

It was the same the following night. The drive back from the Cape had been uneventful—Roger drove the entire way, and we rode pretty much in silence. Déjà vu. Roger vibrated with tension. After the relative calm of the last few days, the stress was pouring off him in heavy waves. When I glanced over at him, I was sure I'd see him tapping his hands on the steering wheel, chewing his lip, bobbing his knee, anything to release the energy thrumming along his nerves. Instead, his hands were steady, his mouth closed, his legs calm. I thought about asking him if he were nervous, but I knew he'd offer me some kind of lie like, "Why? There's nothing for me to be nervous about."

Once we turned from 90 to 87, my sensation of Belvedere House returned—had been with me for some time, gradually rising in volume. By the time we were turning off the Thruway for Huguenot, the skin on my arms and legs was rigid, as if Roger had turned the air-conditioner on full-blast. Rather than taking the back way, down

Soldier, to the house, Roger drove along Main Street. This took us past the turn-off for the college, past Pete's and Prospero's Books—why am I telling you this? You live there. Up the street from Prospero's, I saw Village Hall and almost jumped. I half-expected a sign of what had occurred there to be visible. I don't know what, a heavy black cloud hanging over the place, something like that.

If the sight of Village Hall startled me, then I'm not sure what reaction you'd expect me to have seeing Belvedere House spread across the windshield—a gasp, or a massive shudder—nausea, even. Although this was the place that was responsible for transforming Roger's curse from empty invective to loaded weapon—or the home of whatever was responsible—the only emotion I felt as Roger pulled the car into the driveway was vague relief. How's that for perverse? Better the devil you know, I guess.

After Roger unloaded the suitcases and carried them up to the bedroom, he vanished upstairs into his office. I contemplated pursuing him, cornering him and resuming my quest to persuade him to lift his curse, but the chances of me succeeding seemed slim at best. Slim—how about nonexistent? I hadn't arrived at any better arguments since our cemetery showdown last night. My most effective line of attack continued to be, If I'm wrong, prove it to me, break the curse, which hadn't been that effective.

Instead of going up after Roger, I left the suitcases where he'd laid them on the bed and went downstairs and back out. We'd left the Cape before ten, and even with a brief stop for lunch, were back in Huguenot by three. I took the car to the post office to pick up our mail. No doubt Roger would sequester himself in his office for the rest of the day and most of the night, besides, making up for lost time. At some point, if he hadn't done so, I'd shuffle through our collection of take-out menus, decide which one sounded most appealing—or least unappealing—and call in an order that I'd probably go pick up myself. Later on, I'd channel-surf for a couple of hours before bed. Later still, no doubt I'd be up following Roger around the house. It doesn't take very long for whatever rut you thought you had escaped to reassert itself, does it?

* * *

On impulse, on my way back to Belvedere House, I kept driving, along Founders to Addie and Harlow's. I wasn't sure if they'd be in. I've never been able to remember Addie's schedule at the library, and if she wasn't working, there was a good chance she and Harlow would've gone out. Luck was with me. They were home, and on the pretense of returning the key to the Cape House, I spent the rest of the day with them. When she saw me, Addie said, "You're home early." She didn't argue with me when I said that Roger had been impatient to resume one of his projects—true enough—but she looked concerned all the time we were together. They invited me to join them for dinner—they were planning a trip to a Vietnamese place next to Penrose—and I'm not sure whether they thought it was strange that I accepted. I mean, here I was, back ahead of schedule from a vacation with my husband, agreeing to go out to dinner without him. Addie offered to call and invite Roger. I told her not to bother. He was already engrossed in his work, I said, I'd bring him something from the restaurant.

Unusual or not, they went along with it, and the three of us had a very pleasant meal at the Green House, which was the ground floor of a large house located a couple of blocks over from Penrose. Throughout the ride to and from Poughkeepsie, and the meal itself, Addie wanted to talk about Roger's and my trip, which was a little tricky. She would say things like, "Oh, you went to Marine Salvage? Isn't it great?" and I would force my mouth into a smile and say, "They have so much stuff in there."

The trickiest moment of the evening came when Harlow asked, "And Roger? How was he?" I was in the middle of drinking from the beer I'd ordered, and I almost choked on it. Once I'd brought my coughing fit under control, I said, "Sorry—went down the wrong way. Roger? Roger is—he's coping. There's a lot for him to work through, still; I guess he's doing his best." I'm sure they knew I was lying. My reasons must have seemed mysterious, but they respected whatever was compelling me.

I came home that night tipsy from three bottles of beer and two sizable after-dinner cognacs. I wouldn't say I was drunk—not by the time I said good night to Addie and Harlow and drove the quarter-mile home—but I'm glad I didn't have to drive any further, and I'm glad it was along a quiet street. That would've been just what I needed, my own trip to the Village of Huguenot jail. Maybe I could've made an unholy deal, too.

• • •

The alcohol meant that I went straight to bed, and that I stayed there even when the mattress shifted deep in the night as Roger rose to resume his sleepwalking. It also meant that I was greeted the next morning with a stabbing headache and a tongue wrapped in gauze. Roger was already in his office. I heard his footsteps overhead as I was brushing my teeth. I wandered downstairs and put on a fresh pot of strong coffee. The prospect of breakfast made the dinner I'd enjoyed so much the night before threaten to put in a second, less pleasant appearance. Coffee brewed, I filled a large mug with it and stirred in a generous helping of maple syrup. I know it sounds gross, but it's the only hangover cure that's ever worked for me.

If Roger had picked up where he'd left off, then so would I. Fresh cup of maple coffee in hand, I climbed the stairs to the library, detouring to the bathroom for a couple of ibuprofen. Shortly thereafter, I was online, Googling Rudolph de Castries.

There were something like thirteen thousand hits for the guy. The official homepage was at the University of Illinois at Champagne-Urbana. I started with that. Whoever designed the site had a flair for the baroque that bordered the outright tacky. The background was this sulfurous yellow, while the name—"Locimancy"—and menu options were deep purple. There was a quotation from de Castries in the same, overripe purple: "All things are alive as we make them live," as well as a black-and-white photo of him. Either the site designer had deliberately reversed the picture's colors, or they'd posted a negative. The photo showed de Castries from about the waist up, seated and apparently talking to someone off-camera. He was wearing an over-sized white—which is to say, black jacket over a loose white shirt, but you could tell he was tall and skinny from the way the clothes sagged on him. His hands were surprisingly short, not what you would expect for an artist. The right one was reaching into his jacket pocket; the left was held up—I couldn't tell whether to make a point, or support the cigarette burning in it. His dark hair was long for 1947, the date a subscript gave the picture. There was nothing remarkable about his face. It was young, nose long and bulbous, cheekbones high and flat, eyes dark. There was a kind of merriment in the way the eyes narrowed, the corners of the mouth lifted.

The homepage was bordered by what I took to be stylized roses—

also too purple—until I focused on one and saw it was a hybrid, a cross between a rose and a human skull. Look at it one way, it's a flower; look at it another, it's a skull. Very nice; very subtle.

The remainder of the morning, I spent navigating the website. Tackiness aside, it was fairly complete. I read de Castries's biography. I ran through pictures of him and his associates. I looked at selected examples of his art. I clicked on links to short essays he'd written on painting. I skimmed the single interview he'd given, to an art critic from the *Village Voice*. As I read, I jotted notes on a legal pad. At some point, I leaned over and switched on the printer. I printed de Castries's most famous painting, *Locimancy*, as well as the short essays—all of which shared the painting's title, with "#1" or "#2" to distinguish them—and the interview. When I was finished, I went back and printed the biography, too. Satisfied I'd seen everything the site had to offer, I bookmarked it, logged off, and shut down the computer. I closed my eyes, leaned back in the chair, and exhaled.

The cup of maple coffee was long finished, and hadn't done much good anyway, so I left the library for a shower. Standing with the hot water beating on my neck—another headache remedy—I sifted through the dozens of screens still glowing in front of my mind's eye. I didn't know what I was doing—not really—how any of this was supposed to help Roger and me. It was as much about following a hunch—if not pursuing an obsession. I'd suspected Thomas Belvedere was connected to the house's weirdness, and now I'd not only substantiated that suspicion, I had a chance to work out the details of it. Or so I told myself. To be honest—I don't know if you've ever done this, but when you're in the middle of some big project—for you, I guess it would be a story or a novel—have you ever just stopped where you are and started working on something else? You tell yourself it's related, and maybe it is, but it's not what you should be doing. Maybe you need a break—maybe you've hit a wall—maybe it's sheer perversity. I think—I think there was more perversity to what I was doing than there should have been—as much a feeling of "I'll do whatever I want," as anything.

Which meant that I had spent the morning learning about a guy who'd been born in 1930 in San Francisco to a family with a reputation for artists and eccentrics. Rudolph's father and his siblings had been a varied crew. Daddy had been a sculptor who'd had limited success with his original creations before deciding to reinvent himself as an archaeologist so he could sell his knock-offs of famous Medieval pieces more convincingly. He made a killing at it, was even invited to give a lecture on the Cathedral of Chartres to a private gentlemen's club, but was eventually caught by the police after an irate collector discovered he'd been duped. The story had made the front pages of the San Francisco papers, prompting Rudolph's mother to take what money remained in the bank account and flee to a second cousin's in Greenwich Village. If Daddy de Castries hadn't been bad enough, Uncle Theo and Aunt Marguerite had been into magic. Theo had written an unreadable book whose title I can't remember. *Mega*-something. Apparently, he'd enjoyed playing the part of a sorcerer. As for Aunt Marguerite, she'd become a warlock. Not a witch, she said, witches and warlocks were two completely different things. She was linked to a number of second- and third-tier Hollywood stars, male and female, and was rumored to have consulted with at least one of the city's mayors. If I'd wanted a topic for a novel, some kind of sprawling, multi-generational triple-decker with heavily satiric overtones, I couldn't have asked for a better one. I wasn't planning on novel-writing anytime in the near future, however. Had Uncle Theo or Aunt Marguerite been among the living, I would have considered calling them for advice, but they were long since in their graves—under mysterious circumstances, needless to say.

Shower finished, I toweled myself dry and went to the bedroom in search of clothes. We'd fallen behind in the laundry, lately. I say we, but I mean Roger, since that was one of his duties. After some searching, I located a pair of jeans and an old concert t-shirt that weren't too wrinkled. My headache lingered, though the combination of ibuprofen and hot shower had forced it to retreat to a more tolerable distance. I wandered downstairs to make lunch, which consisted of popping the top on a can of Campbell's Chunky Beef Soup. Over soup and a couple of pieces of only-slightly-stale bread, I tried to organize what I'd learned about Rudolph de Castries himself.

• • •

He'd grown up in Greenwich Village, spending time in the company of the artists his mother and her second-cousin associated with. Mommy, it appeared, continued to have a thing for the artists, despite several disastrous relationships. She tended to be drawn to men whose proclivities led in a more or less straight line to jail. Rudolph's schooling had been erratic, complicated by early alcoholism—the result, it seemed, of too many secret drinks snuck him at this or that party. By the time he was thirteen, he was skipping school for days at a time. Within a couple of years, it was weeks at a time, and when he turned sixteen it was good riddance. In a sense, that was as exciting as his life ever got. You could say he struggled with his alcoholism, but it was more a case of him struggling to find the money to buy the next bottle. Even that wasn't much of a drama. Momma de Castries kept him in cash, except for the times they argued and didn't speak to one another for months. Then Rudolph took whatever work was available, most of it menial. No excitement on that front, either. He was a conscientious employee who was able to hold his craving for a drink in check until the end of his shift. When he was twenty-five, he collapsed on his way home from a friend's gallery opening. By the time anyone stopped to see what was wrong with him, he was dead. The autopsy would deliver the verdict: his liver had disintegrated. He was buried in Queens, given a simple headstone that his admirers would replace with a more elaborate monument two decades later. His mother lived to attend that ceremony, which featured readings by a couple of poets and a talk by an art historian from Columbia, but her life wasn't very happy. Apparently, when she died the month after, hit by a city bus, there were witnesses who claimed she'd deliberately stepped out in front of it.

That had been the short, unhappy life of Rudolph de Castries. It had been redeemed by one thing and one thing only, his art. From the time he'd been a child—before he could write, he could draw, and draw well. The artists who attended his mother's parties tended to patronize him at first, until they registered the intensity in his brown eyes, after which most of them left him alone. A few gave him advice, pointers on how to improve his pictures. He drew incessantly, in pencil and crayon. His small bedroom was wallpapered with his latest efforts, which he'd tear down and replace every couple of months. Not many of those drawings have survived—Rudolph threw the ones he'd stripped from his walls out with the trash—but those that have are striking. Some critic or another described them as Hieronymus Bosch's ideas executed by Michelangelo. The pages were packed full of the elaborate imagery you find in Bosch, but it was rendered with the weight, the solidity, you associate with Michelangelo. One of the visitors to the de Castries residence gave Rudolph five dollars for his pick of the drawings. Rudolph used that to buy a basic set of oil paints and a couple of brushes and began to experiment.

Left to his own devices, Rudolph might have become an interesting enough painter—his early work plays with deliberate flatness in a way that manages to evoke Rousseau and still be its own thing. The subject matter was bizarre as ever. No one's sure how or when Rudolph first encountered *The Garden of Earthly Delights*, but there's no doubting the impression it made on him. From the ages of, say, fifteen to nineteen, as he's running through these different styles like Picasso on fast-forward, Bosch is never far—it's as if he's elaborating that one painting. What Rudolph was doing was sufficiently far outside the mainstream of American painting for there to be no danger of him becoming rich and famous from it. At the same time, it was done with enough talent and originality that he was able to place individual pieces in small shows, and sell one now and again.

I've seen the early paintings—there are a couple hanging in MoMA, and maybe a half-dozen others scattered throughout the Manhattan galleries. I like them even less than Belvedere's stuff. There's no doubt the man who painted them was gifted—the detail in them is remarkable—but most of them resemble covers to bad science fiction novels—*Attack of the Dragonfly People; The Ant-Man vs. The Hummingbird Woman*. They feel like technical exercises. It's as if, here was this talent waiting for its subject matter.

Rudolph found that subject matter when he was twenty. That was when a copy of the book his Uncle Theo had written came into his possession. I've tried to track it down, but it's notoriously difficult to lay your hands on. Theo had it privately printed, and only a hundred copies at that, so it's one of those books you read about instead of read. From what I can tell, it's something of a cult classic. I'm surprised no one's tried to reissue it. Anyway, based on what people who've read the book have said, Theo's book has to do with cities. He had this idea that, once a city reaches a certain size, it comes to life. I don't mean metaphorically; I mean, they achieve consciousness. He uses all this bizarre math to show how this happens. Apparently, the size and shape of the buildings play into it. So does where they're placed in relation to one another. After a city becomes aware, it seeks to manifest that consciousness, which Theo claimed it does through a variety of avatars—apparently, he catalogued a dozen different shapes in which a city can express itself, each more bizarre than the last.

Theo's book captivated Rudolph's imagination. His friends and acquaintances grew used to the sight of him tucked away in a corner, his uncle's book open on his lap, him studying it intently. Theo had had the volume printed and bound on the cheap, and it wasn't long before Rudolph's copy was falling apart. He taped the covers together with some kind of heavy-duty builder's tape, and wound the whole thing around with twine and rubber bands. When it came to who could look at the book, Rudolph was extremely guarded. Once the book was falling apart, this was easy enough to understand, but even before that, he would snap it closed whenever anyone approached. One person—a woman he tried to seduce after he'd emptied a couple of bottles of wine at a party—convinced him to let her have a peek—I can't imagine what she must have been wearing to make him agree, but agree he did. She said the pages he opened to were a mess. The margins were crammed full of Rudolph's handwriting and drawings. He had circled words and phrases in the text and drawn lines between them, as if he were constructing his own text within his uncle's. This woman said that, when she reached out to touch the book, Rudolph slammed it shut and stormed out of the party without another word. Seduction over.

• • •

As was lunch. I left the dishes in the sink and headed back to the library. I couldn't bear the thought of a staring at myself in the monitor for the rest of the afternoon, so I scooped up the pile of print-outs and took them to the couch.

• • •

Rudolph had always been productive. Under the influence of Theo's book, he exploded, tossing off completed paintings like there was no tomorrow. One critic said it was as if Rudolph knew he wasn't long for this world, and was trying to fit a lifetime's worth of work into a few years. Had he lived to be sixty, this still would have been a lot. Much of it's the same. In painting after painting, Rudolph illustrates his uncle's central conceit, going from the southern tip of Manhattan to the northern in the process. There are about a hundred of these paintings. They're executed in the same, quasi-abstract geometric style, some a little more abstract, some a little more concrete. They're sufficiently detailed for you to identify each painting's subject, and they're sufficiently stylized for you to pick up on the underlying shapes structuring each piece. There is something impressive about Rudolph's desire to show Theo's ideas playing out up and down the island—at least in theory. In reality, it's painting after painting of this building, then that building, then another building, all of them bleeding a gray-white fog that coalesces into cryptic shapes—Theo's city-avatars. One critic speculated that, if you were to place all of these canvases side by side, you'd see a vast shape—the soul of the city—forming out of them.

Once he had completed this series, Rudolph began moving in other directions; specifically, he started to write. One of his acquaintances stapled together a bunch of mimeographed pages every other week or so that he called *Dionysia: An Expression of Culture* and tried to charge people a dime for. Rudolph gave him these short, one-to-two-page essays full of typos that the guy pretty much printed as is. The first one had the title "Locimancy," which I don't think is especially good Greek but which was supposed to mean "place magic." Eighteen more followed, all with the same name—the editor was the one who added a number to each to distinguish it from the previous essay. Rudolph was not what you would call a gifted prose-stylist. All that missed school came back to haunt him. He writes what we used to call "Engfish," that kind of English college freshmen tend to use when they're trying to sound smart enough for the rhetorical situation. He's positively eighteenth century in his use of capital letters. Not to mention, what he's trying to express sounds, by and large, insane.

He spends the first couple of essays rehashing his uncle's book. Having laid out the basics of Theo's thought, Rudolph then spends three essays pointing out the flaws in those ideas. For him, there are two problems with Theo's book. One, it thinks too big. It doesn't realize that there's no need, as Rudolph puts it, "to lift our Eyes so High to witness such Grand Processes." Two, it scants artists, especially in their role as "Midwifes" of the Grand Process. Essays six through eighteen are a kind of speculative crash-course in how the artist can "Quicken" a place. They're a mix of circular logic and impossible mathematical formulae. The sentences say things like, "As they Give of themselfs to the Work, therefore shall the Work Give them back Themselfs." The math literally does not add up. I read someone who said that it's as if Rudolph is using the math symbols we know to express his own set of concepts, but my first impression was, the equations were the equivalent of Rudolph's style, attempts to make him seem smarter than he was. After all, who was going to call him on it? How many artists can do math? Or sorcery, for that matter?

The last essay in the series is half-finished, or so the theory goes—it's even less coherent than the others. It's a warning about the ideas he's just outlined that seems to be trying to make the previous essays appear more important by stressing how dangerous they are. At the same time, Rudolph can't resist bragging about how there are places that demonstrate the truth of everything he's said and more. He warns his readers to avoid "the Crooked House" in Red Hook, and cautions against waiting alone at the Eighty-second Street subway platform.

No one knows whether Thomas Belvedere read any or all of Rudolph's essays, but I'm willing to bet that, if Rudolph didn't send him copies with his letters, then the letters themselves expounded his ideas. What Belvedere did see was the first of Rudolph's paintings to come out of these essays, a piece Rudolph also called *Locimancy*. I gather the canvas is pretty big, about six feet high by eight long. On it, he painted a cross-section of the apartment he and his mother shared with her second-cousin, rearranging the space slightly so that the living room sits at the center of the picture. At the center of the center, there's a man, Rudolph's copy of da Vinci's Vitruvian Man— you know, the naked man with his arms and legs stretched out one way inside a circle, the other inside a square. Rudolph includes the circle and square with his copy, which is pretty faithful, except for the face, which he's replaced with his own. The figure is too big for the apartment; proportionally, he's a giant. Rudolph maintains the parchment color of da Vinci's drawing, inside the circle and square, so that you're looking at this reasonably cheerful mid-twentieth-century interior with a faded-yellow heart. The effect—it's as if Rudolph painted around da Vinci's original. There's one other change he makes to da Vinci. Where the figure's eyes and genitals should be, there are three black holes, as if he'd cut those sections out of the canvas.

If you were willing to stretch the point, you could argue for similarities between a painting like this and what Magritte and Dali were doing, but Rudolph had almost nothing in common with the figures who were already dominating American art, Pollock and de Kooning, Motherwell. The only reason—well, not the only reason, but the principle reason *Locimancy* was included in the show where Belvedere first saw it was that the gallery owner had a thing for Rudolph's mother. Most of the contemporary reviews fail to mention the picture at all. The couple that do, dismiss it as an inexplicable lapse on the part of the organizer.

All of which made it more interesting that Belvedere should have been so taken with the painting. With the exception of Rudolph de Castries's work, Thomas Belvedere's interests and influences are fairly conventional. He'd been infatuated with Picasso, only to reject him as too facile, unwilling to pursue any one style far enough to produce anything truly profound—the quality he claimed to find in Pollock's gigantic swirls. You get the impression, though, that Belvedere admired the quality more than he did the pieces he claimed to find them in. At heart, I think, he was uncomfortable with how far away from the figural Pollock and the other Abstract Expressionists strayed. In Rudolph's work, Belvedere must have seen not so much an answer, but the means to an answer.

Nor did it hurt that, once Belvedere was in regular correspondence with Rudolph, Rudolph was advising him to leave the wife and kids who had become more of a burden than Belvedere had anticipated. There's nothing like being told exactly what you want to hear to cement a friendship, is there? If you believed Viola, though, there was more to it than that. Something about Rudolph's ideas spoke to Belvedere. I guessed it was his artist-as-shaman bit—most artists are suckers for that kind of line. I also guessed that, over the summer Belvedere had spent in Huguenot, he had done his best to put Rudolph's ideas into practice.

He would have learned how to do so in the sixth "Locimancy" essay, most of which is taken up with a diagram that sort of resembles the star you put on top of a Christmas tree—there are all these irregular points constructed in precise ratios to one another. Line A is two-thirds longer than Line B, which is three-fifths Line C, and so on. You graph this design onto the space you want to awaken—maybe I should say "into" the place. You work out all the necessary dimensions, then perform a number of gestures at each of the star's points. There's an order you're supposed to follow—first point 13, then point 3, etc.—and you're supposed to complete the ritual within twelve hours. At the end, you go to your easel—strategically positioned, of course—pick up your brush, and start painting. The gestures that are required at each of the star's thirty-one points—sip from a glass of red wine, bow to the left, the right, the earth, the heavens—were simple and repetitious enough to have the feel of the sacred. I could believe that, having gone through the entire process, you would approach your canvas like a priest approaching his altar.

The problem with Rudolph's design is that there's no baseline. Although he tells you what relation the parts of his star must have to one another, he never specifies its proportions relative to the place it's supposed to be awakening. Do you construct it in one room, or do you use the entire building, or do you need the space around the building, too? It's completely self-referential. The "True Artist" will know what to do with the tools Rudolph has given him—which struck me as so much ass-covering. Thomas Belvedere lucked out—either that, or he was a True Artist.

• • •

My headache, which had kept its distance for the better part of the afternoon, finally surrendered around the time I heard Roger pass the library on his way downstairs to order dinner. Funny—there was a time when the prospect of being able to order out for your meal every night would have struck me as the lap of luxury. Now, the prospect of another assortment of aluminum-foil dishes and white cardboard boxes seemed almost unbearably depressing. I left the library and hurried after Roger, but he was gone. He'd taken the car and gone to place his order in person. For a moment, I considered returning to the second floor to read more about Rudolph, then decided I had had enough of his over-heated prose for the time being. Instead, I poured myself a glass of white wine and went outside to sit on the front step and drink it.

The evening was hot, the air tropically humid. Walking out the front door was like walking into a cloud of steam. As I passed through the doorway, there was another sensation—as if the doorway had been stretched tight with some kind of gauze: It was like when you're out walking and you blunder into a spiderweb. I brushed my arms, neck. There was nothing on them. The feeling that there was, however, that there was something all over me, persisted. *More weirdness*, I thought, *terrific.* The sensation wasn't as bad as it sounds—not quite—the heat and humidity definitely had the edge—but it wasn't pleasant, either. If I'd been claustrophobic, this would have been worse. As it was, I was mostly annoyed. No doubt the experience would cease the moment I walked back into the house, but I had come out here to sit and enjoy my drink, and by God, that was what I intended to do. I plopped myself down and raised the glass to my lips. I could still taste the wine, at least.

• • •

There was one last wrinkle to Rudolph de Castries's story, and as the sweat raised itself through what now felt like a film all over me, I considered it. At the very end, about a month before he dropped dead, Rudolph made a series of strange—but given his theories, potentially significant—remarks. Most of them were to random strangers met at this or that party; although a couple were to a guy he was working with at a laundry. Only one was recorded reasonably soon after he spoke it—the young woman to whom Rudolph said, "Mirrors hold more than reflections. There are corners in them around which we do not—we dare not—see," recorded his remark in a letter to a friend the same night, so her report is considered fairly accurate. None of the others saw the light of day for almost another two decades, when the first biography was being researched, and questions remain about their authenticity. That said, apparently Rudolph told several people that he had not understood his own ideas. His co-worker from the laundry claimed Rudolph spent weeks talking about hidden folds and creases that concealed "relentless depths." That was Rudolph's word, the co-worker said, "relentless." It sounded pretty Freudian to me, and I was half-inclined to believe the critic who'd speculated that Rudolph's remarks hinted at an illicit relationship with his mother's second cousin. Other critics didn't give the statements nearly as much credence. Some wrote them off as essentially invented; while those who did accept them dismissed them as the products of a brain severely damaged by alcohol.

It was those corners, those folds and creases and their depths, that concerned me as I drank my wine. Assuming you could believe the reports, in the weeks leading up to his death, Rudolph had learned something about his ideas. For reasons unknown, he'd seen them in a different light, understood new implications to them. If he'd been speaking metaphorically, that could have been the significance of the corners and creases, tropes for his own blindspots to his theories. The question I was interested in was, What if he hadn't been talking in code? What if what you saw was what you got?

• • •

I found it hard to answer that question, however, because the sensation of something clinging to my skin was worsening. It had crept up on me as I was thinking. It was as if I were wrapped in fine plastic, my sweat pooling under it, my fingers cupping the wineglass through it. The feeling extended to my mouth—the tang of the wine seemed mixed with another taste, as if my teeth and tongue were coated with an oily film—even my eyes saw the lawn and street as if through a pair of dirty contacts. Everything had acquired a slight haze. Although I'd already done so without result, I wiped my hand on my arm, almost expecting to watch a layer of something like cling-film tear and come off on my fingers. Nothing. I could breathe, hear—though air and sound seemed delayed, as if they were coming from farther away.

The house—my awareness of the house, the thousand threads that wove my nerves into its walls and windows, had changed. Instead of that sense of the house just beyond the edges of my skin, now it seemed to press against me.

Not panicking was taking more of an effort. Everything in front of me, grass, trees, road, the house across the road, was surrounded by haze—a kind of mist shot through with rainbow streaks—the way things are when you're trying to see through a window that hasn't been cleaned properly. My skin was growing hot—hotter, as if the substance coating it were heating. Breathing was harder. The air seemed thick, almost liquid. Wineglass in hand, I struggled to my feet and walked down the front steps and out across the yard.

I know. Why did I go that way? Why not turn around and run back inside? I don't know. That was just the direction my feet took me. No, that isn't right. It was more a case of when I stood, I had a momentary impression of—of weight, of tremendous heaviness on the other side of the membrane—inside the house. It was unlike anything I'd experienced before, and standing on the front step seemed like standing much too close to it.

By the time I'd put fifty feet between myself and the front steps, I was sucking in air like an asthmatic in the middle of a bad attack. My skin was roasting, as if a great heat-lamp had been focused on me. And the haze—the haze had become clouds of color washing over the scene in front of me. The effect was most pronounced around the house, from which rivers, waterfalls, geysers of color streamed out. Scraps of rainbow chased one another up the walls, over the doors, across the windows. There was something else on the windows—there and gone so fast the only way to see it was to remember and slow down the memory. There, on the front parlor windows, Roger's face had been frozen in anger, the way it had been when he'd cursed Ted. There, on the living room windows, had been Ted, in Afghan dress, carrying his rifle, walking down a dark street. The windows to the library had shown streets I didn't recognize, what might have been desert landscapes. The third-floor windows—I couldn't remember— my eyes traveled up the house, trying to catch another glimpse, and I saw the mountains.

Towering over the house, the yard, steep, grooved slopes rising to stark crests—I'm not much good at estimating heights, but these things were huge. They weren't like the Ridge. These were more like the Catskills, enormous stone pyramids worn down by the millennia. With all the color loose in the air, it was hard to tell their exact shade, but I thought it was sand-colored, tawny. They were—you know how it is with mountains. They're there. They hold their space the way nothing else does—well, maybe the ocean. The late-afternoon sun cast shadows left to right across their slopes, highlighting the snow dusting their summits. I didn't forget to breathe, but for a long moment, that ever-more-difficult process was far away. I could feel them—not the same way I could the house—these were too much for one person to take in like that—but enough to know that they were alive. Or some-thing—they were full of energy, humming with it like great dynamos. Whether they were mountains that were living, or something else that appeared as mountains, I couldn't say, but my apprehension that they were more than rock was completely wonderful and utterly terrifying. It was the feeling I'd had on that long-ago whale watch with my dad, only magnified ten times, fifty times. I couldn't run from them— where was there to run from things like this? I half-felt I should fall down and hide my head in reverence.

A car door slammed. The special-effects show I was the center of stopped—blinked out like a popped bubble. The rainbow haze, the images on the windows, the heat baking my skin, the air too thick to breathe—not to mention the root cause of all of them, the invisible film coating me—fled, exorcised by the sharp clap of metal meeting metal. I bent over, gulping air. When I straightened, Roger was striding across the lawn to me, his expression a struggle between concern and annoyance. I tried to speak, but was too busy taking air in to spare any for explanations. The mountains were still there. Only long enough for me to verify that, yes, they were sand-colored, and then I was staring at the empty sky. Roger said, "What? What is it?"

"I—"

"You what? Are you all right?"

I shook my head side to side.

"What's wrong?"

The best I could do was shake my head again.

"You've seen something, haven't you?" He might have been accusing me of a particularly distasteful crime.

I nodded.

"Another vision of Ted? Of what you think is Ted?"

I shook my head. "No," I said. "Mountains. I saw mountains."

"Mountains?" Roger said. "What mountains? What did they look like?"

"Tall," I said, "sandy. There," I added, pointing to sky behind the house.

"Like the Himalayas?"

"I don't know," I said, "I guess."

Roger gestured toward the line of Frenchman's Mountain. "Not like that?"

"Definitely not."

"My God," he said, "I think you've seen something."

"Do you?" I said, finally finding my voice. "What was it that clued you in? Was it when I said I'd seen something, or was it that part about me seeing something?"

"I mean something important," Roger said. "Come inside—I'll show you." He turned and strode toward the house, ignoring the car and our dinner in his haste. I followed more slowly, stopping at the car to retrieve the brown paper bag on the front passenger seat. Funny, the things that seem important to you. Inside, I deposited the take-out on one of the tables in the hallway and trailed upstairs.

Roger was in his office, standing over the futon to the left. Do you know, for all the times I'd stood outside this room during the wee small hours, I hadn't seen it during the day for weeks? When I'd been here in the a.m., I'd been too occupied watching Roger study his strange map to attend to the rest of the office. It wasn't substantially different from before—the changes I noticed were by and large ones of degree. The bookcases and walls were hung with more maps, more points on which were connected to one another by pieces of thread. Roger had started using different-colored thread. I couldn't tell what each color signified. The tabletop model had gained an extra layer of buildings on all sides, as well as a new group of figures meant to be attackers. There were pictures scattered around it, three-by-fives that appeared to be of Kabul—a few showed American troops in close-up.

"Here," Roger said, ducking his head under a thread as he advanced holding an oversized book out to me. It was open to a two-page spread of mountains. I took the book from him and studied the image. "That was what you saw," he said.

"Could be." I wasn't sure. The photograph showed a cluster of mountains that looked approximately like what I'd seen filling the sky—same worn outline, same grooves carved into the sides, same dull yellow color—but there was something missing from it.

"Those are the Asmai Mountains," Roger said. "From the spot where Ted was killed, they are visible in the distance—if you look straight down the street on which his patrol was traveling, you can see them."

The sensation of life—of energy—that was what the photo lacked. "So you think this is a message from Ted?"

"I 'think' nothing. It can be nothing else."

"Maybe," I said, handing the book back to him. "I wonder why you didn't see them."

"I wasn't here," Roger said, returning the book to a pile on the futon. "Obviously, there was only a certain time at which Ted could communicate with us, and when that moment arrived, he had to send his communiqué, regardless of who was there to receive it."

"You mean, even if it was only me."

"I didn't—"

"Never mind," I said. "I find it interesting that you're willing to believe me on this, but you won't believe any of what really matters."

"It isn't that I don't believe you saw something in the restaurant,"

Roger said, "I don't agree with your interpretation of what you saw. I'm sure it isn't right. It can't be. Don't you see? What you've just seen proves that Ted isn't a monster—that he's continuing to reach out to us."

"That wasn't exactly what I had in mind," I said. "For what it's worth, whatever I saw out there proves nothing one way or the other—except maybe that Ted was involved in it." I held up my hand to block his reply. "What I meant was, you have no problem crediting my viewing mountains on the other side of the globe, but you can't accept that I saw you making your deal in the police cell."

"This again? My Faustian bargain? What will it take for you to abandon this nonsense?"

"Your admitting to it would be nice," I said, "but I'm willing to settle for you lifting the curse."

He crossed his arms. "I have told you already, I am not going to do that. It is a matter of principle. I refuse to validate your representation of me as some type of fiend."

"Even if it saves your son?"

"It will not save Ted. Its sole purpose is my humiliation." Roger pushed past me out of the room. "If you will excuse me, I am going down to dinner."

I went to call after him that I'd brought it in, then thought better of it. If he didn't notice the bag sitting on the hall table, let him search the car for it. Picturing the confusion on his face as he felt under the seats gave me more pleasure than it should have.

I wanted a look at the photos around the model. They were sprinkled with a fine layer of dirt—no doubt taken from or near the place where Ted had died. There were maybe two-dozen pictures, about half of which were of Kabul—including six that showed the square where the ambush had occurred. Judging from the scorch marks and bullet holes decorating the buildings, the photos post-dated the attack. The last picture in the series showed a shallow depression at its center; it took me a second to pick up on the charred ground and process that this was it, this was the spot where Ted had been torn apart by the RPG. Do you know, despite what I'd seen within the last hour, the picture of that scoop out of the earth, that burnt emptiness, was more deeply shocking than any of it? It was like, here was the thing itself—here was death in all its brute simplicity. Roger had lined up that picture, I saw, with the spot on the model where the figures of

Ted and the old man jostled for space with the grenade fragment inside the red circle.

The remaining pictures were of young men I was reasonably sure were other members of Ted's squad. Unlike the photos of the city, which appeared to have been taken all on the same day, the shots of the soldiers went back months. Some guys were in full dress uniform, others in fatigues, still others dressed as Afghans. I didn't know any of their faces. I wondered if Roger did, if he'd recognized them from his and Joanne's visits to Ted's bases. Whether he knew them or not, I was certain that, were I to flip over any of the pictures, I'd find not only their names, but every last bit of information about them and their relationship to Ted that Roger had been able to cram into the space.

On my way out of the office, I paused at the photo of the place where Ted's life had come to an end. Here was the blank spot at the center of things. Without it, the square was just a square, the soldiers just soldiers. With it, the square became a site of loss, the soldiers a company of the grieving.

I also paused to study Roger's doorway map, more crowded with notations than ever. The newer ones were so small it was difficult to read them, but roughly half appeared to be notes on the history of the place. These went back several hundred years, but Roger had employed a personal shorthand that rendered everything except the dates impossible to decipher. The other half of the new notes looked like astrological symbols. I'd never paid much attention to those kinds of things, but I was pretty sure I recognized the symbols for the moon and the crab, Cancer, as parts of short, apparently nonsensical equations. I thought I'd seen this kind of math on more elaborate horoscopes—they had something to do with the positions of the planets—or the stars—or both. The shorthand history and the astrological calculations had been written in gold ink. The center of the map, that white circle with Ted's old mirror inside it, remained pristine.

• • •

As I walked down the stairs to join Roger, an unpleasant comparison occurred to me: Roger's doorway map reminded me of Rudolph de Castries's misshapen star design. The comparison wasn't exact—the second I made it, I was aware of all the things they didn't have in common. Rudolph's design was meant to be realized in three-dimensional space; Roger's appeared confined to the page. Rudolph employed a definite, if irregular, shape; although there was that circle at the center of Roger's map, what appeared to be the point of it, the endless accumulation of detail, didn't seem arranged in any pattern. Rudolph's star was intended to establish certain points at which you would perform further actions; Roger's map was an end in and of itself.

Somehow, though, those differences didn't seem as pronounced as I wanted them to. What was more important—more significant—was the way they both tried to shape space, to identify and delimit the edges of certain events. I don't know. Phrased this way, the similarity sounds as if it was more about me than it was about them. I was reasonably sure Roger hadn't been studying the writings of Rudolph de Castries. If he had, he'd have produced a different map. I'd already asked him about the map; he'd already explained its purpose—and admitted to not understanding why he'd glued Ted's old mirror to the map. If I were to ask him about the latest information he'd added, I knew he would attribute it to his ongoing desire to understand the circumstances of Ted's death in all possible dimensions, including their relation to such larger contexts as the square's history and the position of the heavens.

That last one, though—I mean, it was at least evidence that Roger's obsession was running way out of hand. As if the rest of it hadn't been. I know. In the interest of fairness, I asked him about it over the take-out he'd ordered from the diner. He gave me the answer I'd anticipated, in pretty much the exact words. He was suspicious. Now that I had revealed what I'd see him do—excuse me, what I thought I'd seen him do—everything I said had to be examined for hidden meaning. He ended his explanation with, "What makes you ask?"

"Just curious," I said. "You have to admit, astrology isn't the first reference point you'd choose."

"It wasn't." Touché.

"How did you start?"

"Why?"

"For God's sake, Roger, stop acting like I'm the bad cop and you're the suspect. I'm asking because I want to know. If you don't want to tell me, then say so."

He was silent, chewing his Monte Cristo. Then he said, "I could not find an adequate map. As you will have noticed, you can order a great variety of maps, including satellite pictures. But I could not locate a map that showed me the site where Ted's patrol had been ambushed in sufficient detail, so I decided I would have to draft my own. I began with the location where he had died, and worked outward from there. After I had established the locations and dimensions of the square's buildings, the map still felt—incomplete, full of large, vacant spaces. I suppose you might say my decision to use those spaces to record the specifics of Ted's death was motivated as much by aesthetics—or something approximating aesthetics—as anything.

"Having listed the facts I had, there was still too much white space visible. If I thought about the event mathematically, however, there was plenty left to write. I switched inks and began listing those facts. Along the way, I learned a few more details about what you might call the written side of things and added them. Once I was finished with the math, there was less blank paper to see; less, but still too much. Especially inside the circle I had drawn around the spot where Ted had died—the first thing I had done once I'd established the spot's exact coordinates. All manner of information crowded the circle's circumference, but from the start I would not intrude on it.

"Finally, I recalled Ted's old shaving mirror. I sought it out and added it to the map. For a few days, I was so pleased with my decision that I left the map alone. I attempted to ignore the map, focused on reading and sending off inquiries via snail- and e-mail. No matter how much work I did, however, how tired I was at the end of the day, the map drew my attention to itself—those white patches seemed as large as ice-fields. I started to cast around for other information, turning first to the square's history—what I should call its deep history, as opposed to the more recent events I'd explored—and second to its astrology—as I've said, not in the interest of fortune telling, but as another way to fix what happened to Ted.

"And yes, before you diagnose, I am well aware that Freud would view my activity as the most elaborate kind of sublimation. Because an action can be interpreted one way, though, does not mean it must be. While such was not my conscious intent, I believe I may have been constructing what the Tibetans call a spirit map."

Here we were with the Tibetans again. "Which is?"

"A chart of the course a spirit takes when it exits this world and enters the bardo. Its purpose is to project the spirit's path as best as possible, in order to guide the prayers of those left behind."

"What's next?"

"What do you mean?"

"For your spirit map. You've approached Ted's death in terms of immediate and longer-term history, of science and superstition. What's next?"

"As yet, I'm uncertain. I have not exhausted either the square's history or its astrological dimensions."

I nodded. "What are you praying for?"

"I beg your pardon?"

"You said the purpose of a spirit map is to help direct the prayers of the bereaved. I'm curious as to what this map has told you."

"I don't think about it in those terms—not exactly. I don't engage in formal prayers—I suppose you might say I view my work as my prayer. You know the goal of that work: to see Ted at peace."

"And you won't consider—"

"No," Roger said. "I don't know why you insist on returning to this subject." He stood and carried his dishes to the sink.

"Because I think it'll help," I said to his back.

"You're wrong."

"How do you know? What do you have to lose by trying?"

"It's not a question of what I have to lose. It's what I have to gain, which is nothing." He finished rinsing his dishes, set them on the dishrack, and turned to leave. He said, "Must you continue to raise this topic at every chance you get? Can't you give me some peace?" Before I could reply, he left the kitchen.

Talk about touching a nerve. Melodramatic exits were becoming Roger's specialty. He couldn't see it was a case of methinks the lady doth protest too much. There was a possibility I was mistaken, but with every angry denial, Roger solidified my belief that I was onto something big.

• • •

Unfortunately, it was a big something I had no idea what to do with. I mean, I couldn't very well lift the curse for Roger—I was pretty sure the marriage bond didn't extend that far. Each time I raised the possibility of his doing so seemed to push Roger that much further in the opposite direction. I carried my dishes to the sink and, when I was done with them, walked into the living room.

There was more for me to read about Rudolph de Castries, if I chose. There were at least ten possibly relevant articles online. I didn't choose, though. I had had my fill of the bizarre for one day. I clicked on the TV, and there was the Demi Moore version of *The Scarlet Letter* just beginning. Have I mentioned how much I hate that film? I'm sure I must've. I swear, you and I could not have made more of a hash of that novel if we'd tried. You would think that a novel that's lasted a hundred and fifty years might have something going for it, but, oh no, not when it comes to Hollywood! Sorry. I could rant like this for hours. What a waste! What a waste of a great cast! All that money—wasted! If I wanted a distraction, I could ask for no better, and with Roger safely out of earshot, I was free to yell at the screen all I wanted. I set the remote on the couch beside me, and settled in for two hours of travesty.

During that time, as I was watching Demi strip naked yet again—as if her body could make us forget the compete lack of anything resembling a coherent script—and Robert Duvall off among the Indians—because someone had seen *Dances with Wolves* one too many times—I'm not sure whether I was aware of the house. In retrospect, it seems I must have been. Things were accelerating—I didn't know it sitting there on the couch, but Roger and I had less than twenty-four hours before our drama played itself out. The fat lady wasn't on stage yet, but she was practicing her scales in the wings. For as engaged as I was with the film—and that was pretty engaged; you know how involved you can become with something you actively despise—I must have registered the house's shifting. How could I not have?

The subtle changes I had sensed during my swoon the previous week had become more overt. The places where I had felt the house thinning were now thinned, opening directly onto the long tunnels I'd sensed on the other side of them. What was more, the rest of the house was also thinning. I mean, every last wall was yielding itself to an opening, to another of the tunnels that felt as if they'd been made of emptiness. It was as if, on the level where this stuff made its impression, the house as house was being replaced by the house as conjunction, as crossroads for all these long, blank corridors—if you'd tried to draw what was happening, you'd have come up with some kind of cubist conglomeration of tubes running in and out of one another. The house around me had converged with the house I'd seen when I lost the baby, all those doorways. No matter how incensed I was, yet again, by the battle between the Puritans and the Indians, I must have felt the house disappearing around me.

Rising from the couch, however, as the credits rolled, all I was interested in was going to bed. No surprise—the day's excitement had left me drained. There was a second when I thought I might have felt something—when my connection to the house might have flashed across my skin, and those cold corridors rippled over me—but, if the shiver I gave wasn't the result of fatigue, its cause was nowhere near as intense as what I'd been through that afternoon—really, as my normal awareness of the house—so I chalked it up to exhaustion. I closed up shop downstairs, and headed to bed, the movie's ending, which subverts everything the book stands for, burning in my mind. I wondered if anyone had written an article responding to the film—scratch that, I wondered how many articles had been written in response to the film. I pushed open the bedroom door, and to my surprise found Roger already there, in bed and fast asleep, snoring quietly. One day back from the Cape, and our routine had reasserted itself so strongly I had been expecting to be long unconscious before Roger slipped into bed beside me. Our continuing argument notwithstanding, I was less unhappy to find him here than I would have expected.

• • •

Had anyone asked, I would have said I hadn't the slightest intention of leaving the bed for Roger's nightly sleepwalk. I hadn't the night before, and he'd been fine. I needed rest, and although the sight of him under the covers had given my heart an unexpectedly pleasant lift, I was still pretty pissed at him. When the mattress shifted at three, however, and I swam up out of my dreams, my anger was slow to follow. It didn't catch up with me until I had pursued Roger down the stairs and out the front door.

Summer night or not, it was cold. The damp grass shocked my feet, and I wished I'd taken a sweatshirt with me. The breath steamed from my mouth. My teeth chattered. *This is what you get*, my anger told me as it arrived. *You could be warm in bed right now.*

I could have been, but my curiosity had awakened, too, and for the time being, it hurried me after Roger. He was striding around the house to my left, taking big, exaggerated steps like a kid playing at being an adult. He completed three and a quarter circuits of the house, counterclockwise, at a pace just short of a run, then stood, panting white clouds. As I approached him, I saw his face shining with sweat. He was shivering, too. The air was colder still; although I was warm from having played Roger's version of ring-around-the-house, I could feel the heat emptying from the air. Grass crunched under my feet, brittle with—yes—frost. Roger was staring intently at the stretch of lawn behind the house. It's a relatively narrow strip that ends in a line of tall, skinny pine trees. I wasn't sure what we were doing here, what this spot's connection to Ted was. I supposed the two of them could have practiced throwing or batting the baseball here. With the house's enormous south lawn available to them, though, it was hard to see why they would've chosen this place. I tried to follow Roger's gaze. Nothing.

I did a double take. Nothing was right. He was looking into solid blackness. Where you should have been able to see the silhouettes of a dozen pine trees, the distant lights of cars moving along 32 winking among their branches, there was unbroken dark. At first, I assumed it was because of the hour. There must be a lull in traffic; the businesses along the road must be closed. Including the all-night gas station? That wasn't right. There should have been some light visible. But no—about five yards from Roger and me, the lawn was truncated by blackness like denser night. That was the source of the cold. The grass nearest it wasn't frosted; it was frozen, locked in ice. The line of dark reached straight up from the ground. I craned my head back, and I couldn't see the stars in that part of the sky. It was as if someone had hung a giant curtain behind the house. I'd been more scared this afternoon, laboring to breathe through whatever had covered my mouth, and the mountains looming over the house had been more starkly impressive, overpowering—all the same, facing such pure blackness was unnerving. I don't know how you feel about being in the dark—I mean total darkness, the absolute absence of light. I guess some people are okay with it, but the mere thought of it makes my heart race, the back of my neck prickle. I drew closer to Roger.

Without taking his eyes off the black curtain, he said, "There it is."

No reply came to me. Roger didn't wait for one. He said, "It's something, isn't it?"

I couldn't help myself. I said, "What is it?"

He didn't answer right away, and I assumed he hadn't heard me. I could feel the darkness, out beyond the edges of my senses, the way you'd feel a feather flutter by the air it sent toward your skin. My impression of it as a curtain had been on target. It was huge, but it was also thin, so thin it was barely there. There was something beyond—a space like another room in the house—

"It's mine," Roger said.

"What?"

"Me."

"You're yours?" Why does dream logic have to sound like an old Abbot and Costello routine?

"It's mine."

"Oh," I said, "you mean this." I don't know why I pointed.

"Me."

"It's yours and it's you."

"Where's my boy?"

"Ted?"

"We're supposed to work on his slider." He paused. "He never comes to see me, anymore."

I didn't know where the conversation, such as it was, had just gone. I said, "Ted?"

He turned to me. His gaze was blind. "Do you know my boy?"

"Not really."

"He used to be so good." Roger sighed. "We used to have such a time together. Not anymore." He shook his head.

"What happened to him?"

"He died."

On impulse, I asked, "How did he die?"

"I locked him away. Threw away the key, as they say. Then he died."

"And he's still locked away?"

Roger didn't answer. I looked away from him, and the darkness moved, belled forward and fell back on itself as if a breeze had passed along it. In that movement, I thought I saw a shape—I couldn't tell if it was on the blackness, or behind it. It was—I dropped my eyes as fear made my stomach clench. It was Ted—no mistaking him.

Roger shrugged. "I have to assume. He won't tell me anything. He won't speak to me at all."

The briefest glance I could manage showed Ted more definite. I wanted to flee, run back inside, but my legs wouldn't do what I told them. Through chattering teeth, I said, "Roger, Ted—"

Suddenly, Roger was shouting. *"Where is he? What have you done with him? Where is my little boy? Where is my little boy? Where is my little boy?"*

I thought he'd wake himself. He didn't. I lurched forward, grabbed his arms, and shook him. "Roger!" I said. "Wake up, Roger, wake up. It's just a dream. It's just a dream."

There was a long moment during which he continued shouting, *"Where is my little boy?"* I threw my arms around him, repeating, "It's just a dream; it's just a dream." His body was electric. I was afraid he'd keep shouting till my ears bled—that, or one of the neighbors called the cops. Then, in mid-yell, his voice fell off and he relaxed against me. I kept on with my "It's just a dream," until I heard him saying, "Veronica? What? Are we outside?"

"You were sleepwalking," I said into his chest.

"I was—why are you holding onto me? What happened?"

"You were upset."

"Upset—over what?"

"Ted."

He tensed. "What about Ted?"

"Never mind."

"What do you mean? What about Ted? What was I so upset about?"

"Roger," I said, "you don't want to know."

Taking me by the shoulders, he pushed me away. Still holding onto me, he said, "I want to know."

I glanced at the place where the black curtain had hung. Of course, it was gone. The fear that had transfixed me was gone, too, elbowed aside by anger. "Why?" I said. "So you can throw up your hands, tell me it isn't true, and run back inside? So you can tell me I don't know what I'm talking about? Forget it, Roger." I pulled free of him and started back around the house.

He caught up to me inside the front door. "Veronica."

"I'm going to bed," I said. "It's ridiculously late."

"Don't," he said. "Don't be so angry with me. I'm only trying—"

"I don't know what you're trying to do," I said, spinning to face him. "You certainly aren't trying to find a way out of this for any of us. You hide up there on the third floor all day, and you know what's wrong—you know what's behind all this—and you know what you have to do, too. But you don't—you wait. Why? Because you're embarrassed—you don't want to admit that you did anything so terrible, so despicable. Well here's a newsflash, Roger: I already know. I already know the depths to which you sunk. There's no point in trying to hide it from me, because I saw it—I saw it firsthand. Which means the only person you're trying to deceive is yourself."

"Wait—"

"Do you want to know what you said to me outside? Do you really? You said that you locked Ted away and threw away the key. What do you suppose that means? You're the esteemed literary critic—you're the one with all the books and articles—how do you interpret that statement? What's its symbolic content?"

"I cannot talk to you when you're like this," Roger said.

"Whatever." This time, I was the one who stormed off.

I wasn't expecting Roger to return to bed. I was reasonably sure I'd hear him pass the door on his way up to his office. It's never too early to indulge your obsessions, right? Five minutes after I turned off the light, though, the door opened. Roger came into the room and settled beside me. Trying to make a point, I knew, which woke the anger that had decided to call it a night right up again. Who knew if Roger was going to sleep? There was no way I was, and how much do you want to bet that was his intention?

If sleep wasn't for me, however, I wasn't going to leave the bed. I could lie here quietly as long as Roger could—longer, with the anger fueling me. The delights of marriage. You know, years ago—I must have been about thirteen—I asked my mother and father what they thought the secret of a successful marriage was. I can't remember why; I think it was for a school project. Anyway, I put the question to the two of them over dinner one night. Right away, Dad said, "Compromise—then give in and do what your mother wants," which made her purse her lips and say, "Honestly."

Mom took longer to respond. When she did, she said, "Don't go to bed angry with one another. No matter how long it takes, stay up and work it out." Dad grunted in surprise and said, "I change my mind. What your mother just said." Lying next to Roger—who either ceased pretending to sleep or had developed a remarkable ability to mimic a snore—I thought about that advice. In the beginning,

Roger and I had never gone to bed angry—I mean, there were a few times we hadn't exactly been speaking to one another, but that had been over things like the relative merits of Norman Mailer. Not that those debates weren't important—because they are; I hate people who say, It's all just words, what does it matter?—but compared to what we were in the midst of now, the pros and cons of *Ancient Evenings* seemed a tad less weighty. The past couple of days—if we went to sleep at the same time, we were as likely as not to be in the middle of an argument—of what I supposed was The Argument. Granted, my parents had done their fair share of going to bed angry—you could tell because one or the other of them slept on the living room couch— to be honest, after they'd had a particularly bitter argument, I used to think it was a race—surreptitious, of course—to see who could make it to the couch first. Mom's advice sounded great, but was sometimes hard to practice.

However nasty the fights between Mom and Dad, though, I'd never felt the same gap between them that yawned between Roger and me. I suppose you could say that I wouldn't have been aware of that kind of distance between my parents—I was too young—but we were pretty tightly knit, even after I morphed into the teenager from hell, and I picked up on a lot. There are moments in every marriage—every relationship—where you realize you aren't going to be able to come to agreement on something; you're going to have to try to move past whatever it is. But this—I didn't know what I—we were going to do about this.

My anger hadn't abated, but fatigue was stealing over me, anyway. At least I'd managed to fake sleep longer than Roger had. I saw that curtain of night in my mind's eye, saw the grass frozen into white angles in front of it. Beyond it, there had been—what? Space—like an enormous room—an auditorium on whose stage a production is about to commence. What play? A cross between *A Midsummer Night's Dream* and *Macbeth*, or maybe *King Lear*. Or *Night of the Living Dead*. The principle actor—well, I would be happy to miss his debut. The thing was—for all that this space had appeared across the yard from the house, the sensation I'd had was that it was another part of it. It was like—this isn't right, not exactly, but it was like that science experiment they have you do when you're a kid, when you put a pencil in a glass of water to study the angle of refraction. What had been on the other side of that blackness had been the house—or part of the house—refracted.

When I consider that I fell asleep after one of that day's events, let alone all of them, it's hard to credit. Show me a giant wall of blackness now, or sudden mountains looming over the house, or let me feel as if I'm coated in some kind of film, and I'd be up for a day, maybe two—I guarantee it. It sounds glib to say you can get used to anything, but let's face it, you can—and what I'd seen and felt that day hadn't been the worst. One moment, I was floating on top of sleep; the next, I was diving down into it.

• • •

It's difficult to convey just how normal the following day was. The calm before the storm, you could say—although the weather had been pretty rough already. The eye of the hurricane, then. When we should have been preparing for more wind and rain, we decided to go to the beach, so to speak. That isn't quite true. Throughout that day, I was aware of how still everything was. It was like one of those cheesy old movies where the explorers are going through the jungle, and one of them says, "I don't like it. It's quiet. Too quiet." I wouldn't go so far as to say I had a bad feeling about the silence—it was more a case of, I wasn't sure how to read it. By the time late afternoon rolled around and nothing had happened—I'd been in and out the house a couple of times, once to go to the post office and once to run to Shop Rite, and hadn't seen, heard, smelt, or felt anything even slightly unusual—by the time I was starting to plan dinner, the day's quiet had made me hope—not a lot—that maybe we might have reached the other side of everything. It was a hope that died almost immediately after its birth. Too much had gone on—too much had been set in motion for it all to come to a halt just like that.

In between my excursions, I'd found myself face to face, so to speak, with one of the photos of Ted I'd hung throughout the house— what seemed like a decade ago. It was in the laundry room, where I'd gone in an effort to make a dent in the mountain of dirty clothes heaped on the floor there. If I waited for Roger to get around to it, I'd be naked, and pretty soon at that, so I'd done my best to separate whites from colors and set the washer going. I hadn't brought a book to read while the machine chugged away, nor was there a magazine in easy reach. As I'd killed time debating whether I wanted to run up to the second floor, or go through to the living room and the delights of midday TV, I stumbled across the photograph.

I'd forgotten I'd placed it here. At the sight of it, I sucked in my breath and drew back, blushing as if I'd been discovered spying. The picture was familiar. It was the one of Ted in Afghan dress, looking like the men he was supposed to be fighting, a book—*Bleak House*— open in his hands. Why I'd selected the laundry room for this photo, instead of, say, the wall outside Roger's office, was a mystery. I leaned in closer to study the picture—carefully, as if I didn't want to disturb it. Ted's face wore the concentrated expression of someone laboring over a difficult, but not unrewarding, task. How hard had reading Dickens been for him? Had he finished the book? The question hadn't occurred to me before. How would you find out the answer to such a thing? Would any of his friends know? Considering that photograph, studying it, it was possible to think of Ted as not unlike one of the returning students you get in Comp 1 or 2 sometimes—someone with a good ten or fifteen years on the average college freshman— someone who'd gone out to see what the world had to offer and now was ready for college. You had to admire someone trying to broaden his horizons—especially by reading Dickens, for God's sake. What had he written on the other side? "Even here, I can't escape this guy."

But as the washer had gurgled and churned, I'd heard Roger saying, "Boy, the best part of you dribbled down your mother's leg." He might as well have been standing in the laundry room with me. "And when you die, may you know fitting torment." Another voice had accompanied his: that of the thing in the corner—the house— that house that Roger had built, so to speak. "Blood and pain," it whispered, and the words had slithered around the room. Turning away from the picture, I'd departed the laundry room for the idiot comforts of the TV.

Blood and pain, I heard as I stood in the kitchen hours later. They were the kinds of things you sealed covenants with, weren't they? Wasn't that what the priest said during mass, during the consecration: "This is My blood, the blood of the new covenant"? You drank that blood, and you were included in the pact. Pain was part of the deal; there was no blood without pain. The pain authenticated the blood.

Roger spent the day in his office. We passed each other at breakfast, and at lunch, with the bare minimum of conversation—in fact, I don't think we said anything at all during breakfast. On some abstract level, I wasn't happy about that but, really, what was there to say? We were like a pair of actors who can't stop repeating a scene. "Lift your curse." "No!" *Exit Roger.*

• • •

If all of this were a movie, and me its director, this would be the moment where I'd have me reflecting on my marriage. I'd probably have Roger doing so, as well. You'd have a shot of me opening kitchen cabinets and sifting through them, followed by a shot of Roger, picking up a book from his desk and opening it—very symbolic actions—then there would be some kind of scene from earlier in the film—just a snippet, shown slightly out-of-focus to make it clear this is a memory—a mutual memory. I imagine I'd choose the first class I had with him. Why not begin at the beginning, right? From there, we'd alternate among those three locations, the action in each advancing a little more each time. Now I'm running water into a pot, Roger's writing on a legal pad, and we're in bed together. Did I mention there's a song playing on the soundtrack? Of course there is. Something slow, full of anguish, regret, and possibly a string section. If I wanted to be artsy, I'd choose an aria from some opera or another—but you have to expect the studio heads would insist on something more commercially viable. Fine. I'm sure Bryan Adams would be available. By this time, the song would be nearing its guitar solo. I would be slicing tomatoes, Roger would be staring at a map, and the two of us would be standing in front of the judge, holding hands as we recite our vows. There's time for one more set of images, maybe two. You'd show me—first turning off the burner and removing the pot from the stove, then standing looking out the kitchen window, arms crossed, forlorn. Roger would put down his pen, raise his glasses, and we'd see him looking out his office window, arms crossed, forlorn. Parallelism, you understand. As for the memories, the Greatest Hits of Veronica and Roger, Volume 1, what would the last two be? Would you want them to be ambiguous—me watching Roger sleep in his hospital bed; the two of us in the car returning from the Cape—or would you prefer to keep them relatively happy—the waiter setting our main courses in front of us at the Canal House; the two of us walking on the beach? Marriage as a three-minute montage—you want to remind the audience of the good times the protagonists have shared, set them up so that what's coming next has real impact.

None of that would've been inappropriate. All of it happened— we had had good times together—great times together. There were moments I was as happy with Roger as I've ever been, and given the right set of circumstances, I might have indulged in just such a mental movie of our relationship. Except—well, except for everything else, for the other movie advertised on my inner marquee. This one's title was *Roger Croydon: The Dark Side*—a bit over the top, but essentially on target. I don't have to tell you what scenes it showed.

When you're in a relationship—at first, you can't believe how much you have in common, right? You find similarities all over the place, no matter how much of a stretch they seem to anyone else. He likes the Yankees and you're from New York? It must be fate. That doesn't last for too long. At some point, you start to notice the differences. If you're lucky, either those differences are minor enough to be insignificant—lovable quirks—or they complement each other—the whole "opposites attract" thing. If you're unlucky, those differences become glaring and irreconcilable. What started with you noticing the other person likes to put butter on the bread for their tunafish sandwich ends with one or the other of you packing your things in cardboard boxes you got from the liquor store. When you're fifteen and your boyfriend turns out to be an alien, it's rough. Your world is over; how will you ever love again; blah-blah-blah. When you're twenty-six and you've seen beneath the mask your sixty-five-year-old husband puts on so he can look at himself in the mirror each day, it's a combination of completely depressing and terrifying. I'd known there was a lot to Roger when we got together. He'd been around for longer than I had—a lot longer—and nobody's perfect. But there had been a connection there. I had felt it. We had been inevitable. A consecration of its own, remember? Of course, inevitable doesn't mean eternal, and as I boiled water for the spaghetti that would accompany the vegetable sauce simmering on the stove, I had the sickening thought that maybe I'd—we'd made too much of all this. Maybe Roger and I had never been meant to have anything more than a fling. We might've been together for a couple of years, even, but when all was said and done, we'd been supposed to go our separate ways. If that were the case—

No, I thought, *I got pregnant—there was the baby—our baby. And what happened to that child?* my inner devil's advocate asked. *Your*

*husband sacrificed it to guarantee his revenge on his older son. Quite the
candidate for Father of the Year, wouldn't you say?*

So why did I stay? Why didn't I pick up my purse and car keys
and drive as far away from that house as fast as I could? I mean, that's
the question you always ask in these kinds of stories, isn't it? Sooner
or later, you say, "Why didn't she leave? Why didn't she get out while
she could?" In the film, that's why you have that montage of happy
memories—to justify the decision to stay. "Oh, look, she still loves
him." As importantly, "He still loves her," so she's making the right
decision. I did love Roger—despite everything, the feeling refused to
die—but that emotion wasn't foremost in my mind. I wouldn't call
what was duty, but it wasn't that far removed from it, sort of a, "You
made your bed," sentiment.

Maybe watching that wretched adaptation of *The Scarlet Letter*
the previous night had stirred the idea; although I doubt it. It's one
of the things I've always responded to most strongly in Hawthorne's
novel, Hester Prynne's refusal to evade the consequences of her decision. She made a choice, and she will accept whatever comes as a
result of it. She could run away, she knows that, but that would be
dishonest. Speaking as a feminist, I find it one of the most frustrating
things about Hester's character. "No," I want to say, "what are you
doing? Don't you realize that by doing this you're only propping up
a corrupt system? You can leave—go!" But she doesn't go—it's as if,
through staying, she owns what happened. I don't want to sound as if
I thought, "Gee, I'll be just like Hester." It's more a case of using her
example to describe a similar impulse within myself. I'd like to say I
stood in the front door with my keys in hand, or even that I made it
as far as backing the car out of the driveway. Those would have been
more dramatic, wouldn't they? And they'd make it appear I'd struggled
more to avoid what was coming next. I didn't, though. Keys and purse
remained where they were on the hall table. Instead, I drained the
pasta, plated it, and ladled the sauce over it.

• • •

As for Roger, I'm not a hundred percent certain, but I'd be willing
to bet he spent his day attending to the map by the door. Although
the nine sheets of paper that composed it were overcrowded with
his handwriting, with letters, numbers, and occult symbols in blue,

black, red, green, purple, and gold ink, he would have been unable
to see anything but the few remaining white patches—to you or me,
barely noticeable; to him, vast empty spaces, ice-fields stretching to
the horizon. There was still more research to be done, more facts to be
collected. His most recent acquisitions, he'd read three times already.
The books he'd had longer he'd half-memorized. He didn't read them
so much any more as let his eyes drift across the pages, on the lookout
for information—facts, connections—that might have eluded him.
The clock was ticking; I was seeing the Asmai Mountains over the
house; Ted was near.

What a relief it must have been when a new fact caught his
gaze. He must have run to the doorway with it burning in his mind,
like a prophet taking dictation from God. Once the detail had been
recorded, he would have stood back and admired his work, happy
that that much more of the paper's unforgiving whiteness had been
occluded. Did his eyes stray to the circle at the center of his construction? To the silver window of the mirror glued there? I imagine
him doing his best not to look at it and being unable not to catch
a glimpse of his reflection. Did he see anything else in there? In the
strip of office shining in the center of the map, did he see a figure
standing as if across the room from him? Did he turn, his son's name
on his lips?

• • •

Shortly after I finished my dinner and put Roger's in the oven to keep
warm, the phone rang. I wasn't expecting anyone to call, although I
felt a surge of hope that maybe Addie was calling to invite me out for
another meal with her and Harlow. She wasn't. I picked up the phone,
and heard my mother saying, "Veronica? It's me. It's Mom."

Talk about the last person on earth you would have expected. I
mean, since our little chat after my wedding, I literally had not heard
from her once. Encounters with the supernatural included, there have
been few times in my life I've been speechless. This was one of them.

"Hello?" Mom called. "Is anybody there? Veronica? Are you
there?"

"Mom," I said. "Hello."

"You *are* there," she said. "I was afraid I'd dialed the wrong number—I hate when I do that."

"No," I said, "you dialed the right number."

"I know it's been a long time since we talked," Mom said. "You haven't called me at all—but before you jump down my throat, let me say that I haven't called you, either. I know that. The telephone works both ways. The last time we spoke—I've been very upset about the way that went. You said some very hurtful things to me, when I was only expressing my opinion, which I think I have a right to do as your mother. But I didn't call to argue. All that is past, now, so let's try to put it there. How are you doing?"

"I'm hanging in there," I said, because, really, I hadn't heard from this woman in years, and I'm supposed to open up to her, forget everything she said?

"And—Donald? Your husband—what is his name? I assume you're still married."

"Roger. And yes, we're still married."

"Roger, that's right," she said, as if she hadn't remembered it all along. "He's well?"

"More or less," I said. "To tell you the truth, he's been having kind of a rough time recently."

"Oh? Why is that? His health?"

"His son. He died not that long ago."

She inhaled sharply. "I'm very sorry to hear that. What was it, drugs?"

"A rocket-propelled grenade," I said. "He was in the Army. He was killed in Afghanistan."

"How terrible. Were you close?"

"Not really. But it's done a number on Roger."

"Of course, of course. I can't think of anything worse than losing your child. However much you fuss and fight, you never stop loving them. Please tell him I'm very sorry."

"I will."

"Has he spoken to anyone about it?"

"Just me."

"No one professional?"

"No."

"Encourage him to. After your father died, I was a wreck, I don't mind saying. You weren't any help. You were busy with your own grieving, I know. For a little while, I felt like I was losing my mind. You have no idea how bad it was. At times, I just wanted to join your father. Fortunately, I went to see Father Gennaro and he put me in touch with a very nice nun who did grief counseling. I don't have her number, but I can give you her name."

"That's okay. If he goes, we'll probably use someone local."

"Of course. How about you?"

"I'm coping."

"It must be difficult for you. I've never known anyone in exactly the same situation—we did have a friend who married a widow, but they were both young and her children were young. I'm sure you haven't known what to say. How could you? Do any of your friends have children, yet? You're not pregnant, are you? I assume you would have called me if I'd had a grandchild."

I was this close to telling her about the miscarriage. The information trembled on the tip of my tongue, razor-sharp. I swallowed my phrasing and substituted, "Not yet."

"Are you planning to have children? With your husband's age—how old is he?"

"Sixty-five."

"I thought he was closer to sixty. In that case—well, you need to take that into account. Not to put too fine a point on it, but it's no easy job raising a child, let me tell you. You want to be sure you're going to have all the help you can get, for as long as you can get it."

"We're not thinking about it right now."

"It's nice to be a young mother—I was with you, and that let me stay in touch with you much better than a lot of older women."

"How's California?" I asked.

"Very nice. The weather is gorgeous, naturally, although it isn't always perfect. It's very expensive, you won't be surprised to hear that, but I'm fortunate that your father left me very well provided for. Between the death benefit from his job and the life insurance policies, I'm—let's just say I can afford to live out here. I do some work with Aunt Shirley—actually, I've become quite involved in the business. I'm basically her partner; although neither of us puts it that way. The job's given me enough money to take some wonderful vacations. Last year, Bob and I went to Hawaii, and the year before that—"

"Wait a minute. Who's Bob?"

"Bob—what?"

"You just said you went to Hawaii with someone named Bob."

"Did I?"

"Yes, you did. Bob who?"

"Bob Foyle. He's—someone I met. Through your aunt."

"And you're seeing him? What am I saying? You went to Hawaii with him. Of course you're seeing him."

"Bob has been very good to me. He's a travel agent—"

"Thus the trip."

"Is there a problem with me seeing someone? Is there a problem with me being happy?"

"Are you going to marry him?"

"No. I've been married once, and while I loved your father dearly, once was enough. Bob agrees with me—he's divorced—actually, he's been married twice; as he says, 'Two times too many.'"

"You're living together, aren't you?" Talk about things you'd never expect to say to your mother.

"I don't see that that's any business of yours."

"Which is tantamount to an admission. Oh my God."

"It's not as if we could get married, even if we wanted to. Bob's looked into it, and he could have his first marriage annulled—he was very young—but the Church won't do anything about the second. And I refuse to be married in a civil ceremony. How tacky."

Thanks, Mom. "So you decided you'd just move in together."

"I don't know what you're getting so upset about, Veronica. Everybody does it, these days. It's the way of the world."

"Is that what you'd tell Dad?"

"As long as I don't marry anyone else, I don't think your father will care."

I laughed. "It's funny. I used to worry that Dad would have been disappointed in me, in the choices I'd made. After this, though—"

"Oh, he would have been."

"Excuse me?"

"Well, he would have. He used to have such high hopes for you—we both did. He had no doubt you'd make something of yourself. After the two of you had had one of your arguments, he would say things like, 'She'll make a fine lawyer.' I assume you haven't gotten your doctorate, since you haven't mentioned it. No man you brought home would have been good enough for your father—no daughter's choice ever satisfies her father—but someone old enough to be your grandfather? Someone with a full-grown son? I mean, you know what you are to him."

"I cannot believe you're saying this to me."

"I'm only telling you what your father would have thought. I knew the man for twenty years. I think I have a pretty good idea what his views were. He would not have approved of you and—Roger. In fact, he would have been very disappointed."

"This is incredible."

"Don't kill the messenger."

"I have to go," I said, hating the quaver in my voice.

"It's not my fault."

"I'll talk to you later," I said, and hung up.

I was expecting it to ring the next moment, my mother's angry voice reaching across the country to me. I stood with my hand hovering above the receiver, unable to decide whether I'd answer it or just pick it up and let it drop. The kitchen shimmered, then fractured as tears flooded my eyes. I hated that my mother could get to me like this, that she knew exactly the right button to push. Of course my dad wouldn't have approved of Roger—not in the abstract, anyway—but he would have come around once they'd had a chance to meet one another, spend some time together, maybe go to a baseball game. I had been Daddy's little girl, true, and there was no doubt he'd wanted what he thought was best for me—but he had also been a pragmatist, and I was reasonably sure that, once he'd seen how serious Roger and I were, he would have decided that, like it or not, this was the way things were going to be and he'd have to accept them.

I wiped my eyes, tasting salt in the back of my throat. I knew what this was really about—this was Mom feeling insecure about Bob the boyfriend and trying to distract attention—and at the prospect of Bob, a fresh wave of tears spilled down my cheeks. I didn't begrudge my mother her happiness—really, I didn't. Dad had been gone a long time, and there was nothing wrong with her finding someone new. Although there was no one who could replace my father—warts and all—that didn't mean I wasn't prepared to give whomever Mom picked a chance. It was just—a guy who'd been divorced twice? Once, and it's like, Who knows who was at fault? Look at Roger and Joanne. Twice, though, and you start to wonder. Why does this keep happening to this guy, i.e. what's wrong with him? How did he convince my mother, the woman who told me that sex was a sacred gift from God that could only be enjoyed fully within the bonds of marriage—how did this guy, this travel agent, seduce my mother into shacking up with him? Yes, after about seventeen, when I had my first serious boyfriend, I decided Mom's ideas about sex were positively Medieval, but that didn't mean I wanted her to come to the same conclusion.

The floor creaked behind me. Roger stood there, looking puzzled. My hand was still stretched over the phone. "Are you trying to make someone call you?" he asked.

"More like the opposite," I said, dropping my arm.

"I thought I heard the phone ring."

"You did. It was my mother."

"That was unexpected—wasn't it?"

"And how," I said, sniffling.

"She upset you—obviously."

"It's stupid. She called to tell me about her new, live-in boyfriend, Bob the twice-divorced travel agent." I laughed. "When you say it out loud, it sounds kind of funny."

"Is this her first boyfriend since your father died?"

"The first she's moved in with. The first she's told me she moved in with. I don't know. There were other guys she went out with, before she moved to Santa Barbara. None of them was serious. At least, I don't think any of them was serious. It used to annoy me that she wasn't more connected to the guys she was dating. I complained to my friends that it was like living with a fourteen-year-old flirt. Irony sucks, you know?"

Roger nodded. "That it does. Safely confined to the pages of novels, it's an interesting rhetorical device; encountered loose in the real world, it's a beast with steel claws and mirrors for eyes."

"Hey—that's pretty good."

"Thank you—now if only I could remember it."

"The perils of age."

"The insolence of youth."

"Do you want some dinner?" I asked. "There's a plate warm in the oven."

"That was why I came down in the first place. The odors of your cooking reached all the way to the third floor and drew me down from my lonely garret."

"Get yourself something to drink—there's beer in the fridge if you want it—and I'll grab the plate. Do you want bread?"

"No thanks. Is there salad?"

"There is. All we have for dressing is blue cheese, though."

"That'll do just fine."

My mother's call had given us a fresh topic for conversation. Seated at the kitchen table, Roger with his dinner, me with a glass of wine, we batted her words back and forth, speculating on the situation that had given rise to them as if she were a character in a novel. Roger's eyebrows lifted when I told him what she'd said about my father.

"Do you think she's right?" he asked.

"Yes and no."

"A balanced answer."

"He would have been—concerned," I said. "He would have worried about both our motivations, especially yours. He wouldn't have been very comfortable with me as the object of desire of an older man."

"Especially one closer in age to him."

"Yeah. He would have talked to me—he would have done his best to talk me out of being with you."

"Would he have succeeded?"

"No."

"That's a relief to hear."

"There would have been some kind of falling out. Maybe we wouldn't have spoken for a while. In the end, though, he would have come around. What about you?"

"Beg pardon?"

"Your father, I mean—or maybe your mother. What would they have thought of you marrying me?"

"Hmm," he said. "Do you know, I've never once asked myself that question."

"Because you know what the answer would be, and you don't want to think about it?"

"Oh, I don't know. Joanne would have offended their sensibilities much more than you. They weren't as concerned with the North-South divide as some. Mother wasn't at all; Father—every now and then, when he'd gotten good and drunk, Father would ramble on about the damn Yankees and how they were responsible for—basically for everything that was wrong with the world today. If only folks were more like him and his, things wouldn't be in such an awful mess. I remember once—not long before his death, he went on this same ramble and, when he reached the part about people being more like him, I said, 'What? You mean drunk?' It was a good line, one that had occurred to me years prior and that I had finally gained the daring to use. His hand darted out and slapped me so hard I fell off my chair. He caught me on the side of the head—for about a week, my left ear rang from the blow.

"But I digress. Drunk, Father would have found Joanne a damn Yankee bitch who thought her piss was Perrier and her turds caviar (one of his favorite sayings). Sober, he would have been profoundly uncomfortable around her. Mother—I remember my mother as always indulging me. While I have no doubt that Mother would have done her best with Joanne, she would have been acutely aware of the class difference, which would not have been helped in the slightest by Joanne herself, who would have been constitutionally unable not to patronize my parents."

"I'm glad we can talk about your ex-wife so much."

"I'm merely settling myself into their viewpoints. Where I grew up, there certainly were marriages where a substantial age difference existed between spouses. The majority of those were because the man in question's first wife had died, in general leaving him with one or more children in need of a mother. Since his age also meant he had accumulated some share of material goods, he had more to offer than the difficulties of raising someone else's resentful children. There was security to be had. I have the impression that these matches were tolerated quite well.

"There were cases, though—one or two—where the man in question abandoned his still-undeceased wife in favor of a younger woman. In one instance, the man lived with his infatuation for a year, then returned home. In the other, he divorced his former love and married the new one. Both men were regarded as damned fools/damned old men, with the 'damned' intended to be not only disparaging, but in some measure descriptive. They had surrendered to their lust, you see. This is not to say that the rest of the community was any purer. There was more than one child who looked nothing like its legal father. But these men had made a show of themselves—shown everyone else, I suppose, their own secret passions. That second couple—the ones that married—they were together almost fifty years, till he was ninety and she seventy, and by most reports quite happy, yet he never stopped being that damned old man.

"All of which is by way of saying that my parents' initial reaction would most likely have been shock and horror at their son's behaving like a damned old man, leaving behind a wife of thirty years for a younger woman—and a student of his, at that. If they could have kept the news from family and friends, I have no doubt they would. These days, everyone is more understanding than they used to be, but their appetite for scandal remains undiminished. Who doesn't love to see the mighty brought low, a big college professor acting like a goat in a pepper patch? The public implications of my decisions—the consequences for them—would have been foremost in their minds."

"And I would be, what? The siren whose song caused you to toss yourself onto the rocks?"

"Possibly. Probably—although they would have felt more comfortable blaming me. To them, I would have appeared some type of academic Don Juan, seducing pretty students willy-nilly."

"Willy-nilly?"

"It's a colloquialism. Perfectly acceptable in this kind of discourse."

"If you say so."

"My best guess is, the two of them would have treated you with formality so complete as to be absolutely freezing. You would have been an object of horror and fascination to them—especially Father, whose talk when he was in his cups would have been full of clumsy innuendoes and poor puns. God, I can almost hear him, now. We'd take them out to eat. He already would have had a few at the house, and when it was time to order and I chose something like chicken breast, he'd leer at the waitress and say, 'Ey-yeah, my boy's always enjoyed his breast—always liked it young and tender.'"

"Yikes."

"To say the least."

"So that would have been that."

"Pretty much. We would have been only too happy to watch them go; they would have been only too happy to leave. They would have found me—I almost said, 'a monster,' which isn't exactly true, but isn't that far from the truth, either. I can hear my mother saying, 'This is not how you were raised,' and while few if any parents counsel their children to avoid middle-age affairs and divorces, in a sense she would have been right. I—I stepped outside the bounds of what my parents knew. I behaved in ways that would have been alien and alienating to them. You might say I revealed hidden depths to them, but these would not have been depths they wanted to witness."

"What about the baby?"

"The baby?"

"The baby I—I lost. What if I hadn't miscarried? Would that have helped?"

Roger looked up at the ceiling. "Maybe. Since it was the reason for our actual marriage, I'm sure it would have added to the scandal—initially, at least. Mother was fond of babies, though. Even Father was a sentimentalist when it came to diapers and lullabies. He was worse when he was drunk. He'd want to hold any baby within a fifty-foot radius and talk nonsense to it. Slurred nonsense. Since he was both extremely assertive and not particularly coordinated after five or ten beers, he was a major source of anxiety to anyone with newborns at family parties. He dropped my cousin, Arthur."

"God."

"Arthur was fine—frightened, but fine. His father, Uncle Edwin, was so incensed he took a swing at Father that was clumsy enough for even Father to avoid. In return, he broke Uncle Edwin's nose."

"What a nightmare."

"Family gatherings were ever an adventure."

"We wouldn't have let him near our baby."

"How would we have stopped him?"

"Given the baby to your mom?"

"Maybe."

"You said she knew how to handle him."

"What I mostly meant by that was, when he hit her, she hit back, hard."

"Oh. Not much fun for a baby."

"No. Who knows? Maybe the old man would've dried out. If he'd lived long enough, maybe he would have followed Rick into rehab—I say followed, because there is no way he would have done such a thing himself. It would have taken something like my younger brother's constant pestering—which he can do; he can be very persistent—to convince him to lay aside the bottle. Maybe he and my mother would have mellowed with time. I can't picture them ever attending any kind of couples therapy. It's the problem with the dead. Not only do they remain as they were, they remain as they were to you. No matter what you may learn about them after they're gone—no matter how much you may come to understand them intellectually—emotionally, they will always be the same."

"I'm not so sure," I said. "I feel differently about my father now than I did when he died."

"No, you don't," Roger said. "You think you do, but what you feel now is what you felt all along. What you experienced when he died was the aberration."

"I'm reasonably sure I know my own feelings."

"Are you?"

"Yes."

"Fine, fine. I should be getting back upstairs. Always more to be done."

"Always."

"This has been nice, though. It's been nice not to argue for a little while, to talk."

I stood as he cleared his plate and carried it to the sink. My wine was long gone. I contemplated a refill, decided against it. As Roger went to exit the kitchen, I said, "Roger?"

He stopped. "Yes?"

"Why can't you see Ted?"

His face was instantly furious. "Why—what are you saying? Why can't you leave this alone?"

I held up my hands. "I'm not trying to be confrontational. Honestly, I'm not. I just want to know why it's been me."

"That was not Ted you saw."

"Okay, say for a moment it wasn't. It was, but maybe you're right. What about all the other stuff? Why me? Why not you?"

His eyes would have burned through metal. When he spoke, it was as if he were strangling. "I don't know," he said, and left.

• • •

So much for us talking again. Yes, I'd been reasonably sure he'd react this way, but hope springs eternal and all that. A civilized conversation, and I was ready to believe we could discuss what really mattered. In retrospect, I know that Roger must have felt like I was continually setting him up, constructing these increasingly elaborate dialogues that always ended in the same place. That I was right didn't help, either.

When the kitchen was clean, I decided to skip TV for a change. Instead, I went up to the library, switched on the computer, and logged online. Since he'd told me about the circumstances of its creation, the compulsion that kept him adding to it, Roger's doorway map had been on my mind. It was the heart of his days, and I suspected it lay near the heart of everything, all the weirdness. How, I couldn't say. Roger had called it a spirit map, a name he'd said he'd borrowed from Tibetan Buddhism. I called up Google, typed in "spirit map," and hit Enter.

• • •

Sifting through the 17,000 or so responses that popped up took some time. I didn't want a guide to Scottish distilleries. Nor did I want the eight steps for enhancing my spirituality. Arlington High's cheerleading homepage was right out. I entered new terms, refined the search, but the only effect adding "Tibetan," "Buddhism," or "Tibetan Buddhism" had was to summon links to sites about Tibet, Buddhism, and Tibetan Buddhism. Thinking that perhaps spirit maps didn't rate their own site—or that Roger had confused the terminology and it went by some other name—I clicked on the Tibetan Buddhism pages and skimmed them. It wasn't the most exciting way to spend an evening. A lot of the art the sites displayed was beautiful, strange and striking, but I'd never been particularly interested in comparative theology.

I found descriptions of the bardo, about which Roger had been broadly accurate. I also read about *The Book of the Dead*, the Lord of the Dead with his black and white pebbles and mirror of karma, and the six realms of the Wheel of Life. I wouldn't say I became an expert on the ins and outs of Tibetan Buddhism, but I learned enough to know that spirit maps were not among its paraphernalia. I mean, if you wanted to stretch a metaphor, you could say that *The Book of the Dead* was itself a sort of general spirit map, since it described the stages of the bardo and how to navigate them, but if you wanted the kind of individualized guide Roger had discussed, you had to turn elsewhere. Either he'd been mistaken, or he'd lied.

It was a strange thing to lie about, though; you have to admit. Inclined as I'd become to suspect Roger, I couldn't understand why he'd feel the need to deceive me about the origins of the spirit map. Unless, I supposed, there were no deeper origins—the map was just something he'd dreamed up and his reference to the Buddhists was an attempt to disguise how completely personal it was. Or, if he were embarrassed about its source—which seemed unlikely to the point of absurd—until I Googled "spirit map" one last time and, on a hunch, added "Dickens."

What came up was a link to a site called *The Occult Dickens*, which was in fact the manuscript of a book this guy—Christopher Graves, self-described independent scholar—had been unable to find a publisher for. So he'd posted all three hundred and fifty pages of the thing online. Briefly put, the book was a survey of Dickens's interest in the occult and how it informed his fiction. Not, in and of itself, an unpromising topic—to be honest, it struck me as a lot more interesting than the latest effort at relating *Bleak House* to the tax laws of the day. What had cost Graves a publisher, I was sure, was his insistence at the outset on the validity of nineteenth-century spiritualism, which transformed a well-researched study into a lengthy tract, and took Dickens's novels from stories about things seen to arguments about things unseen.

Anyway, there was a search box for the manuscript, so I entered "spirit map." The page that appeared was titled, "Dickens, Collins, and the 'Spirit Map.'" I scrolled down. The story came from a couple of Wilkie Collins's letters. Apparently, Collins had visited Dickens while Dickens and his family were staying in Paris. (I'm not sure why the Dickenses were in France in the first place; Graves didn't say.) During their time together, Collins and Dickens went for walks around the city, and, on one of them, while they were basically window-shopping, they came upon a bookstore. Collins was excited because he found all these books about French crimes—a kind of true crime collection that he snatched up and I gather used in some of his fiction.

Dickens picked up an oversized volume that Collins said looked on the verge of collapsing into dust at any moment. The expression on Dickens's face when he touched its covers was one of distaste—Collins noticed and asked him what was wrong; Dickens replied that whatever the book had been bound with had a particularly greasy feel to it. He was ready to replace it unread, then changed his mind and flipped it open. Apparently, it was a treatise on witchcraft. Intrigued, Dickens paged through it, stopping every now and again to read a passage to Collins, who was equally fascinated. He encouraged Dickens to buy it, but Dickens dismissed the idea—although, Collins thought, he was tempted.

During this time, Collins and Dickens started planning to collaborate on a play, *The Frozen Deep*, about a polar expedition. Before settling on that plot, they kicked around a few others, including at least one of which drew its inspiration from that unnamed book. It would concern a father whose vanity and selfishness had caused a rift between him and his son, after which his estranged son had been killed in the Crimea. Desperate with grief, the father turns to a mysterious woman—possibly a gypsy—who promises to put him in contact with his son. This woman would employ a spirit map, Dickens said, which the book he'd leafed through had described as a way to lead the dead back to this world from the next. The man would have a daughter—or a niece—who would urge him not to follow this course. There might be a suitor for the daughter/niece who would do something heroic. Collins was intrigued—he saw the possibility for some nice ghostly effects—but, in the end, the two of them couldn't arrive at a satisfactory ending for the story. The one they liked the best involved having the father descend into madness and the daughter burn the spirit map, but Collins was inclined to make the mysterious gypsy a con artist who'd prayed on the father's grief, while Dickens thought the gypsy should have some kind of connection to the family—possibly another daughter the father had never acknowledged, or the son's wife. After what Collins said was a pleasant evening bandying about possibilities, the two men passed on the story in favor of one about an Arctic expedition.

Having completed the anecdote, the book went on to discuss the importance of the spirit map to understanding Dickens's later fiction. I didn't bother with this part. What concerned me was the truth of the Collins story. I stood and walked to the bookshelves. Roger had three or four copies of Peter Ackroyd's biography of Dickens, one here, one in his office, and at least one more at school, before I added the one I'd bought for his class. There was plenty about it he didn't care for, especially what he described as its "blatantly unnecessary concessions to postmodern self-indulgence," but for sheer volume of information on Dickens, he admitted, the Ackroyd was hard to beat. I slid the biography down and opened to the index. Five minutes, and I'd confirmed the outlines of the story. There was no doubt Roger knew it. The relevant paragraph in this particular copy had a penciled check beside it, and I was sure that, were I to open the copy in his office, I'd find the margins heavily annotated.

After receiving word of Ted's death, how long would it have taken

Roger to remember Collins and Dickens's idea for their collaboration? Once the first, unbearable surge of grief had ebbed, how long before Roger recalled Dickens's plot about the father whose son is taken from him in war? The similarity to his situation was more than remarkable. It was downright uncanny, one of those times you feel yourself brushing up against powers and intentions far greater than your own. It isn't so much that life imitates art as it is that life and art converge on some third thing—I don't know what to call it.

However superficial it might be, Roger would have been stung by his resemblance to the father in the play. He'd always identified himself with Dickens's heroic young men, whether Nicholas Nickleby, David Copperfield, or even Pip. It wasn't something he'd ever told me, but once I'd learned the circumstances of his early life—the nightmarish upbringing, the rise to better circumstances—I mean, you don't need much interpretive ability to realize that what Roger found in those heroes was himself, his story retold for him. He'd never had to identify with one of Dickens's failed fathers—now, as his life took on the shape of another of Dickens's plots, he was at best a Micawber, at worst a Krook or a Scrooge. Talk about pouring salt into your wounds. It must have seemed that even the writer he loved best had, in an obscure way, judged him and found him wanting.

The first time I'd stopped in at Roger's office at school, he'd declared, "The great writers are forever out ahead of us." He was pontificating, showing off. I didn't care. He said, "We are always catching up to them—always trying to catch up to them, because as soon as we are sure we have—the moment we have arrived at a reading that we are gospel-positive explains a novel once and for all—we realize that there is something else, something left over, something we could not bring under our critical control. In fact, there are several such somethings, each of them suitable to form the core of an entirely new interpretation of the text. Just when we are about to say that we have Dickens, he wriggles free from our grasp. I have written one reasonably long book about him; he has been a significant part of three of my other books; and thirty-five of my articles have addressed his work from various perspectives. You would think that so much writing would have exhausted Dickens for me. It has not. I continue to find new things to say about the work of a man I first read years before you were born. I have more to say about him, and he has more to say about me.

"Yes," Roger nodded, "about me. Dickens's novels—no less than any great literature—define us. They lend shape to the lives we inhabit and color our understanding of them. I am no critical solipsist, but I do believe that, in reading Dickens, we read ourselves."

I'd always admired that sentiment—admired and envied it, since I couldn't say I'd ever felt that way about any writer—even with the ones I admire the most, with Hawthorne and Dickinson, I've been aware of the distance between us, the gap in our sensibilities. However narrow that gap may draw, I've never been able to close it. To tell the truth, I'm not sure I'd want to. My life is mine, you know? But I couldn't help thinking it must be nice to so identify with a writer that his work is a kind of home to you. Until, that is, the walls start to shriek and the windows run with blood, and you find yourself in a completely different story than you'd anticipated.

Roger wouldn't have bothered researching the spirit map, not right away, at least. He had nothing but contempt for that kind of stuff—witchcraft, Ouija boards, séances, all deeply annoyed him. He dismissed them as exploiting the gullible. He would have done his best to put the idea from his thoughts. But as he walked the night hours away, his head brimming with memories of Ted and of his own father—as he stood at the edge of Belvedere House's lawn and watched those same memories spill across the house's windows—did he glimpse one more image on the living room window, what couldn't properly be called a memory but which had taken place nonetheless? What had he seen? Two men sitting beside a fire, talking? Both were bearded: the one's enormous, flourishing down his chest, over his tie; the other's an extended goatee that appeared to have sprung out of control. The one's hair was short, well-combed; the other's curling up and around his head. The one's eyes were mild, unremarkable; the other's large, liquid, expressive. Roger knew Dickens—and Collins—well enough to have heard their conversation. He would have winced at the description of the father's character as shrill, vain, and selfish. He would have wondered at the construction of what was essentially his situation. He would have listened attentively to Dickens's short-hand description of the sprit map and then—

• • •

The sun's final rays were flaring on the library's windows. The sky over Frenchman's Mountain was pink and red; the mountain itself a long silhouette fringed with fire. Squinting at the glare, I looked down on Founders Street. A couple—both of them in their fifties, I guessed—was walking hand in hand. As I watched, the woman pointed to Belvedere House and said something to which the man nodded. Tourists, probably up from the City for the day to visit the quaint town of Huguenot. Maybe one or both of them had attended SUNY. They were just about old enough to have lived in the house when it had been broken up into apartments. I fought the impulse to run downstairs and ask them if this was the case, if they knew anything about the house worth telling. Stupid. I had information. I had more information than I knew what to do with. Alcoholic painter-shamans; magic formulae for bringing houses to some kind of weird life; malevolent entities offering sinister deals; ghosts trapped who knew where by paternal curses; strange visions and sensations; and, to cap it all off, a spirit map. I wasn't living one horror story; I was the screaming heroine in a B-movie marathon. The sun dropped below the horizon. The couple continued on their way, toward the Reformed Church. What is it Freud says, about every action being overdetermined? Bingo.

• • •

Inspired—was that the right word?—by Dickens, Roger had constructed his own spirit map, built a pathway for Ted to travel. No—that was too cut-and-dried a way of putting what had happened, wasn't it? No doubt he'd told himself the same story he'd told me. He needed a better map. There might have been some truth to it, too. All the while he'd been drafting that map, though—What? Had he investigated the book with the greasy covers? It was possible; although hard to believe he could have obtained a copy without me knowing. Well, an original copy. Someone could have mailed him copies of the relevant pages in a regular envelope, or e-mailed them. He might have hit a dead-end in his research, but just knowing that such a thing had been proposed—I could imagine him speculating about it, asking himself how a spirit map would function, how it would lead the dead back from wherever they'd gone—or been sent. His logic wasn't hard to reconstruct: he'd disclosed most of it when he'd shown me the changes he'd made to his office—was that months ago? The place where Ted had died—the doorway through which he'd been forced out of this life—was the ideal place from which to try to bring him back into it. Going to Afghanistan, however, was out of the question, so you would need a substitute. The map was his re-creation of that space symbolically, supplemented by the tabletop model with its dirt and fragment. It was all the wildest wishing—except that Roger had made it here, in the heart of a space that was different—quickened. Before his last collapse, Rudolph de Castries had claimed he hadn't understood his own ideas. Was this what he hadn't realized, that a space changed by desire might respond to further desire?

But it was desire that wouldn't stand still, desire at odds with itself. At the center of everything, all the plots swirling around him, was Roger, unable not to hurt his son as badly as he could, and then unable to stop trying to reverse what he couldn't admit he'd done in the first place. As it was, he'd laid a path to a door he refused to open. Talk about wanting to have your cake and eat it, too.

Of course, I could be wrong. For all I knew, the house was behind this. Observing Roger's activities, it had intuited their purpose and done what it could to give the impression they were succeeding—but in such a way as to cause him—and me—maximum anguish. If this were the case, it had done a pretty good job.

• • •

I turned back to the library. That was enough research for today. I shut down the computer, switched off the light, and closed the door behind me. Instead of heading for the first floor, I walked down the hall the other way, to the bottom of the third-floor stairs. I didn't climb them. For the moment, I'd had my fill of confrontations with Roger, big and small. What I wanted was a look out the window there, in the direction of the mountains I'd seen yesterday. I wasn't expecting them to be there again, and they weren't. The sky was still light, empty of even the slightest cloud. It was more a case of me wanting to see the place where they'd been, as if that space had been altered by their occupying it, as if there was a trace I'd be able to see, or sense—an afterimage, so to speak. I stood in front of the window searching the sky—trying to see through it, to wherever those huge forms had come from.

Nothing. For a moment, I was sure they were almost there, just out of range of my vision, and then that certainty passed. I don't know what I would have done if they had revealed themselves. I guess I was staring at the sky as much to see them not appear, if that makes any sense. Mind-blowing as another glimpse of them would have been, I think I would have been happy, too—this mad kind of happiness.

When I finally abandoned the window, the hallway was darker, the consequence of my prolonged sky-gazing. A few feet in front of me, walls, floor, ceiling vanished. Blinking, I stepped forward, stopped. That sense of the house changed—reconfigured—no longer so much a house as the meeting point for dozens of corridors leading off to who knew where—lit up my nerves like lightning. Like a tank crashing into a mud hut, that level where the weirdness lived—the not-place that had been drawing ever closer—broke through into this one—into what you might call real life.

The sensation—imagine leaning against a wall and having it jerked away from you—now double that, triple it, multiply it by twenty, forty—as if you've been leaning on not just one, but every wall in the house and they've all been yanked away at the same time. Vertigo does not begin to do the experience justice. This was falling away from myself in every possible direction. That what I could see around me appeared exactly the same didn't help. It made what was happening worse, the dislocation more extreme. For want of a better term, I had been wired into the house, as if it were a giant spiderweb whose every vibration carried itself to me. In less time than it takes to describe, that web had been stretched distances too far to know the end of.

I swayed, staggered, and put out my hand to the nearest wall to steady myself. It was like touching the side of a glacier. I jerked my hand away, overbalanced in the other direction, and sat down hard. My hand had been shocked numb—I pressed it to my chest. The hallway was still dark. My eyes should have adjusted by now, and I understood that my other sense of the house was overlapping my vision. I was seeing the mouths of passages black as emptiness, black and freezing. The numbness in my hand was fading, replaced by pain. I wanted out of there. It was all I could do not to bolt in any direction, including right in front of me. I glanced behind me, to where I'd just been gazing out the window, and saw nothing. So much for fleeing upstairs to Roger. I screamed his name anyway, loud as I could, loud enough to guarantee he'd drop whatever he was doing and come running. *"ROGER!"* I screamed it again. *"ROGER!"* My voice sounded strange, as if, instead of bouncing around the inside of the hallway, it had fled long distances. I should have heard Roger's feet hurrying down the stairs. I did not. The only sound in that space was the breath rushing in and out of my mouth.

Then I did hear something, a trio of sounds, one right after the other, so close they might have been the same noise: bangbangbang. They seemed to come from miles away. A pause, and they repeated. The front door. Someone was knocking on the front door, pounding on it hard enough to rattle the glass. Absurdly, I almost called, "Just a minute." Just a minute what? I'm in the middle of a terrifying supernatural event?

Bangbangbang. With the third set of knocks, I realized that the scene around me hadn't changed, hadn't dissipated with the noise downstairs. Which meant that the sound wasn't separate from the terrifying supernatural event. It was part of it. I was on my feet, the hyper-vertigo, the pain licking my palm, put to one side as I focused on the front door. On the other level, the walls might have disappeared, but the doors held their places. It was strange, but I was less concerned with that strangeness than I was with the presence I could feel on the far side of that door, an absolute intensity, an inferno of heat—or cold; it didn't matter; either way, it would consume anything it came into contact with.

It was as if a figure—not just wreathed in flame, but made of flame, were standing on the porch. I had been in the presence of that same blast-furnace once before, in the diner on Martha's Vineyard. The other week, it had only been for a fraction of a second, and my mind had collapsed. Now, it was demanding admission, and even from this far away, my consciousness trembled. But it—Ted, say his name; it was Ted standing out there; Ted flaming with his father's curse and however much rage of his own; Ted crashing his tortured fist against the door. He was knocking—maybe that meant—

The doorknob clicked. We hadn't locked it. I was forever telling Roger we should, especially with living in one of the biggest houses in town—but he insisted there was no reason to. Huguenot wasn't that kind of place. From time to time, I at least locked the doorknob, if not the deadbolt, but not today. I doubt it would have mattered anyway. Creaking faintly on its hinges, the front door swung open and Ted stepped into the house. He'd knocked not to request, but to announce.

• • •

This wasn't the first time he'd been inside Belvedere House since he'd died—I'd been aware of him on a couple of occasions. It was, however, the first time he'd entered this deliberately—this theatrically—and when the house was in however you'd describe this state—dissolution? Everything was quiet. Ted was there, no mistaking it. I couldn't see him—thankfully—but I could feel him so strongly, it was as if I could, this ruined shape orbited by shrapnel. He was taking a look around, surveying the front hallway as if assessing the way I'd redecorated it. Although I was certain he could see me where I was, I held my breath, trying not to make a sound while a fresh surge of extreme vertigo tried to push me off my feet and my palm sang with pain. I knew it wouldn't work, yet when I heard the floorboards shifting as he walked towards the second-floor stairs, and then the sharp moans of the stairs as he climbed them, I almost fainted with terror. He wasn't in a hurry, but he wasn't taking his time, either.

This is it, I thought. The words chased each other around my brain. *This is it this is it this is it*. Ted had returned as he'd been unable to previously. What had started with his first visit to us was going to be completed by his second.

He was almost at the top of the stairs. My nerves shrieked at the proximity. I had to move. There was no way I wanted to be standing here when he arrived. *Move!* I told myself, *Move!* My feet stayed where they were. Ted's presence had overloaded the channels that should have carried messages from my brain to the rest of my body. *Move!* I thought, while, *This is it*, continued to play like an idiot mantra. One more stair to go—

I grabbed the doorknob to my left, pulled the door open, threw myself into the room beyond, and hauled the door closed behind me so hard it bounced open again, sending me racing frantically after it. Ted's footsteps hurried up the hall as I caught the door, swung it closed, and fumbled with the lock. It was one of those push-in ones, that you have to press forward and twist in order to secure, and as Ted drew nearer, I couldn't get the thing to catch. He was right on the other side of the door, his presence loud as a thunderstorm. The lock took, and I clasped my hands to my head. Ted's feelings roared against me, pain like a mouthful of razor blades, rage like a sea full of icebergs heaving into one another, and underneath them, an eagerness that was maybe the most powerful of the three, an anticipation sharp and jagged as broken glass. I crouched down, hands pressed against my temples as if to keep my head from flying apart. Scratch the "as if": with Ted that near, it was like standing next to a jet engine. You aren't sure what's going to get you first, the noise or the flame, but there's no doubt something will.

The door—I had to back away from the door, put what space I could between myself and Ted. I was sitting on the floor. I kicked against the door, pushing myself across the floor like a kid playing a game. I continued to retreat that way until the foot of the guest room bed caught me in the back. All the time, my eyes did not leave that door. In a way, it was—on the level where Ted existed, there were no walls. Whatever might appear to be standing to either side of the guest room's door; however solid its pale-blue surface might seem, there was nothing. Where there should have been drywall and wood beams and insulation and wiring, there were openings to nowhere, one to the right of the door, one to the left. None of the other walls were any more substantial. All that was reasonably solid was the door. The whole thing was like some kind of avant-garde theatrical set, the freestanding door with the bed on one side to represent a room. As far as I could tell as I climbed up onto the bed and kept moving backwards, there was literally nothing to keep Ted from going around either side of the door.

He didn't, though. For I don't know how long, he stood in the hallway, the absolute-zero burn of what he was, raging into the room. I'd closed the shutters, so to speak, locked the doors and windows, but the paint blistered and sloughed off; the wood charred and started to smoke; the glass clouded and bubbled. I was trapped. The guestroom was cut off from Ted's childhood room to my right, and the bathroom to my left. There was a decent-sized closet in here, but I had no desire to trap myself in a smaller, more confined and therefore more vulnerable space.

Ted banged on the door. I jumped and tried to squeeze myself into the corner the bed abutted. Ted hammered on the door. The wood leapt under his assault. At this rate, the door would give way in a minute, maybe less. I looked around desperately for a weapon, which was a laugh. How was I going to hit someone whose very appearance would blast what remained of my mind into oblivion? There was nothing, anyway. Even if I'd wanted to throw a blanket over him and run past him into the hall, the bed was bare.

The noise was deafening. The door groaned, leaned in toward me. *Not now*, I thought, *not now. I've learned so much!* That's how it goes in these kinds of narratives, isn't it? You gather the information, digest it, and use it to resolve the situation, i.e. defeat the monster. This was too soon. I needed another day or two to sift through what I'd learned and come up with a plan. I guess Ted had watched enough horror movies to want to pre-empt that plot. Either that, or I'd already had my chance with Roger, and what was happening was the result of my failure to fulfill the requirements for a happy ending by now.

The knocking stopped. I stayed where I was, positive that Ted was preparing for a final attack on the door that would splinter it into kindling. It was probably as close as I'd ever been to death— the most serious circumstance in which I'd found myself—but none of the thoughts you'd expect to rush to the fore were anywhere to be found. I'd always assumed I'd make a deathbed conversion—or re-conversion—to Catholicism. Say a quick Act of Contrition: Sorry, God, hope there's no hard feelings. I wouldn't go so far as to say I'd planned my repentance, but that isn't too far from the truth.

With Ted about to burst into the room and do who knew what to me, however, last-minute reconciliation with the Almighty was the least of my concerns. To be frank, it wasn't really a concern at all. I was caught—suspended where I was, all my energies focused on the conflagration on the other side of the door. I wasn't even that concerned about what was going to happen to me. I knew it would be unimaginably horrible, Ted's revenge for whatever he thought my role in all this had been. I was in a state of almost complete anticipation.

As I was poised, I heard something, a new sound—Roger's voice, sounding as far away as Ted's knocking on the front door had. He was calling my name, a question mark at the end of it. "Is that you?" he said. "I thought I heard knocking." He was at the top of the third-floor stairs, which sent up their own chorus of groans as he started down them, still saying my name.

At his approach, Ted—faded. He didn't disappear. It was more as if he stepped around one of the new corners the house contained and concealed himself. The effect on me, on my nerves—you know what it's like on a hot, sunny day, when a cloud slips in front of the sun? If the air cools at all, it's only by a degree, but you welcome the respite from that constant downpour of light and heat all the same.

• • •

Roger's footsteps carried him past my door, my name dopplering as he went. He paused at the top of the stairs, shouted down them for me, waited, then returned along the hallway. On his way, he noticed the guest room door closed and paused. He tried the handle. Despite myself, my stomach squeezed. "Is anyone in there?" he asked. "Veronica? Is that you?" He thumped on the door. "Hello?"

"It's me," I said.

"Veronica?"

"Yes."

"What's the matter? Is something wrong?"

I didn't know how to answer that.

"Is everything all right?"

"No."

"No? Well—can you open the door?"

That was a good question. Maybe not the sixty-four-thousand-dollar question, but good nonetheless. Ted was lurking nearby, much, much too close for any kind of comfort. On the other hand, so long as Roger was around, he appeared to need to keep his distance. The curse, for once working to my advantage. I didn't want to send Roger away any sooner than was absolutely necessary. "Hold on," I said.

"What is it?" Roger asked when he saw me.

"Ted."

Hope and suspicion flitted across his face. "What do you mean?"

"I mean Ted is here—in the house. He's very, very close."

"What makes you so sure?"

"Because he just spent the last five minutes trying to break the door down. That was the banging you heard."

Roger frowned. "Why would Ted do that?"

"You tell me."

"Is this—did you see him?"

"No."

"Then what makes you so sure it's Ted?"

"I can feel him," I said. "Trust me, Roger, it's Ted. Who else would it be?"

"I haven't the slightest idea. Since you didn't actually see Ted, however—"

"For God's sake—what do you think, that some new ghost is going to stroll in, now? 'Oh, hey, I hear the haunting's good here.' Will you listen to yourself?"

"All right. What does he want?"

"To scare the crap out of me. How should I know?"

"And you think he's near?"

"It's not a matter of thinking, Roger. I know it."

"Where is he?"

"Close. He's just out of sight."

"Where?" Roger asked, throwing his hands out right and left. "Is he here? Or here?" He turned around. "Is he lurking behind me?" He looked up, down. "Is he on the ceiling? Under the floor?"

"It isn't like that." How to explain everything to him? "The house is different. It's changed—I think Ted has changed it. Things aren't as—solid as they used to be. There are new spaces in it, places where Ted can remove himself and watch us."

"You're asking me to take a lot on faith, Veronica."

This was ridiculous. "How can you say that, after everything that's happened to us? I've never lied to you. I've always been straight with you. What do you think, that was me hammering on the door? And then what? When I heard you coming, I hurried and locked myself in the guest room? What's the sense in that?"

"I don't know."

"Yes, you do. You do know. You don't want to admit it, but you do. You're such a coward. I never realized that before, but you are. You're the biggest coward I've ever met."

"Now wait one minute," Roger said, but I lost the rest of his sentence because Ted chose that moment to reappear. From whatever oblique angle he'd chosen to conceal himself, he walked out into the open, looming over Roger's shoulder. I had barely enough warning— my awareness of him spiking—to cover my face and twist away. As it was, the little I'd glimpsed—less than in the diner: the edge of a cheek threaded with what might have been barbed wire—was enough to set a flock of screams loose from my throat.

"Veronica!" Roger said. "What is it? What's wrong? What are you seeing?"

"Ted!" I screamed, hands pressed as tightly over my eyes as those of any six-year-old trying not to see the monster in the closet. "It's Ted!"

"Ted?" he said, as if this were the first he'd heard of the idea. "But—how can that be?"

This close to Ted, my mind was a shack in an earthquake. "Make him go away! For God's sake, make him leave! Please!"

"Ted?" Roger said, turning. "Is that you? Ted? Son?"

"He's right there! Can't you see him? Can't you see anything?"

"No," Roger said. "I—wait—at the other end of the hall—what? Hold on, I'm—Ted? Is that you?" Before I could tell him not to, Roger was running for the stairs to the first floor, shouting, "Ted?" as he went.

"Roger!" I yelled, "Don't leave me!"

There was no reply, only the clatter of his feet on the stairs, the diminishing sound of his calls.

I backpedaled into the guest room. Ted's presence roared around me. I struck a wall, something that jabbed me in the kidney—the closet door. Ted's feet scuffed on the threshold as he stepped into the room. Eyes still closed and covered with one hand, I fumbled for the doorknob with the other, struggling to resist the temptation that had raised itself—more a compulsion to drop my hand from my eyes, open them, and meet my fate. There was no way I was coming out of this. The best I was doing was delaying the inevitable. My arm trembled. An awful fascination, to look at Ted directly, to see him as he truly was, despite the consequences—almost because of the consequences—joined the temptation. He was no more than five steps away, moving with the pace of a man who has all the time in the world. When the closet door popped open, I forced myself inside. So much for avoiding the smaller, more confined, and therefore more vulnerable space. I grabbed the doorknob with both hands and braced my feet against the frame. *What would it be like?* a little voice asked somewhere in my head. *What would it be like to surrender, to stop trying to prop up your mind and just let it crumble?*

The door shuddered as Ted smashed into it. Apparently, he'd decided it would be more fun to break the door down than it would be to tear it open, which he could have done easily. I wasn't exactly

Sheena, queen of the jungle. For the instant that we were both in contact with the door, I—my body—it was like being plunged into a vat of liquid nitrogen. The jolt was enough that my mind stopped. There was a stutter in the film, and then Ted was crashing into it again. Another stutter, and the doorknob almost yanked itself out of my hands. Stutter, and the door banged so hard it flung me back, through a curtain of dresses I'd hung in here until I could sort through them and decide which were going to the Salvation Army. Several of them dropped onto me, and as Ted struck the door and I heard mixed in with the *Wham!* the creak of wood starting to part from itself, I struggled to pull the dresses off me. My dinner churned at the back of my mouth. When Ted hit the door this time, the wood moaned. I freed myself from the last dress, hung onto the heavy coat hanger that had supported it, and scrambled for the back of the closet. If ever there was a time to discover the house had secret passageways, this was it. At least the closet was deeper than I'd remembered.

On the other side of the line of dresses, there was a pause. The doorknob turned, clicked, and light spilled into the closet. He'd tricked me, the son of a bitch had convinced me he was intent on bursting through the door so I'd keep my distance and all he had to do was reach for the handle. His silhouette filled the doorway, and I swear, even obscured by the light and the clothes, there was something about Ted—about his shape—that was so wrong, so fundamentally off, that the dinner I was already struggling to keep down came bubbling up out of my mouth in one long stream.

There was no time for wiping my mouth. Ted's outline shifted and he entered the closet. Before he'd completed that move, I was on my feet and running as fast as my legs would carry me in the opposite direction. By all rights, that should have slammed me into the back of the closet immediately. I should have knocked the wind out of myself and fallen to the floor, pretty much at Ted's feet. Instead, the closet kept going—went on and on, its walls forming the sides of a corridor down which I sprinted. Yes, part of me was thinking, *This is impossible. How can this be happening?* But it was too far removed from my feet pounding on the floor, arms pistoning, to have any effect.

• • •

There was light ahead, a single bulb set in the ceiling. By its dull glow, I saw that the walls had gone from the unfinished wood of the closet's interior to something like sheetrock. They'd been painted creamy white a long time ago. Huge patches had since fallen off and lay crumbled across the wooden floor. What remained was mapped by cracks. Where the walls were bare—what was underneath was dark. There was no time to stop and examine it. Ted was behind me, a storm nipping at my heels. I ran under the bulb and saw what looked like a door ahead.

A second later, I was through it. Or—not through it so much as caught in it. It was as if—it was like running into a more substantial version of the membrane that had coated me the day before—as if the air had turned to taffy. Everything slowed down. I was looking at a room I'd never seen before. It was a living room, but of a house substantially smaller than Belvedere House. Its walls were the same off-white as the stretch of corridor behind me, only slightly less riddled with cracks. To my left, sunlight streamed through a pair of dirty windows. Across from me, there was what looked like an old radio, a heavy brown box flanked by a pair of armchairs whose floral prints had seen better days, as had that on the loveseat under the windows. There was a sewing basket next to one of the chairs, and a bottle of amber liquid poorly concealed behind the other. To my right, an upright piano clustered with framed black-and-white photos stood on the near side of a doorway. The air was brown with unfiltered cigarette smoke. Through the doorway beside the piano, I heard voices—one voice, really, raised and shouting, "Don't you walk away from me, mister!"

From the other side of that doorway, Roger walked into the room. I was so surprised I said, "Roger!" before I knew what I was doing.

He didn't respond, and I saw that he had changed into different clothes. When I'd seen him ten minutes ago, he'd been wearing a polo shirt, jeans, and loafers; now, he was dressed in a white, short-sleeved dress shirt, black slacks, and black shoes. Head down, he crossed the room to the radio and began to fiddle with its dial.

Yelling, "Do you hear me? You do not walk away from me when I am talking to you!" Ted charged through the same doorway, rattling the photos on the piano as he passed.

I screamed and tried to turn, ready to take off back up the corridor at my back, but there, out of the corner of my eye, was a shape in the dimness—a figure that, even obscured, made me close my eyes and pull my head away. Ted was still behind me—but paused, caught in the same clogged air that held me. What was in front of me—

For one thing, there was nothing wrong with this Ted's appearance. His face was flushed, but it had been red the first time I'd seen him standing outside the apartment door. His speech was thick, his gait unsteady, but he appeared as alive and healthy as he ever had. His clothes were the mirror image of Roger's, except that his pants were held up by suspenders, and a badly knotted black tie flattened against his shirt. He caught Roger by the arm and spun him around so hard that Roger almost fell over. "Are you deaf?" Ted said. "Is there something wrong with your ears?"

Roger said, "I just came in to warm up the radio for you."

"Well, isn't that thoughtful?" Ted pushed Roger, who staggered backwards, his hip striking the corner of the radio. "If I want to listen to the Goddamned radio, I believe I am capable of switching it on myself."

Roger's head shot up, his mouth tight with pain, his eyes furious. Ted's shoulders registered his surprise. "Would you look at this?" he said. "That appears to be a spark of rebellion I see lighting up your face. Is that true? Am I watching you in the act of breaking the Fourth Commandment? Are you going against the word of God Himself? Do you not remember what the Bible says? Is that possible?" He punctuated each question by stabbing his index finger against Roger's chest. "Exodus chapter 20, verse 12: 'Honor thy father and mother: that thy days may be long upon the land which the Lord thy God giveth thee.' What part of that don't you understand? Huh? What part? Huh? Huh?" The index finger stabbed like the needle of a sewing machine. Roger tried to cover his chest with his arms. Ted flung them away and continued jabbing him.

Before Ted could catch him, Roger ducked under his arms and ran to the doorway. Ted overbalanced, driving his finger into the radio with a crack. "Son of a bitch!" he shouted, drawing his hand to his chest and then waving it about like a flag. He wheeled to face Roger, who cringed where he was. "I cannot believe I have lived to see this day," Ted said, shaking his hand. "First you walk away from your father while he is talking to you, and then," he held up his hand, "you raise your fist against him."

"I didn't," Roger said.

"Is there no end?" Ted said, throwing back his head as if appealing to a sympathetic God for his answer. He brought his hands to his throat and began unknotting his tie, wincing when he moved his injured finger. Once the tie was loose, he threaded it out from under his collar and tossed it onto the closer armchair. Next he reached his hands to his shoulders, slid his thumbs under his suspenders, and eased them down, drawing his arms up through them as he did.

Roger was a study in terror, his face pale as china, his back hunched, his knees bent.

Ted finished pulling his shirt out of his pants and said, "I may not be able to make you respect me as a father—it's a sad, sad day, and Almighty God will hold you to account for breaking one of His Commandments, you can be sure of that. I wouldn't be surprised if there's some hellfire waiting for you, and a whole host of devils waiting to try their pitchforks on you. No, I would not be surprised in the least. You may not respect me as a father, but you will respect me as a man. Even crippled by treachery, I reckon I can show you a thing or two. Come on, then. You think you're so much better than me—let's see."

Roger's hands were up, palms out. "Pa, I'm sorry. I didn't mean anything."

"It's too late for sorry," Ted said. "Sorry is a train that left the station a long time ago."

"No, Pa," Roger said, "no."

"No?" Ted said. "You're still contradicting me? Boy, the Devil has gotten into you and taken hold something powerful."

"Stop," Roger said. "That isn't what I meant. I'm sorry, Pa, truly."

Left hand curled into a fist, Ted strode toward Roger, who was crying, his cheeks shining with tears, his mouth open in anguish, his entire body trembling. He dropped to the floor as Ted drew near him, sheltering his head beneath his arms as if Ted were the atomic bomb he'd been warned about in school.

Standing over him, Ted said, "Well, what's this? It appears Satan isn't quite so big as all that. It appears Satan fears the wrath of a righteous man." He nudged Roger with his shoe. "Get up, Satan. Get up and take what's coming to you."

"I'm sorry, Pa," Roger sobbed. "Honest I am."

"I swear before the Throne of the Living God," Ted said, kicking Roger now, "if you don't stand on your own two feet like a man, I will kick the living shit out of you. Get up. I won't say it again."

Groaning with dread, Roger stood. "Sorry, Pa."

"Shut up," Ted said. "Boy, if you're going to act the part of the big man, you'd best be prepared to play the role to the bitter end." His left hand whipped up and around. *Crack.*

Roger's head rocked back, his legs wobbled, and he collapsed, his nose and mouth scarlet. Ted's right foot lashed out. Roger yelped as it connected with his left leg, high on the outside. Ted kicked him again, on the shin, again, in the stomach. Roger screamed. His face was wet with tears, snot, blood. His white shirt was decorated with red spots and splatters. "You might have done better than that," Ted said. "Still, I expect that's chased the Devil out of you for a time. Now you know, boy. You know what's waiting for you if you feel like wearing a man's clothes before you're ready for them. And that was with my good hand incapacitated. You think about that. You ponder what the old man might've done if he'd had the use of both his hands. You hear me?"

"Yes, sir," Roger mumbled through crushed lips.

At my back, Ted pushed forward through the thickened air like a swimmer forcing his way upstream. The hairs on the back of my neck stood up, my heart surged, my ears popped, and before I knew what I was doing I was running across the living room, the air around me once more fluid. The other Ted said to Roger, "Now get up and go wash your face." Despite my urgency, I gave both figures a wide berth. Neither spared a glance in my direction. My destination was the doorway behind them. I spared a last look at Roger—at this Roger—who scrambled to his feet, his nose obviously broken and leaking more blood, his face drawn with fear.

Then I was in the next room, for a second time caught on the threshold by what felt like an enormous sheet of clear plastic. In front of me was the dining room. Or, a kind of minimalist approximation of a dining room. Except for a tall lamp standing off to the right, the room was unlit. A card table occupied center-stage. Seated on folding chairs to either side of it, Roger and Ted faced each other. Three more folding chairs—all empty—crowded the table's far side. As they had been in the previous room, Roger and Ted were dressed alike, this time in workshirts, jeans, and boots. The card table was stacked with dishes and cutlery. I was—my head swam at the sight of the two of them. Obviously, I wasn't—well, I wasn't in Kansas, anymore, but I'd just left these two in the other room. If I hadn't felt Ted making his way towards me, striding against air that refused to yield for him as it had for me, I'd have ducked my head back out for another look.

There was no time. My nerves were trying to tear themselves out of my skin. It looked as if there was an opening in the wall across from me. I pushed, my ears popped, and I was through to the room. Circling the table, I hurried across the floor. Roger picked up the topmost plate from the pile and held it out to Ted, asking, "May I have some bread?"

"Certainly," Ted replied, extending his right hand over the dish. One blink, his hand was empty, miming the act of passing a slice of bread. The next, it was full of a snake, coiling around Ted's wrist, twisting its head back and forth in the air, hissing at Roger—who stared calmly as it dropped from Ted's hand to his plate. The plate tilted as the snake slapped it; Roger had to maneuver to keep the snake from sliding off onto the table. I don't know much about reptiles, but this was not a garden snake. It was blue-black, its back covered in electric green loops. Once it was secure on Roger's plate, it wasted no time. It slid up his arm, raising its head as it went, and when it reached his shoulder, opened its mouth and drove its fangs into his head, behind his left eye. Roger didn't flinch, sitting calmly as the snake's venom pumped into him, the rest of it wrapping around his neck like a hideous scarf.

"Is that enough?" Ted asked.

"Plenty, thanks," Roger said, as a stream of blood escaped the snake's mouth and dribbled down his face.

I'd shouted when the snake appeared, a second time when it struck Roger. I do not like snakes, and the appearance of one sent me around the room that much faster. All the same, seeing it latched onto Roger like an oversized leech, I had to fight the urge to run over to him and try to pull it off. I think I already knew that it wasn't really Roger sitting at the table—or, it wasn't the Roger who'd chased down the stairs after Ted. This was Roger from years—decades ago. But that didn't make the sight of the four-foot snake looped around his neck any less horrifying.

Footsteps thumped on the floor to my rear. Ted was gaining. I ran the rest of the distance to the door, only to realize I'd been mistaken. There wasn't any opening here, just a black rectangle painted on the wall. In the half-light of the room, I'd mistaken part of the backdrop for an actual exit. Panic stabbed me. My hands shot out, racing over the wall in search of a way out. My left hand brushed the doorway, and it shifted, rippled. In a second, I had torn aside the heavy drape on which the black rectangle had been painted and run through it to the opening it concealed. Another hallway stretched in front of me, this one full of doors—some open, some closed—set on either side. Each door was flanked by a pair of tiny glass lamps in which candles danced weakly. I sprinted ahead, throwing the curtain back in hopes of tangling Ted.

There was a door—open, the room beyond lit—at the far end of the hall. I aimed for that. To my right, my left, doors flashed by. I caught scenes—pieces of scenes. Hand trembling madly, Roger held out a butter knife as Ted stalked toward him, murder in his eyes. Ted lay on an undersized bed, smoking a cigarette and looking bored while Roger sat on the end of the bed and read an invisible book out loud to him. One room—I wasn't sure, because it was too confusing, but I could have sworn I saw Roger standing in front of the home-made map in his office, two men looking over his shoulders—only, they were both Roger, too, except that one was wearing a baggy black coat over a loose white shirt, the other a blue morning coat over a gray vest and white shirt around whose high collar an oversized gray bowtie had been tied.

The room at the end of the hall was in front of me. I was so focused on finding the next door that it was all I could see—there, in the wall to the left, a varnished plank of wood whose doorknob had been polished to a brassy shine. I entered and crossed the space easily, my hand closing on that doorknob before the room's other contents registered. Or maybe I should say, its inhabitants. Two figures stood at the center of what was otherwise a plain box of a room. One I knew right away. Standing with her hand on the shoulder of a young girl was my grandma, looking exactly as she had when she'd babysat me when I was younger, green cardigan over a white mock-turtleneck, jeans, the plain white sneakers she called tennis shoes and I thought of as grandma-sneakers. The half-glasses she was constantly losing track of hung, as they always had, from a cheap chain around her neck. Her hair—she was a redhead, too, right up until she died; her hair never went yellow, the way it does for most redheads as they age—her hair was piled on top of her head, held in place with a dozen different hair-pins and barrettes. Her face was the one part of her that was different, and that not by much. It was made-up—so far as I knew, not a day in her life went by that my grandma didn't at least wear lipstick, even if she was staying at home. It wasn't obviously disfigured or anything. No, it was that her face was drawn, pale, her features fighting a losing battle against great pain.

Seeing her stopped me where I was. For what couldn't have been more than one, maybe two seconds, but that felt like hours, everything else—the fear churning my gut, Ted's presence raging against my nerves, the feel of the house, (which I haven't said anything about)—all that was on hold. Seeing her stunned me—and it was her, not another trick. The air was heavy with Jean Naté, her favorite perfume, which she always wore too much of. What registered as shock was a knot of emotions, love, and grief, and fear, and something else, something like awe.

I barely noticed the girl on whose shoulder my grandmother's hand rested. She was little more than a head of red hair tied into a ponytail, denim jacket and jeans. Maybe six, maybe seven, but I wasn't especially interested. My tongue was flopping around my mouth like a fish out of water, trying to find something to say. "I love you." "I miss you." "Are you all right?" "What's happening?" "Help me"; all rushed through the door at the same moment and got stuck in it.

The hallway to the room echoed with Ted's slow-motion progress, his boots striking the floor like distant thunder. His presence was a firestorm, scorching my mind. No time. There was no time. My cheeks were wet with tears I hadn't realized I'd been crying.

My grandmother said, "Poor bunny. My poor, poor bunny. We must stay awake and see evil done just a little longer." Her voice was thick, as if she were speaking through a mouthful of dirt.

"What?"

"Poor bunny," she said. She tried to say something else. All that came out was a dry, choking sound.

"I don't understand," I said. "Please, what do you mean?"

Grandma's mouth opened and closed. Silence.

The girl in front of her stepped forward and opened her mouth, sticking out her tongue. Wet with saliva, an oversized ring shone on it. I knew who she was: the girl from the carousel, the one who'd spurned my gift of the ring I'd taken, only to swipe it from the air when I dropped it in the bucket. What was she doing here, with my grandmother?

Ted was about to enter the room. I said, "I love you," opened the door, and left them both.

I was back in the house—our house, Belvedere House. The door snicked behind me and I was standing in the second-floor hallway, outside Roger's and my bedroom. The hall was dark, though not as absolutely so as it had been when Ted appeared. I could glance to either side and see the windows there. This was simply night. Roger was here, chasing shadows downstairs. I moved to the top of the first-floor stairs and shouted his name.

No answer. I doubted he was—wherever I'd just been, but he could be outside. I started down the stairs, calling, "Roger!" as I went.

• • •

You could hardly call the six seconds or so it took me to reach the first floor a respite—I hadn't heard the bedroom door open yet, but was sure it would any moment—but it gave me the briefest of opportunities to catch my breath. I wouldn't say I collected my thoughts—those had been burned and scattered by Ted's constant proximity—and my emotions were still reeling from my encounter with Grandma and the little girl—yet the pause was sufficient for me to be aware—more aware of the house. Maybe I should say of the house's absence. Once I'd plunged down the corridor behind the guest room closet, my sensation of the house, already changed, had changed more, the end of the series of transformations that had taken it from a solid, stable structure to an increasingly temporary and unstable arrangement of space; then from that shimmering instability to little more than the locus of dozens of passageways to who knew where; and now, from that common meeting-point to something entirely different. Not an organization of space, or the conjunction of other, organized spaces— the house had lost all form, all pretensions to arrangement altogether. Fleeing through its hidden rooms, I had felt Belvedere House as a heaving sea washing against me, an Arctic ocean full of pieces of flaming wreckage. When I'd emerged back into the house proper, that feeling had come with me.

I hesitated at the foot of the stairs, called for Roger. Still no answer. I checked the front parlor, the living room. Empty, the two of them, except for the moonlight pouring in over the furniture. It was the kind of light you get with a full moon, that pale, silver illumination. I hadn't realized we were due another full moon so soon. Hadn't the moon just been full? Yes, yes, it had. While we were on the Cape—I remembered it hanging just over the pines the first or second night we'd arrived. It didn't stay at full for more than three days—certainly not this long. What was going on? Did I have time for this? Obviously, it was part of Ted's end-game. Ted seemed to be holding his place inside our room; although, with these final changes to the house, it was almost impossible to be sure where everything and everyone were in it. Taking a deep breath, I crossed to the living room windows.

After two steps, the temperature began to drop. Three, and my skin was rigid. Four, and I exhaled white clouds. Halfway across the room, the air was as cold as I'd ever known, the kind of cold you feel on a February day when the wind chill takes the mercury down to minus fifteen or twenty. My face was numb—my fingers, too. Each time I inhaled, it seared my lungs. By the time I was at the window, I couldn't feel the clothes on me. Tears welled up in my eyes, freezing on the lashes. Why keep going, right? Because it got colder—that meant there was something to see. Through tiny icicles, I gazed out windows thickened by frost.

The moon was full, casting light over the scene in front of me from high in the sky. The moon—there was something wrong with it, beyond its being full. The patterns on it—the dark areas that give the Man in the Moon his face—were different—rearranged into an image I couldn't distinguish but that hurt my eyes to look at. The landscape the moon shone on was dominated by a river, its near shore maybe ten yards from the house, its far side at least a mile away. I thought I could make out buildings on that other shore, but the river was bright as mercury—it caught the moonlight and flung it back up, clouding the air with white light like a fog. I could hear the river, rasping as it slid through its banks—like the biggest snake ever, miles long. In the far distance, blocking the sky under the moon, there might have been mountains, which might have shared the outline of the peaks that had towered over the house yesterday—

But it was too much. The cold was too intense for me to stay where I was a minute—a second more. I was shivering madly, every square inch of skin stiff, legs wobbling, teeth not even chattering—my jaw was clenched shut, my entire head shaking. Wherever—whatever this was a view of, I had to leave. Feet numb, I stumbled towards the

door to the hall, crashing into the couch on the way. I caromed off it
and stumbled out the door.

• • •

To find myself, not in the hall, but a new room. It wasn't much more
than an oversized wood crate. Walls, ceiling, floor consisted of unfinished wood planks stacked, hung, and laid side by side. They were
gray, weather-beaten, held in place by rusted nails and rife with splin-
ters. From the ceiling, half a dozen primitive mobiles hung at the ends
of as many lengths of frayed rope—each mobile a large metal hanger
from which a trio of smaller ones dangled. From the smaller hang-
ers, four or five figures swung from pieces of thread. The figures had
been scissored from newspaper. Some were silhouettes of the moon,
sun, and stars. Others were the shapes of adults and children. A few
of the newspaper shapes appeared to have been cut on the lines of
machine guns, knives, and—I swear—Belvedere House. There were
no windows in the place, but beams of sunlight stole into the room
through gaps between the planks. There were no doors, either, except
the one that had admitted me here—which, a glance back showed,
was now blocked by a badly fitted door that looked as if it formerly
had opened on a better room. The space was hot, stifling with the
smells of sawdust and rot—the reek of a dead deer left lying on the
side of the road for days. Even as my still-aching stomach threatened
to find more to bring up out of itself, the rest of me soaked in the heat
like a sponge. The inside of this place might as well have been an oven
someone had turned up to 450. In a matter of minutes, I'd be unable
to stand it. After the living room, however, I could not only tolerate
it, I was grateful for it.

A sound tickled my ear, so soft I barely picked it up. A voice—
Roger's voice?—speaking in the whisper of a whisper. "Ted!"

The voice that answered was the air shattering itself into thunder,
a 747 roaring directly overhead. "THIS IS ABOUT YOU LEAVING
MY MOTHER FOR SOME TEENAGED SLUT. THIS IS ABOUT
YOU BREAKING UP A THIRTY-EIGHT-YEAR MARRIAGE SO
YOU COULD GET YOUR DICK WET. THIS IS ABOUT YOU
SPITTING IN THE FACE OF THE WOMAN WHO GAVE HER
LIFE TO YOU."

Ted's voice seemed to come from everywhere, as if a ring of concert-sized speakers had been set around the outside of the room and the volume on every one turned all the way up. The room shook with the force of it. The mobiles swung wildly. The beams of sunlight trembled. Fine dust lifted from the walls. An assortment of insects— mostly centipedes and beetles—lost their grip on the ceiling and walls and rained down. I covered my ears, crouching as if making myself smaller would help. My ears were ringing, so I almost missed what the first voice said, "I didn't mean—"

Ted's voice cracked the air open. "ARE YOU DISHONORING YOUR FATHER? ARE YOU BREAKING ONE OF THE COMMANDMENTS THAT GOD HIMSELF CARVED IN FIRE?"

"Now wait just a minute—"

"RESPECT? LIKE THE RESPECT YOU AND YOUR WHORE SHOWED MY MOTHER?"

"Swear to God—"

"YOU THINK CAREFULLY, NOW. YOU THINK ABOUT WHETHER YOU WANT THE USE OF THOSE HANDS, HOW PRECIOUS BEING ABLE TO SEE OUT OF BOTH THOSE EYES IS TO YOU. YOU THINK ABOUT WHAT GIRL'S EVER GONNA WANT TO LOOK AT YOU SMILING THROUGH A MOUTH OF BROKEN TEETH. BECAUSE I'LL DO ALL THAT, BOY; AS SURE AS GOD'S IN HIS HEAVEN AND THE DEVIL'S IN HIS HELL, I'LL DO ALL THAT AND MORE. IT'S MY RIGHT, AND I HAVE NO TROUBLE EXERCISING IT. IT'S YOUR DECISION. DO YOU WANT TO TAKE THOSE FEELINGS, PUT THEM IN A BOTTLE, AND PUT A CORK IN THAT BOTTLE, OR WOULD YOU RATHER GET DOWN TO BUSINESS?"

The room shuddered as if it were in the middle of an earthquake. The walls swayed and creaked. The mobiles danced and jangled against one another. Nails gave up their hold on the planks and popped free. A plank in the wall to my left came loose and tumbled to the floor. Sunlight poured through the gap.

Roger's voice said, "That is enough!"

"THIS IS ABOUT YOU BRINGING DISHONOR TO OUR FAMILY. I WILL BEAT YOU DOWN. THIS IS ABOUT YOU MAKING YOURSELF A LAUGHING STOCK. YOU WILL SHUT

YOUR MOUTH, OR I WILL PUT YOUR FACE THROUGH THAT WALL."

"I didn't—"

"IT'S TOO LATE FOR SORRY. I WAS HAPPY TO LET YOU RUIN YOUR LIFE. BOY, THE DEVIL HAS GOTTEN INTO YOU AND TAKEN HOLD SOMETHING POWERFUL. BUT YOU COULDN'T LEAVE WELL-ENOUGH ALONE, COULD YOU?"

Another plank—this one in the wall across from me—tore itself free and flopped to the floor; I raised my hand against the sunlight that raged against my eyes. A pair of mobiles tangled together and plummeted from the ceiling like the metal abstraction of a bird. A third plank, also from the wall to my left, wrenched itself loose and joined its fellows below. As it separated from the wall, its nails tore away with such force that they flew across the room in all directions, including mine—I ducked and a nail struck my head anyway, hard enough to sting. It was past time for me to leave this place. I stood, managed the two steps to the misfit door—which was rocking from side to side—and had it open and was through before Ted's voice had completed its last crashing syllable.

For the third time, a hallway opened in front of me. My eyes, still sun-dazzled, took their time adjusting to the dimness. The strong, antiseptic smell of industrial cleaner—and, underneath it, the unlovely stink of urine—and another odor I couldn't name right away, something rich, metallic—pushed themselves into my nose and I sneezed. Roger's voice—was back. Only, it wasn't in my ear. It was ahead, down the corridor on the left. There were metal bars to either side of me and, for once, I knew where I was, the Huguenot holding cells. I walked forward, past empty cell after cell—more, I was sure, than made up the actual jail—Roger's voice becoming clearer as I proceeded. "This," I heard him saying. "Here—you want pain—take it."

There he was, his back to me, standing beside his bunk, facing the far corner of his cell. That corner—I had a hard time seeing it past Roger, but there was someone standing there, deep in the shadows. Roger swayed like a drunk. I saw his right hand raised—pressed over the heart that was dying in his chest, as he tried to fight it long enough to complete his deal. To the right, Ted slumbered on—

No, he didn't. I spared a glance in his direction, then, when I understood what I'd seen, did a double-take. While events in Roger's cell were playing out essentially as I'd seen them in the pavilion on the

Vineyard, the scene across the hall was something out of a Renaissance painting of Hell. Ted was in there, but—where do I begin?

The cell was different. Instead of bare concrete and metal bars, its walls were tall bookcases, each of them hung with an assortment of maps. At the center of the room was a heavy table, to which Ted had been chained by the wrists and ankles. He was naked, and his chest—his chest, his hips, his thighs—they had been—I don't know what the technical term is—flayed, I guess. The skin hung off them in long, ragged strips that looked like bloody crepe paper. What had been exposed—red muscle, shockingly white bone—bore the marks of further abuse. In some places, cut back until you could see what lay wet and shining beneath it. In others, pierced by long, white needles that quivered as Ted—still alive—moved on the table. In a couple of spots, what should have been inside had been lifted outside. A gray-purple coil of what I realized was intestine had been heaped on Ted's belly and fixed there by a pair of the needles. One eyeball had been extracted from its socket and left on Ted's cheek, a needle inserted into the emptied cavity. This close, the smell I'd been unable to identify was obvious. It was the copper stench of the blood that ran from Ted's wounds in bright runnels, that had spattered the maps in Pollock loops and swirls. Ted's mouth opened and closed, but the needle fixed in his throat prevented anything more than a meaningless croak from escaping.

As if that wasn't bad enough, Ted wasn't alone. He was in there, too—I mean, there were two of him. Seated on the chair Roger kept at the table, dressed in the desert fatigues he'd had on the last time I'd seen him—alive—this other Ted rested his chin on his steepled fingers and stared at himself spread out on the table. They were—the two of them were Ted—or, not exactly—not like the Ted who was pursuing me through the house, the Ted whose rage burned somewhere too close. They weren't that—I don't know—intense—although the one who'd been tortured on the table wasn't too far from it—but they were more—say substantial than any of the other Teds I'd encountered so far.

Behind me, Roger said, "Anything—take whatever you need. Whatever you need."

I was close enough to see past him to the figure he was addressing. Standing in the shadows, his features frozen in a wide, idiot grin, Roger heard the promise he made to himself, nodded, and collapsed into a cloud of rubble and dust, like a skyscraper falling in on itself. Within that swirl of debris, I thought I saw something—a patch of skin covered in scales the size of my hand—but I wouldn't swear to it. Roger—the real Roger, the Roger who'd just struck the deal that would cost us all so much, everything—fell onto his bunk. A hand touched my shoulder.

• • •

"Veronica?" I was on the floor, hands over my head, cursing myself for having been so distracted, before I realized who was standing behind—over me. "Roger?"

"Yes," he said, "it's me."

To be safe, I peeked at his feet. There were the frayed edges of his favorite jeans lying over the tops of his new loafers. I stood, Roger catching my arm as I did and helping me to steady myself. I must have looked—you can imagine: soaked in sweat from all the fleeing, my face with the thousand-yard stare of someone who's seen way too much. We were—I was no longer in the jail. It had been replaced by the front hallway. Moonlight burned on the windows. His hand still on my arm, Roger said, "What happened? What's happening?"

To my surprise, I could speak. "The end." Melodramatic, maybe, but otherwise true.

"I didn't find him," Roger said. "I kept thinking Ted was just ahead of me—that I had caught a glimpse of him going from the foot of the stairs to the parlor, then from the parlor to the dining room, and so on through the house. It was—it was as if we were back playing one of the games he'd loved when he was a child, a kind of hide-and-seek, the goal of which was for him to stay a little in front of me. He would laugh merrily as I chased him, until the suspense became too much, at which point he'd turn around and rush into my arms. This time, though, that didn't happen. The pursuit went on and on and on. I—you're going to think I've suffered a breakdown, but I followed him through rooms I've never seen. There wasn't time for me to stop and examine them, but I swear I ran through an art gallery—a room the size of the library that was hung with paintings. I don't know why this should sound any stranger than what I've told you already, but they were all the work of Thomas Belvedere. Another room was some kind of museum, full of glass cases and glassed-in tables I almost crashed into. I couldn't get a good look at their contents. It seems to me—I left my watch upstairs, but it seems to me that I was a long time doing this. Look—the moon's up."

My stomach dropped. A look out a front window confirmed the worst. There was that disfigured moon—higher in the sky, now—pouring its corpse light over the yard, which was no longer the yard. It had been replaced by thirty feet of rock and sand that ran to the shore of a vast river shining pewter-bright. Of course it was the same view I'd had from the living room window, except that I wasn't freezing to death seeing it.

"What is it?" Roger asked. "What's wrong?"

There was some kind of town or city on the far shore. I could make out rows of squat buildings—the light in the air prevented me distinguishing much more. Beyond the town—I still couldn't say for sure if the shapes bulking there were the same mountains that had stunned my eyes—was it yesterday?

"Veronica?"

I felt it, too, all of it. This was no adjunct to the house, no extra, oversized room—this was the house, was continuous with it. The change I'd sensed in the house—the move from form to formlessness, from structure to sea—whatever pretensions to landscape the view outside might have, it was that seething ocean given room to stretch out.

"Veronica," Roger said, grabbing my arm. "What is it? What do you see?"

Eyes straight ahead, I said, "What do *you* see?"

Roger squinted. "To be honest, not much. The moon seems particularly bright. Although—the yard looks darker. There are no lights on in anyone's house, are there? Is it that late?"

The sound of the river, that scraping, was louder, clearer. A wave passed up it in a way that made me think of flesh rippling. The impression that this was one segment of an enormous snake was stronger than ever; I swear, had it hauled itself up out of its bed and sought another course, I wouldn't have been that surprised. I would have lost my mind at the sight, but it wouldn't have surprised me. I said, "You mean, you don't see anything."

"Nothing," Roger said. "Should I?"

"I don't know."

"What do you see?"

"Everything's different."

"How so?"

"To start with, there's a river."

"A river?" Roger peered out the window.

"It's big—maybe a mile wide."

"And it's out there?" He pointed.

"Yes, and you can't see it, I know."

"It's just—a river—and one so big, at that—are there any houses?"

"I can't tell on this side, but there seems to be a town or city on the far shore."

"What do the buildings look like?"

"Buildings—I don't know. I'm not sure what you're asking. None of them is especially tall. It's hard to tell with the glare from the moon, but they look kind of blocky."

"Mountains," Roger said, "do you see any mountains?"

"I think so."

"Kabul," Roger breathed. "It's Kabul. It has to be." He turned to me. "Are you sure about all of this?"

"Why would I make it up?"

"That's not an answer."

"Yes, I'm sure," I said. "I'm not sure it's Kabul, but that's what I see."

"What else could it be?"

I didn't have an answer to that one.

Roger reached for the doorknob.

"Wait!" I said. "What are you doing?"

"Opening the door."

"That's not—you can't do that—we don't know what'll happen—"

Roger turned the knob and pulled the door. It swung open, admitting a breeze that smelled of dust and cordite. Nothing had changed. There was the river, the town, the mountains, the moon presiding over it all. I knew, then—I'd already thought, This is it, when Ted had entered the house, but this was really it. However this story was going to end, this was the stage on which it was going to do so.

"Well?" Roger asked.

I burst into tears.

Whatever he'd anticipated, it wasn't this. The expression on his face—a combination of arrogance, triumph, and fear—slid into confusion. "Veronica?"

"It's still there," I said. "Are you happy? It's still there."

"But—"

"Why can't you see it?" I said. "Why can't you see what's right there in front of you?"

"Veronica—"

"Don't you understand what this means?"

"Of course I do. It means my boy has come back to me. He's finally home."

"Goddamn you!" I shouted. "Why do you keep doing this? Why do you keep lying? Don't you get it, Roger? This is it. This is the end of the mess you made when you struck your deal with that thing in your cell. This is where your cursing of Ted has led you—us—all of us. Here—now—can't you drop the act?"

The confusion on Roger's face congealed into anger. "If this is, to borrow your phrasing, 'it,' I don't understand why you can't let go of this ridiculous obsession with making me confess to something that isn't true."

"Because I was there. I saw what you did. I saw you promising that thing whatever it wanted."

"That's irrelevant! What I may or may not have done in a moment of weakness has no bearing whatsoever on what's happening. Ted has returned to his father. That's what this is about."

"You can't believe that. You're too smart—I can't believe you don't understand what's really happening here. You have to know you're lying to yourself."

"I know nothing of the kind."

"Lift the curse, then. If that has nothing to do with this, lift it."

"No."

"Oh my God," I said, "I get it."

"Get what?"

"It's not that you're fooling yourself—you are, but not the way I thought. It isn't that simple. You don't want to lift the curse because you're afraid that it'll make Ted go away."

Roger's look of anger faltered. "That's not—"

"That's it. You don't care that he's suffering—you think that, as long as you keep him around, as long as he isn't gone, lost once and for all, there's a chance for, what? Some kind of reconciliation?"

Roger was silent.

"You can't see him, can't hear him, can't touch him—but I can.

I'm there to assure you Ted's around. That's what you're up to in your office, isn't it? You've been looking for a way to make him visible to you. Maybe not at first—maybe you did believe he was in the bardo; maybe you were trying to help him exit it—that doesn't make any sense."

"That's because it isn't true," Roger said. "Once again, you're inventing a scenario in which I play the role of villain. How you do enjoy painting me the monster. Has it ever occurred to you to give me the benefit of the doubt?"

"You're not a monster. You're just like your father, that's all."

"I beg your pardon?"

"I'm sure he would have insisted he wasn't a monster, either. He would've quoted the Bible at me to justify breaking your nose, or tormenting you. 'Honor thy father and mother,' right? Especially thy father."

"Of all the things you have said to me—you could have said to me—this is by far the worst, the most hateful."

"Oh please. Don't try to take the moral high ground, here. You aren't the victim. You know it and I know it. But you have a chance to be something else, Roger—you've got a chance to lift this curse and be something your father never was—to be more than he was."

That almost did it. There was a long moment where I honestly thought I'd gotten through to him and we were going to get out of this. His face seemed to relax, as if he'd decided it was time to abandon this posturing and finally make things right. I could see him trying to arrive at the right set of sentences to break the curse. Then—that process ground to a halt. Whatever sentences he'd thrown together fell to the floor and shattered. His mouth tightened, and he said, "I am not my father. I will never be that man."

In the front yard—what had been the front yard—there was movement, down by the river. I glanced at it, turned away immediately. The air was too full of white light for me to distinguish him clearly, but it was Ted.

"What is it?" Roger asked.

Not looking in that direction, I pointed. "Ted."

"Ted, or what you've mistaken for him?"

"It's Ted. He's standing on this side of the river."

"How can you be sure?"

"I can feel him," I said, which was true. Ted was unmistakable, a beacon of cold fire. The stew of emotions that had assaulted me before was past the boil. His agony, his anger, most of all his eagerness, that overpowering desire, bubbled up and out of him. His desire, his greed, burst against me, and I understood what he wanted. Roger, of course. He wanted Roger to leave the house and come join him by the bank of the grinding river. I said, "He's waiting for you."

"He is?"

I nodded.

He licked his lips. "Out there—in the dark."

"Beside the river."

"You're certain."

Now was not the time for qualifications. "Yes."

Roger's forehead was shining with sweat. He grimaced and wiped it. His breathing had grown heavy. I assumed he was working himself up to stride out onto the front porch and across the yard. Judging from the sweat and the breathing, he did not find the prospect of doing so appealing. No surprise, there. Whatever he might say to me to save face, he knew what was waiting for him. I thought I would give him another five seconds before suggesting that he wouldn't have to do so if he lifted the curse. I wasn't sure what I'd do if he refused—which, let's face it, he was more likely to do than not. I couldn't see myself being able to keep him inside if he decided to brazen it out, but I did not want him going to Ted. While I was afraid that, in the end, there would be no other choice, I was holding out hope that the extremity of the situation would force him, at long last, to break the curse.

How surprised was I, then, when Roger said, "I can't." For a moment—a good two- or three-second moment—I literally could not process the words that had come out of his mouth. When I could, I said, "You what?"

"I can't do it," he said. "I can't go to Ted."

"Why not?"

"I—I don't know. I can't, that's all."

"All right," I said. "You know what this means?"

"What?"

"It's time to renounce the curse."

"No." He shook his head.

"Excuse me?" The anger—the fury that swept over me was unlike anything I'd known. It blew through me, this hurricane of resentment and rage that actually took my vision—for an instant, I was so angry it blinded me. Almost before I knew what I was doing, my fist lashed out and caught Roger next to the eye.

The blow took him completely by surprise. His head rocked with the force of it and he backed toward the doorway. He hadn't finished raising his hands and I'd hit him again, a punch in the mouth that scraped my knuckles and burst his lip. Hands up, he retreated onto the front stoop. I swung again, missed, struck his shoulder on the next try. I was—I swear, I've never been that angry at anyone. If I'd had a knife, I could have cut him to ribbons cheerfully.

Doing his best to bat my hands away, Roger backed toward the top of the stairs, talking all the way, his bloody lips asking me what I was doing, what was wrong, what was the meaning of this. The questions rolled off me. I was sick of talking, sick of endless dialogues that led nowhere, sick to death of trying to argue Roger into admitting the truth. This—the confusion scrawled on his face, his hands struggling to keep up with mine, the thud when my fist found his arms, his sides, his gut—was infinitely more satisfying. It was almost sexual; it was that visceral, that immediate.

I'd never—I want to say I could count the number of times I've hit someone on one hand, but even that's an overstatement. I could count them on one finger. In the fourth grade, I gave Katy Britten a black eye for calling me a slut. That was the extent of my combat-related experience. I've never been a fan of violence, never liked violent art, movies, TV shows, whatever. That wasn't all—if you'd asked me if I thought I'd be able to hit Roger, to hurt him, I'd have said absolutely not. I don't know why. The one fight I'd witnessed him in, he hadn't done especially well. It's just socialization, I guess. He's the man; you're the woman; he fights; you don't. To be fair, I don't think he was trying as hard as he might have—as he would've if he'd known how totally committed I was to hurting him. Fast—from start to finish, it was over so fast. Roger went to take another step away from me, and found nothing there—we'd reached the stairs. He threw his arms forward, trying to catch himself from falling, and I hit him in the chest. Still trying to find his footing, he tipped back and fell down the front stairs.

As falls went, it could have been worse. He landed on his ass and back; although I think his ass took most of his weight. A cloud of dust puffed up around him. He looked at me, his eyes wide, his mouth a bloody o. His lips were moving, speaking almost the last words my husband would say to me, and I was too busy exulting in the power coursing through my fists, my arms, to hear what they were. I think one of them was "Why?"—that would make sense, wouldn't it? He tried to wipe his mouth with the back of one hand, but only succeeded in smearing blood across his cheek. I saw the red on his face—and I saw it streaming from his freshly broken nose as he tried to avoid another kick from his father's polished shoe—I saw it leaking from the place where the snake had fastened itself to him—I saw it dried on his lips as they pronounced his curse on Ted—I saw it flush beneath his cheeks as he told the judge he would marry me. As quickly as it had swept me up, the wave of anger dropped me. Where I'd been strong, powerful, relentless, an Amazon taking my destiny in my own hands, now I was hollow, burnt-out, dizzy and sick at what I'd done.

From his position next to the river, Ted watched events unfold with keen interest. My rage had fled, and Ted was there, waiting for Roger to join him. What was the way out of this? There had to be one, right? Absurd as it sounds, part of me still hadn't abandoned the idea that something was going to save us. Either Roger would give in and break the curse, or I'd finally understand all the reading I'd done in the last few days and know how to defeat Ted. It wasn't too late, not yet—

Except that nothing was coming to me, nor was Roger any closer than he'd ever been to taking back the words he'd uttered months ago. Months? God—I had one of those seconds where it's like, you simultaneously think, *But that happened yesterday, didn't it?* and, *Wasn't that ten years ago?* Roger had been watching to find out if I intended to descend the stairs and continue attacking him, or if I was content to maintain the high ground. Since I hadn't charged down after him, he pulled himself to his feet, one eye on me in case I changed my mind. He held up his hands, both of them bloody from his efforts at cleaning his mouth, and let them fall to his sides. He said, "That was a bit excessive, don't you think?"

"Your son is waiting for you," I said. "If you turn around and walk in a straight line, you'll go right to him."

"Veronica—I told you, I can't."

"He's waiting for you."

"Honey, I can't do this. I'm sorry, but I can't."

"It's about ten yards."

"Dammit, Veronica, I said I'm staying right here."

"No, you're not," I said. "You're going to turn around and walk in a straight line to Ted."

"I will not."

"Goddamn you!" I shouted. "You will walk your Goddamn ass to your Goddamn son or I swear to Christ I will come down there and I will claw your eyes out. This is what it's come to, Roger. You're out of options. I'm out of options. You got what you wanted. Ted has come back to you. You own that. You drink your cup of blood. You accept what you wanted and go to him. Be a man, for God's sake."

Roger looked behind him. "It's dark. It's all dark."

"Walk in a straight line. He's there."

"I can't believe—you swear he's awful, yet you're willing to send me out to him like this."

"I didn't bring him here—I didn't make him what he is."

"So that's it? That's all there is?"

"Unless you want to lift the curse, yes, that's all."

He was about to reply. I didn't give him the chance. I spun on my heel, marched back inside, and slammed the door. I snapped all the locks; Roger would have no trouble hearing them. If he wanted in, I wasn't sure I'd be able to keep him out—it wouldn't be that hard to smash the window and reach through to release the locks. I was afraid he might try to do that, and I wasn't sure what I'd do if he did. Watching him standing at the foot of the stairs, watching me, because I couldn't follow my actions all the way through and walk away from the door, I was certain he'd call my bluff. At the very least, I assumed he'd hold his position.

He didn't. After I don't know how long of looking at me, Roger took a deep breath, said something he thought I'd be able to hear or read on his lips—I couldn't do either—and headed towards the river. He walked slowly, hesitantly, the way you do when you're moving through your house in the dark. I kept expecting each step forward to be his last, that he'd run back to the house as fast as he could. He didn't. Moving ever more slowly, he continued to advance, unseeing, toward Ted, who trembled with anticipation. The closer he drew to Ted, the harder it was to see him. The combination of light from the moon and river and wanting to keep my eyes from Ted made Roger less and less distinct.

• • •

How could I let him go, right? How could I stay where I was while my husband walked toward what had to be his death? Why didn't I end this, unlock the door and call out to him to stop, come back, we'd find another way through this? Because it was his decision. He had the choice between releasing Ted and going to meet him. The most I could do was force him to choose. I wish I could say that the tears were streaming down my face as he went, that I sobbed and whimpered, but mostly I was anxious, eager for this to be over. I had had enough. Enough of Roger's mania, enough of Ted's haunting me, enough of the whole sick and sad affair that my life had become. Peace—I was desperate for peace. I was thinking—praying, *Let this do. Let this satisfy him.* If it wasn't the ending I'd wanted, let it at least be an ending.

• • •

About two-thirds of the way to Ted, Roger stopped. My first thought was that his nerve had failed and he'd gone as far as he could. Ted would have to come the rest of the way to him. No, that wasn't it. Hard as it was to see Roger through this white glare, I was pretty sure something was different. The tilt of his head, the way he was carrying himself, changed, as if he could see part or all of what lay in front of him, as if he'd gone so far into this landscape that he couldn't help seeing it. There was no way to know how much of it was visible to him, but he didn't appear to notice Ted. Even if he'd managed not to collapse or run screaming in the opposite direction, he would have registered the sight of his son somehow. Roger bent down, dragged his fingers through the dust at his feet, and stared at his hand. He straightened up, wiped his hand on his jeans, and stared at the river. He took one step forward, then a second.

I couldn't watch—he was too close to Ted, who had flared like a bonfire doused in gasoline. Nerves in flames, I backed away from the door to the foot of the second-floor stairs. That was too close by far. I retreated up the stairs to the second-floor hall. My brain still felt as if it were burning inside my skull. I stumbled up the stairs to the third floor. That wasn't any better, nor was there much point in continuing to the attic. The entire house—what had been the house—was ablaze with Ted. My skin felt wreathed in fire—for the briefest instant, it was as if I were standing beside Ted when the RPG struck the ground and made him the heart of a momentary sun. Blue-white tongues of flame played across my fingers, and I realized that the sensation that was consuming my nerves was about to take the rest of me with them. My legs wouldn't carry me any further. Tongue too dry to cry out, I dropped to the floor. In some distant corner of my mind, I wondered if there would be anything left of me. My body shook as if I were having a seizure. Darkness rimmed my vision, consciousness fleeing for what promised to be the last time. There was time for me to hope I wouldn't end up in the same place as Ted, then nothing.

• • •

That nothing lasted until late the following morning. While I was wrapped in it, there were no dreams, no memories recycled into new configurations—only a distant pain that gradually drew closer. It was that pain—a feeling as if the entire inside of my body had been scraped raw—that finally brought me back to the house. Funny—my first thought wasn't relief at being alive, or wonder at what had occurred, or concern for Roger. The first priority to present itself was an urgent need to use the bathroom. Somehow, despite everything that had happened, I'd managed to avoid wetting myself, and now my bladder was demanding to be relieved from its duty. Not until I'd done the necessary did those other concerns announce themselves. Half-sure the desert landscape would remain to greet my eyes, I peered out the bathroom window. There was green, the lawn, with Founders and the neighbors in their familiar places. The sheer happiness and relief that slice of view brought me was replaced almost immediately by a thick, sinking dread. *Roger?* I thought.

• • •

He wasn't in any of the places I searched for him, inside the house or out. I knew he wouldn't be. Right from the start, before I'd been over the entire house from attic to basement twice, then driven to his office, then wandered around campus, then wandered around town, then tried to retrace the paths of his walks and runs—by which time the sun had lowered behind the mountains and I was fainting with hunger—from the second his name occurred to me, it was followed by an answer. Gone. That answer wanted to bring along a longer explanation, in which the words "your" and "fault" featured prominently, but I refused them admittance. After a stop at the diner for a plate of scrambled eggs and dry toast, I returned to Belvedere House in case Roger was waiting for me. He wasn't.

After I'd been through the house a third time, I called the police and told them my husband had gone out last night and not returned. The officer who spoke to me asked a couple of questions, then suggested I stop into the station and fill out a missing person's report. I took his advice, but before I did, I climbed the stairs to Roger's office.

I'm not sure what I was expecting to find. When I'd looked in here during my searches, something had struck me as off, though not in a way that seemed to have any bearing on the task at hand. Moving more slowly, now, I flipped on the light and entered the room. More maps than ever overlapped on the bookcases, the walls. The threads that connected them, however, had been severed, every last one, the ends hanging limply from the stickers Roger had used to secure them. The air was heavy with a sharp, oily smell, which came from the table, whose model was splashed with what had to be red—scarlet paint. How had I missed that before? The figures of the soldiers had been knocked over, the buildings thrown out of alignment, as if someone had taken hold of one end of the table and shaken it, produced a scale-model earthquake. Paint pooled heavily around each figure, streaked the buildings' walls. The soil Roger had sprinkled the table with lay in wet clumps. Most of the photos surrounding the model lay under a layer of bright red. I picked one up by the edge and wiped it against the edge of the table. The spot where Ted had been killed glared at me. I dropped it as if I'd been bitten.

The map at the door I studied the longest. Roger's writing had crowded out almost every bit of available space, but it was as if he'd thrown a bucket of water onto it: his script had run together into a gray mess, the paper warped and wavy beneath. Here and there, individual words and symbols had survived the deluge, half a sentence about trade routes converging in Kabul, a fraction—fifteen over negative seven—bracketed and followed by a minus, the astrological sign for Cancer, a backwards hook and a straight line that might have been Arabic. At the center of it, the narrow bar of Ted's shaving mirror, Roger's long-ago, failed birthday present—his attempt at carrying on paternal tradition. The mirror was dark. I bent to study it, and saw that the backing was charred, the glass scorched, as if a fire had erupted inside it, burning its reflections away.

EPILUDE

THREE ENDINGS

"That isn't the end," Veronica said, "but what came next, I can summarize. I went to the police, dickered with a cop who told me Roger couldn't be considered officially missing until twenty-four hours had passed, filled out a missing persons report anyway, then endured a set of surprisingly probing questions from the cop who'd given me the hard time. He wanted to know what I'd done to my hand. I told him I'd been so frustrated at not being able to find my husband, I'd punched a door. Nodding, making sympathetic noises, the cop asked if I was sure that was what had happened—maybe it was my husband I'd hit, and that was why he hadn't returned home yet? I could feel my cheeks reddening, but I did my best to play it as anger at this clod for having dared suggest such a thing. Who knew I'd be getting Huguenot's answer to Sherlock Holmes? I returned to the house, accompanied by Sherlock and his partner, because I'd mentioned the state of Roger's office, and that sounded like something that should be checked out. I was half-sure I'd be leaving it in cuffs, on suspicion of involvement in my husband's disappearance.

"That didn't happen, though the cops stayed much longer than they'd planned. I'd become so used to the sight of Roger's office that I hadn't realized how profoundly strange it would appear to anyone seeing it for the first time. It prompted an extensive conversation with my friend from the station about Roger's recent history, which I narrated as thoroughly as I dared while his partner called for backup. I'm not sure why they needed the extra help. They fed me some line about more eyes on the scene of an investigation having a better chance of noticing things, but I think they were freaked out by what they'd walked into and wanted someone else there with them. Before what turned out to be a long night was over, I'd narrated the last few months, in part and in whole, to three different cops. Not one of them failed to ask me about the scrapes on my knuckles, and not one of them failed to look dissatisfied with my explanation.

"The last cop to interview me—or interrogate, I suppose; although it didn't seem much like an interrogation. We were sitting at the kitchen table, me with a Coke, him a glass of milk, while the others continued to pore over Roger's office. Anyway, once I'd reached the end of my story—Roger, I said, had told me he was going out for a walk around nine and never returned—this guy, (who'd kept asking me to backtrack and explain something I'd said ten minutes ago) put down his milk and said, 'Mrs. Croydon, I hope you won't take this the wrong way, but it feels like there's more you have to tell us. I could be wrong, and I'm not accusing you of anything, I want to make that clear. It's just—your story—it feels like there's more to it. A lot of times, women—if there are problems at home: maybe the husband drinks a little too often; maybe he's too free with his hands—they don't want to talk about it. They feel embarrassed, ashamed, like it's their fault this guy has an impulse-control problem.

"'Understand, I'm not saying anything like that took place here. But from everything you've said, your husband, Roger, has been under a lot of stress. My son's fifteen—he drives me insane, but, God forbid, if anything ever happened to him, I don't know what I'd do. You don't need to be much of a psychologist to know your husband's in a bad way—all you have to do is take a look around that study of his. Someone in that state of mind—they're not really themselves, are they? Anything they might do—it's not like they're really doing it, is it? It's the stress; stress makes people do all kinds of things they'd never do otherwise.'

"He paused. This was my opportunity to say, 'Tell me about it,' or 'You have no idea,' pick up the baton and carry it the next lap. Except, what would I say? Believe it or not, this was a real problem for me. There was no way I could discuss any of the weirdness that had invaded our lives, not in the slightest, without signaling to the guy across the table that I was in deep psychological trouble. There was no way to hint at what had happened, to package it in a more acceptable wrapper. Once I started to talk about it, I'd be unable to stop until this guy and his friends had me on my way to the psych-ward at Wiltwyck Hospital.

"I realize this sounds like a no-brainer to you, but you have to understand, what I'd seen—all of it—was bursting to get out. On a much more immediate level, I felt this almost irresistible pressure—I mean a literal force somewhere behind my mouth that threatened to erupt at any minute in a flood of words. It wasn't guilt—what I'd done to Roger had been my only option, and when you came right down to it, what more had I done than force him to finish what he himself had started? No, the desire that wanted to run riot with my tongue predated guilt. Call it astonishment, shock at your own experience.

"Fortunately for me, I had my Coke to sip as I debated how to respond. I watched the cop watching me—studying me. No doubt I'd already given myself away. I set the glass down and said, 'I'm sorry. I honestly don't know what you're talking about.'

"So why did I call the police, right? Why so soon? Why not wait until Roger had been gone a week—at least a couple of days?"

"Something like that had occurred to me," I said, although I had an idea of the answer.

"Because Roger was gone," Veronica said. "I didn't know what had become of him—I still don't—but I was certain—right from the start, I knew I wasn't going to see him again. Ever. Going to the cops was—it's what you do, when someone disappears, especially if—"

"You've got nothing to hide."

"Yeah. That's not exactly how I would put it—I think I'd go for, 'You're not responsible'—but same difference. The longer I waited, the worse it would look, so I decided not to wait at all. As it was, a certain amount of suspicion fell on me anyway. One look at Roger's office, and the extent of his obsession was clear. Why hadn't I gotten him some help? I had tried, I explained, check with Dr. Hawkins. I gave her permission to speak to them about the outlines of our meeting, which I assumed would satisfy the cops. I was wrong. As far as they were concerned, I hadn't done enough, and if I weren't directly responsible for Roger's disappearance, which I think one or two continued to suspect, I was indirectly to blame. I can't say if that one or two ever approached the DA with their suspicions, but it wouldn't surprise me to learn they had.

"You aren't happy with my explanation. I can see it."

"I don't—"

"My shrink thought there was more to me calling the cops, as well. He said it was a red flag that, my protests to the contrary aside, I was profoundly guilty, and going to the police was my way of admitting this.

"Oh, yes, I went to see a psychiatrist, the winter after Roger disappeared. By then, everything had quieted. Despite my suspicions about their suspicions, the cops didn't charge me with anything. The news reports had come and gone—actually, the TV news was never that interested. I think there were two segments on channel 6, one announcing that Roger had vanished, the other covering the search the cops did of the rail trail. The local papers had more. I don't know if you read *The Times Herald-Record*, but one of their reporters wrote about Roger, on and off, for something like three weeks. She'd taken a class with Roger, herself, back in the eighties. I think she interviewed everyone he'd ever talked to for longer than five minutes. I spoke to her twice. She even managed to squeeze a few words from Joanne. Talk about blood from a stone. In the end, though, she moved on, as did the cops. The detective in charge of the case told me they were leaving it open but, for the time being, they'd followed all their leads as far as they could. If I received any new information, I should call him, immediately. Should anything come across his desk, he'd be on the phone to me right away.

"The funny thing is, when I heard this—the guy drove down to the house to tell me they were moving the case to Inactive—I started crying, sobbing, telling him, No, no, he couldn't do this. I knew what this meant; they thought Roger was dead. The detective did what he could to reassure me. He kept patting my arm, saying that wasn't it at all. He was sure Roger had just gone someplace for a little rest; that was all. No doubt he'd be back in touch with me very soon, now. I refused to be consoled. I cried and cried and cried, and then I cried some more. 'I can't believe he's gone,' I sobbed.

"It wasn't a performance, either. I honestly could not believe that Roger would never return. Or—it wasn't so much that I couldn't believe it. It was more that I couldn't accept it. I know; I know. You're sitting there thinking, *You're the one who sent him into Ted's arms. You threatened to claw his eyes out, for crying out tears. What else did you expect?* That's absolutely true—I knew that—and I knew that there had been no other way. I'd exhausted all possible options. Intellectually, I could justify what I'd done—what I'd been forced to do—all day.

The problem was, I couldn't accept it. For weeks after the detective's visit, as summer decayed into fall, and fall was swept aside by winter and that string of bad storms we had that year—every weekend, another storm barreling up the coast and vomiting another foot of snow on us—I debated walking into the police station and turning myself in. I wouldn't be able to admit what I'd done, of course, but I thought that, if I could concoct a plausible enough story, I could be punished, anyway.

"I spent hours planning the perfect crime in reverse. I finally decided that my best chance was to claim I'd taken Roger to the Mid-Hudson Bridge in the middle of the night, poisoned him, and pushed him over the side. That seemed the most likely way to account for the lack of a body. The problem was figuring out how I would have convinced him to come with me to the Bridge at three a.m., and, once there, to have consumed the poison. If I were going to do this, I had to do it right. My biggest fear was that the cops would see through me, tag me as a grieving, de facto widow who'd lost her mind.

"When all was said and done, I didn't plead guilty—I can't say confess. There was no story I could come up with that didn't have holes in it big enough to drive a truck through. Instead, I started to drink. Scotch was my choice—not because I liked it any better than I ever had, but because it hit me so much faster than beer did, and because it bit into my tongue and burned my throat all the way down to my stomach, and because a glass of it—I mean four fingers' worth, straight up—removed me from myself far enough for me not to feel like screaming all the time. You won't be surprised to hear that my sleeping had gone the way of the dinosaur. For a short time, the Scotch helped that. Then it made it worse. I would be up until two, three, four in the morning, wandering the house, glass in one hand, bottle in the other. I preferred single-malt. None of your blended crap for me. The house—I haven't told you, have I? I couldn't feel the house anymore. Ted going nuclear had been the last thing. I wasn't sure if it had fried my circuits, so to speak, or if he'd consumed every-thing there was to be aware of, but for the first time in months, all I was aware of was myself.

"That isn't to say that nothing weird happened. One night—this was in December, right around Christmas—Ted disappeared from all the pictures of him I'd hung around the house. I was befuddled enough that it took me a while—a long while—to figure out what was wrong. When it dawned on me that the eight-by-ten photograph of the flag and blue background I was staring at was supposed to have Ted in its foreground, I raced from room to room, hallway to hallway, to check the other pictures. Empty, every last one of them. I didn't know what it meant. I was afraid that Ted had left his photos and was on his way for me, a notion that half a bottle of Glenkinchie made seem a lot more convincing. I waited out the rest of that night in my car, the heater on full for the cold, the radio tuned to the campus heavy-metal show to keep me awake. The next day, Ted had returned to his pictures, and I wondered if he'd ever left them in the first place.

"I could go on, but you get the idea. I was in rough shape. Pretty soon, the Scotch stopped working as well as it had, and not long after that, it stopped working altogether. I was still drunk, but being so now took me closer to what had happened. Here I was, my knuckles scraping Roger's teeth. Here he was, lying on his back in the dirt, his mouth a bloody mess as he looked up at me. 'That's all there is?' he asked. I didn't forget the other things—how could I? Not his cursing Ted; not my flight through the house's hidden rooms. All of it was tangled together. I spent hours in Roger's study, which I hadn't bothered to clean up. I stared at the tabletop, where the paint had long-since dried and darkened. I trailed my fingers over the maps—although I avoided the map by the door. However dark that mirror appeared, I didn't want to chance looking into it and seeing something looking back.

"December slid into January. January gave way to February. The house was a wreck, the kitchen table lost under a mountain of fast-food bags and boxes; empty, unrinsed Scotch bottles competing for space up and down the halls, in most of the rooms; the air smelling of alcohol and must. Funny how far you can fall so fast. Once the sun went down, I sat on the front step, sometimes wearing a winter coat, a couple of times wrapped in a blanket, gazing at the spot where Roger had lain after I'd knocked him down. Two feet of snow covered it. One night, I got down on my hands and knees and dug through the snow with my bare hands—I don't know what I expected to find. I can imagine what the neighbors must have thought. Did I mention I brought a bottle out with me? I'd sit there until my teeth were chattering and I couldn't feel my fingers or toes, then I'd fumble the stopper out and let the Scotch scorch my mouth. For a moment, I'd have the illusion I was warm.

"You want to know the craziest part of all this? Throughout this time, I continued to teach, adjuncting at SUNY and Penrose. I didn't need the money. Roger had added my name to the accounts and investments after we were married, and he'd employed a good accountant. I was comfortable enough not to need the pennies slave labor—I mean being an adjunct—paid. I can't say why I kept getting into the car and going to work. It wasn't for the social contacts, that's for sure. I went in for my classes, my office hours, and that was that. With the exception of Harlow and Stephen, none of the faculty at either school had much to say to me—except for those people who wanted to ask me what had happened to Roger, which is to say, those people who wanted to tell me their theory of Roger's fate. I can remember how astounded I was the first time someone stopped me—it was this woman I knew at Penrose—to ask me these incredibly personal questions. How had our sex life been? Had I kept Roger satisfied? I mean, really. She concluded her inquisition by declaring that Roger was 'obviously' in Mexico with another former student, but I shouldn't blame myself, and as long as he'd left me the money, I was better off without him. If I hadn't been in my near-perpetual state of hangover, I would have walked away as fast as I could. That, or taken a swing at the bitch.

"So I wasn't teaching for the wonders it did for my personal life, that's for sure. I liked the students well-enough, but I've never been one of those teachers who develops close bonds with their students. It's one of the things I've always liked about the classroom, the relative impersonality of it. You stand up in front of this group of people, and all you have to do is deliver information to them, impart skills where you can. You're a means, not an end. Yes, I knew they were talking about me outside of class. I didn't blame them. In their position, I would have; and at least none of them was talking to me. I guess it was playing—escaping into the role that appealed to me.

"During the fall, I'd managed to fulfill my teaching duties reasonably well, but after the long Christmas break, starting up again at the end of January was much more difficult. By the time Valentine's Day was approaching, it was all I could do just to show up to class on time and in reasonably clean clothes. I couldn't focus on the reading I assigned long enough to complete it myself, so I improvised these crazy lectures that followed tangents as far as they'd take me in an hour. Some of the students took notes attentively—some always do—and I'm sure I must have offered a few tidbits of useful information—not about the subject we were supposed to be addressing—but the classes were slipping away from me. I'd collected two sets of papers from each class that I hadn't so much as thought about. When a student asked me when they could expect them back, I went off on him. Here I was, following in Roger's footsteps, but without having written the shelfful of books that might buy me a measure of indulgence. No, at this rate, it would be another week before the chairs of both English departments called me into their offices and delivered some kind of ultimatum."

Veronica paused. I waited, then said, "What did you do?"

"I had—you wouldn't call it a moment of clarity, not exactly—it was more a moment of less obscurity. Late one Tuesday night, I phoned both chairs and told them versions of the same story. I hadn't been feeling well lately—very run down, feverish, glands swollen—and had finally been to my doctor, who told me it was a sure case of mono and ordered me on bedrest for the next month. I was sorry to call them this late, it was just, I'd spent the last three hours trying to find someone to take my classes, and no one could, and I didn't know what to do. I was very convincing. Each of them sounded relieved. Clearly, they'd already heard complaints about me. This provided them with a solid explanation. Within an hour, I'd handed over my classes for the next four weeks, at least. The following morning, I went to my regular doctor and got him to give me an emergency referral to a psychiatrist—in Albany. I didn't want to be caught going out of anyone's office locally. There was one more night in the house. The morning after, I packed a bag, got in my car, and headed north on the Thruway. Once the shrink had heard my story—the less-edited version—I figured there was a fair-to-middling chance he'd recommend some hospital time for me. If he didn't, I planned on finding a local motel, anyway.

"As it turned out, I was right. I spent six days in a surprisingly comfortable bed, after which I checked into a motel in Delmar. There's no need to go into the gory details. Suffice it to say, I got the help I needed. After one extra week off, I picked up my classes again, and finished the spring semester in much better shape than I'd started it in. My evaluations weren't the greatest, but what did you expect?

"And that was that. It's hard to know where to end. There's always a little more to tell. I cleaned up Belvedere House after I returned from Albany. I thought about selling it, but the deed's in Roger's name—

it's the one thing he didn't add me to—and the process of changing that—especially since he's officially missing, not dead—is more complicated than I can be bothered with, right now. Ditto having Roger declared legally dead. You'd be surprised how many people have urged me to do that. It's not that I think he's coming back. It's just—well, I'm not going to do it, all right?"

"Fine."

"I've kind of lost interest in literature. I teach it when I have to, but the focus of my freshman comp classes has shifted more to the visual arts, to painting. I'm writing about painting, too."

"Belvedere?"

"And de Castries."

"I thought you said you didn't care for either man's work?"

"I did. It's—I spent so much time on each of them, it seemed a shame not to do something with my research. We'll see what happens. Maybe I'll do a Ph.D. in art history. I try not to pay attention to the news—so much of it is so depressing—but there are times I can't help noticing what's going on. Like now, the whole situation in Iraq. Maybe there was a case to be made for going in—I don't know. But I keep thinking, it's like, we were all traumatized on 9/11, and now we're going to pass that on, as if trauma's some kind of disease that compels you to spread it to someone else." She stood from the couch and stretched, throwing her arms out to either side. "What time is it? God, I'm exhausted."

I consulted the clock. "Four."

"Wow." She ran a hand through her hair, turned in the direction of her room. "I guess that's all—"

"Actually," I said, "there's one more thing."

"There is? What can I possibly not have told you?"

"Roger. What happened—what do you think happened to him?"

Veronica crossed her arms. "I don't know. How could I?"

"You couldn't—I don't think. But you spent a great deal of time imagining him at other moments. I find it hard to believe you haven't done the same for this one."

Her face darkened. "This doesn't seem the slightest bit intrusive to you?"

"Under normal circumstances, yes, horribly. After all that you've told me, not at all." I added, "If you want to know what the end of the story is, that's it."

There followed a long pause during which I thought Veronica was staring—glaring—at me, as if to discern…it was hard to say what, what further quality she was attempting to assess, since she already had judged me fit to hear things I would have assumed reserved for the priest in the confessional, if not the privacy of her own conscience. I was exhausted, my brain stuffed full of the seven course meal Veronica had served. Perhaps I had heard all that was necessary. Perhaps, but like the diner who must have the last piece of chocolate mousse cake, and so overrules his body to lift the fork to his mouth, I wanted to know the last detail. I shifted under Veronica's eyes, but did not look away.

At last, her face lightened, and I understood that she hadn't been glaring at me. She hadn't seen me at all; her gaze had been directed inward, to a question or scruple I only could guess. Arms still crossed, she sat on the edge of the cushions. "Fair enough," she said, though her mouth had the cast of someone preparing to taste a bitter drink. "You're right. I spent hours mulling over Roger's fate, speculating, constructing what I thought were plausible scenarios—although, really, when it comes to this kind of thing, how do you judge plausibility? Wrong word. What you're after is an ending that feels right, which no doubt means it's a fiction. I mean, how often does life conclude like that?

"Last night, I told you that I'd talked to one of the guys from Ted's outfit, Gene Ortiz—Woodpecker. I called him after Roger disappeared, but I didn't say why. It was because I thought I knew what had become of Roger. A narrative had presented itself to me fully formed: I woke up one morning, tongue thick, head aching, and there it was waiting for me.

"In this version, as Roger draws nearer to Ted—remember I said there was that moment he hesitated, his body language changed, and I realized he was seeing something? Well, he does, only it isn't the view that presents itself to me. Where Ted is standing waiting for him, Roger sees a path—an alley, bordered by low buildings, houses whose mud walls he recognizes at once. He's in an alleyway in Kabul. The sky is dark. The moon is up. From the position of the stars, he knows with stomach-dropping certainty what night this is. He runs to the end of the alley and looks around. He doesn't recognize the street he's on. He goes to turn left, decides on right instead. The street is deserted. He runs to the next intersection. He doesn't—wait, he does know where he is. If he crosses this street, there should be an alley ahead to the left—yes, he has his bearings, now. If he follows this narrow, crooked passage, he should come out at the square where Ted and his patrol are to be ambushed. If he can catch them before they enter it—or at least warn them—

"Roger's legs pound harder than they have since he was twelve and racing to make it home before the deadline his father had set. He's half-expecting his heart to start shouting, but when he stops, it's to catch his breath. Truth be told, he's happy—elated—the fear that had gripped him on the front step melted by the chance he's been given, the opportunity to make everything right.

"He sets off for the ambush site once more, doing his best to pace himself. On his way, he checks the sky. From the strip of it he can see, there isn't much time left. The alley forks. He chooses left when he should have picked right, and is a hundred yards the wrong way before he realizes his mistake. Cursing himself, he doubles back, grabbing a robe from atop a heap of clothing behind a house and struggling into it as he runs. It's occurred to him that, if he hurtles into the square in his jeans and polo short, the assassins may take it as a cue to open fire. He needs enough of a disguise to buy himself fifteen, twenty seconds. He pulls the robe closed, and there's the square ahead. He can see the movie theater's silhouette rising above its fellow buildings. Is that someone on the roof?

"As he approaches the end of the alley, a debate springs up in his mind. He knows where the attackers are positioned. Should he try to disable one of them, use that weapon to kill the others? Or should his priority be warning Ted? Then his legs have carried him out into the square and there is Ted's patrol spread out across it—dammit, he's too late; there's no time—the best he can do is warn them, which he's already doing. He's yelling at the top of his lungs, an inarticulate howl that draws all the soldiers' weapons in his direction. 'Not me, you idiots!' he wants to shout, but the clock is ticking. Any second now, the old man, the Judas goat, will come running out and the ambush will begin.

"He runs up to Ted, his heart straining with joy at the sight of his son, alive and well in front of him after everything. He wants to throw his arms around Ted, wrap him in a hug and tell him all is forgiven, but he has to warn him, first, which he's doing, a stream of information pouring out of his mouth as he gestures wildly, pointing at the spots where the attackers are concealed. Ted's eyes are wide. He's stepped forward to meet this man who looks exactly like his father but cannot be him, because that's impossible, and who's yelling about an ambush, men with guns all around them. He's so focused on Roger that he doesn't hear the RPG cough—but Roger does, and the instant before they're both blown out of this life, he moves to embrace Ted. That's how he dies: arms outstretched to the son who's backing away from him.

"This conclusion arrived with the force of revelation. There was no doubt in my mind that this was Roger's fate. So I set about trying to clarify it, which was why I called Woodpecker. Needless to say, I didn't tell him the real reason I was contacting him. I said I'd found Ted's death very troubling and was now in therapy to help me come to terms with it. My therapist had suggested I might find it helpful to talk to someone who'd known Ted. The CO had identified Gene as Ted's best friend. Would he mind talking to me?

"If I'd been waiting for some kind of confirmation, however, a telling detail that would verify my narrative of Roger's end, I was disappointed. Trying not to appear any more interested in the old man who'd halted the patrol and so set them up than I was in the rest of the story, I asked Woodpecker what he remembered about him. Not much, he said. He was just an old man waving his arms and shouting. Did he have a beard? I asked. Could you understand what he was saying? To be honest, Gene said, he wasn't too sure about anything when it came to the old man. The attack had happened so soon after he appeared. He guessed the old man must've had a beard, because all the men in those parts wore facial hair. No, he couldn't understand a word coming out of the guy's mouth. Do you know what became of his body? I asked. He didn't. Probably in an anonymous grave somewhere on the outskirts of Kabul. If I would excuse him for saying so, he thought that body, and those of their attackers, should have been left to rot where they were. That was all right, I said, I didn't mind.

"So, compelling as it may have been, my scenario remained speculative. There was sufficient uncertainty in Gene Ortiz's account of the attack for my version of events to slot into it. In the absence of corroborating evidence from Gene, though, or any of the other soldiers—I talked to the four men I could get in contact with—the story I had stayed more invention than hypothesis. As the weeks crept on, everything that had argued so forcefully in its favor—especially its irresistible neatness—increasingly seemed to count against it. It was too *Twilight Zone*—ironic, but not necessarily logical. Ted allows Roger to go back in time to insure that he—Ted—will be killed. You see what I mean?"

I nodded.

"The second ending I arrived at more deliberately. While I was recuperating in Albany, I told the first scenario to my shrink. He'd heard more of the supernatural events I'd been through than the cops had—not as much as you; you've heard pretty much everything—because by then it cost me too much effort to conceal them, to create parallel situations that would account for the same results. He didn't believe any of it—he was quite candid about that, said he thought I'd created this massive hallucinatory structure to mediate my experience to myself—but he encouraged me to discuss the supernatural moments in depth. He said it would help him map the parameters of my delusion. When we'd reached the end of the story, he asked me what had become of Roger. I told him I'd thought I knew, but wasn't sure anymore, and gave him my exercise in irony. He agreed it didn't make much sense if you considered it closely, but he was fascinated by it all the same, especially what he called its '*mis-en-abyme*' quality. 'Roger goes into the past in order to create the situation that will end in him going into the past in order to create the situation that will end in him going into the past, and so on.' What I'd created was a wonderful symbol for Roger's obsession with Ted's death and its destructive effects on him and me.

"He gave me an assignment—write a new ending for Roger and Ted, a more hopeful one. He handed me a legal pad and a pen, and I had till our appointment the next morning to see what I could come up with. It was hard to conceive of any finish to this story that didn't include pain and suffering. I went through the entire pad—fifty sheets torn off and crumpled into yellow balls I threw at the garbage can in mounting frustration—until all I had was the cardboard backing. I spent a restless night, irritated at my inability to fulfill what appeared to be a straightforward-enough task. I could have tossed off something simple and banal—Roger and Ted go to heaven and everyone's happy—but that wouldn't do. For the assignment to serve its purpose, whatever I wrote would have to feel right in the same way the first ending had.

"An hour before that next appointment, the edge of an idea

presented itself to me, and I started to write, using the backing and keeping my handwriting tiny. I was almost late completing it. I ran into the office, panting, and thrust the cardboard into the doctor's hands. He raised his eyebrows, but he read what I'd written."

"Which was?"

"I'm getting to that," Veronica said. "This version of events begins at the same moment as the previous one, with Roger stopping in his progress toward Ted, cocking his head as something becomes visible to him. In this case, it isn't an alleyway in Kabul—what he sees in the darkness ahead of him is a corridor whose familiarity he can't place right away. Its walls are strange, irregular. He advances and realizes that they're the bars of jail cells. He's back in the holding area where he and Ted spent what was left of the night after their confrontation. The lights are out, but the air outside the windows is lightening. Dawn will arrive soon. The same time he—throat dry, Roger searches for his cell, the cell in which he—there it is. Empty, he's relieved to see. He looks across at Ted's cell.

"Which isn't empty. In fact, it's full, crammed with—he walks forward until he's standing outside it. Instead of bare concrete and metal bars, its walls are crowded with tall bookcases, from each of which hangs an assortment of maps. The center of the room is dominated by a heavy table, to which—Roger has been thinking, *It's my study, how did that get here?* when his brain catches up to what's chained to the table. It's Ted, naked and—cut open, tortured. His chest, hips, thighs, are bare red meat, the skin dangling from them in long, ragged strips. His heart, breathing, everything stopped, Roger sees that those exposed places have suffered further violation, cut into windows for what lies beneath, or transfixed by long white needles. In more than a few places, what should have remained inside has been lifted out. Gray loops of intestine have been coiled on Ted's belly and held there by a pair of the needles. An eyeball has been loosened but not severed, left to lie on Ted's cheek, a needle inserted in the evacuated socket. There's blood everywhere, pooled under the table, splattered across the maps, dotted on the ceiling. The sharp tang of it forces itself into his nostrils and mouth before he has a chance to cover either. Roger is stunned, forced out of himself by what he can't close his eyes to. In some, faraway part of his mind, he's screaming, awash in horror, tears pouring down his face as he slams his fists against the bars. Here, though, he's silent—until, that is, Ted moves, shifting on the table as much as he can. The needles quiver, so many gauges to his continuing agony. Roger groans.

"Without thinking, Roger puts his hand on the cell door, which resists his pull at first. He's afraid it's locked—who has the key? Then, with the scream of metal surrendering its grip on itself, the door slides open. He enters the cell with a combination of reverence and deliberateness. He doesn't linger, doesn't waste time playing voyeur to Ted's wounds. He walks to the table, surveys Ted from head to foot, and begins removing the needles, grasping hold of the end of each one and sliding it out of Ted's eye socket, ear, throat, chest, arm, hand, stomach, groin, leg, foot. The needles slide out easily, making small, wet sounds as they exit. Roger drops them on the floor, where they clatter against one another. With his throat free, Ted moans in earnest, flinching as Roger continues his work.

"The last needle removed, Roger directs his attention to Ted's other wounds, cupping his eyeball in his palm and gently returning it to its socket, folding flaps of skin back in place, lifting lengths of intestine—carefully, oh so carefully—and depositing them inside his son. When he has seen to Ted's final hurt, Roger holds up his hands, stares at the blood and gore clinging to them. He places them on Ted, who leaps at the touch, and starts to move them over him, as if rubbing Ted's blood back into him. Where Roger's hands pass, Ted's skin is whole, healed. Ted screams as Roger's hands join muscle to bone, skin to muscle, skin to skin. He twists against the chains that bind him to the table still.

"Once Ted's body has been repaired, Roger takes Ted's head in his hands. The terror and pain that have played across Ted's face throughout Roger's actions drain away, replaced first by calm, then recognition. 'Dad?' Ted says. Roger releases Ted's head and, walking around the table, snaps the chains holding his wrists and ankles as if they're plastic. He helps Ted to sit up, then off the table, steadying him as he regains his footing. When he's sure Ted isn't about to collapse, Roger looks at him directly and says, 'Son—Ted—I am sorry; I am so very sorry. This has—all of this, I fear, has been my doing—my responsibility. The fruit of my words—my curse, to call it truly. I was—I was—it isn't enough—I was angry. I'm not trying to excuse myself—there is no excuse, none at all.' Roger lowers his head and drops to his knees. 'What is there left for me to do except beg for your forgiveness? I am sorry, my boy—oh God, I am so sorry.'

"Roger doesn't know what to expect. He wouldn't be that surprised if Ted were to chain him to the table, grab a handful of needles from the floor, and return the favor. Such a prospect terrifies him. It's obvious suffering can extend far beyond the normal limits here. But he's ready to accept it as no more than his due. Ted crouches beside him. Roger tenses but keeps his eyes downcast. He's breathing heavily, trying to will himself to embrace whatever is to come. Ted leans toward him, and takes Roger into a hug, wrapping his arms around him and pressing him against his bare and bloody skin. Roger almost panics—there's a half-second where he thinks Ted is going to crush him—before he understands what's happening and returns his son's embrace.

"That was where I left them, reconciled at last. The shrink was intrigued. He was full of questions, too. Why hadn't I had Roger confront Ted as I'd seen, which is to say, imagined, him, i.e. in his mind-numbingly horrifying state? Why hadn't Ted said more? What did I think he would have said? And, most importantly, what happened next? Where did they go?

"The answer to his first question seemed obvious. If Roger had seen Ted as I had, his brain would have been fried, which would have complicated my assignment of writing a happy ending for him considerably. That was fair enough, the shrink said, but he found it interesting that I'd inserted Roger into my hallucination of the house—of course that was how he thought of it; although, he'd been quick to add, hallucinations were facts, too. In placing Roger inside my imaginary landscape, I was, the shrink said, validating my view of the situation. I didn't have an answer to that, or to his other questions. I assumed Ted hadn't spoken more than he did because a) his throat had been tortured and b) he hadn't known what to say. I mean, who would? What you'd mostly feel would be relief at not being tortured anymore, don't you think?"

"I do."

"That, and probably a boatload of anger, too. That anger would have to be affected, though—softened—by Roger releasing him—healing and releasing him. I don't know."

"What about his last question. Where did they go?"

"Someplace else," Veronica said. "He tried to get me to take it further. I guess he wanted an ending that was more definitively happy, but this was as far as I could go. I couldn't imagine what a happy afterlife—what heaven would be for the two of them. A never-ending baseball game, with all their favorite players on the field? After everything we'd been through, that kind of thing sounded juvenile. If you wanted to split hairs, I wasn't sure Roger deserved heaven. I couldn't speak about Ted, but Roger had done a number of things that were less than good, which I didn't know if even my cardboard scenario would balance. Sure, Roger might repent his actions and be forgiven, but that wouldn't mean he wouldn't have to atone for them. So to speak, he might be headed for a long stay in Purgatory. The shrink and I debated this for a long time, actually—well beyond when my session with him was supposed to be over. I had enough Catholic school to hold my own. If you're going to entertain these notions, it's important to do so with some kind of integrity, you know?

"From everything I'd experienced, however, I wasn't sure that the Catholic schema mapped the other world with any accuracy. I guess I could have pictured Roger and Ted resting in peace—asleep in the dark—but, when all was said and done, I wasn't concerned enough to settle on an image—to feel the need to settle on a further image. As long as Roger and Ted were reconciled, that was enough.

"Funny thing is, a couple of months later, I wasn't so sure that the situation I'd invented wasn't right. I can't say what triggered it, but I couldn't stop thinking about what had happened to Roger—where he'd gone. The psychiatrist had done his best to convince me that Roger had, for all intents and purposes, run away, that the parts unknown he'd headed for were most likely North Dakota, or Saskatchewan, or the Yucatan. I never bought it—even under the influence of the medications he put me on, I knew what I'd seen, heard, felt—but insisting on that seemed counterproductive, so I nodded and went along with the shrink's picture of Roger pumping gas somewhere on the Canadian border.

"Anyway, one day, Roger popped up in my thoughts, and, for the next few weeks, his fate—again—occupied my waking hours. I wasn't as frantic as I'd been the first time I dwelt on it. The question was compelling, but not painfully so. Or, it wasn't that painful. During this time, I started wondering if what I'd written in the hospital mightn't have been true. I appreciate how crazy that sounds—I realized it at the time—but consider: I had been—call it plugged in to all the weirdness at a level it's hard to describe, and while that connection had been a casualty of Ted's final conflagration, its effects might have lingered. They would almost have to have lingered. How could they not? If there were still some residue of my previous experience—if my brain had been—reshaped, say—couldn't that have led me to produce an apparently fictional piece that was more factual than I was aware? The reasoning seemed plausible enough to me, so for a time I took what I'd written as fact—or close enough. It was consoling."

"But that wasn't all," I said.

"No, there was a problem. It took a while for me to recognize, but eventually, I did."

"Let me guess. The certainty you felt about this ending wasn't any different from your feeling about the first ending. If that had been wrong—"

"Yes."

"Was that it, or were there any other endings?"

"One more," Veronica said. "This was last fall. Over the course of the summer, I'd lost faith in the second scenario—or, if you prefer, I'd come to recognize it as the fiction it had always been. There'd been no dramatic moment of revelation. The process had been more gradual, a slow-but-steady accumulation of doubt that eventually tipped the scales away from that explanation. The summer had been especially long. For the first time in years, I wasn't teaching during either of the summer sessions at the college, nor did I have any other job lined up to help distract me from the fact that Roger had been gone close to a year. I had had three hundred and sixty-five days, give or take a few, of an empty house, of unlocking the front door and knowing there was no one waiting for me, of eating meals in front of the TV in the living room, because what was the sense of sitting in the kitchen, let alone the dining room, alone, of walking from floor to floor with only Ted's photographs for company? The world went on—it had never stopped going on. Fighting went on in Afghanistan. We invaded Iraq. We made threatening noises at Syria and Iran. There were times—if I'd had a match, I could have burned Belvedere House to the ground. Well, maybe not. As soon as I'd be struck by that impulse, that desire to see the house in flames, collapsing, and I'd wonder how I could bring that to pass, my firestarting would be brought up short by another thought. The house was all that was left of Roger.

"Strictly speaking, that wasn't true. There were all those books and articles, page upon page where his voice spoke as passionately and intelligently as ever. The house was a place Roger had worked on with his hands—his sweat had made it over, twice. I could slide my hand along the banister for the second-floor stairs and hear Roger telling me how the original had been broken off—all of it—during a particularly frenetic house party, and then refastened with an assortment of tapes, so that when he and Joanne bought the house, the banister was more danger than protection. They'd gone to all kinds of lengths to find a craftsman who could match the original, then, because they'd spent so much money doing that, Roger had insisted on the thriftiness of installing it himself. 'It's fortunate,' he'd said, 'that my father bestowed upon me such a treasure chest of obscenities, for I believe I had the opportunity to dig down to its bottom before that job was done.' He'd had an easier time with my renovations, which had been more cosmetic than structural; although he'd muttered plenty as I insisted he and his grad student cronies move this couch against that wall. Roger was part of the house, so much so that I wouldn't have been surprised to find him pacing its walls."

"Did you?"

"Meet Roger? No, never. There were times I was immensely afraid that I would. I would be reading in the library, and I'd be overcome by the certainty—not that Roger was watching me, or waiting outside the door—but that he would be, that it was only a matter of time before he returned to torment me for what I'd done to him—what I'd forced him to do. Times like these, the happy ending I'd given him fell apart and blew away like dandelion seeds. If I didn't catch myself, if I didn't insist that Roger was gone to wherever it was he'd went, and that his going there had been the only solution to the crisis he'd given birth to—if I didn't do that, I would be consumed by fear and guilt, unable to read or even watch TV, as sad—as heartsick—as I'd ever been.

"My solution to the prospect of a long summer alone in Belvedere House was to leave it as much as I could. I contacted friends I hadn't heard from or seen since undergrad—since high school, in one case— thank God for the Internet, right? The majority of them were happy to hear from me, and, when they got the *Reader's Digest* version of what had happened with Roger, invited me to visit them. Most of them lived in the Northeast, although one girl had relocated to Montana— but she invited me to Billings, and I drove the four-thousand-plus miles to her and back. I even flew out to my mother and her live-in boyfriend, who wasn't as bad as I'd feared. Don't get me wrong. He was a jerk, just not as big a jerk as I'd anticipated. With my husband safely out of the picture, Mom found me easier to deal with. Suffice it to say, I won't be returning there any time soon."

"What about the last ending?"

"I'm getting to that. By the time fall classes started, the ending that had struck me as so compelling now appeared so much wishful thinking. The shift was more disappointing than upsetting. It had been nice to picture Roger in a softer light. After I'd abandoned that conclusion, I wondered if it mattered whether I knew, or thought I knew, Roger's fate. Practically speaking, it didn't. He wasn't coming back to me, in the flesh or—my anxieties aside—the spirit. What was important was that he'd faced Ted.

"Regardless of what you think you believe, down on the deeper levels, things go their own way. This past January, when we had those really cold days, and the snow wore a patina of ice, so that the sunlight pooled on it in puddles and ponds of brilliance, and the house was an island in a lake of fire—on one of those days, while I was making lunch in the kitchen, I had a vision of Roger. Not in any kind of supernatural way, you understand. This picture of him came to me, that's all.

"He was in a dark place—not pitch-black, more the kind of heavy dim of a cloudy, moonless night. The landscape around him was arid, parched soil littered with rocks. Beyond about thirty feet in any direction, the dim congealed and it was difficult to distinguish anything, but it seemed—something about the image gave the impression the desert was all there was. Roger was walking, shuffling his feet to avoid smashing his toes into or tripping over the larger rocks. His head—he'd stuck his head out as far in front of him as his neck would allow, his eyes narrowed. His arms were bent, his hands out and open as if waiting to make contact with—I couldn't say what. There was no accompanying narrative, no frame of damnation or redemption—only the vision of Roger, alone in the dark. Compared to other images that had occurred to me—I'd already started reconstructing the story of our time together (I had been almost from the moment Roger disappeared), and I'd spent a good deal of time trying to get inside Roger's head, occasionally succeeding. I'd imagined him standing outside Belvedere House during the period of his nightly walks after Ted died; I'd watched him watching his time with Ted playing out on the house's windows and known with nearly absolute certainty that this was what had happened. Compared to that, this felt tentative, speculative, the kind of strange, random production your brain spits out sometimes.

"My picture of Roger wandering a vague wasteland hasn't changed. There's been no eureka moment, or even the more quiet realization that, at long last, I've found the truth. For what it's worth, the vision hasn't faded, but that could change. Tomorrow, I could decide that this ending is no more valid than any of its predecessors. No doubt, before too long I'd arrive at a fourth one.

"For the moment, however, these are your choices, irony, reconciliation, or endless solitude. There are times—I have this fantasy that, someday years from now, I'll stop for gas on my way through some little, out-of-the-way town, and the guy pumping the gas—I won't recognize him at first, because he'll look a thousand years old, his skin lined and grooved like the bark of a tree, his hair blizzard-white—yes, it'll be Roger. I'll be speechless. I'll wait till almost the last possible moment, then grab him by the arm and confront him."

"What will he say?"

"Nothing," Veronica said, and laughed. "He might recognize me, but that'll be it. When I ask him what happened? where did he go? where has he been? he'll stare at me blankly, no matter how much I shake him or how many questions I yell at him. When the manager comes out to ask me if everything's all right, he'll tell me that Roger doesn't say much of anything to anyone—that folks around these parts assume he's either had an accident or suffering from Alzheimer's. So even if I see him again, I won't learn anything, won't know what destination he went to, much less what happened to him there and how he returned. I won't know if maybe he did run away, flee what his life had become and try to start over again—if the shrink was right after all, or partially right, or whatever."

"How does the fantasy end?"

"I drive away, I guess. What would there be to stick around for?"

No answer presented itself.

Veronica stretched. "God, the sun'll be up soon. How did I let you talk me into staying up so late?"

"The demands of narrative?"

"Or a guilty conscience?"

"I didn't—"

"I know, I know," Veronica said. "For what it's worth, I appreciate your hanging in there to the bitter end. Although it's not as if you got nothing out of the experience—how long will it be until this sees print?" Before I could protest, Veronica said, "Just make sure you change the names to protect the innocent—or me, anyway."

She stood, and I followed her lead. My legs were stiff, my back sore, and I could look forward to a maximum of three hours' sleep. The demands of narrative, indeed. I assumed Veronica was heading off to bed, but she lingered, gazing out the windows at the night's fading remnants. "You know," she said, "for the longest time after Roger—left, I couldn't read his work. I'd wander into his office, which I finally cleaned up, and pull down an issue of *Dickens Studies* or *Victorian Quarterly* that contained one of his articles, and I couldn't do it. My hands would tremble, my eyes fill up with tears, and the words on the page would swirl together. At first, once everything had calmed down—once I'd calmed down—it was comforting to think that Roger's voice had been preserved in all these pages. Over time, though, my inability to read more than two sentences he'd written became a source of torment. I couldn't turn back the cover of my copy of *Dickens and Patrimony*, which Roger had inscribed to me after I'd taken his class, without the waterworks starting. I couldn't wait them out, either. As far as Roger was concerned, my supply of tears appeared to be endless. There were times I'd sit tracing my fingers over the pages, as if mere contact with his words would suffice.

"Eventually, though, my reaction tapered off, then stopped altogether. There was no magic cure—only time. Once I could read Roger's writing again, I went through all of it, some pieces three or four times. I reread *Dickens and Patrimony* compulsively, pen in hand, jotting down notes, comments in the margins. A few were scholarly, most weren't. They were the kind of personal remarks I might have made to Roger himself: 'nicely put'; 'you've got to be kidding'; 'do you really believe this?' Others were more intimate than that, details from our time together that seemed related to whatever topic was at hand.

"Anyway, there was this one passage, right at the end of the book, that I kept returning to. I'd marked it the very first time I'd read the book. Now, I underlined it. A little later, I highlighted it. At this point, I think the book pretty much falls open to it. Let's see if I can quote it. Who am I kidding? Of course I can quote it.

"'Dickens's work is full of insufficient and absent fathers. Of course we can read this as expressing his continuing outrage at his own father for John Dickens's failings. Yet, the matter is more complicated. For not only does Dickens's accusation turn on his father, it also turns on himself, as if he is secretly afraid that he is not as far-removed from his father's failed character as he would wish. And not only does his accusation light on the individual, it also falls on those institutions of society and government that, like a father, are supposed to provide security and order but instead default to insecurity and chaos. There is no doubt that Dickens became increasingly conservative as he aged, but that conservatism was accompanied by; indeed rooted in; a deep skepticism regarding paternal authority.

"'Nor is the issue settled there. For such characters as David Copperfield and Pip, their dead fathers exert profound influences on their lives. Those fathers are oddly active absences. Indeed, it does not seem too much an exaggeration to say that, dead, Dickens's fathers have a much greater effect on their sons' lives than ever they could have hoped for during life, for worse and for better. In his great long novels no less than *A Christmas Carol* Dickens presents us a world through which the dead glide, in which fathers' deaths become their bequests to their children.'

"Take that for what it's worth," Veronica said.

Upstairs, my son woke with a snort that immediately ascended into a cry. "I'm sorry—I have to get him," I said, heading for the stairs.

"Sure," Veronica said. "Good night—or good morning."

"Good night," I replied, already taking the stairs two at a time.

Robbie was standing up in the porta-crib when I opened the door, his hands clutching the railing, his face tilted up to the room's darkness, mouth open wide, cheeks wet with tears. In the bed, Ann stirred. I hurried to Robbie and hoisted him out of the crib, murmuring consolations as I carried him to the rocking chair. As I settled into the chair with him and started to rock, his crying tapered off. He sniffled, wriggled into a more comfortable position, and closed his eyes with a hitching sigh. "There," I whispered. "Daddy's good boy."

Downstairs, I heard the door to Veronica's room open and close. It would remain shut until later that same day, when the rest of us went out to P-town; then, she would pack her things, make her bed, and leave before our return.

I shifted in the rocking chair, trying not to disturb Robbie too much as I sought a more comfortable position. A second night without sufficient sleep had taken its toll. Fatigue tugged at my eyelids.

My head nodded forward. My arms and legs were heavy as lead. It was not out of the question that I would succumb to sleep in the rocking chair, my son in my arms; in fact, it was highly likely. My mind, though, was alight with the story I'd been told, burning with details I hadn't begun to sort through. I was full of the joy that comes with discovering a story.

Robbie started, opened his eyes.

"Shhh," I said. "That's all right. Daddy's here. Daddy's here. Shhh. Daddy's good boy. Daddy's good boy."

AFTERWORD

I

I'm fond of saying, when I speak about *House of Windows*, that I wrote my second novel first. By this, I mean that many of the novel's elements, especially its knotty, damaged characters, are the kind of things a writer might better include in the second book, after having gained an audience's trust with a first novel populated by sympathetic characters. But the statement is true on a more literal level, too. I began the story that would grow into *House of Windows* while taking a break from writing another story that was stretching into a novel (and would eventually become my second published novel, *The Fisherman*). Up until this point in my writing life, my goal had been to finish and submit for publication one story per year. All my fiction had appeared in *The Magazine of Fantasy & Science Fiction*, and I tried to have the next story done and in the mail before the current one was published. It was a low-stress schedule intended to keep me writing by setting modest goals. Matters grew complicated with *The Fisherman*, however, which from the start ran long. Adding another wrinkle to the situation, I was scheduled to do my first big reading, at the KGB Bar's Fantastic Fiction series, with the late, great Lucius Shepard, and I wanted to have something new to read for the event. I had thought this would be *The Fisherman*, but increasingly, that was looking unlikely.

On top of this, I had been struck by an idea for a new story. I was teaching Henry James's brilliant ghost story, "The Jolly Corner," in a section of Honors English at SUNY New Paltz. If you don't know

335

the story, it concerns a man who's haunted by the ghost of the life he could have led. It's one of my favorites. Reading it as an undergraduate had opened my eyes to James, after I had been unmoved by *The Turn of the Screw* during my senior year of high school. While reading it this time through, I had the thought, *What if you had someone who couldn't be haunted by a ghost?* This rapidly clarified to a father who couldn't be haunted by the ghost of his son. This clarification was rooted in a dinner conversation I'd had with my dear friends, Bob and Kappa Waugh, about a former professor of mine at New Paltz. I had known the man when he was married to his second wife, but I was aware that there had been a first wife, and children from that union, one of whom had died under unclear circumstances. I mentioned this in passing to Bob and Kappa, and they filled in the missing parts of the story. There had been a great deal of bad feeling on the part of one of the children of that first marriage toward the new wife, which had flared into intermittent conflict, which eventually had led to the father, my old professor, disowning his child. Later, that child was killed in a misadventure overseas.

It was an astonishing story, in no small part because I had always known the man it concerned as both kind and exceedingly gentle, to the extent that it was difficult to imagine him engaging in any action as rash, as melodramatic, as disowning one of his children. Yet there were the specifics to flesh out my plot, a father who discovers he cannot be haunted by the ghost of the son he disowned, and who was then killed. I would set the story at Bob and Kappa's summer house in Wellfleet, far out on Cape Cod. This had been the setting for my first published story, "On Skua Island," and I liked the idea of returning to it for this new piece. *Who knows?* I thought. *This could be the beginning of a series of stories set at the Cape house. Visitors could appear with their weird tales to tell.* I rewrote the opening line to "The Jolly Corner" as a gesture to my immediate influence, and set off writing.

At this point in my writing, I was very self-consciously revisiting the major tropes of the horror field. Already, I had produced stories about a mummy and an animate skeleton. With this new piece, I was interested to see what I could do with the haunted house. In the village of New Paltz, which is and is not my village of Huguenot, there is a wonderful old Queen Anne–style house on Huguenot Street called the Deyo House. Like many of the buildings on the street, it's owned and maintained by the local historical society. I added a story to it, tweaked its history to make it available for private purchase at the time it was being turned over to the historians, and had my house to be haunted.

After *House of Windows* was published, my friend, the writer Nick Mamatas, told me that it was a good book, but a typical first novel, in which the writer tries to fit in everything they can between its covers. It's not an unfair description. This time, once it had become apparent that I was (again) writing a novel, I had embraced the idea. If this story was going to be a book, I declared, then it would be one by which I could stand or fall. Were I to be struck by a bus the day after the novel was done, I liked to say, I would leave behind something with which I was satisfied. To be honest, even had this not been my first novel, I suspect it still would have been information dense, as it were. I've pretty much always been of the John Irving school of "Less isn't more, it's less. More is more."

A good deal of that *more* consisted of subjects about which I was passionate. Dickens, for one. As was the case with Henry James's fiction, my first exposure to Dickens (junior year in high school, when I had waited until two days before the test to secure a copy of *Great Expectations* that I tried to read in a pair of marathon late-night sessions) had not gone well. Not until I was in my later twenties and decided to give Dickens (and *Great Expectations*) another try did I appreciate what he had been up to in his fiction, after which I became a dedicated fan. Like James, Dickens could still be slow going, but the rewards of the effort repaid it dramatically. With both writers, there was frequently the sense of watching a consciousness in the process of understanding, or attempting to understand, what was happening around it. I loved this, and found it congenial to my idea of what might be included in a story involving the supernatural—particularly, an extended or ongoing experience of it. At the same time, Dickens and James were skilled practitioners of melodrama, which seemed equally appropriate to the horror story. Upon reflection, I suppose there were other ways by which I could have imported my enthusiasm for Dickens into the narrative, but since the frame narrative of Bob and Kappa's Wellfleet house involved a gathering of a group of academics, making Roger Croydon a Dickens scholar at SUNY Huguenot appeared the most direct course of action. This allowed me, too, to refract what I was doing off Dickens's fiction in a more self-conscious way.

I included more recent allusions, as well. The school at which Veronica Croydon completes her undergraduate education, Penrose College, was a nod to Carol Goodman's fine *The Drowning Tree*. Veronica's grandmother's mention of "Aunt Eleanor" was a reference to the protagonist of Shirley Jackson's masterful *The Haunting of Hill House*. The story of Rudolph de Castries and his *Locimany* essays was an attempt to link my narrative to Fritz Leiber's brilliant later novel, *Our Lady of Darkness*. And the novel as a whole bears the impress of my deep admiration and love for the fiction of Peter Straub, especially *Ghost Story* and *lost boy lost girl*. (In fact, the spring after the novel was published, a contemporary attempted to dismiss it as "mid-eighties Straub," a put-down I was happy to take as a compliment.)

Some references, however, escaped me, even as I was making them. Perhaps a year on from *House of Windows*'s appearance, a reader commented that Roger's curse reminded her of Lear's disowning of Cordelia in Shakespeare's tragedy. The connection struck me like a baseball bat to the forehead. Of course *King Lear* was present in the text, and in a major way, at that. It was among the first of Shakespeare's plays I read, the second semester of my freshman year in college, as well as the one to which I had most often returned, in part because another professor had told me it was the greatest of Shakespeare's plays. I had studied it as a graduate student; I had taught it in surveys of British literature. That I could have been blind to such an obvious influence left me dumbfounded.

On the other hand, I had spent ten months of intense effort writing and revising the book, trying to keep track of its various elements. It was not inconceivable that there could have been aspects of it that had sailed by me, hiding, so to speak, in plain sight. In an odd sort of way, it was reassuring to think that I had produced a book capable of surprising me. This proved to be the case, too, as with the passing of time I came to understand that the novel I had written engaged not only the trope of the haunted house, but that of the curse, not to mention of the deal with a sinister power. Veronica's passion for Hawthorne, I saw, had told me more about his presence in the novel than I had realized.

II

Having alluded to the novel's difficulties finding a publisher in its acknowledgements, I'm not sure I need to revisit that material now. I came close to placing *House of Windows* with an editor at one of the major houses, but he was overruled by his superiors. After the first round of rejections, I revised the book, focusing on its chronology. Originally, Veronica had related her story from beginning to end, starting with Roger and Ted's history and moving forward from there. In the new version, I began with Ted's angry appearance at Veronica's apartment door, and reshuffled the rest of the material. But the second round of submissions was no more successful than the first, and I might have given up on the novel had I not encountered Jeremy Lassen, then one of the co-owners of Night Shade Books, at the 2007 World Fantasy Convention in Saratoga Springs. Already, I had been thinking of Night Shade as one of the smaller presses to which the book might be submitted next. (I'm pretty sure I had broached the idea to John Joseph Adams, who had edited his first anthology with them; he read the novel in draft and encouraged me to try Night Shade.) During the convention, I found myself standing with a group of writers and editors, of whom Jeremy was one. Somewhat clumsily, I steered the conversation to this novel I was searching for a home for, and succeeded in making it sound sufficiently interesting for Jeremy to tell me to have my agent send him a copy. To their credit, Night Shade accepted the book and showed what I later realized was an unusual degree of loyalty to it, publishing it first in hardcover, then redesigning it for its paperback edition.

Although I wouldn't say that the novel was widely reviewed, what attention it received tended to be not just positive, but the kind of enthusiastic essay a writer hopes for. To name a few, Matt Cardin in *Dead Reckonings*, Richard Larson in *Strange Horizons*, and Mark Tiedemann in *The Internet Review of Science Fiction* wrote detailed, insightful analyses of the novel, which gave me hope that there was an audience for the book. Not long after its publication, I received an e-mail from Peter Straub telling me how much he had enjoyed the novel, which has to count as one of the best messages I've ever been sent. Then, at the 2011 World Horror Convention in Austin, I had the slightly surreal experience of standing with Peter at a buffet table while he asked me questions about the book. In the years since its appearance, *House of Windows* has continued to be the subject of occasional, thoughtful reviews, which never fail to delight me, as well as kind notes from writers such as Robert Shearman, Victor LaValle, and Adam Nevill, which have left me humbled and grateful. (From what I can tell, a good percentage of the novel's fans reside in Toronto. I'm not sure what that signifies, except the superior literary acumen of Toronto's inhabitants.) Indeed, it was Jaime Levine's overwhelmingly positive response to the book that led to this new edition of it, and the chance to reflect on it.

So many novels appear and vanish without a trace that it's remarkable to me *House of Windows* has endured as long and as well as it has. I'm more thankful than I can say to everyone who has bought, read, and reviewed it. Working on this afterword has reminded me how much the original composition of the book I owed to the love and support of my wife, Fiona. I can think of no better way to conclude this than by thanking her, again, for all of that—and for everything else, too.

Rifton, NY

SUGGESTIONS FOR FURTHER READING

Charles Dickens	*Great Expectations*
Nathaniel Hawthorne	*Selected Stories*
Shirley Jackson	*The Haunting of Hill House*
Henry James	"The Jolly Corner"
Fritz Leiber	*Our Lady of Darkness*
Peter Straub	*Ghost Story*
--	*lost boy lost girl*

READING GROUP QUESTIONS

1. At the beginning of the novel, Langan makes reference to melodrama, to describe Charles Dickens's work but also Roger Croydon's life. It's a description Roger himself appears to endorse; life, he tells his students, is as extravagant as anything in any of Dickens's novels. What do you think of this? Is melodrama, in fact, a more fitting way to approach our lived experience than a more sedate realism? What can melodrama allow a writer to represent that another approach might not?

2. What effect does Roger's disowning Ted have on your view of his character?

3. While in Dr. Hawkins's office, Veronica sees and describes one of Thomas Belvedere's paintings, which shows a cross-section of a black and yellow funnel cloud, through which strange, quasi-cartoonish figures flit. What do you think this painting hung in the therapist's office signifies to the novel as a whole?

4. While at the carousel on Martha's Vineyard, Veronica has a brief encounter with a young girl. Why does Langan include this moment?

5. What exactly do you think Roger comes face to face with in his police cell? What do you make of the way Langan describes it?

6. Why is Roger ultimately unable to lift his curse? Do you think it would have made a difference if he had?

7. In discussing Roger's fate, Veronica offers three possible scenar-

ios. Does any of these seem more satisfying to you? Less? What is the effect on the narrative of not settling on a single fate for him?

8. At the very end of the novel, we're shown the narrator of the framing sections comforting his toddler son, who has awakened crying. Why do you think Langan chose to conclude the novel with this image? How does it connect to elements in Veronica's story?

JOHN LANGAN lives in upstate New York with his wife and son. His debut collection, *Mr. Gaunt and Other Uneasy Encounters*, received a starred review from *Publishers Weekly* and was nominated for the Bram Stoker Award. His fiction has appeared in Ellen Datlow's *Poe*, John Joseph Adams's *By Blood We Live* and *The Living Dead*, and *The Magazine of Fantasy & Science Fiction*.

Printed in the USA
CPSIA information can be obtained
at www.ICGtesting.com
JSHW031707140824
68134JS00038B/3555